SINCE YOU'VE BEEN GONE

Also by Morgan Matson

Amy & Roger's Epic Detour

Second Chance Summer

SINCE
YOU'VE
BEEN

**SIMON &
SCHUSTER**

London · New York · Sydney · Toronto · New Delhi

A CBS COMPANY

First published in Great Britain in 2014 by Simon & Schuster UK Ltd
A CBS COMPANY

Originally published in the USA in 2014 by Simon & Schuster BFYR
An imprint of Simon & Schuster Children's Publishing Division,
1230 Avenue of Americas, New York, BY 10020

A CIP catalogue record for this book is available
from the British Library

1 3 5 7 9 10 8 6 4 2

Simon & Schuster UK Ltd
1st Floor
222 Gray's Inn Road
London WC1X 8HB

www.simonandschuster.co.uk
www.simonandschuster.com.au

Simon & Schuster Australia, Sydney
Simon & Schuster India, New Delhi

PB ISBN 978-1-47112-266-8
Ebook ISBN 978-1-47112-267-5

Printed in the UK by CPI Group (UK) Ltd, Croydon, CR0 4YY

For Amalia

ACKNOWLEDGMENTS

Justin! They say only the good die young, but only the best would be able to take a 400+ page manuscript, read it over a weekend, come back with the most wonderful notes—and repeat, four times. You may be right; I may be crazy, but THANK YOU for all your patience and insight and amazing notes and humor—and for never making me feel like I was in the ninth, two men out and three men on. I'm beyond grateful to you.

Thank you to Emily Van Beek, superagent extraordinaire, who always takes such good care of me.

Lucy Ruth Cummins is a genius. Thank you so much for the most gorgeous cover EVER and for letting me feel such a part of the process. Ponies Butterscotch and Snickerdoodle are on their way. And thanks to Meredith Jenks for the unbelievable photos!

Jessi Kirby, where would I (or this book) be without you? Thank you so much for your friendship, your kindness, your encouragement, and for sharing your lovely stretch of beach with authors in need. I couldn't have done this without you.

I am lucky enough to be part of a wonderful community of writers who give me so much support and teach me so much just by their awesome examples. Thanks and hugs and cupcakes to: Lauren Strasnick, Rosa Lin, Leslie Margolis, Rachel Cohn, Jordan Roter, Anne Heltzel, and Liz Werner. Thanks also to Janet and Lee Batchler.

Thanks to Alexandra Cooper, for so many things, and especially that very first two-hour talk about this book, at a Starbucks in Texas.

Thank you to the fantastic team at S&S—Danielle Young, Anne Zafian, Mary Marotta, Paul Crichton, Bernadette Cruz, Chrissy Noh, Katy Hershberger, Katrina Groover, and Venessa Carson. I couldn't be in better hands.

Thanks and love to my family—Mom, Jason, Amanda, and Katie.

And thank you with all my heart to Amalia Ellison—road trip companion, partner in crime, travel buddy, best friend.

Duncan

You have to trust me, here. We're friends.

Cecily

I don't think we are.

Real friends are the ones you can count on no matter what.

The ones who go into the forest to find you and bring you home.

And real friends never have to tell you that they're your friends.

1
THE
LIST

The list arrived after Sloane had been gone two weeks.

I wasn't at home to get it because I was at Sloane's, where I had gone yet again, hoping against hope to find her there. I had decided, as I'd driven over to her house, my iPod off and my hands gripping the steering wheel, that if she was there, I wouldn't even need an explanation. It wouldn't be necessary for her to tell me why she'd suddenly stopped answering her phone, texts, and e-mails, or why she'd vanished, along with her parents and their car. I knew it was ridiculous to think this way, like I was negotiating with some cosmic dealer who could guarantee this for me, but that didn't stop me as I got closer and closer to Randolph Farms Lane. I didn't care what

I had to promise if it meant Sloane would be there. Because if Sloane was there, everything could start making sense again.

It was not an exaggeration to say that the last two weeks had been the worst of my life. The first weekend after school had ended, I'd been dragged upstate by my parents against my wishes and despite my protests. When I'd come back to Stanwich, after far too many antique shops and art galleries, I'd called her immediately, car keys in my hand, waiting impatiently for her to answer so that she could tell me where she was, or, if she was home, that I could pick her up. But Sloane didn't answer her phone, and she didn't answer when I called back an hour later, or later that night, or before I went to bed.

The next day, I drove by her house, only to see her parents' car gone and the windows dark. She wasn't responding to texts and still wasn't answering her phone. It was going right to voice mail, but I wasn't worried, not then. Sloane would sometimes let her battery run down until the phone shut off, and she never seemed to know where her charger was. And her parents, Milly and Anderson, had a habit of forgetting to tell her their travel plans. They would whisk her off to places like Palm Beach or Nantucket, and Sloane would return a few days later, tan, with a present for me and stories to tell. I was sure that's what had happened this time.

But after three days, and still no word, I worried. After five days, I panicked. When I couldn't stand being in my house any longer, staring down at my phone, willing it to ring, I'd started driving around town, going to all of our places, always able to imagine her there until the moment I arrived to find it Sloane-free. She wasn't stretched out in the sun on a picnic table at the Orchard, or flipping through the sale rack at Twice Upon a Time, or finishing up her pineapple slice at Captain Pizza. She was just gone.

I had no idea what to do with myself. It was rare for us not to see each other on a daily basis, and we talked or texted constantly, with nothing off-limits or too trivial, even exchanges like *I think my new skirt make me look like I'm Amish, promise to tell me if it does?* (me) and *Have you noticed it's been a while since anyone's seen the Loch Ness monster?* (her). In the two years we'd been best friends, I had shared almost all of my thoughts and experiences with her, and the sudden silence felt deafening. I didn't know what to do except to continue texting and trying to find her. I kept reaching for my phone to tell Sloane that I was having trouble handling the fact she wasn't answering her phone.

I drew in a breath and I held it as I pulled down her driveway, the way I used to when I was little and opening up my last birthday present, willing it to be the one thing I still didn't have, the only thing I wanted.

But the driveway was empty, and all the windows were dark. I pulled up in front of the house anyway, then put my car in park and killed the engine. I slumped back against the seat, fighting to keep down the lump that was rising in my throat. I no longer knew what else to do, where else to look. But Sloane couldn't be gone. She wouldn't have left without telling me.

But then where was she?

When I felt myself on the verge of tears, I got out of the car and squinted at the house in the morning sun. The fact that it was empty, this early, was really all the evidence I needed, since I had never known Milly or Anderson to be awake before ten. Even though I knew there was probably no point to it, I crossed to the house and walked up the wide stone steps that were covered with bright green summer leaves. The leaves were thick enough that I had to kick them aside, and I knew, deep down, that it was more proof that nobody was there, and hadn't been there for a while now. But I walked toward the front door, with its brass lion's-head knocker, and knocked anyway, just like I'd done five other times that week. I waited, trying to peer in the glass on the side of the door, still with a tiny flicker of hope that in a second, any minute now, I'd hear Sloane's steps as she ran down the hall and threw open the door, yanking me into a hug, already talking a mile a minute. But the house was silent, and all I could see through the glass was the historical-status plaque just inside the door, the one that proclaimed the house "one of Stanwich's architectural treasures," the one that always seemed covered with ghosts of fingerprints.

I waited another few minutes, just in case, then turned around and lowered myself to sit on the top step, trying very hard not to have a breakdown among the leaves.

There was a piece of me that was still hoping to find this had been a very realistic nightmare, and that any minute now, I'd wake up, and Sloane would be there, on the other end of her phone like she was supposed to be, already planning out the day for us.

Sloane's house was in what was always called "backcountry," where the houses got larger and farther apart from each other, on ever-bigger pieces of land. She was ten miles away from my place, which, back when I'd been in peak running shape, had been easy for me to cross. But even though they were close, our neighborhoods couldn't have been more different. Here, there was only the occasional car driving past, and the silence seemed to underscore the fact that I was totally alone, that there was nobody home and, most likely, nobody coming back. I leaned forward, letting my hair fall around me like a curtain. If nobody was there, it at least meant I could stay awhile, and I wouldn't be asked to leave. I could probably stay there all day. I honestly didn't know what else to do with myself.

I heard the low rumble of an engine and looked up, fast, pushing my hair out of my face, feeling hope flare once more in my chest. But the car rolling slowly down the driveway wasn't Anderson's slightly dented BMW. It was a yellow pickup truck, the back piled with lawnmowers and rakes. When it pulled in front of the steps, I could see the writing, in stylized cursive, on the side. *Stanwich Landscaping*, it read. *Planting . . . gardening . . . maintenance . . . and mulch, mulch more!* Sloane loved when stores had cheesy names or slogans. Not that she was a huge fan of puns, but she'd always said she liked to picture the owners thinking them up, and how pleased with themselves they must have been when they landed on whatever they'd chosen. I immediately made a mental note to tell Sloane about the motto, and then, a moment later, realized how stupid this was.

Three guys got out of the truck and headed for the back of it, two of them starting to lift down the equipment. They looked older, like maybe they were in college, and I stayed frozen on the steps, watching them. I knew that this was an opportunity to try and get some information, but that would involve talking to these guys. I'd been shy from birth, but the last two years had been different. With Sloane by my side, it was like I suddenly had a safety net. She was always able to take the lead if I wanted her to, and if I didn't, I knew she would be there, jumping in if I lost my nerve or got flustered. And when I was on my own, awkward or failed interactions just didn't seem to matter as much, since I knew I'd be able to spin it into a story, and we could laugh about it afterward. Without her here, though, it was becoming clear to me how terrible I now was at navigating things like this on my own.

"Hey." I jumped, realizing I was being addressed by one of the landscapers. He was looking up at me, shielding his eyes against the sun as the other two hefted down a riding mower. "You live here?"

The other two guys set the mower down, and I realized

Morgan Matson

I knew one of them; he'd been in my English class last year, making this suddenly even worse. "No," I said, and heard how scratchy my voice sounded. I had been saying only the most perfunctory things to my parents and younger brother over the last two weeks, and the only talking I'd really been doing had been into Sloane's voice mail. I cleared my throat and tried again. "I don't."

The guy who'd spoken to me raised his eyebrows, and I knew this was my cue to go. I was, at least in their minds, trespassing, and would probably get in the way of their work. All three guys were now staring at me, clearly just waiting for me to leave. But if I left Sloane's house—if I ceded it to these strangers in yellow T-shirts—where was I going to get more information? Did that mean I was just accepting the fact that she was gone?

The guy who'd spoken to me folded his arms across his chest, looking impatient, and I knew I couldn't keep sitting there. If Sloane had been with me, I would have been able to ask them. If she were here, she probably would have gotten two of their numbers already and would be angling for a turn on the riding mower, asking if she could mow her name into the grass. But if Sloane were here, none of this would be happening in the first place. My cheeks burned as I pushed myself to my feet and walked quickly down the stone steps, my flip-flops sliding once on the leaves, but I steadied myself before I wiped out and made this more humiliating than it already was. I nodded at the guys, then looked down at the driveway as I walked over to my car.

Now that I was leaving, they all moved into action, distributing equipment and arguing about who was doing what. I gripped my door handle, but didn't open it yet. Was I really just going to go? Without even trying?

"So," I said, but not loudly enough, as the guys continued to talk to each other, none of them looking over at me, two of them having an argument about whose turn it was to fertilize, while the guy from last year's English class held his baseball cap in his hands, bending the bill into a curve. "*So*," I said, but much too loudly this time, and the guys stopped talking and looked over at me again. I could feel my palms sweating, but I knew I had to keep going, that I wouldn't be able forgive myself if I just turned around and left. "I was just . . . um . . ." I let out a shaky breath. "My friend lives here, and I was trying to find her. Do you—" I suddenly saw, like I was observing the scene on TV, how ridiculous this probably was, asking the landscaping guys for information on my best friend's whereabouts. "I mean, did they hire you for this job? Her parents, I mean? Milly or Anderson Williams?" Even though I was trying not to, I could feel myself grabbing on to this possibility, turning it into something I could understand. If the Williamses had hired Stanwich Landscaping, maybe they were just on a trip somewhere, getting the yard stuff taken care of while they were gone so they wouldn't be bothered. It was just a long trip, and they had gone somewhere with no cell reception or e-mail service. That was all.

The guys looked at each other, and it didn't seem like any of these names had rung a bell. "Sorry," said the guy who'd first spoken to me. "We just get the address. We don't know about that stuff."

I nodded, feeling like I'd just depleted my last reserve of hope. Thinking about it, the fact that landscapers were here was actually a bit ominous, as I had never once seen Anderson show the slightest interest in the lawn, despite the fact that the Stanwich Historical Society was apparently always bothering him to hire someone to keep up the property.

Two of the guys had headed off around the side of the house, and the guy from my English class looked at me as he put on his baseball cap. "Hey, you're friends with Sloane Williams, right?"

"Yes," I said immediately. This was my identity at school, but I'd never minded it—and now, I'd never been so happy to be recognized that way. Maybe he knew something, or had heard something. "Sloane's actually who I'm looking for. This is her house, so . . ."

The guy nodded, then gave me an apologetic shrug. "Sorry I don't know anything," he said. "Hope you find her." He didn't ask me what my name was, and I didn't volunteer it. What would be the point?

"Thanks," I managed to say, but a moment too late, as he'd already joined the other two. I looked at the house once more, the house that somehow no longer even felt like Sloane's, and realized that there was nothing left to do except leave.

I didn't head right home; instead I stopped in to Stanwich Coffee, on the very off chance that there would be a girl in the corner chair, her hair in a messy bun held up with a pencil, reading a British novel that used dashes instead of quotation marks. But Sloane wasn't there. And as I headed back to my car I realized that if she had been in town, it would have been unthinkable that she wouldn't have called me back. It had been two weeks; something was wrong.

Strangely, this thought buoyed me as I headed for home. When I left the house every morning, I just let my parents assume that I was meeting up with Sloane, and if they asked what my plans were, I said vague things about applying for jobs. But I knew now was the moment to tell them that I was worried; that I needed to know what had happened. After all, maybe they knew something, even though my parents weren't close with hers. The first time they'd met, Milly and Anderson had come to collect Sloane from a sleepover at my house, two hours later than they'd been supposed to show up. And after pleasantries had been exchanged and Sloane and I had said good-bye, my dad had shut the door, turned to my mother, and groaned, "That was like being stuck in a Gurney play." I hadn't known what he'd meant by this, but I could tell by his tone of voice that it hadn't been a compliment. But even though they hadn't been friends, they still might know something. Or they might be able to find something out.

I held on to this thought tighter and tighter as I got closer to my house. We lived close to one of the four commercial districts scattered throughout Stanwich. My neighborhood was pedestrian-friendly and walkable, and there was always lots of traffic, both cars and people, usually heading in the direction of the beach, a ten-minute drive from our house. Stanwich, Connecticut, was on Long Island Sound, and though there were no waves, there was still sand and beautiful views and stunning houses that had the water as their backyards.

Our house, in contrast, was an old Victorian that my parents had been fixing up ever since we'd moved in six years earlier. The floors were uneven and the ceilings were low, and the whole downstairs was divided into lots of tiny rooms—originally all specific parlors of some kind. But my parents—who had been living, with me, and later my younger brother, in tiny apartments, usually above a deli or a Thai place—couldn't believe their good fortune. They didn't think about the fact that it was pretty much falling down, that it was three stories and drafty, shockingly expensive to heat in the winter and, with central air not yet invented when the house was built, almost impossible to cool in the summer. They were ensorcelled with the place.

The house had originally been painted a bright purple, but had faded over the years to a pale lavender. It had a wide front porch, a widow's walk at the very top of the house, too many windows to make any logical sense, and a turret room that was my parents' study.

I pulled up in front of the house and saw that my brother was sitting on the porch steps, perfectly still. This was surprising in itself. Beckett was ten, and constantly in motion, climbing up vertiginous things, practicing his ninja moves, and biking through our neighborhood's streets with abandon, usually with his best friend Annabel Montpelier, the scourge of stroller-pushing mothers within a five-mile radius. "Hey," I said as I got out of the car and walked toward the steps, suddenly worried that I had missed something big in the last two weeks while I'd sleep-walked through family meals, barely paying attention to what was happening around me. But maybe Beckett had just pushed my parents a little too far, and was having a time-out. I'd find out soon enough anyway, since I needed to talk to them about Sloane. "You okay?" I asked, climbing up the three porch steps.

He looked up at me, then back down at his sneakers. "It's happening again."

"Are you sure?" I crossed the porch to the door and pulled it open. I was hoping Beckett was wrong; after all, he'd only experienced this twice before. Maybe he was misreading the signs.

Beckett followed behind me, stepping into what had originally been an entry parlor, but which we had turned into a mud-room, where we dropped jackets and scarves and keys and shoes. I walked into the house, squinting in the light that was always a little too dim. "Mom?" I called, crossing my fingers in my jean shorts pockets, hoping that Beckett had just gotten this wrong.

But as my eyes adjusted, I could see, through the open door of the kitchen, an explosion of stuff from the warehouse store one town over. Piled all over the kitchen counters were massive quantities of food and supplies in bulk—instant mac and cheese, giant boxes of cereal, gallons of milk, a nearly obscene amount of mini micro cheesy bagels. As I took it in, I realized with a sinking feeling that Beckett had been totally correct. They were starting a new play.

"Told you," Beckett said with a sigh as he joined me.

My parents were a playwriting team who worked during the school year at Stanwich College, the local university and the reason we had moved here. My mom taught playwriting in the theater department, and my dad taught critical analysis in the English department. They both spent the school year busy and stressed—especially when my mom was directing a play and my dad was dealing with his thesis students and midterms—but they relaxed when the school year ended. They might occasionally pull out an old script they'd put aside a few years earlier and tinker with it a little, but for the most part, they took these three months off. There was a pattern to our summers, so regular you could almost set your calendar to it. In June, my dad would decide that he had been too hemmed in by society and its arbitrary regulations, and declare that he was a *man*. Basically, this meant that he would grill everything we ate, even things that really shouldn't be grilled, like lasagna, and would start growing a beard that would have him looking like a mountain man by the middle of July. My mother would take up some new hobby around the same time, declaring it her "creative outlet." One year, we all ended up with lopsided scarves when she learned to knit, and another year we weren't allowed to use any of the tables, as they'd all been taken over by jigsaw puzzles, and had to eat our grilled food off plates we held on our laps. And last year, she'd decided to grow a vegetable garden, but the only thing that seemed to flourish was the zucchini, which then attracted the deer she subsequently declared war on. But by the end of August, we were all sick of charred food, and my dad was tired of getting strange looks when he went to the post office. My dad would shave, we'd start using the stove inside, and my mother would put aside her scarves or puzzles or zucchini. It was a strange routine, but it was ours, and I was used to it.

But when they were writing, everything changed. It had happened only twice before. The summer I was eleven, they sent me to sleepaway camp—an experience that, while horrible for me, actually ended up providing them with the plot of their play. It had happened again when I was thirteen and Beckett was six. They'd gotten an idea for a new play one night, and then had basically disappeared into the dining room for the rest of the summer, buying food in bulk and emerging every few days to make sure that we were still alive. I knew that ignoring us wasn't something either of them intended to do, but they'd been a playwriting team for years before they'd had us, and it was like

Morgan Matson

they just reverted back to their old habits, where they could live to write, and nothing mattered except the play.

But I really didn't want this to be happening right now—not when I needed them. "Mom!" I called again.

My mother stepped out of the dining room and I noticed with a sinking feeling that she was wearing sweatpants and a T-shirt—writing clothes—and her curly hair was up in a knot on top of her head. "Emily?" my mom asked. She looked around. "Where's your brother?"

"Um, here," Beckett said, waving at her from my side.

"Oh, good," my mother said. "We were just going to call you two. We need to have a family meeting."

"Wait," I said quickly, taking a step forward. "Mom. I needed to talk to you and Dad. It's about Sloane—"

"Family meeting!" my dad boomed from inside the kitchen. His voice was deep, very loud, and it was the reason he was always getting assigned the eight a.m. classes—he was one of the few professors in the English department who could keep the freshmen awake. "Beckett! Emily!" he stepped out of the kitchen and blinked when he saw us. "Oh. That was fast."

"Dad," I said, hoping I could somehow get in front of this. "I needed to talk to you guys."

"We need to talk to you, too," my mother said. "Your father and I were chatting last night, and we somehow got on—Scott, how did we start talking about it?"

"It was because your reading light burned out," my dad said, taking a step closer to my mom. "And we started talking about electricity."

"Right," my mother said, nodding. "Exactly. So we started talking about Edison, then Tesla, and then Edison *and* Tesla, and—"

"We think we might have a play," my dad finished, glancing into the dining room. I saw they already had their laptops set up across the table, facing each other. "We're going to bounce around some ideas. It might be nothing."

I nodded, but I knew with a sinking feeling that it wasn't nothing. My parents had done this enough that they knew when something was worth making a bulk supermarket run. I knew the signs well; they always downplayed ideas they truly saw promise in. But when they started talking excitedly about a new play, already seeing its potential before anything was written, I knew it would fizzle out in a few days.

"So we might be working a bit," my mother said, in what was sure to be the understatement of the summer. "We bought supplies," she said, gesturing vaguely to the kitchen, where I could see the jumbo-size bags of frozen peas and microwave burritos were starting to melt. "And there's always emergency money in the conch." The conch shell had served as a prop during the Broadway production of *Bug Juice*, my parents' most successful play, and now, in addition to being where we kept household cash, served as a bookend for a listing pile of cookbooks. "Beckett's going to be at day camp during the week, so

Morgan Matson

he's all set. Annabel's going too," my mother said, maybe noticing Beckett's scowl.

"What about camping?" he asked.

"We'll still go camping," my dad said. Maybe seeing my alarmed look, he added, "Just your brother and me. The Hughes men in the wilderness."

"But . . ." Beckett looked into the dining room, his brow furrowed.

My dad waved this away. "We aren't going until July," he said. "And I'm sure this idea won't amount to much anyway."

"What about you, Em?" my mom asked, even as she drifted closer to the dining room, like she was being pulled there by gravitational force. "Do you have your summer plans worked out?"

I bit my lip. Sloane and I had made plans upon plans for this summer. We had concert tickets purchased, she had told me she had mapped out something called a "pizza crawl," and I had decided we should spend the summer seeking out Stanwich's best cupcake. Sloane had a plan for both of us to find "summer boys," but she had been vague on just how we were going to accomplish this. We'd blocked off the weekends we would drive upstate to the various flea markets she'd spent the last few months scouting, and I'd already gone through the drive-in calendar and decided which nights we needed to block off for the double features. She'd planned on making friends with someone who had a pool, and had decided this would be the summer she'd finally beat me at mini golf (I was weirdly naturally skilled at it, and I'd discovered that Sloane got strangely competitive when there were stuffed-animal prizes involved). I wanted to learn the zombie dance from "Thriller" and she wanted to learn the dance from £ondon Moore's new video, the one that had sparked all sorts of protests from parents' groups.

At some point, we were going to need to get jobs, of course. But we'd decided it was going to be something unchallenging that we could do together, like we had the summer before, when we'd waitressed at the Stanwich Country Club—Sloane earning more tips than anyone else, me getting a reputation for being an absolute whiz at filling the ketchup bottles at the end of the night. We'd also left lots of time unscheduled—the long stretches of hours we'd spend at the beach or walking around or just hanging out with no plan beyond maybe getting fountain Diet Cokes. It was *Sloane*—you usually didn't need more than that to have the best Wednesday of your life.

I swallowed hard as I thought about all these plans, the whole direction I'd planned for my summer to go, just vanishing. And I realized that if Sloane were here, suddenly having my parents otherwise occupied and not paying attention to things like my curfew would have meant we could have had the most epic summer ever. I could practically see that summer, the one I wanted, the one I should have been living, shimmering in front of me like a mirage before it faded and disappeared.

"Emily?" my mother prompted, and I looked back at her. She was in the same room with me, she was technically looking at me, but I knew when my parents were present and when their minds were on their play. For just a moment, I thought about trying to tell them about Sloane, trying to get them to help me figure out what had happened. But I knew that they'd say yes with the best of intentions and then forget all about it as they focused on Tesla and Edison.

"I'm . . . working on it," I finally said.

"Sounds good," my dad said, nodding. My mom smiled, like I'd given her the answer she'd wanted, even though I hadn't told them anything concrete. But it was clear they wanted this off their plates, so they could consider their children more or less sorted, and they could get to work. They were both edging toward the dining room, where their laptops glowed softly, beckoning. I sighed and started to head to the kitchen, figuring that I should get the frozen stuff into the freezer before it went bad.

"Oh, Em," my mother said, sticking her head out of the dining room. I saw my father was already sitting in his chair, opening up his laptop and stretching out his fingers. "A letter came for you."

My heart slowed and then started beating double-time. There was only one person who regularly wrote to me. And they weren't even actually letters—they were lists. "Where?"

"Microwave," my mother said. She went back into the

dining room and I bolted into the kitchen, no longer caring if all the burritos melted. I pushed aside the twelve-pack of Kleenex and saw it. It was leaning up against the microwave like it was nothing, next to a bill from the tree guy.

But it was addressed to me. And it was in Sloane's handwriting.

****

JUNE

One Year Earlier

"You sent me a list?" I asked. Sloane looked over at me sharply, almost dropping the sunglasses—oversize green frames—that she'd just picked up.

I held out the paper in my hands, the letter I'd seen propped up by the microwave as I headed down that morning, on my way to pick her up and drive us to the latest flea market she'd found, an hour and change outside of Stanwich. Though there hadn't been a return address—just a heart—I'd recognized Sloane's handwriting immediately, a distinctive mix of block letters and cursive. "It's what happens when you go to three different schools for third grade," she'd explained to me once. "Everyone is learning this at different stages and you never get the fundamentals." Sloane and her parents lived the kind of peripatetic existence—picking up and moving when they felt like it, or when they just wanted a new adventure—that I'd seen in movies, but hadn't known actually existed in real life.

I'd learned by now that Sloane used this excuse when it suited her, not just for handwriting, but also for her inability to comprehend algebra, climb a rope in PE, or drive. She was the only person our age I knew who didn't have a license. She claimed that in all her moves, she'd never quite been the right age for a permit where they were, but I also had a feeling that Milly and Anderson had been occupied with more exciting things than bringing her to driver's ed and then quizzing her every night over dinner, geeking out on traffic regulations and the points system, like my dad had done. Whenever I brought up the fact that she lived in Stanwich now, and could get a Connecticut license without a problem, Sloane waved it away. "I know the fundamentals of driving," she'd say. "If I'm ever on a bus that gets hijacked on the freeway, I can take over when the driver gets shot. No problem." And since Sloane liked to walk whenever possible—a habit she'd picked up living in cities for much of her life, and not just places like Manhattan and Boston, but London and Paris and Copenhagen—she didn't seem to mind that much. I liked to drive and was happy to drive us everywhere, Sloane sitting shotgun, the DJ and navigator, always on top of telling me when our snacks were running low.

An older woman, determined to check out the selection of tarnished cufflinks, jostled me out of the way, and I stepped aside. This flea market was similar to many that I'd been to, always with Sloane. We were technically here look-ing for boots for her, but as soon as we'd paid our two dollars apiece and entered the middle school parking lot that had been converted, for the weekend, into a land of potential treasure, she had made a beeline to this stall, which seemed to be mostly sunglasses and jewelry. Since I'd picked up the letter, I'd been waiting for the right moment to ask her, when I'd have her full attention, and the drive had been the wrong time—there was music to sing along to and things to discuss and directions to follow.

Sloane smiled at me, even as she put on the terrible green sunglasses, hiding her eyes, and I wondered for a moment if she was embarrassed, which I'd almost never seen. "You weren't supposed to get that until tomorrow," she said as she bent down to look at her reflection in the tiny standing mirror. "I was hoping it would be there right before you guys left for the airport. The mail here is too efficient."

"But what is it?" I asked, flipping through the pages. *Emily Goes to Scotland!* was written across the top.

1. Try haggis.

2. Call at least three people "lassie."

3. Say, at least once, "You can take my life, but you'll never take my freedom!"

(Say this out loud and in public.)

The list continued on, over to the next page, filled with things—like fly-fishing and asking people if they knew where I could find J.K. Rowling—that I did not intend to do, and not just because I would only be gone five days. One of my parents' plays was going into rehearsals for the Edinburgh Fringe Festival, and they had decided it would be the perfect opportunity to take a family trip. I suddenly noticed that at the very bottom of the list, in tiny letters, she'd written, *When you finish this list, find me and tell me all about it*. I looked up at Sloane, who had set the green pair down and was now turning over a pair of rounded cat-eye frames.

"It's stuff for you to do in Scotland!" she said. She frowned at the sunglasses and held up the frames to me, and I knew she was asking my opinion. I shook my head, and she nodded and set them down. "I wanted to make sure you got the most of your experience."

"Well, I'm not sure how many of these I'll actually do," I said as I carefully folded the letter and placed it back in the envelope. "But this is awesome of you. Thanks so much."

She gave me a tiny wink, then continued to look through the sunglasses, clearly searching for something specific. She had spent most of the spring channeling Audrey Hepburn—lots of winged black eyeliner and stripes, skinny black pants and flats—but was currently transitioning into what she was calling "seventies California," and referencing people like Marianne Faithfull and Anita Pallenberg, who I'd never heard of, and Penny Lane in *Almost Famous*, who

I had. Today, she was wearing a flowing vintage maxi dress and sandals that tied around her ankles, her wavy dark-blond hair spilling over her shoulders and down her back. Before I'd met Sloane, I didn't know that it was possible to dress the way she did, that anyone not heading to a photo shoot dressed with that much style. My own wardrobe had improved immeasurably since we'd become friends, mostly stuff she'd picked for me, but some things I'd found myself and felt brave enough to wear when I was with her, knowing that she would appreciate it.

She picked up a pair of gold-rimmed aviators, only slightly bent, and slipped them on, turning to me for my opinion. I nodded and then noticed a guy, who looked a few years younger than us, staring at Sloane. He was absently holding a macramé necklace, and I was pretty sure that he had no idea that he'd picked it up and would have been mortified to realize it. But that was my best friend, the kind of girl your eyes went to in a crowd. While she was beautiful—wavy hair, bright blue eyes, perfect skin dotted with freckles—this didn't fully explain it. It was like she knew a secret, a good one, and if you got close enough, maybe she'd tell you, too.

"Yes," I said definitively, looking away from the guy and his necklace. "They're great."

She grinned. "I think so too. Hate them for me?"

"Sure," I said easily as I walked a few steps away from

her, making my way up toward the register, pretending to be interested in a truly hideous pair of earrings that seemed to be made out of some kind of tinsel. In my peripheral vision, I saw Sloane pick up another pair of sunglasses—black ones—and look at them for a moment before also taking them to the register, where the middle-aged guy behind it was reading a comic book.

"How much for the aviators?" Sloane asked as I edged closer, looking up as if I'd just noticed what she'd picked up.

"Twenty-five," the guy said, not even looking up from his comic.

"Ugh," I said, shaking my head. "So not worth it. Look, they're all dented."

Sloane gave me a tiny smile before putting her game face back on. I knew she'd been surprised, when we'd first started this bargaining technique, that I'd been able to roll with it. But when you grew up in the theater, you learned to handle impromptu improv. "Oh, you're right," she said, looking at them closely.

"They're not that dented," the guy said, putting his comic—*Super Friends*—down. "Those are vintage."

I shrugged. "I wouldn't pay more than fifteen for them," I said, and saw, a moment too late, Sloane widen her eyes at me. "I mean ten!" I said quickly. "Not more than ten."

"Yeah," she said, setting them down in front of the guy, along with the square-framed black ones I'd seen her pick up. "Also, we just got here. We should look around."

"Yes, we should," I said, trying to make it look like I was heading toward the exit without actually leaving.

"Wait!" the guy said quickly. "I can let you have them for fifteen. Final offer."

"Both of these for twenty," Sloane said, looking him right in the eye.

"Twenty-one," the guy bargained lamely, but Sloane just smiled and dug in her pocket for her cash.

A minute later, we were heading out of the stall, Sloane wearing her new aviators. "Nicely done," she said.

"Sorry for going too high," I said, as I stepped around a guy carrying an enormous kitten portrait. "I should have started at ten."

She shrugged. "If you start too low, you sometimes lose the whole thing," she said. "Here." She handed me the black sunglasses, and I saw now that they were vintage Ray-Bans. "For you."

"Really?" I slipped them on and, with no mirror around, turned to Sloane for her opinion.

She look a step back, hands on hips, her face serious, like she was studying me critically, then broke into a smile. "You look great," she said, digging in her bag. She emerged with one of her ever-present disposable cameras, and snapped a picture of me before I could hold my hand up in front of my face or stop her. Despite having a smartphone, Sloane always carried a disposable camera with her—sometimes two. She had panoramic ones, black-and-white ones, waterproof ones. Last week, we'd taken our first beach swim of the summer, and Sloane had snapped pictures of us underwater, emerging triumphant and holding the camera over her head. "Can your phone do this?" she'd asked, dragging the camera over the surface of the water. "Can it?"

"They look okay?" I asked, though of course I believed her.

She nodded. "They're very you." She dropped her camera back in her bag and started wandering through the stalls. I followed as she led us into a vintage clothing stall and headed back to look at the boots. I ducked to see my reflection in the mirror, then checked to make sure her letter was secure in my bag.

"Hey," I said, coming to join her in the back, where she was sitting on the ground, already surrounded by options, untying her sandals. I held up the list. "Why did you mail this to me? Why not give it to me in person?" I looked down at the envelope in my hands, at the stamp and postmark and all the work that had gone into it. "And why mail anything at all? Why not just tell me?"

Sloane looked up at me and smiled, a flash of her bright, slightly crooked teeth. "But where's the fun in that?"

★★★★

MISS EMILY HUGHES
15 DRIFTWAY LANE
STANWICH, CONNECTICUT
06831

1. Kiss a stranger.

2. Go skinny-dipping.

3. Steal something.

4. Break something.

5. Penelope.

6. Ride a dern horse, ya cowpoke.

7. 55 S. Ave. Ask for Mona.

8. The backless dress. And somewhere to wear it.

9. Dance until dawn.

10. Share some secrets in the dark.

11. Hug a Jamie.

12. Apple picking at night.

13. Sleep under the stars.

I sat on my bed, gripping this new list in my hands so tightly, I could see the tips of my fingers turning white.

I wasn't sure what it meant, but it was something. It was from Sloane. Sloane had sent me a list.

As soon as I'd taken it out of the envelope, I'd just stared at it, my brain not yet turning the symbols into words, into things I could parse. In that moment, it had been enough to know that she had sent me something, that she wasn't just going to disappear and leave me with nothing but questions and memories. There was more to it than that, and it made me feel like the fog I'd been walking around in for the past two weeks had cleared to let in some sunlight.

Like the others she'd sent—one appearing every time I went away, even if it was just for a few days—there was no explanation. Like the others, it was a list of outlandish things, all outside my comfort zone, all things I would never normally do. The lists had become something of a running joke with us, and before every trip I'd wonder what she was going to come up with. The last one, when I'd gone to New Haven with my mom for a long weekend, had included things like stealing the bulldog mascot, named Handsome Dan, and making out with a Whiffenpoof (I later found out Anderson had gone to Yale, so she'd been able to include lots of specifics). Over the years, I'd managed to check off the occasional item on a trip, and always told her about it, but she always wanted to know why I hadn't done more, why I hadn't checked off every single one.

I looked down at the list again, and saw that something about this one was different. There were some truly scary things here—like skinny-dipping and having to deal with my lifelong fear of horses, the very thought of which was making my palms sweat—but some of them didn't seem so bad. A few of them were almost doable.

And as I read the list over again, I realized these weren't the random items that had accompanied my travels to California and Austin and Edinburgh. While many of them still didn't make sense to me—why did she want me to hug someone named Jamie?—I recognized the reasoning behind some of them. They were things I'd backed away from, usually because I was scared. It was like she was giving me the opportunity to do some things over again, and differently this time. This made the list seem less like a tossed-off series of items, and more like a test. Or a challenge.

I turned the paper over, but there was nothing on the other side of it. I picked up the envelope, noted her usual drawing where most people just wrote their addresses—this time she'd drawn a palm tree and a backward moon—and that the postmark was too smudged for me to make out a zip code in it. I looked down at the list again, at Sloane's careful, unmistakable handwriting, and thought about what was sometimes at the bottom of these—*When you finish this list, find me and tell me all about it.* I could feel my heart beating hard as I realized that this list—that doing these terrifying things—might be the way I would find her again. I wasn't sure how, exactly, that was going to happen, but for the first time since I'd called her number and just gotten voice mail, it was like I knew what to do with myself. Sloane had left me a map, and maybe—hopefully—it would lead me to her.

I read through the items, over and over again, trying to find one that wasn't the most terrifying thing I had ever done, something that I could do right now, today, because I wanted to begin immediately. This list was going to somehow bring me back to Sloane, and I needed to get started.

S. Ave in number seven had to mean Stanwich Avenue, the main commercial street in town. I could show up there and ask for Mona. I could do that. I had no idea what 55 Stanwich Avenue was, but it was the easiest thing on the list, by far. Feeling like I had a plan, some direction, for the first time in two weeks, I pushed myself off my bed and headed for the door.

"Emily?"

"*Oh* my god!" I yelled this as I jumped involuntarily. My brother was in my doorway—but not just leaning against the doorframe like a normal person. He was at the very top of the frame, his legs pressed against one side of it, his back against the other. It was his newest thing, after he'd seen it done in some ninja movie. He'd terrified us all at first, and now I just habitually looked up before entering a room. To say Beckett had no fear of heights was an understatement. He'd figured out how to scale the roof of our house when he was five, and if we were trying to find him, we all started by looking up.

"Sorry," Beckett said, not sounding sorry, shrugging down at me.

"How long have you been there?" I asked, realizing that while I'd been absorbed in my letter, my brother had come into my room and climbed to the top of my doorframe, all without me noticing.

He shrugged again. "I thought you saw me," he said. "Can you drive me somewhere?"

"I'm about to go out," I said. I glanced back at Sloane's list, and then realized I had just left it sitting out on my bed. Our cat was only in the house about half the time, but he seemed to have a preternatural ability to know what was important, and he always destroyed those things first. I picked up the letter and placed it carefully back into the envelope, then tucked it into my top dresser drawer, where I kept my most important things—childhood mementos, pictures, notes Sloane had slipped into my hand between classes or through the slats of my locker.

"Where?" Beckett asked, still from above me.

"Stanwich Avenue," I said. I craned my neck back to see him, and suddenly wondered if that was why he did this—so that we'd all have to look up at him for a change, instead of the other way around.

"Can you take me to IndoorXtreme?" he asked, his voice getting higher, the way it did when he was excited about something. "Annabel told me about it. It's awesome. Bikes and ropes courses and paintball."

I was about to tell my brother sorry, that I was busy, but there was something in his expression that stopped me, and I knew that if I went without him, I'd spend the whole time feeling guilty. "Are you going to want to spend a lot of time there?"

Morgan Matson

I asked. "If I drop you off at this Extreme place? Because I have somewhere I need to go."

Beckett grinned. "Hours," he said. "Like, all afternoon." I nodded, and Beckett lifted his foot and did basically a free fall down the doorframe, stopping himself before he hit the ground and jumping to his feet. "Meet you at the car!" He raced out of my room, and I glanced back to my dresser.

I caught my reflection in the mirror above it, and I ran a brush though my hair quickly, hoping that Mona—whoever she was—wouldn't be someone that I needed to impress. I was wearing a vintage T-shirt Sloane had insisted I buy, and a pair of jean cutoffs. I was tall—I had a good four inches on Sloane, unless she was in one of her heel phases—and the only really interesting thing about me were my eyes, which were two different colors. One was brown, and one was brown and blue, and Sloane had freaked out the first time she'd noticed it, trying out all sorts of different eye shadow combinations, trying to see if she could get them to turn the same color. My hair was brown, pin-straight, and long, hitting halfway down my back, but anytime I'd talked about cutting it, Sloane had protested. "You have such princess hair," she'd said. "Anyone can have short hair."

I tucked my hair behind my ears, then pulled open my top drawer to make sure the list and the envelope were still safe. When I was sure they were, I headed downstairs, turning over and over in my head what I was about to do—*55 S. Ave. Ask for Mona.*

2
APPLE
PICKING
AT NIGHT

Beckett was already sitting in the passenger seat of my car when I made it outside. I drove an old green Volvo that my dad had bought off a student who was transferring to a school in California. I had never met the student, but I felt like I knew a lot about him despite that, because the car was covered in bumper stickers. *Save the Whales, Who Doesn't Love Purple Martins?, This Car Climbed Mount Washington*. Along the back windshield was a deconstructed school sticker that read *Unichusetts of Massaversity*, but there wasn't, among all of them, a Stanwich College sticker, which pretty much made it clear why the owner of the car had transferred. I had tried to get them off, but they had proved almost impossible to remove, and so now I was just used to them, and to the occasional honks of anger—or solidarity—I got when other drivers thought they were reading my opinion. The left rear door was jammed, it took a long time for the heat to get going in the winter, and the gas gauge was broken—it was permanently stuck in the center, showing half a tank even when I was running on fumes. I'd learned, over time, just to be aware of when I'd last filled up and how much I'd driven. It was an inexact science, but since I'd never actually run out of gas, it seemed to be working.

The biggest issue with the car, however, was that the roof was always open. The panel that closed the sunroof had been long gone when my dad bought the Volvo, and I just hoped it had been there when the car climbed Mount Washington. I had a tarp I could put over it for when it was raining in the summer, and my parents had gotten the set construction guys to cut a piece of wood that fit inside and made it nearly airtight in the winter. Sloane had loved this part of the car, and had never wanted the roof covered, even when we had to crank the heat and bundle up in blankets. She was always stretching her hand out to let the wind run through her fingers, and leaning forward into the sunlight that spilled down onto the seats.

"All set?" I asked as I slipped on my black Ray-Bans and slammed my door. I'd asked out of habit more than anything else, since Beckett was clearly ready to go. I started the car and pulled out of the driveway, after making sure that there were no strollers or runners heading our way.

"Who's Tesla?" Beckett asked as I started to head toward downtown. I'd looked up IndoorXtreme's address on my way downstairs, wanting to minimize any and all delays that I was sure would be caused by expecting Beckett to know where we were going. And despite the fact that when I was his age, I'd mastered the New York subway system—or at least the stops in Brooklyn—my brother and I had had very different child-hoods. I'd been the child of two struggling playwrights, moving wherever my parents were workshopping a play, or where they'd managed to land adjunct professor or writer-in-residence gigs. We lived in Brooklyn, in San Francisco, in Portlands both Maine and Oregon. I was usually sleeping on the couch in the apartments we were subletting, and if I did happen to have my own bedroom, I never hung up my boy-band posters or keep-sakes, since I knew I wouldn't be there for long. But everything changed with *Bug Juice*. My miserable summer at camp had led to a Broadway play, a subsequent terrible movie, and then countless community theater and school productions, the play taking on a life of its own, my parents an overnight success after ten years of struggle. But most importantly, the play led to my parents securing two tenure-track positions at the same school, which even then I'd known was a big deal. And so we'd moved to Stanwich, and while my brother claimed to remember our early, horrible apartments, for the most part, he'd never known anything but security, his posters hung firmly on his walls.

"What?" I asked, glancing up from the directions on my

phone, weighing whether Beckett could be trusted to read them to me, or if he'd lose interest and start playing *SpaceHog*.

"Tesla," Beckett said carefully, like he was trying out the word. "The play they're writing?"

"Oh," I said. I had no idea who that was, but at the moment, didn't really care. My parents' play was not my priority—Sloane's list was. "I'm not sure," I said. "Want to look it up?" I handed over my phone, and Beckett took it, but a moment later, I heard the *SpaceHog* theme music.

I was about to tell him to try and pay some attention to the directions, when he said, his voice quiet, "You think this one's going to last?"

"The play?" I asked, and Beckett nodded without looking up from the game, his curls bobbing. I took after my dad, with my straight hair and tallness, and Beckett was like a mini version of our mother—her curly hair, her blue eyes. "I don't know," I said honestly. It seemed like it would, but they had certainly had false starts before.

"Just 'cause Dad and I were supposed to go camping," Beckett said, punching the screen of my phone hard, making me wince. "We had a whole plan and everything. We were going to eat fish we caught for dinner and sleep outside."

"You don't even like fish," I pointed out, only to get a withering look in return.

"That's the *whole point* of camping—to do stuff you wouldn't normally do."

"I'm sure it'll still happen," I said, crossing my fingers under the steering wheel, hoping it would be true. Beckett looked over at me, then smiled.

"Cool," he said. "Because—" He stopped and sat up straight, pointing out the window. "There it is."

I made the left into the half-filled parking lot of a huge building; I was pretty sure it had once been a warehouse. I put the car in park, but while the engine was still running, Beckett unbuckled his seat belt and got out, racing for the entrance without waiting for me. Under other circumstances, this might have bothered me, but today, I was thrilled to see it, since it seemed to prove that he wouldn't care that I left him there while I headed off to Stanwich Avenue. As I got out of the car, I glanced at my gas gauge, even though this was pointless, and realized I probably needed to fill up soon—yet another reason to drop Beckett off and go. I followed my brother across the parking lot and inside, heaving open a heavy steel door, the handle shaped like a mountain peak.

IndoorXtreme was big—a huge, open space with ceilings that might have just been the tallest I had ever seen. There was a counter with a register, and shoe and equipment rentals, but the rest of the space seemed devoted to all the ways you could injure yourself in air-conditioned comfort. There was a half-pipe with skateboarders flying down one side and up the other, a bike course with jumps, and, along the back, a vertical climbing wall, with climbers making their way up or rappelling down.

Morgan Matson

The wall had hand- and footholds along it, and it stretched up almost to the top of the ceiling. The whole place seemed to be made of steel and granite, and was painted mostly gray, with the occasional splash of red. It was cold, and the low hum of the industrial air conditioner mixed with the shouts from the skateboarders and the just-louder-than-background-music techno.

Beckett was waiting for me by the counter, having hoisted himself up to see the options, his feet dangling off the ground. He informed me that he wanted the all-inclusive kids' pass, which included everything except paintball, and even though I winced at the price, I got it for him, figuring that the longer Beckett was occupied, the more items on Sloane's list I might be able to accomplish. I'd just planned on the one, but maybe I could even do two. Maybe, if I somehow figured out how to do the really frightening ones, I could have this thing done inside of a week.

I paid the bored-looking guy behind the counter, whose name tag read *Doug* and who picked up a thick paperback the second we walked away, leaning his elbows on the counter to read. Then Beckett ran over to a bench carved to look like a boulder—or maybe it actually *was* a boulder—and started putting on the climbing shoes that Doug had swapped for his sneakers. "So are you all set?" I asked, not even sitting down. I was already planning out my route to Stanwich Avenue. If I didn't stop for gas, I could be there in ten minutes. "I told you, I have those . . . errands to run."

"I'm good," Beckett said, Velcroing his shoes and jumping to his feet. "See you in a couple hours?"

"Great," I said, and Beckett gave me a grin and ran off toward the climbing wall. As I looked around, I realized that this was actually the perfect place to leave him. I had no doubt my brother would be occupied all afternoon. I decided to wait just a minute more, so I wouldn't feel like the worst sister in the world, and watched Beckett take his place in line for the climbing wall, hopping from foot to foot the way he did when he was really excited about something.

"Eight?" I turned and saw two things, neither of which made sense. Frank Porter was standing in front of me, and he was holding out a pair of shoes.

I knew who he was because everyone knew Frank Porter, one of the undisputed stars of Stanwich High School. He was never off the High Honor roll, he was a National Merit Scholar, he'd been sophomore and junior class president. He seemed to actively be trying to make the world—or at least our school—a better place, constantly circling petitions and founding clubs and organizations, always trying to save a program or monument or bird. He would be a lock for valedictorian if it weren't for his girlfriend, Lissa Young, who was just as disciplined and dedicated as he was. They'd been together since something like ninth grade, but they weren't one of the couples constantly making out against the lockers or having screaming fights in the parking lot. They just seemed like a unit, like even their relationship was focused and properly directed. I had heard that they went off every summer together to an academic enrichment program—so I didn't understand why Frank Porter was currently standing in front of me. He was one of the few guys in our class who seemed totally comfortable when there were formal events and he had to wear a suit and tie, which was why it was a little jarring to see him now, wearing a gray T-shirt with *Xtreme Attitude!* written across it, in a font that looked like graffiti. *Frank*, his name tag read, just in case I had any doubt this was him.

The shoes that were extended to me drooped a little, and Frank tilted his head to the side. "Emily?"

I nodded, a little surprised, even though we'd been in the same school for three years. Since Sloane had come to town, I'd happily existed by her side. People called out to her by name and waved at me, and I had a feeling that the majority of my class would, like the landscaping guy, identify me as "That girl who's always with Sloane Williams" or something along those lines. And I never minded—even just being Sloane's friend made me much more interesting than I ever would have been on my own.

"Hi," Frank Porter said, giving me a quick smile. "How are you?" Despite the T-shirt, Frank looked the same as he did during the school year. He was tall, maybe six-two, and lanky. He had reddish-blond hair that was cut short and neatly combed, and curled just slightly at the nape of his neck. His eyes were a light brown, and his skin was freckled. Even in his

T-shirt and holding a pair of rentable shoes, Frank somehow radiated authority. It was like you could see him moving beyond the world of Stanwich High, with no doubt he would succeed wildly—running for office, chairing a board, inventing something tiny and electronic and essential. He just had that air about him—competent and trustworthy and, especially, wholesome. If he hadn't clearly had grander ambitions, I could have seen him in ads for peanut butter and heart-healthy breakfast cereals. When Sloane had first come to Stanwich High, she had looked him up and down and asked, not unappreciatively, "Who's the Boy Scout?"

"Hey," I stammered when I realized I had been staring at him silently for a moment too long. Frank was looking at me, like he was waiting for something, and I remembered, much too late, that he'd asked me a question, and I still hadn't answered it. "I mean, good."

"Did you need these?" Frank asked, lifting the shoes. I couldn't think why I would, and shook my head. "Oh," he said, retracting them. "I heard someone over here needed climbing shoes, and I thought it was you. I guessed on the size." He glanced down at my flip-flops, and I did too, then immediately wished I had gotten a pedicure recently, as the vestiges of the last one I'd gotten with Sloane—bright red, with a cat done in black dots on the big toe—had mostly chipped off. "But was I at least right?" he asked, looking up from my feet. "Size eight?"

"Um," I said. I realized that I was waiting for someone else to jump in and direct this interaction, but unfortunately, there was just me, doing a very poor job of it. If Sloane had been here, she would have known what to say. Something funny, something flirty, and then I would have known what to say too, whether to chime in, or make the kind of joke I only ever seemed to be able to make around her. I didn't know how to do this by myself, and I didn't want to have to learn. Also, I didn't think I'd exchanged more than a few sentences with Frank Porter in three years, so I wasn't sure how we were spending this much time talking about the size of my feet. Which was, incidentally, something I wasn't super thrilled to be talking about, since they were bigger than I liked. "It's just because you're tall," Sloane had always said to me, with the confidence of someone with tiny feet. "Otherwise, you'd look weird. Or tip over."

"Nine," I said finally, leaving off the *and a half* because, really, why did Frank Porter need to know my shoe size?

He shrugged. "Well, I'm still learning the ropes." If Sloane had been next to me, I would have said *So to speak* or *That's for sure* or some other punny remark, since there were actual ropes here and Frank had pretty much opened up the door for a joke like that. But she wasn't, so I just looked away, trying to find my brother somewhere on the line for the climbing wall, so that I could just verify that he was okay and I could leave.

"Porter!" We both turned and I saw Matt Collins, who I knew from school but wasn't sure I'd ever spoken to, dangling in midair from one of the rappelling ropes. He was wearing a T-shirt like Frank's, along with a bright-red helmet, and was turning slowly on his rope, kicking at the wall to spin himself around. "Tonight. We're hitting the Orchard, right?"

The Orchard had, at one point, been a functioning orchard, but the land was now just sitting empty, and it had become the place for parties, especially in the summer. It had the benefit of existing in the hazy border between Stanwich and Hartfield, the next town over, which meant the cops tended to stay away, mostly because, rumor went, nobody was sure whose jurisdiction it was. I had gone a few times, mostly that spring, when it had been Sloane and Sam and me and Gideon. The Orchard conjured, for me, memories of sitting close to Gideon and rolling a bottle between my palms, trying to think of something to say.

Frank nodded, and Collins—even though his name was Matthew, everyone, even teachers at school, called him by his last name—grinned. "Aw yeah," he said. "The C-dawg's going to meet some sweet ladies to-night!"

The woman climbing next to him, who looked like she was in her thirties, with impressive and serious climbing gear on, frowned at him, but Collins just smiled wider at her. "And how are *you* today?"

Frank just sighed and shook his head.

"Well," I said, starting to edge toward the exit. Even though I couldn't see Beckett, I was sure he was fine. And I really didn't want to keep having this incredibly awkward conversation with Frank Porter. I needed to get to Stanwich Avenue, and

I'd already spent much more time here than I'd planned on. "I should . . ." I nodded toward the door, taking a step toward it, hoping Frank didn't feel like he had to keep talking to me just because he thought I was a customer.

"Right," Frank said, tucking the unnecessary, too-small shoes under his arm. "It was nice to—"

"*Heya!*" Collins ran up to us at full speed and crashed into Frank, nearly toppling him over and knocking himself off-balance, windmilling his arms to stay upright. He was still wearing his helmet, which didn't really do a lot for him. Collins was a head shorter than Frank—it looked like he was even a little shorter than me—and on the heavier side, with a round face, a snub nose, and dark blond hair.

"Collins," Frank said in a resigned tone of voice, as he helped to steady him.

"So what's up? What are we talking about?" Collins asked, his eyes darting over to me. He frowned for a moment, then smiled wide. "Hey," he said. "I know you. Where's your friend? It's Emma, right?"

"Emily," Frank corrected him, "Emily Hughes." I looked over at him, shocked that Frank knew my last name. "And I thought you were supposed to be spotting on the wall."

"This guy," Collins said, as he clapped a hand on Frank's shoulder. He turned to me and shook his head. "I mean, I've been here a month and he's here two weeks and is already ready to run things. So impressive!"

"Spotting?" Frank persisted, but Collins just waved this away.

"Everyone's fine," he said. "And I actually *was* spotting. I *spotted* you two talking over here and I wanted to join the convo. So what's the word?" He looked over at the shoes under Frank's arm. "You climbing?" he asked me. Without waiting for a reply, he took the shoes from Frank, looked down at my feet, then at the back of the shoes where the size was written. "Not with these you're not. I'm guessing you're more like, what, a nine and a half?"

I just looked down at my feet for a second, letting my hair swing forward and cover my face, which I had a feeling was bright red. Did I have to respond to that? People weren't under any obligation to admit to their shoe size, were they? But I had a feeling that if I tried to deny it, Collins would challenge me to put the smaller shoes on, and would probably soon be taking wagers from onlookers. I took another step away and started to turn for the door, when the scream ripped through the air, overpowering the techno. It sounded markedly different from the happier yells that, I realized, had just become background noise. The three of us turned in its direction, and I saw that it had come from the serious climbing woman, who was leaning back in her harness and pointing up at the very top of the wall—where my brother, I realized with my heart sinking, was merrily walking.

"Holy crap," Collins said, his mouth hanging open. "How'd

that kid get up there? And where's his harness? Or helmet?"

Before I could say anything, Frank and Collins had taken off in the direction of the wall, and I followed. A crowd had gathered, and most of the climbers were rappelling down, out of the way.

"Emily!" Beckett yelled, waving at me, his voice echoing in the huge space. "Look how high I am!"

Both Frank and Collins looked at me, and I twisted my hands behind my back. "So, that's my brother," I said. I tried to think of something to follow this, like some explanation as to why he was currently humiliating me and jeopardizing IndoorXtreme's insurance policy, but nothing else came.

"What's his name?" Collins asked.

"Beckett," I said. "But I'm sure he's fine. He just—"

"Bucket?" Collins asked, then nodded as though this made sense. "Hey, Bucket!" he yelled up at my brother. "I'm gonna need you to come down from there, okay? Wait," he said, shaking his head. "First, put your helmet back on and come down. Actually," he amended, taking a small step closer, "first put on your harness, *then* your helmet, then come on down from there. All right?"

Beckett looked down at the crowd that was now staring up at him, then at me, and I tried to silently convey to him that he should absolutely do this, and as quickly as possible.

"Okay," he said with a shrug, picking up his harness and snapping himself back into it.

The people below seemed to let out a collective sigh of relief and the crowd began to break up, people starting to climb the wall again or heading back to the bike course.

"See? All good," Collins said, waving up at my brother, who was buckling the chin strap underneath his helmet.

"This is why you were supposed to be spotting," Frank said, shaking his head as he strode toward the climbing wall.

"He's coming down," Collins pointed out, and my brother had indeed started to find the first foot- and handholds to take him back down to earth. "You don't need to go up there." But either Frank didn't hear this or chose to ignore it, because he started climbing up the wall with a sense of purpose, heading toward Beckett. "Ruh-roh," Collins said quietly, looking up at the climbing wall, his brow furrowed.

"It's really okay," I said. "My brother climbs stuff that high all the time."

"I'm not worried about Bucket," Collins said. "I'm worried about Porter."

I looked up at the wall. Frank was almost halfway up now, moving his hands easily from one handhold to the next. He seemed fine to me. "Um, why?"

Collins took off his helmet, and wiped his hand across his forehead. His hair was dark from sweat and plastered down against his head, making him look like he had a bowl cut. It wasn't the best look on him. "Porter's got a fear of heights."

I looked around, at all the many things in this establishment that would involve climbing or skating or jumping over high things. "Oh," I said. I tried to think of some way to ask why he worked here without being insulting. "But . . ."

"I know," Collins said, talking fast, sounding defensive. "My uncle said the same thing when I got Porter the job. But he's *great* with all things paintball," he said, and I nodded, wishing I'd never said anything. "And there's nobody better at the bike course," he went on. "Dude can straighten jumps like nobody's business. Also, he's the most competent one here, so that's why he's the one in charge of the bank deposits. I was *terrible* at that." I nodded; I could easily believe this. "But heights?" Collins leaned a little closer to me and shook his head. "Not his strong suit."

I looked up at Frank, who was now pretty high, almost at the level of Beckett. "Then why is he climbing?" I asked, feeling myself get a little panicky on Frank's behalf.

"Because he's Frank Porter," Collins said, and I heard a note of bitterness in his voice for the first time. "Captain Responsible."

I looked back at the wall, thinking that despite this, maybe things would be okay—when I saw Frank reach for the next handhold, glance down, and freeze, his arm still extended.

"Told you," Collins said softly, not taking any pleasure in the statement.

Frank was now holding on to the wall with both hands, but he still wasn't moving. "What happens now?" I asked, feeling like I was seeing something that I really shouldn't be.

"Well, sometimes he pulls it together," Collins said, his

voice still quiet. "Otherwise, there's a big ladder in the back."

"Oh no," I said, trying to look away but finding that it was impossible. It was clear to me that this was all because of Beckett—which meant, as far as Frank Porter was concerned, it was all because of me.

"I know," Collins said, wincing.

Beckett had now reached the same level as Frank, and he said something to him that I couldn't hear. Beckett kept on climbing down and I realized that he was now below Frank, who still hadn't moved.

Doug from the front desk had come out to stare at the spectacle, his book abandoned on the counter. "Ladder?" he asked Collins, who nodded.

"I think so," he said.

A second later, though, Beckett changed direction and climbed back up until he was level with Frank again. He said something to him, and Frank shook his head. But my brother stayed where he was, still talking to Frank. And after a long pause, Frank reached down for the handhold just below him. Beckett nodded, climbed down two handholds, and motioned for Frank to come down to where he was, pointing out the footholds. After another pause, Frank moved down to the next level again. It was painfully clear to me that my ten-year-old brother was talking the IndoorXtreme employee down the climbing wall, and I just hoped that it wasn't as obvious to everyone else in the facility.

Morgan Matson

"Nice," Collins said, as he watched the progress—slow, but incremental—on the wall. "Does your brother need a job?"

"Ha ha," I said a little hollowly. I was watching with a tight feeling in my chest, and I didn't really let out a full breath until Beckett jumped the last few feet to the ground and then looked up at Frank Porter, pointing out the remaining handholds for him and giving him an encouraging thumbs-up. Frank half stumbled down to the ground, and when he turned around, I could see that his face was almost as red as his helmet. Doug shrugged, then turned and trudged back to the register.

"Porter!" Collins yelled. "You complete moron. I thought I was going to have to get the ladder and pull you out like a damn cat!" The worried friend who had been there just moments before was gone, and I realized Collins had changed back into the guy I was used to from school, the one who was constantly pulling pranks and asking out the most popular girls in highly public ways that invariably backfired.

"Beckett," I called, gesturing for him to come to me. My bother nodded, unclipped himself from his harness, and held up his hand for a high-five, which Frank listlessly returned. Now that he was safely on the ground, I could practically feel the embarrassment coming off Frank in waves.

Beckett reached me, and I grabbed him by the neck of his T-shirt, not wanting to let him out of my sight, in case he decided to scale the half-pipe or something. "See you around,"

I said to Collins, just out of habit, but without any expectation that this would be true.

"Yeah," Collins said, and I could tell he was saying this the same way—just something you say, not something you mean. "Sure." He headed toward Frank, who was still standing by the wall, and I watched him go for a moment before I looked down at my brother, who had the sense to at least pretend to look ashamed of himself.

"Sorry," he said quickly. "I just wanted to see the view from the top, and—"

"Let's go," I said, steering him toward the front counter, Beckett dragging his feet and talking fast, trying to stall.

"We don't have to leave," he said. "I just won't go on the wall. I can still do the bike course, right? Em?"

I didn't even respond to this as we reached the counter and Beckett pulled off his climbing shoes. I wasn't happy about leaving, because it meant I probably wouldn't get to Sloane's list today. But I had a feeling that even if I didn't take Beckett away, he might be asked to leave, making this even more embarrassing than it already was. I pushed Beckett's climbing shoes across to Doug, who was back to reading his paperback. *A Murder of Crows*, the cover read, featuring a fierce-looking bird about to alight on a flaming sword. He stood and got Beckett's sneakers without looking up from his book.

"But, *Emily*," Beckett whined.

I just shook my head. And we walked out to my car in

silence as I tried to steel myself for what I was going to have to do. I usually didn't play the Big Sister card—Beckett and I got along fine, mostly because there were seven years between us, we'd never been competing for the same things, and I usually felt more like his babysitter than his sibling. But this was one of the instances where I knew I had to do it, since my parents certainly weren't going to step up, not right when they'd begun a play. I put the key in the ignition, but didn't turn it yet as I faced my brother, who was sitting cross-legged on the seat, glaring down at his hands. "Beck, you can't do stuff like that," I said. I suddenly wondered if it would have been better if Beckett had gotten hurt at some point during the years he'd been climbing, so he'd have a healthy degree of fear, or at least some understanding of the consequences. "You shouldn't be taking risks like that. I don't care what you climb at home. There were other people around. You could have been hurt, or you could have hurt them. It's called being reckless."

I started the car and headed home, Beckett not speaking, still looking down. I knew he was mad at me and figured he would probably sulk the rest of the drive, so I was surprised when he spoke up as I turned onto our street.

"But I wasn't," Beckett said. I wasn't sure what he meant, and it must have been clear, because he went on, "I wasn't hurt. Nobody else was, either. And I got to see a really great view. So what's that called?"

I just shook my head, knowing somehow that there was a

flaw in his logic, but not exactly sure how to articulate what it was. "Just . . ."

"I know, I know, be more careful," he said as I pulled in to the driveway. He contradicted this immediately, though, unbuckling his seat belt and jumping out before I'd even put the car in park. "I'm going to Annabel's. See you later," he yelled as he slammed the door and took off running behind our house. Annabel lived at the other end of the block, and she and Beckett had spent most of last summer finding shortcuts between the two houses that they guarded closely and refused to disclose.

I watched him go, then picked up my phone. I had pressed the button to call Sloane automatically, when I realized what I was doing. I hung up—but not before I'd heard the phone was still going directly to her voice mail, the one that I'd heard a thousand times, the one that she'd recorded with me next to her as we walked down the street. Toward the end, you could hear me laughing. I set the phone down on the passenger seat, out of easy reach. But it always felt like nothing had really happened until I'd talked to Sloane about it. I was used to recapping my experiences to her, and then going through them, moment by moment. And if she'd been here, or on the other end of the phone, I could have told her how bizarre it was that Frank Porter was working at IndoorXtreme, about Collins, and what I'd heard about their evening plans—

I suddenly understood something and glanced up at my bedroom window, picturing the list in my drawer. I got now

Morgan Matson

what Sloane meant by number twelve. It wasn't just a bizarre fruit-gathering mission. She wanted me to go to the Orchard.

I waited until ten before I left. By this point, Beckett was in bed and my parents had retreated to their study at the top of the house. All their patterns from a few years ago were coming back, and this was how they had worked then: they would write all day in the dining room, usually forgetting about dinner, and then head upstairs, where they would go over that day's pages and plan out the next day.

When I was thirteen, the last time this had happened, it wasn't like I'd had much of a social life, or anywhere at all to go at night, so I'd never explored the possibilities their writing afforded. But now, things were different. During the school year, I had a pretty strict midnight curfew that Sloane—who had no curfew whatsoever—had figured all kinds of techniques for getting around. Now that my parents were otherwise occupied, I had a feeling my curfew had become more theoretical than something that would be enforced. But just in case, I scrawled a note and left it up against the TV in the kitchen, so if they found me gone, they wouldn't call the police.

As I'd gotten ready in my room—this basically just meant putting on jeans instead of shorts, grabbing a sweatshirt, and adding a swipe of lip gloss—I'd stared down at the list. While I still didn't understand a few of the others, I *really* didn't get this one. It didn't seem like it was going to be a challenge, since it wasn't like I'd never been to the Orchard before. We'd gone there one afternoon a week before I went upstate and Sloane disappeared. We'd had milkshakes—vanilla for me, coffee for her—and lain out on the picnic tables for hours in the sun, just talking. We'd been a number of times this past spring, usually at night, but occasionally during the day, when Sloane wanted a place where we could hang out in peace, working on our tans or just walking up and down the rows of trees, talking about anything that came to our minds.

I kept the Volvo's lights off until I reached the street, even though the curtains in my parents' study were drawn. And once I'd made it down the street without my cell lighting up with calls and texts asking me where I thought I was going, I figured that I was in the clear.

I turned my lights on and my music up, a Luke Bryan album I'd downloaded last month but not listened to until now, and headed in the direction of the Orchard. I was halfway through the album when I turned off the main road and on to the side street that would lead me there. Out here, the houses got farther and farther apart until there was nothing but empty land and, tucked away on an almost-hidden drive, the Orchard. I slowed as I got closer. The entrance was always, by design I was sure, blink-and-you'll-miss-it. I was contemplating turning around and backtracking when I saw the fading sign and the narrow gravel driveway. I put on my blinker, even though I hadn't seen any other cars on the road, and turned in, pausing for a moment to look at the sign.

It was almost lost in the overgrown bushes on the side of the road, and so faded with weather and time that whole parts of it could barely be seen. Without meaning to, I glanced down at the underside of my wrist before looking away and driving on.

****

MARCH

Three months earlier

"It's just up here," Sloane said as she turned around in the car to face me, pointing. "See the driveway?"

"I can't believe you've never been to the Orchard," Sam said from the driver's seat, and I heard the capital letter in his tone.

"No, remember?" Sloane asked, and I could hear a laugh tucked somewhere in the edges of her words. "Because I'd never been before we came here last month."

"That doesn't mean Emily couldn't have gone on her own," Sam said, shaking his head. Sloane turned her head back to look at me again and we exchanged the tiniest of smiles—probably not even perceptible to anyone but us. I didn't want to contradict Sam, or argue with him, but of *course* I wouldn't have come here if I hadn't been here with Sloane, and we both knew it.

She raised her eyebrows at me with a bigger smile, and I understood her meaning perfectly—she was asking something like *You're having fun, right? Isn't this great? Are you okay?*

I smiled back at her, a real smile and not an *I need a rescue* smile. The last thing I wanted was to upset the evening that she'd worked so hard to arrange. Her smile widened, and she turned back to Sam, moving as close to him as her seatbelt would let her, reaching over and running her hand through his curly hair.

Gideon and I were sitting on opposite ends of the backseat, in contrast to the snuggling that was going on in the front. I was half on the seat and half pressed against the door handle, which probably wasn't really necessary, as we were riding in an enormous SUV and it looked like there was probably room for several people in the space between us. I looked across the expanse of the dark backseat at Gideon, who I had met just a few hours before.

Sloane had been talking up Gideon Baker for weeks, ever since she and Sam had become whatever they were now. "We don't need a label," Sloane had said, when I'd tentatively asked what, exactly, they were doing. She'd smiled at me and straightened her vintage cardigan. "You know I hate those." But when whatever they were doing had become more serious, suddenly I had started hearing a lot about Gideon, Sam's best friend, who was also single. And wouldn't it be so great if . . . ?

That sentence had always trailed off, never really stating

what exactly she was asking, but always with a hopeful question mark at the end. Somewhere along the line, I'd agreed that it *would* be so great, which was how I now found myself wearing more makeup than usual, sharing a backseat with Gideon, going to someplace called the Orchard.

Gideon took up a lot of space in the car—he was tall, with broad shoulders and big hands and feet, and when we'd been sitting across from each other in the diner booth an hour before, and Sloane had been stealing fries off Sam's plate, I'd asked him if he played any sports. He looked like an athlete—I could practically see him featured on the Stanwich Academy website, a lacrosse stick slung over one shoulder. But he'd just taken a bite of his burger as I asked this. He'd chewed, swallowed, taken a sip of Coke, wiped his mouth, then said, "No." And that had pretty much been the extent of our conversation so far.

"What is this?" Sam asked, letting out a sigh as he slammed on the brakes. I leaned forward and saw that we were now behind a long line of cars, and that there was a bottleneck around the entrance to a gravel driveway.

"It just means that this is *clearly* the place to be," Sloane said, and I could hear in her voice how happy she was. Happy we were going there, happy to be with Sam, happy that I was there in the back, with a boy of my own, not a third wheel.

We edged closer to the turnoff, Sam sighing loudly and drumming his fingers on the steering wheel. I glanced across the car at Gideon again, trying to think of something to say, when I saw the sign. It was out his window, and I edged a little away from my door handle, trying to get a better look. It was dark out, but the SUV's headlights—which were sci-fi bright, and also clearly made out of something expensive and fancy, unlike my Volvo's regular old lights—were right on it, illuminating it.

"Do you guys see that?" I asked, pointing at the sign, aware as I did so that my voice felt a little scratchy—it was the first thing I'd said during the car ride. Everyone turned to look, but Sam just shrugged.

"It's the sign from when this used to be an actual orchard," he said. "It's always been there."

I moved over a little farther into the middle, trying to get a closer look. It was mostly faded, but you could tell that it had been brightly painted at some point. *Kilmer's Orchards!* it read in stylized script. *Apples/Peaches/Cherries. Berries in Season! Pies!* Underneath this, there was a cartoon-style drawing of two cherries, attached at the stem. They had faces and were smiling big, looking up like they were reading the message at the top. I looked at all the exclamation points, now faded and unnecessary, selling a product that no longer existed. You could also tell the sign had been hand-painted, and not by a professional—the cherries were admittedly a bit lopsided—which somehow made things worse.

"What?" Sloane asked. I glanced over at her, and saw

she was looking at me, and that she could tell something was wrong.

"Just . . . that sign," I said, hearing how silly it sounded. It was something I would have said easily if it were just Sloane and myself, but the presence of the guys in the car changed this. "I don't know," I said, forcing a laugh and moving back to my side of the seat. "It just . . . seemed really sad, I guess."

Sloane had started to reply when Sam laughed and drove on, talking over her. "It's just a sign, Emily."

"I know," I said, trying to keep my voice light as I looked out my own window. "Never mind."

Sam leaned over and said something I couldn't hear to Sloane, and I watched the trees passing slowly in the darkness. I was wishing I'd never said anything at all when I felt something touch my arm.

I jumped, and looked over to see Gideon, his seat belt unbuckled, suddenly sitting close to me, right in the center seat. He gave me a half smile, then picked up my arm and brought it a little nearer to him.

He had literally kept his distance from me all night—so why was he holding my arm? I took a breath to say something when he pulled a thin Sharpie from his pocket. He nodded down at my arm, and then held up the marker, like he was asking if it was okay.

I nodded, mostly just because I was so thrown. He uncapped the marker, then started drawing on the inside of my wrist. The marker strokes felt feathery and light against my skin, almost tickling me but not quite. I tried to lean over to see what Gideon was drawing, but he pulled my arm a little closer to him and turned it slightly, carefully toward him and away from me. I was still trying to get my head around the fact that this was happening, and I was suddenly glad that Sloane and Sam were oblivious in the front seat, because I knew how strange this must look.

Gideon's head was bent over my arm as he worked, and I couldn't help but notice the texture of his dark hair, so short it was almost a buzz cut, and how big his hands were, how it seemed like, if he'd wanted to, he could totally encircle my wrist with two fingers. The car lurched over a bump, and my arm flew up, almost smacking him in the face. He looked over at me and I gave him a tiny, apologetic smile. He waited a moment, steadying my arm, holding it with both hands— maybe to make sure there were no more bumps—and then started working again, drawing faster than before. He straightened up and capped his Sharpie just as Sam parked the car.

I pulled my hand back to see what he'd done and saw, to my surprise, that he'd drawn the cherries from the sign. He was clearly a much more talented artist than the sign painter, but he'd managed to capture them perfectly in their slightly irregular glory. One of the cherries was saying something, and I lifted my wrist closer to my face to see what it was.

Don't worry, Emily! We're not sad!

I smiled at that, running my fingers over the words, their neat block print. I looked up at Gideon, who was still sitting close to me. "Thank you," I said.

Sam cut the engine, and the car's interior lights flared on. I could see Gideon much more clearly now as he ducked his head like he was embarrassed and slid over to his side of the car. But before the lights started to dim again, I saw him smile back at me.

★★★★

The Orchard looked, from my parking spot, about the same as it had the last time I'd been there. It was a huge open space, covered with grass that was always flattened by cars driving and people walking over it. People tended to park haphazardly and then congregate by the picnic tables that ringed the space, left over from the Orchard's previous incarnation. There were still some ladders to be found leaning up against the trees, but most of them had at least a rung or two broken, and only the bravest—or drunkest—people ventured up them. More than once, I'd seen someone go crashing to the ground when a rung had collapsed under their feet. Sometimes people were organized enough to get a keg, but mostly they brought their own beverages with them, and there was usually some enterprising person selling not-quite-cold cans of beer, for a heavy markup, from a cooler in the back of their car.

It looked like I was still on the early side—you knew a night was really getting going when there wasn't any room to park on the grass and people ended up parking on the road that led to the turnoff. Orchard etiquette dictated you parked, at minimum, half a mile up the road so as not to attract cops' attention.

An open convertible, stuffed with people, screeched into the spot next to me and parked at an angle. I didn't recognize anyone, but before I could look away, a few of them glanced at me as they got out of the car. I turned away quickly, and in that moment, I suddenly realized what I had done. I had been so focused on following Sloane's list that it was just now hitting me that I had shown up to the town party spot, all by myself. The only people I'd ever seen alone at the Orchard were creepy guys from Stanwich College, trying to pick up high school girls.

The Volvo's engine started to whine and I reached forward to turn it off, then sat back against my seat. Reading the list and making the plan for tonight, it had seemed like Sloane was here with me. But this was the reality. I was alone at the Orchard, and had no idea what I was supposed to do next. I could hear, across the clearing, the low bass of music thumping and occasional shouts or laughter. I couldn't make out anyone clearly, but I could see that there were a lot of people there, groups of friends in clusters. Was I supposed to just walk in there by myself?

A car swung in to park on the other side of me, and I picked up my phone, pretending to be absorbed in it, until I realized

Morgan Matson

that nobody had left the car—and, in fact, the couple inside had started furiously making out in the front seat.

It was enough to get me out of the car, slamming my door and locking it shut. I looked ahead of me, to the Orchard. For just a second, I tried to rationalize that maybe I could just go home now—after all, I'd shown up here, and Sloane hadn't provided any other instructions. But even as I was thinking it, I knew that wasn't what she meant. And if I was going to do this, I needed to do it right. I took a big breath and made myself put one foot in front of the other as I walked to the clearing, wondering what it was that I normally did with my hands.

I was just not used to having to do things like this on my own. It had been me and Sloane, joined at the hip for the last two years, and she was so good at this kind of stuff—utterly fearless about walking into places she hadn't been before, or talking to people she didn't know—that any skill I might once have had in that department had withered away, since I knew Sloane would lead the way. And before she had moved to town, I had been part of a group of other freshman girls, and we had basically navigated the first year of high school by going everywhere in a pack.

I realized, with my heart sinking as I got closer to the clearing, that I had to deal with the fact that I had nowhere to go. There were about forty people here, and I recognized about a third of them—mostly people from Stanwich High, but a couple of Stanwich Academy people who were familiar from parties I'd been to with Gideon, when we'd gone with Sloane and Sam.

Different groups had staked out the picnic tables, with people sitting on the tables and the benches, everyone talking and laughing and clearly here with their friends. Nobody else was wandering around alone.

I could see, a little farther into the rows of trees, various couples either making out or arguing, and beyond them, a small group smoking. There was a guy at the edge of the picnic tables with a keg and a stack of red Solo cups, an open cooler at his feet, and a steady drift of people walking in his direction. I thought about going over there, just to have something to do, but then what would I do afterward? I was sure everyone was looking at me; I could practically feel it. Everyone noticing that I was standing alone, out of place and friendless. Half the people there probably thought I was a narc.

I could tell that I was only a few minutes away from crying—or panicking—and to stave off this reaction, I stuffed my hands into my back pockets and tried to look around with a purpose, like maybe I was just trying to locate the friend that I was meeting, the people who were waiting for me. As I looked around, I saw Collins, leaning on a ladder in what I'm sure he thought was a suave pose, talking to Callie Dwyer, who was one of the most gorgeous and popular girls in school—someone who couldn't be further out of his league. Callie looked bored and a little discomfited, and it didn't seem like Collins had noticed yet that she was slowly edging away from him.

At the picnic table closest to him was Frank Porter, sitting with a group that I recognized he spent time with at school, but none of whom I knew particularly well—they were the super-focused high achievers. I looked away quickly, before either of them saw me staring, suddenly worried that they'd think I'd come here to tag along with them because I'd overheard their plans at IndoorXtreme.

I looked down at my feet, at my chipped polish, like it was somehow fascinating, wondering how long I had to stay here before I could consider this one done and go back home again.

I felt a hand on my shoulder and jumped, startled, then turned around to see Gideon standing in front of me.

"Oh," I said, surprised to see him—especially since I'd been thinking about him earlier. I suddenly hoped that this wasn't clear in my expression. I realized after a second that this had not been the most polite reaction, and quickly added, "I mean, hi. How are you?"

"Okay," Gideon said, giving me a half smile. He looked at me for a long moment before he spoke again. "It's good to see you, Emily."

"You too," I said automatically, then wondered a second later if it really was. While I was happy to have someone to talk to and I was no longer the most pathetic person at the Orchard, I didn't particularly want to talk to Gideon, especially after the way we'd left things.

Gideon looked the same as he had the last time I'd seen him, the night in May when everything had crashed and burned.

I'd gotten used to his tallness when we were hanging out—or whatever it was we'd been doing—every weekend, but it had been long enough since I'd seen him that it struck me again. His blue eyes were still inscrutable, and his dark hair looked freshly cut. I was surprised and a little impressed he'd come over to me. I knew that if I'd seen him here, I wouldn't have done the same thing. But maybe that's how pitiful I'd looked standing here on my own—he'd felt he needed to come and rescue me. "So," I said, after a long pause when it became clear Gideon wasn't going to say anything. "How have you been?"

"Well," he said, then took another pause. Gideon had always skipped the small talk with me, always thought about his answers and always wanted real answers in return. He had never given the flip, easy responses like everyone else. I thought now that we were no longer the something we'd once been, he'd stop this and go back to the superficial. But apparently not. "I'm all right," he finally said. He turned his head slightly to the right, and nodded behind him. "Sam wanted to come out tonight, so . . ."

I lost whatever else Gideon was saying as I followed his nod and saw Sam. Just the sight of him was enough to make my stomach drop. He was leaning against a picnic table, and there was a girl sitting on top of it, talking to him, smiling wide and gesturing big, telling him some story while Sam nodded occasionally, one eyebrow raised. Why hadn't I put this together as soon as I'd seen Gideon? He and Sam went places together, especially places like the Orchard. Before I could look away,

Morgan Matson

Sam's gaze drifted from the girl and landed on me. We just stared at each other for a moment, my heart thudding, before I looked away, down at the ground.

I could still sense his eyes on me, and I felt myself get closer to panic, wondering if he was going to come over, if I was going to have to talk to him. But when I glanced back, I saw that he was looking away, clearly barely listening to the girl at his side. And I could feel myself relax a little. Of course he wasn't going to come over here. He had always been a coward.

"Emily?" I made myself focus back up at Gideon, who was looking at me with his eyebrows raised, waiting for an answer to a question I hadn't heard him ask.

"Sorry," I said quickly. "What was that?"

"Nothing," Gideon said, with a smile that disappeared immediately. He took a breath, and I realized he looked nervous, that he was swallowing hard. "Emily. I—"

"Sorry," I said, quickly, needing to cut off whatever he was about to say. I wasn't even sure what it was, only that he would probably want some explanation for what had happened, and I much preferred to keep that can of worms closed. "I just . . . I have to go," I said, starting to edge away from him. "I actually— there's someone I need to talk to."

Gideon just looked at me in silence, and I could feel a long-dormant frustration bubbling up to the surface. Half my conversations with Gideon seemed to consist of these long, charged pauses, and after a while I'd just found it exhausting—like being a character inside a Pinter play. Like there were all these meanings that I was supposed to understand in his silences, but never quite did. "Okay," he said slowly.

"Bye," I said, then I turned and walked away, toward the guy with the keg, simply because I couldn't think of any other options. I realized only after it was going to be too late to change direction—without it being super obvious—that I was going to pass Sam. I tried to keep my eyes fixed in front of me, but couldn't help glancing in his direction just as I passed. The girl next to him was still talking, her gestures bigger than ever, while he just looked on, impassive. It was something that had always really bothered me about him: he rarely laughed at anything, making you feel like you were somehow obligated to entertain him. And even though I didn't want it to, when you did get him to laugh, it somehow felt like an achievement. I pointedly looked away before our eyes could meet again, keeping my head down until I got to the keg.

The guy selling the beer was perched on one of the more rickety-looking picnic tables with a girl next to him, sitting close. I didn't recognize either of them—I was pretty sure they went to Hartfield.

I waited for a moment, until it became clear that he was not paying attention, then cleared my throat and said, "Um, beer? Please?"

"Five bucks," the guy said, not looking away from the girl, even when I pulled a crumpled bill out of my pocket and handed it to him. He pointed to the remaining red cups, and then toward the keg.

"Thanks," I said, taking a cup and walking toward the keg while the girl burst out laughing. Even though I knew it wasn't about me, I still felt my heart pound as I pressed the spigot. The keg was nearly tapped, and I'd never been great at working them to begin with, so I mostly got a cup of foam. It didn't really matter to me, though, since I was basically just using it as a prop. I took a tiny sip, wincing at the warm, metallic taste, wondering how much longer I had to stay.

An hour later, I had solved the problem of looking like a total loser hanging out alone by removing myself from public view. I had found a spot in the rows of trees, the ones away from the picnic tables that nobody would be climbing as a dare, and had sat down, my back against one of them, trying not to cry. I had known, of course, that Sloane wasn't here anymore. But I hadn't quite understood what that meant until tonight. As I'd walked across the Orchard with my beer, I'd seen people I knew from school, and occasionally they would give me half a nod, but some people's eyes slid right over me, as though without Sloane by my side, I'd become invisible. I'd pretended like I had somewhere to go, biting my lip hard as I walked into the trees and then sat down.

The reality of life without Sloane was, it turned out, much worse than I'd imagined. The reality was me, sitting by a tree with a prop cup of beer, totally alone, while other people laughed with their friends. I poured the beer out onto the tree's roots and pushed myself to my feet. I was going home. I had surely spent enough time at the Orchard to satisfy Sloane's list, though I had no idea what it might have accomplished beyond making me feel the loss of her even more sharply.

I stepped out of the trees and back onto the grass, and noticed a moment too late that I had basically fallen into step with two people also heading the same direction. After a second, I saw that they were Frank and Collins, and I felt my heart sink.

"Hey!" Collins said, smiling big at me. He was wearing a rose-colored polo shirt that fit him a little too tightly and long khaki cargo shorts. "Where'd you come from, Emma?"

"Lee," Frank corrected.

"*Lee?*" Collins asked, squinting at me, tilting his head to the side. "No, I don't think that's right."

"Emily," Frank explained, his voice patient. "We went through this like four hours ago at work." He looked over at me and gave me a half smile. "Hi, by the way."

"Hey," I murmured. I figured they were probably heading to the keg, and I looked longingly toward the cars—I was so close to just being alone, and not having to have any of these strained conversations any longer. "See you guys," I said, turning off toward the parking lot, counting down the seconds until this would be over.

"We're, um, actually," Frank said, nodding ahead, and I realized they were heading to their cars as well, in the same direction as me—and I had just made this more uncomfortable than it needed to be.

"Oh, right," I said quickly. "Right. Cool." There really didn't seem to be much to say to that, and we walked along silently, all in a row, like we were a gang in a movie musical. "See you guys," I said, as soon as my car came into view, and then realized a second later that I'd just repeated myself. But I didn't really care, at this point. I just wanted to go home.

"Laters, Emma-*lee*," Collins said, emphasizing the last syllable of my name. He stopped in front of a maroon minivan and pointed his clicker at it. A moment later, the side door slid open with a jerking movement, finally jolting to a stop. He glanced proudly at the open door and gave me a faux-modest smile. "Not bad, huh?"

I wasn't sure what to say to that—or even why he'd opened that door, not the driver's door—but before I had to think of something, Collins held out his hand to Frank for a fist-bump, gave me a wink, climbed in through the side door, and maneuvered his way into the front seat. Then he peeled out of the Orchard, fast, his door sliding shut as he pulled away.

I walked to the Volvo and unlocked it as I realized Frank was getting into a blue pickup truck a few cars down from me. He gave me a nod, and I gave him a half smile before I ducked into my car and started the engine. I turned on my lights, starting to breathe a little easier now that this whole strange, stressful evening was coming to a close. I didn't even wait for Frank to leave first, but stepped on the gas, just wanting to get home. I had almost made it to the top of the road, by the sign, when my car started to slow down. I pressed harder on the gas, but the car didn't speed up, instead just rolling a few more feet and then sputtering to a stop. I shifted the car into park and cut the engine, then waited a few seconds and tried to start the car again. But the car didn't start—the engine revved once, then died. Was it the battery? I looked in a panic at the dashboard, like this might tell me something, and my eyes landed on the gas gauge, still right at a half tank, and I realized what had happened. I was out of gas.

I closed my eyes for a long moment, as though maybe I would wake up to find this had all been a terrible dream. But no. I opened them, saw headlights approaching behind me, and realized that things were only going to get worse.

It was Frank's truck. I tried to start the car once again, like maybe there was a special secret reserve tank that would be activated, but of course, nothing happened. I could hear Frank's engine rumbling behind me, and I cranked down my window and stuck my hand out, motioning for him to go around. It was narrow here at the top of the road, but there was enough room to get out if you drove on the grass. And he was in a truck, so it wasn't like it would be a problem for him or anything. When Frank didn't move, I motioned him around again, wishing he would just leave so I could figure out what to do here. But a second later, his hazards switched on, flashing red every

Morgan Matson

few seconds, and Frank got out of the driver's side and headed toward my car.

I looked away and bit my lip hard, feeling like I was about five seconds from bursting into tears. All I wanted to do was to go home. Why was that so impossible? And why was Frank Porter insisting on witnessing my humiliation? Suddenly, I was mad—furious—at Sloane. I didn't want to be here. I didn't want to be dealing with any of this. I was only here because she'd told me to go here. And if she'd hadn't left, if she'd been where she was supposed to be, none of this would be happening.

"Hey." I looked over and saw that Frank was leaning down to speak to me through my open window, his face closer to mine than I'd been expecting. I drew back slightly, clutching my keys in a hand that I realized was shaking. "Are you okay?"

"Fine," I said, trying to make myself smile at him, wishing more than anything that he would just leave me alone. Frank looked at me for a moment, and I wondered if I had insulted him by trying to pretend that things were fine when they so clearly were not. I couldn't help but wish that it had been any-one else behind me. Of course Frank Porter was going to come over and make sure I was okay, while I knew most people would have just gone around me without a second thought. "I mean," I added after a moment in which Frank hadn't moved, "I'm out of gas. But it's okay. I can handle it."

"Really?" A car behind Frank's honked its horn, loud, and Frank made the same *go around* motion that I'd given to him.

The car screeched around us, followed by two others, and I felt myself start to get panicky, as I realized that I was completely blocking people's way out. Frank turned back to me. "Why don't I drive you to get some gas?"

"Oh, that's okay," I said automatically. "I'll be fine." A second later, though, I realized I hadn't thought through what I was going to do here. Call my parents, wake them up, and tell them to come get me because I was stranded at a party they didn't know I had gone to? It was not a good option. I had a feeling they'd be more upset about being woken up—and having a subpar workday tomorrow—than about the party itself. Could I call a tow truck? But I didn't know how much that would be, or if there was enough money in the conch to cover it.

Two more cars zoomed around us, one driver yelling something as he went that was lost in the roar of his engine. One of them veered close to the car, and Frank took a step closer to the window. "Come on," he said, and our heads were almost level now as he rested his hand on the open window frame. "There's a place not too far up the road. It'll take no time."

I looked ahead to the dashboard, to the useless gauge, and considered my options. Going with Frank Porter to get gas was, unbelievably, the best of the lot. Another car zoomed around us, the driver leaning on his horn as he went. "Emily?" Frank prompted.

"Yes," I said quickly, realizing that Frank was being incredibly nice in offering this, and probably didn't have all night to stand around while I dithered. I took a long breath and then let it out. "Let's go."

We drove in silence up the road together. Frank and I had pushed the Volvo to the side of the drive, almost right up against the sign with the cherries. Then he'd opened the passenger side door for me, and I'd gotten in, not remembering to say thank you until he'd closed it and was walking around to the driver's side. As I sat in the truck, buckling my seat belt as the lights dimmed, I realized I was in a *boy's* car. Not that I'd ever spent much time picturing the inside of Frank Porter's vehicle, but it wasn't what I'd expected. It wasn't spotlessly clean, maybe with some SAT prep books neatly stacked in the backseat. There was *stuff* everywhere. On the floor in front of me there was a digital camera, a thick biography on John Lennon, and a baseball cap with a robot where the team name normally was. In the backseat, I could see a pair of sneakers and an iPod and a bag from the art supply store on Stanwich Avenue. In the front cupholder, there was a fountain soda cup, the straw bent, and in the back one, a tiny origami frog. I was trying to process all of this, but it pretty much came down to a revelation that hit me like a punch to the stomach—Frank Porter was an *actual person* and, despite his ubiquitous presence on campus, one I knew nothing about. And that made the fact that we were going to do this all that much stranger.

Frank pulled open the driver's door and got in, turned off the hazards, and started the engine. The stereo came to life, but not playing music, just the sound of people laughing and clapping before Frank reached over, fast, and hit the button to turn it off. He didn't comment on this, and so I didn't either as we pulled out onto the dark, quiet road. Frank turned right, the opposite direction of going back to town. I actually had no idea where we were heading now, and was very grateful that he seemed to know where the nearest gas station was.

Being so far out from the lights of town—and with no houses around—it was pitch-black, the truck's headlights bright against the darkness and the stars above taking over the sky, seemingly twice as many of them as I saw at home. I glanced at his profile, lit up by the dashboard lights, then out the window again, trying to get my head around what was happening. I was alone with Frank Porter, in the dark, in a confined space.

The truth was, I really just wasn't used to being by myself with guys. Even with Gideon, when we were alone together, it was usually at a larger party, or with Sam and Sloane. I couldn't remember when—if ever—it had just been me and a guy, alone in a car, on a dark road.

"So did you have fun tonight?" Frank asked, looking over at me after we'd been driving in silence for several minutes, me pulling my feet up to avoid stepping on John Lennon. I didn't respond right away, and he added, "Until the car troubles, I mean?"

"Oh," I said. I looked down and saw that the truck was a stick shift, and that Frank was driving it with ease, moving between the gears without even looking down. "Um, it was

Morgan Matson

okay," I said, feeling like the last thing Frank Porter needed was a recap of how terrible my night had been. He nodded and looked out at the road, and I realized after a moment too long that it was now my turn to ask him a question. If it had been Sloane in the car and not me, she and Frank would have been talking and laughing like old friends, and would have established their own inside jokes by the time they'd reached the gas station. And if it had been the three of us, I would have been able to sit quietly, happily, joining in with the laughter, feeling part of it, comfortable enough to jump in with a comment or an aside, but knowing the weight of the interaction wasn't on me. "Did you?" I finally asked. "Have fun, I mean? Tonight?" Managing to mangle this simple question, I looked out the window, rolling my eyes at myself.

There was a small pause, and Frank cleared his throat before responding. "Yeah, sure. I mean, it was fine." I nodded, and looked back out the window, thinking this was the end of our attempt at a conversation. But a second later, he added, "I don't usually go there. It's not really our scene. Mine and Lissa's," he clarified after a tiny pause, as though I didn't know what *we* he was a part of. I nodded again, and realized that, in fact, I'd never seen him at the Orchard before. "But Collins asked me to come along as his wingman, so . . ." He shrugged.

"How, um," I said after another too-long pause, "how did that go?" I had a feeling I knew, since the girl Collins had been hitting on hadn't seemed too thrilled about it.

"The same way it always does," Frank said, shaking his head.

I turned to look out the window again, feeling relieved, like we had made enough small talk, and now Frank Porter wouldn't feel obligated to try and carry on a conversation with me. He switched on his brights, and the outside world was much clearer, showing us things that had been hidden in the shadows before—including a possum that was dashing across the road, right into the path of the truck.

Frank slammed on the brakes. I was jolted forward into my seat belt, and felt something slide out from under my seat and hit me on the ankle. Thankfully, the possum didn't freak out and play dead in the middle of the road, but just kept running, disappearing a second later into the trees on the other side. "Sorry about that," he said, glancing over at me as he downshifted and started to drive again, more slowly this time. "You okay?"

"Fine," I said. I reached down and picked up what had slid out from under the seat. It was a CD case, the cover showing a mournful-looking guy on a curb in the rain, holding a microphone. Something about the picture made me think it was a few years old. *Curtis at the Commodore*, it read in stylized cursive. Frank looked over at me, and I quickly set the CD down on the seat next to me, hoping he didn't think I was pawing through his stuff. "Sorry," I said quickly. "This was just under the seat, and when you stopped—"

"Right," Frank said, reaching over for it and dropping it behind his own seat. "Thanks." He looked straight out at the road, and I wondered if I'd looked at something I shouldn't have. But since I had no idea how to apologize for that, I didn't even try. Before the silence could get uncomfortable, I saw the bright neon lights of the gas station up ahead. *Route 1 Fuel*, the sign read. It probably would have stood out in the daylight as well, since there was nothing around it, like it had popped up from the ground. Especially after the darkness of a road without streetlights, it seemed to appear almost like a mirage. But it was a mirage I was very happy to see at the moment. It was small, just four pumps and a mini-mart that looked very mini indeed. I could see a yawning employee behind the counter, and a flickering neon sign in the window that read *Snacks Drinks Candy*.

"I'm really—," I started, then stopped and tried again. "I mean, I'm just glad that you knew about this place. All the way out here."

Frank nodded as he swung up to one of the fuel pumps, pointing at the trees behind the very mini mini-mart. "See those?" he asked. "That's the habitat of the gray tree frog. There were plans last year to expand the convenience store, add a car wash. Lissa and I spearheaded the petition that shut it down."

"Oh," I said, nodding. This was impressive, and while I was happy for the gray tree frog, I also couldn't help but wish that we had gone to a gas station where someone wouldn't have a grudge against Frank—and by association, me. "Well, I'll just be a second," I said, unbuckling my seat belt and opening the door.

"I'll come in," Frank said, unbuckling his own seat belt,

apparently not worried that management would kick us out before we could get gas. I didn't feel like I could say no, though, so I just headed up to the mini-mart, Frank pulling open the door and holding it for me before I could even reach for it. "Thanks," I muttered. I walked up to the counter, hoping that in a place this small, they would sell something I could put gas in. "Um, hi," I said, and the guy behind the counter straightened up from where he'd been leaning over a folded section of the paper, a pencil in his hand. It looked like he'd been doing the word search, a few words already circled.

"Hey," he said, as Frank came to stand next to me. Frank leaned forward, turning his head to the side, and I realized he was trying to look at the word search. "What do you need?"

"Do you have something I can put gas in?" I asked, looking around the store, but only seeing the normal mini-mart stuff—bags of chips, sodas in refrigerated glass cases, candy and magazines.

He nodded and pointed toward the back of the store. "Against the wall."

"Thanks," I said, hurrying back there, not wanting to take up any more of Frank Porter's time than I already had. But I wasn't really sure Frank minded all that much, because I saw him lean forward, looking at the newspaper.

"You doing the word search?" I heard Frank ask as I reached the back of the store. I found the very small section that seemed to deal with car maintenance stuff—motor oil and funnels and tire pressure readers. I found a giant plastic container with a nozzle attached, but I really didn't think I'd need that much, plus I wasn't sure I could afford it, especially considering I'd also have to buy the gas to put inside it. After I'd overpaid for beer I hadn't drunk, I only had twenty dollars on me. I had an emergency credit card, but it was linked to my parents' card, and I really didn't think I wanted them to see that I'd been buying gas in the middle of nowhere at one a.m.

I returned to the counter with a container about a third of the size of the giant one to find Frank and the guy both leaning over the counter, the newspaper between them.

"*Renaissance*," Frank said, tapping his finger on the newspaper, and I somehow wasn't surprised at all that Frank Porter was now doing the word search with the mini-mart employee. The guy leaned closer, then nodded and circled the word.

"Backward," the guy said, shaking his head. "They always try and get you that way."

"Is that it?" Frank asked, looking down at the paper. "Any left?"

The guy must have noticed me then, as he straightened up and reached for the container, scanning it and giving it back to me. "And the rest on pump four?" I asked, handing him my twenty.

"Nicely done," Frank said. He nodded down at the search, which was now just a collection of pencil circles, the list of words crossed out, and the few lone letters that didn't fit in anywhere. "Emily, check it out."

"Oh," I said, not really sure what to say about this, since I'd never before been in the position to need to compliment some-one's word search. What was I supposed to say? That it looked really thorough?

But before I needed to decide this, Frank was already moving on, plucking my receipt from the counter and starting to fold it absentmindedly. "You ever do Sudoku?" he asked.

"Nah," the guy said, tucking the pencil behind his ear. "Not my scene."

"You have to try it," Frank enthused as I turned to leave, suddenly feeling like I was in the way. "Once you get the hang of it, it's addictive. Oh, man. You have no idea."

I heard the guy laugh before the door closed, and I walked over to the pump. I tried to concentrate on fitting the nozzle into the container, and then not spilling the gas everywhere as it started to fill up, but really I was trying not to think about how acutely aware I was that there were two types of people—the type who could talk to anyone and make friends with them, and the type who spent parties hiding and sitting against trees.

"Hey." I looked up and saw Frank coming to stand next to me. "You okay? I was going to help."

"I think I have it," I said. The numbers had started to slow down, and when they stopped, I put the nozzle away, firmly closed the container, and then bent down to lift it—but it didn't budge.

"Let me get that," Frank said, bending down as well to grab one side of it. We hoisted it up together, and only then did it occur to me that I could have filled up the container in the truck bed, and made things easier for us. It was just one more thing that had gone wrong tonight, and I added it to the list. "James said we should keep it in the back," he said as we placed the container into the truck bed. "And even after it's empty, you should keep the container in your trunk unless you want your car to smell like a filling station."

"James?" I asked as I walked around the back to the passenger side. I hadn't noticed a name tag, but maybe Frank had, or maybe they'd just bonded while doing the word search.

"Yeah," Frank said, nodding toward the guy inside the store, who waved at us. "Nice guy. I think he's going to give Sudoku a try."

We got into the truck, and Frank started the engine and dropped a piece of paper into the cupholder with the origami frog—which was when I noticed that what had been my receipt was now folded into a crane. I wanted to ask him about it, but instead, I just put on my seat belt and looked out the window. If Sloane had been there, sitting next to me, I could have gotten her to ask with one look. She would have done it, too. She had never, in the two years I'd known her, backed down from any kind of challenge.

We were halfway back to the Orchard before I broke the silence and spoke up. Our interaction was coming to an end; I could almost see it shimmering in the distance like the finish line at the end of one of my long cross-country races. "Thank you again," I finally said after silently trying out a few different versions of this. "I really appreciate it. I swear, I've never run out of gas before."

"And I bet you won't again," Frank said. He nodded toward his dashboard, which was lit up like a spaceship, bathing his whole side of the car in a cool blue light. "Mine starts flashing and beeping at me if I get below a quarter of a tank, so I'll usually fill up immediately just to get it to stop."

"The gauge on my car is broken," I explained. Normally I wouldn't have shared this, but I didn't want Frank Porter to think I was some kind of airhead, in addition to being the sister of a preadolescent adrenaline junkie. "So I just try and be aware of how much I've driven."

Frank glanced over at me, eyebrows raised. "I'm surprised you haven't run out before now."

"No, I'm usually really careful," I said. "But this week . . ." My voice trailed off when I realized I wasn't about to tell Frank these kinds of details about my life: Sloane vanishing, me driving all over town looking for her, the list. "It's just been a little crazy," I finally supplied.

He nodded as he made the turn back into the Orchard. It looked like, while we'd been gone, the evening had started to wind down—there were only a handful of cars still parked there. Frank pulled up next to my car, and even though I'd just been expecting he would drop me off, he helped me lift the container down and then held it steady while I filled up. I dropped the empty container off in the trunk, and when I walked back to the driver's side, I saw that Frank was reading the bumper stickers that covered the left side. He looked at me, and I could see the question in his eyes, but I looked away as I got behind the wheel and crossed my fingers. I turned the key, and after a moment of sputtering, the car came to life again.

"Working?" Frank asked, leaning in my window a little.

"Working," I said. I tapped on the gauge. "But don't look at this. It's always stuck on half empty."

Frank leaned closer, contemplating it. "I would say it's half full." He smiled at me, and a moment later, I got the joke. But rather than laughing, or saying something in return, I just gave him a tight smile and stared ahead at the steering wheel. Frank turned to head back to his truck, and I suddenly wondered if this had been incredibly rude.

"But seriously," I said, leaning out the window a little, "thank you. Let me know if there's anything I can do to pay you back."

He nodded and held up a hand in a wave as he turned his truck around to leave. But then he stopped and leaned across his truck to look down at me. "Actually," he said through the open window. "There is something. Can you teach me to run?"

This was so not even close to anything I'd expected him to say that I wasn't sure how to react at first. This might have been apparent in my expression, because Frank went on quickly. "I mean, I know how to run. I just want to get better at it, maybe train for a 10K or something. You're on the cross-country team, right?"

I nodded at that, trying to disguise my shock that Frank had any idea what I'd been involved in at school—or, honestly, that he knew anything about me at all. And after I'd started missing practices and meets regularly this past spring, I wasn't sure that I would still be on the team come fall. But I didn't think that he needed to know any of that. "Sure," I said, easily. I was pretty certain that this wouldn't come to anything, that he would forget he'd asked me, and the next time I saw Frank Porter, it would be at the first day of school in September, when he would be welcoming us all as the senior class president. He had probably only asked so that I wouldn't feel like I owed him anything. "Anytime."

"Great," Frank said. He gave me a smile, then pulled forward, signaling as he turned to leave, even though there was no reason for it. I watched his brake lights until they faded from view, then I turned on my iPod, connected to the ancient stereo via a line in, put my car in gear, and headed for home, ready to put this entire night behind me.

I opened the door slowly, so the hinges wouldn't squeak, and stepped over the threshold. It was almost one thirty, and I held my breath as I waited for lights to turn on and my parents to thunder down the stairs, furious and demanding explanations. But there was only silence, punctuated by the loud ticking of the grandfather clock that had been in the house when we moved in and had proven too heavy to lift. I let out a breath just as I felt something brush against my legs.

I froze. Heart hammering, I looked down and saw that it was only the cat. "Move," I whispered to him as he sat down on the threshold and started washing his paws, like he didn't know that he was sitting right in the path of the door. We'd been in Stanwich a year before he showed up, mewling at our door one night. I was thrilled to be finally getting a pet, which had never been possible before. But even though we put a collar on him and filled his food and water dishes, it quickly became clear that he was not going to be a typical housecat. He came and went as he pleased, mostly living outside in the garage, only spending large amounts of time in the house once it got cold out. But just when you had given up on him ever turning up again, there he would be in the kitchen in the morning, waiting impatiently by his dish, like he'd never been gone. My dad had named him Godot, and over the years, we'd all gotten used to his *I'll be there if I feel like it* presence.

"Come on," I said, nudging him with my foot, but gently, since I just had flip-flops on, and Godot was not shy about using his claws when he felt offended. But it was late, I was exhausted, and it been a long enough day, without having to deal with our cat. I wanted to go upstairs, cross *Apple picking at night* off the list, and then fall into bed. But just as I'd taken a breath to tell the cat to move again, something occurred to me. Had I earned the right to cross it off? I had gone to the Orchard at night, but

I hadn't picked an apple, and I wasn't sure how literal Sloane wanted me to be with some of these. So before I could really think it through or talk myself out of it, I was pulling the door closed, startling the cat, who hissed at me halfheartedly and then stalked away into the night.

By the time I got back to the Orchard, I could see that the last few remaining cars were gone. The place was deserted, empty except for the occasional red cup left crushed on the ground. Now that I was here by myself, the place no longer seemed like the scary battlefield it had been earlier, and I found myself walking easily though the same space I had been tiptoe-ing around the edges of only hours before. I walked across the grass, my eyes adjusting to the darkness, my path lit by the moon that had come out of its cloud cover. As I walked through the rows of trees, I looked for one with a mostly intact ladder, one that wasn't as visible. I figured this was my best bet, since the really prominent ladders were the ones that got jumped on by drunk people, and those were the ones with most of the rungs broken. But the ladder I finally picked seemed to be in one piece, except for the first rung, which I skipped. I climbed it carefully, and when I reached the top and hadn't gone plunging to the ground, I felt myself relax. I was up in the branches of the tree, and I could also see the view from up here—the parking lot with only my car now in it, the endless dark roads that led back to town.

It was months away from being apple season, but I was

Morgan Matson

hoping that there would be a few. The apples I did see looked like the tiny, sour ones, and I had resigned myself to one of these when I spotted one, just a little out of reach. It wasn't as big or as perfectly formed as a supermarket apple, but it was the best one that I could see. I grabbed it, and made sure to hold on to the ladder with my other hand as I gave it a hard yank. It came free of the tree, and I polished it on my tank top before I turned around and leaned back against the top step. Then, making sure I was balanced, I took a bite.

It wasn't bad. It wasn't quite ripe yet, but it wasn't bad. And it really was pretty up here—maybe Beckett was onto something after all. I leaned more fully against the ladder and looked out at the view as I ate my apple, slowly, in the moonlight.

3
55 S. AVE.
ASK FOR
MONA

I stood in the parking lot in front of 55 Stanwich Avenue and stared at the sign in front of me. *Paradise Ice Cream*, it read in neon-colored letters. *Where Every Cone Is a Dream!*

I was in a small shopping plaza off one of the main roads that ran through town. I had been here many times before, but I had never paid attention to the numbers, so hadn't know what 55 was until I'd pulled into the parking lot, following the directions on my phone. There were only a handful of stores in this shopping plaza—Captain Pizza, which was our go-to to-go pizza place; a beauty supply store; a running shop where I'd bought my last pair of sneakers; an accountant's office; and at the end, Paradise Ice Cream.

It was the day after I'd gone to the Orchard. When I'd woken up that morning, out of habit, I'd reached for my phone to call Sloane, not remembering the current situation until a few seconds later. But unlike the previous two weeks, the realization didn't send me into a tailspin. I'd gotten a letter from her, after all. I had instructions. I'd already crossed one of the items off the list, and I was sure I could do the rest just as quickly. I had a plan.

I took a deep breath and crossed the parking lot, passing Captain Pizza as I walked, my stomach growling at the scent of the fresh-baked pizza wafting out, despite the fact that it wasn't even noon yet and I'd just eaten breakfast. Through the window, I could see a blond girl behind the counter, leaning close to a guy standing by the register, smoothing his hair down and giggling.

I pulled open the door to the ice cream parlor and stepped inside, and a blast of cold air hit me. The place was very bright, with white walls and tables, and fluorescent lights overhead. It wasn't huge—five tables with chairs, a long counter with the ice cream below in glass cases, and a freezer that displayed ice cream cakes and pints to go. There were large framed posters covering most of the available wall space. There was something about the photography, or maybe the way the models were styled, that made me think these hadn't been changed in a few years. They all pictured people holding cups or cones of ice cream and looking blissfully happy about it. *Take a Chance!* read one that pictured a smiling woman with a cone stacked five scoops high.

What's Your Ice Cream Dream? read another, with a pensive-looking little boy contemplating a sundae.

There was a girl behind the counter wearing a shirt with a rainbow across the front. I guessed she was around my age, maybe a little younger. She hadn't looked up when I'd entered the store, but instead was examining the split ends at the end of her braid.

"Hi," I said, as I stepped up to the counter. She had a name tag pinned to her shirt that read *Kerry*, and I felt myself deflate a little as I looked at it. Because of course she couldn't have been Mona—that would have made this too easy.

"What can I get you?" she asked, looking away from her hair and picking up the ice cream scoop from where it was resting in a cup of water.

"Oh," I said quickly. "No. I mean—I don't want any ice cream." Kerry stopped shaking off the ice cream scoop and gave me a look that clearly said *Then what are you doing here?* I swallowed hard, and tried to make myself get through this. "I was . . . Is Mona here?"

"No," Kerry said, looking at me strangely. I didn't blame her.

I nodded, wondering if I maybe should have started with buying some ice cream; maybe that would have made this process go a little easier. I stood there for a moment, trying to think of how to ask this. It would have helped if I had any idea who Mona was, or if I knew why I was supposed to ask for her. "I just . . ." I started, not exactly sure how to describe what I needed when I knew so little about it myself. I took a breath and decided to just tell her, trying not to care how crazy it sounded. "A friend of mine left me a note, saying to come here and talk to Mona. So . . ." I stopped talking when I realized I didn't know how to finish this sentence, without demanding that Kerry somehow procure her. This had already become much more humiliating than I had imagined it would be, which was, in a weird way, kind of liberating.

"Well, Mona's not here," Kerry said, speaking slowly and deliberately, like maybe the reason I was still standing in front of her, not ordering ice cream, was that I didn't understand English well. "So if you're not going to get something, you can't—" The store phone rang and she picked it up. "Hello, Paradise," she said, keeping her eyes on me the whole time, like maybe this was all part of an elaborate ruse to rob the place. "Hey, Mona. No. Not a customer. Just—"

"Is that Mona?" I asked quickly, leaning across the counter. Desperation was making me brave, and any sense of dignity I had when I entered the place was long gone. "Can I talk to her?"

"No," Kerry said into the phone—but probably to me, too—taking a step back. "Just some girl who didn't order anything. Wanted to talk to you." She listened for a moment, then lowered the phone. "What do you want?"

"Okay, so my friend," I babbled, speaking fast, lest Kerry change her mind, "she left me this list—her name's Sloane

Williams, I don't know if that matters. Anyway, on the list, it said to come here and ask for Mona. So that's . . . what I'm doing."

Kerry just raised her eyebrows at me. "Did you get that?" she said into the phone. She tilted her head slightly to the right, listening to something that was being said on the other end. "Oh," she said, looking at me. "I don't know why she didn't just start with that then. Okay. Yeah, I'll ask her. Talk to you later." She hung up and I looked in dismay at the phone on the counter, wondering if I should have tried to get on the phone with Mona myself. Kerry reached under the counter and pulled out a manila folder. She flipped through the papers inside, tilting them away from me so I couldn't see what they were. She stopped, then looked up at me. "What's your name?"

My heart was starting to beat harder now, but not from nerves—because it felt like I was getting close to something. "Emily," I said, wondering if I should show some ID. "Emily Hughes."

She nodded and pulled out a piece of paper and set it down on the counter. "You were supposed to be here last week," she said. "Mona thought you didn't want the job."

I just stared at her. "Job?"

Kerry rolled her eyes, clearly losing any patience she'd once had with me. "Yeah, the job," she said. "The one you applied for? Mona's the manager?" She shook her head and reached back underneath the counter, and I pulled the piece of paper closer to me so I could read it.

Morgan Matson

Sure enough, it was an application to work at Paradise Ice Cream. It had been filled out for me in Sloane's handwriting. There was Sloane's email and phone number, but my name and work experience. Sloane had put herself down as my emergency contact, and under *Additional Info* she had added, *I am a really hard worker, a wonderful friend, really punctual, funny, loyal, thoughtful, all-around awesome. Oh, and humble too.*

I smiled as I read this while simultaneously feeling like I might burst into tears. The only thing that prevented this was imagining what Mona, or Kerry, or whoever, must have thought of this bizarrely confident application.

"Can I have this?" I asked, holding on to the application as Kerry stood up again, holding two white T-shirts.

"No," she said, sounding exasperated with me, as she pulled it back and placed it in the folder. "We need to hold on to it. So we have your information in case you burn the place down or something." She looked at me closely after she said it, clearly thinking I might be capable of this. "Anyway, I'm sure Mona mentioned the salary when you applied. So we need someone five shifts a week, two of those have to be weekends, and Mona does the scheduling tonight, so she can e-mail you."

I blinked at her. "You mean I got the job?" Kerry didn't even bother responding to this, just flipped through the folder again.

"Mona wanted to know if your friend was still interested." She pulled out another paper, and I could see it was Sloane's handwriting again, this time filling out her own application. I saw, in the section that dealt with scheduling, Sloane had written in all caps, *NEED SAME SHIFTS AS EMILY HUGHES!!!*

I got it then, finally. She'd had a plan for us to work together after all. And judging by how empty Paradise was, she had picked the ideal place. Unlike last summer, when our marathon chat sessions were always being interrupted by people who wanted their food brought to them or their orders taken, this would have been the perfect job for us. We would have gotten paid to hang out all day, with minimal customer interference.

Kerry gave a loud sigh, and I realized I hadn't answered her. "No," I said quickly. I noticed that Sloane had left the *Additional Info* section on her own application blank. "She's . . . not available for it any longer."

"Okay," Kerry said, putting Sloane's application back in the folder. "Do you want the job or not? Because if not, we need to call the other applicants."

I thought about it as I looked at the two neatly folded white T-shirts on the counter. It wasn't the worst idea in the world. I needed a job, after all. And Sloane had gotten me one. She had put this on the list, after all, so that I'd know about this job even after she'd left. And I had a feeling that it most likely wouldn't be super demanding. I nodded. "Yes," I said. "I'll take it."

"Great," Kerry said, sounding decidedly unenthusiastic about this as she pushed the shirts in my direction. "Welcome to Paradise."

By the time I made it home again, it had turned into the hottest part of the day. The Volvo's air conditioner was barely functional, so normally I didn't even try it. But when I'd attempted it today, only hot air had come out at me, and I'd quickly turned it off. Normally, the open roof let a breeze in, but instead, it just felt like I was sitting directly in a sunbeam I couldn't get out of. I made a mental note, as I pulled into the driveway, to get the wooden piece for the roof from the garage, if only to cool the car down by providing some shade. As I walked up to the front door, new employee T-shirts in hand—they had rainbows on them like Kerry's had, I'd been dismayed to see—I was regretting the fact I hadn't gotten any ice cream after all.

I let myself in, careful not to make too much noise in case my parents were working. But when I passed the dining room, it was only my dad sitting at the table. His laptop was open, but he was leaning back in his ergonomic wheelie chair, reading a thick book, highlighting occasionally, so focused on his task, I was pretty sure he didn't even sense me in the doorway.

I found my mom in the kitchen, washing off a peach. She turned when she heard me, giving me a tired smile, and I had the feeling they'd been working all morning. "Hey, Em," she said. She looked down at the shirts under my arm. "Did you go shopping?"

"I got a job," I said, shaking out one of the shirts and holding it up so she could see it. "Paradise Ice Cream."

"Oh," my mother said, raising her eyebrows. "Well, that's . . .

good. And I'm sure it'll be nice and cool in there, right?" Without waiting for a response, she went on. "Did you eat?" She looked around, then held out the fruit in her hand to me. "Peach?"

"No, thanks," I said, crossing to the fridge, grabbing a bottle of water from the door and taking a long drink.

"I meant to ask you," my mother said as she patted her peach dry, "is everything okay with you and Sloane? It feels like we haven't seen her around in a while."

"Oh," I said. I looked down at the scuffed wood of the kitchen floor, debating what to tell her. Only yesterday, I'd wanted nothing more than to tell my parents, to get their help to find her. But that was before the list. And the list made me feel like Sloane had a plan, and me running to my parents for help wasn't part of it. "She's out of town for the summer," I said, looking back at my mom, rationalizing that, technically, this wasn't even really a lie.

"Oh, that's too bad," my mom said, her brow furrowing. My mother felt everything quickly, and deeply, and cried at the drop of a hat. It was the reason none of us ever wanted to sit next to her when we saw sad movies. "That's going to be hard for you, Em."

My mother took a bite of her peach, but I could tell that there were more things she was about to ask; I could practically feel them, questions like *where* and *why* and *for how long*, questions I couldn't begin to answer. So before she could ask, I said quickly, "So Beckett seems pretty excited about this camping trip." I was almost positive that he was away at day camp, but I looked up to check the doorway, just in case.

"Yeah," my mother said with a smile. "Your dad, too." I nodded, figuring that this meant the trip was still on, and I hadn't done the wrong thing by basically telling my brother as much. "Though I don't know why," my mother said as she shook her head, rotating the peach, looking for a perfect bite. "Sleeping outdoors when you've got a perfectly good bed has never—"

"Andrea, listen to this," my dad said, bursting into the kitchen. He was holding a thick book in his hands, and talking fast and excited. "Tesla and Edison were *friends* when he first came from Paris. Edison called him a genius."

"Scott," my mother said. "I was in the middle of talking to Em." But I could tell that she was only partially in the kitchen with me now. It was like I could practically feel her wanting to get back to the play, and I was pretty sure she'd already forgotten about Beckett and camping.

"It's really fine," I said quickly, backing out of the kitchen. "You guys go write."

My mother bit her lip and looked at me, and I gave her a bright, *Everything's okay here* smile and headed upstairs, but not before I heard them start to talk, their voices excited and overlapping, saying words like *laboratory* and *patent* and *alternating current*.

I took the stairs up to my room slowly, feeling the temperature seem to rise with every step. I flopped down on my bed and looked up at the ceiling, where I could still see the tape marks left over from the rotating pantheon of teen heartthrob posters I'd put up during my middle school years. I reached for my phone, which was, of course, free from any texts or missed calls. And even though I knew it would probably just go to her voice mail, I found myself pressing the button to call Sloane. Sure enough, her voice mail recording started, the one I knew by heart. I waited until the beep, then took a breath and started.

"Hey, it's me. I got the job, the one at Paradise. So thanks for setting that up for us." I said the word automatically, but a second later, reality hit me like a punch to the gut. There would be no *us* at Paradise. Just me, working in a T-shirt with a rainbow on it. "I'll have to tell you what happened. It was really funny, this girl thought I was crazy." I listened to the silence, the empty space where Sloane's voice should have been, already laughing, asking me questions, reacting in just the right ways. "Anyway. I'll talk to you soon."

I hung up and, after a moment, pushed myself off the bed. I dropped my new T-shirts into my drawer and pulled out Sloane's list. I didn't think I was going to be able to get anything else done today—I knew I'd have to do some brainstorming before tackling the others. I carefully crossed off number seven, then returned the list to its envelope and the envelope to the drawer. Then I looked around, at a bit of a loss.

I didn't want to stay in my room—I actually didn't think it would be healthy to, if I wanted to avoid heatstroke—but

Morgan Matson

I didn't want to tiptoe around my parents downstairs. And I didn't want to go over to campus, or go downtown by myself. I was starting to get a jumpy, claustrophobic feeling. I needed to get out, but I'd technically just come back. And where was I supposed to go? I kicked off my flip-flops and tossed them into my closet, where they landed on my sneakers and gave me my answer.

Without thinking twice, I pulled the sneakers out of the closet, then reached for the drawer that held my workout clothes. I wasn't sure it was going to make anything better, but it was the only thing I wanted to do at that moment. I was going for a run.

****

JUNE

Two years earlier

I shook out my arms and tried to pick up my pace, trying to ignore how my breath was coming shallowly. I hadn't run since school had ended two weeks before, and I was feeling it with every step. I'd made the cross-country team as a freshman, but had lagged behind the rest of the team and wanted to get my times up over the summer so that I would have a chance of making it again in the fall, when I knew the competition would be more intense.

Since there were too many people and too many excuses to slow down in my neighborhood, I'd gone out of my way to run in this one. It was a good ten miles from my house, and I had a feeling my return might end up being a walk—and a long one, at that. I'd spent almost no time in this part of town, Stanwich's backcountry. There weren't any sidewalks, but running on the road didn't seem to be that big a deal, since there were also almost no cars.

I was just debating if I could keep going, or if maybe the time had come to give up and start walking, when I saw the girl.

She was pacing back and forth in the driveway of a house, but she stopped as I approached, and shielded her eyes from the glare. Then, to my astonishment, she started waving at me—but not the normal kind of saying hello waving— the kind of waving castaways on islands did to flag down passing ships.

"I'm so glad you're here," she called, as soon as I got within earshot. "I've been waiting for you!" I slowed to a walk, then stopped in front of the girl. She looked around my age, except that she was dressed much better than any- one I knew—wearing a silky flowing top with her jean shorts, bright-red lipstick, and mascara. But contrasting all of this was the fact that her hair was underneath a towel, which she'd twisted into a turban.

"Me?" I asked, trying to catch my breath, glancing behind me to see the road was still empty. But she couldn't have meant me—we'd never met before. I would have remembered that, I was sure of it.

Morgan Matson

"Well," the girl acknowledged with a smile, "someone like you. Someone who didn't look like a total scary weirdo. Although at this point, honestly, I probably would have taken that, too. But you're like the first person to show up here in like an *hour*, I swear. I was worried that I was suddenly in a zombie movie where all of humanity had disappeared." She stopped and took a breath, and I just blinked, trying to keep up with what was happening here. She spoke fast, and seemed to be a combination of stressed out and on the verge of cracking up, which was a mixture I wasn't sure I'd ever seen before.

"What—" I started, then stopped, when I realized I wasn't sure what to say here. "Are you okay?"

"No," she said, then seemed to rethink this. "Well, I mean, I'm, like, physically fine. I'm just . . ." She took a breath. "Can you help me break into my house?" She pointed behind her, and I felt my jaw fall open.

It was an absolutely enormous mansion. It looked old, stately, and very grand. It was the kind of place I could imagine steel barons owning, a house where black-tie parties were thrown, where duchesses and senators were invited to dinner, where grave, white-gloved butlers would open the front door.

"I live here!" the girl continued. "I swear, I'm not trying to steal anything. I just locked myself out." She shook her head, then reached up to steady the towel. "And normally, I'd be all whatever, just take a walk or work on my tan or something. Because my parents are coming back at *some* point. You know, most likely. But I'm a little worried my hair's about to turn permanently green." After she said this, she started to laugh, closing her eyes and bending forward slightly, her shoulders shaking.

Even though I didn't know what was funny, and was still trying to figure out what was going on here, I felt myself smile as well, like I was about to start laughing too, just to be in on the joke.

"Sorry," she said, straightening up and letting out a breath, pulling herself together. "The situation is just so ridiculous."

"Why is your hair about to turn green?" I asked.

The girl grimaced and pulled off her towel. I felt my eyes widen as I took a tiny step back. Her hair was coated in a bright green mask that looked like it was hardening into a helmet shape. "You're only supposed to leave it on for twenty minutes," she said, reaching up to tentatively touch her hair. "And it's been, like, an hour. Or more. Probably more. Oh, god."

"Sure," I said, "I mean, how can I help?" As soon as the words were out of my mouth, I was surprised I'd said them. But I had meant it, 100 percent.

"Oh, thank you so much," the girl said, her shoulders sagging with relief. "We just moved in a few weeks ago, so it's not like I even know where the best places to get in are.

But I'm pretty sure there's an open window I can get to, if you just give me a boost."

"Okay," I said, and the girl grinned at me and headed up the driveway. I followed, and noticed she was barefoot, and that the chipped bright-red polish on her toes seemed to match her lipstick. The house was even more impressive the closer I got to it, and I suddenly realized I'd seen it before. When we'd first come to Stanwich, when my parents were house-hunting, the realtor had driven us past it, talking about how it was one of the town's architectural landmarks, using words I'd never heard before, like *portico* and *vestibule*. "Your house is amazing," I said as I followed her around the side, gazing up at it.

"Thanks," she said with a shrug, clearly not as impressed as I was. "Okay, see that window?" She pointed up to a window that looked worryingly high, but that I could see was open, the beige curtains inside blowing in the faint breeze.

"Yes," I said slowly, trying to figure out how—even with my help—this girl was going to get up to it.

"So I think if you just give me a hand, I should be able to get in," she said. "And then I can wash this stuff off. And hopefully it won't have done permanent damage, or made my hair fall out, or anything like that."

"I'm sure it will be fine," I said, even though I had no knowledge whatsoever about this. I regretted it immediately— the leader of the pack of girls I was friends with would have rolled her eyes and asked, *how*, exactly, I knew that. But this girl just smiled at me.

"Thanks so much," she said. Before I could reply, the girl was striding forward, examining the window, hands on her hips. "I think this should be doable," she said, though she sounded less confident than she had a moment before. She looked at me, and I suddenly wished that I looked more pulled together—which was ridiculous, because I'd been running. But this girl looked so cool, I couldn't help but be aware that I was wearing my old, too-short running shorts, and an ancient sheer T-shirt of my mom's that read *Williamstown Theater Festival Crew.* "Thank god you're tall," she said. "I'm so jealous. I wish I was."

"You're not that short," I said, since I only had about four inches on her.

"I am, though," she said, shaking her head, and I noticed, getting a little worried, that her hair didn't move at all when she did this. "Oh my god, when I was in Copenhagen, it was the *worst.* Everyone there is tall. I was practically the shortest person around. You would totally have fit in. I love your T-shirt, by the way. Is it vintage?"

"Um," I said, looking down at it, thinking that *vintage* was probably not the right word for it, but nodding anyway. "Kind of. It was my mom's."

"Awesome," she said. "You can tell. Cotton only thins out like that with years of washing. I know a consignment shop in San Francisco that would pay you at least a hundred bucks for that." She seemed to realize that we'd gotten away from the mission at hand, because she turned back to the window.

As I looked up at it, I couldn't help but wish that Beckett had been with us, since he would have been able to get up there, no problem.

"Okay," the girl said, looking from the window and back to me. "Maybe if you give me a boost?"

"Okay," I echoed, trying to sound more sure of this than I felt. I met her eye, and we both started laughing, even though I couldn't have said why.

"Oh my god," the girl said, clearly trying to regroup. "Okay. Okay okay."

I made a cradle with my hands, and she stepped into them. And while I tried my best to push her up, this quickly turned into the girl basically standing on my back while she grabbed for the windowsill.

"Are you okay?" she asked. "I'm so sorry. I can't believe this. Am I hurting you?"

"It's fine," I managed as I tried to stand up and give her another boost.

"Got it!" she said triumphantly, but when I straightened up, I saw this was maybe a little optimistic, as she was hanging on to the sill, but seemed much closer to falling to the ground than getting herself into the window. "Um, sort of."

"Here," I said, grabbing one of her feet that was kicking in space as she tried to hoist herself over. "Maybe if I give you another push?"

"Yes!" she said. "Great idea. You're a genius at this." I held on to her foot, and she pushed off my hands and was able to swing one leg, then another, over the sill. She fell over the window with a thump that I could hear even from the ground. "Ow," I heard her mutter from inside.

"You okay?" I called up.

A second later, her green head appeared in the window. "Fine!" she said. "Thank you so much! You saved my life. Or at least my hair." She smiled at me, and then disappeared from view. I figured she'd gone to wash off the green mask, but found myself waiting by the window for just a few moments more, wondering if this was over. When she didn't come back, I turned and walked down the driveway. As I got to the end and turned right on the road, in the direction that would take me back home, I realized that I didn't even know the girl's name.

When I started running in the same direction the next day, my muscles protested—loudly. But I didn't even think about not going, though I hoped it wouldn't make me seem like a stalker. It just felt like I'd seen the first five minutes of a movie, and I had to know what happened next. And if the girl wasn't there, I wasn't going to knock on the door or anything. I was just hoping that maybe she'd be outside

Morgan Matson

again. When I got closer to her house, I felt my hopes deflate as I realized that the driveway and sidewalk were empty. It seemed totally obvious now that they would be. Did I just expect that she would be hanging outside, waiting around? I turned to head home, and as I did I noticed that there was writing on the ground, in chalk, the letters a mix of capitals and cursive.

Hey, running girl!! Thanks so much.
Hair is fine. ♩ xo, SW

On the third day, I didn't even try to run. My legs were killing me after trying to do two long runs when I was still out of shape. I'd gotten my mother to drop me off about a mile away, telling her that I wanted to scout a new run. I think normally she would have asked more questions, but Beckett had been throwing a temper tantrum in the backseat and her attention was divided. She told me to give her a call if I needed a ride home, reminding me not to be gone too long, since we had a family dinner planned.

If it had been one of the girls from school that I'd been trying to impress, I would have worn something different. One of my nicer dresses, the skirt my mother had just bought for me, the kind of clothes that always made me feel like I was pretending to be someone else altogether. But I found myself reaching for another one of my mom's old T-shirts, the ones I only normally used for running or hanging around the house. I also put on some lipstick, even though I didn't have anything close to bright red. As I looked in the mirror, I realized I still felt like myself, but a new version of myself, one I'd never tried out until today.

I walked slowly toward the girl's house, trying to get my courage up. I had decided, back when I was getting ready, that I was going to go up and ring the bell. She'd left me a note, after all, and wasn't that kind of like an invitation? But the closer I got, the more I began to question if I would actually be able to do this. Ring the bell of a mansion, and then when someone came to the door, ask for—who, exactly? The plan was seeming stupider and stupider the closer I got, but I made myself walk all the way up to the base of the driveway. The chalk message was gone, no doubt washed away in the thunderstorm that had woken me up at two a.m. I looked up the driveway for a moment longer, then lost whatever bit of courage had gotten me this far and turned to go.

"Hey!" I looked up and saw the girl leaning out of a second-story window. She smiled at me. "Hang on, okay?" I nodded, and her head disappeared inside.

I shifted from foot to foot, smoothing my shirt down, wondering why I felt so nervous. I was nervous around my friends at school, but that was more nervousness that I would say something stupid or find myself kicked out of the group. This was something else entirely.

Morgan Matson

"You came back!" I looked up and saw the girl was heading down the driveway, walking fast, then running for a few steps, then walking again. As she got closer, I saw she was holding a pair of sandals in one hand, swinging them by their long leather straps. She reached me and dropped them next to her on the ground. "I'm so glad you're here! I wanted to thank you, but then realized I had no idea how to do that. Look!" She bent forward and shook her hair at me, and I realized that it was intact, and not the slightest bit green.

"No damage?" I asked, as she flipped her head back up.

"None!" she said happily, pulling one end into her eyeline to examine it, then tucking it behind her ear. "I mean, as far as I know. Watch, it'll all fall out next Tuesday."

"Delayed reaction," I said, nodding. "Or what if you've discovered some magical chemical compound that only is activated when you've left it on too long? And that's why they tell you not to do it."

"Love it," she said. "The hair mask is my radioactive spider." I laughed, and didn't even really have time to worry that I was boring her or sounding stupid before she asked, "What's your name?"

"Emily," I said, and she smiled, like that was just the name she'd been hoping to hear.

"It's so nice to meet you," she said. "I'm Sloane."

****

RUN, EMILY, RUN!

Galveston	Glen Campbell
Any Way You Want It	Journey
Crash My Party	Luke Bryan
Heat of the Moment	Asia
True North	Jillette Johnson
Take On Me	A-Ha!
The Moment I Knew	Taylor Swift
Just Like Heaven	The Cure
It Goes Like This	Thomas Rhett
Mr. Blue Sky	ELO
All Kinds of Kinds	Miranda Lambert
Nightswimming	R.E.M.
What About Love	Heart
The Downeaster "Alexa"	Billy Joel
Short People	Randy Newman
Dancin' Away with My Heart	Lady Antebellum
Take Me Home Tonight	Eddie Money
You Make My Dreams	Hall & Oates
Even If It Breaks Your Heart	Eli Young Band
Aw Naw	Chris Young
The Power of Love	Huey Lewis & The News
This	Darius Rucker
Fancy	Reba McEntire

Morgan Matson

Run	Matt Nathanson feat. Sugarland
A Lot to Learn About Livin'	Easton Corbin
Centerfold	J. Geils Band
Quittin' You	The Band Perry

I was seriously out of running shape. I could feel it in how my calves started to ache right away, how my breath was labored after the first mile. My participation on the cross-country team had gotten very sporadic as school was ending, and I hadn't run at all since I'd come back to find Sloane gone. But it was still sad that, after doing this for most of my life, I could become so bad at it so quickly.

Running was the one activity I'd done regularly from child-hood on. Looking back, it was clear why my parents had nudged me to join kids' races and running clubs and, if one of them was teaching, encourage me to go down to the college or university track and practice. It was cheap and didn't require a team or being in the same place all the time—money and consistency being in short supply when I was growing up.

Sloane, on the other hand, had had more lessons than I'd even really known were options. She could ride horses and ball-room dance, in addition to ballet and tap. She could sail, play tennis, speak conversational French, and, for some reason I'd never been clear on, could play doubles bridge. I had learned to swim at camp, but mostly I just ran. For most of my life, it had been the one athletic thing that I could do well, which was why it was so embarrassing to find myself now limping through the first mile.

I turned up the volume on my iPod, as if this would give me a corresponding surge of energy. It didn't, but I pushed myself to go faster, even as I was gasping for breath. I was listening to a new mix, complete with embarrassingly motivational name. The mix was filled with the kind of music I listened to but never admitted to—country and eighties pop. It had the same playlist repeating again after the end; my iPod's loop function was broken, and when it got to the end of a playlist, it just froze. It had been acting wonky ever since I'd left it in the car and an unexpected rainstorm had come through the open roof and drenched it.

I was running a loop near my neighborhood that I'd discovered last year. It took me right along the water, which meant that it was cooler and I would sometimes get a breeze, which I was seriously in need of at the moment. Usually, this was an easy five-mile run, but usually, I wasn't this out of shape.

I rounded a bend in the road and saw that there was someone running ahead of me. It was a guy, and maybe around my age. . . . He turned his head to adjust the iPod strapped to his arm, giving me a glance at his profile, and I felt my feet stumble and then slow when I recognized it was Frank Porter.

It didn't look like he'd noticed me. He was back to looking straight ahead, white earbuds in his ears. I slowed even more—I was pretty much just walking with bounce now—and tried to figure out what to do. If I pushed myself, I could run past him, but then I'd have to keep going fast until I could make it home. Also, then Frank would be looking at the back of me unless I *really* kept up my pace and disappeared from his view. And I had grabbed the first pair of shorts I'd seen in my drawer, and they had *GO SH!* printed across the back. This was supposed to mean *Go Stanwich High,* but apparently nobody had realized until we'd all prepaid for them that it looked like *GOSH!* was written across our butts. But running fast seemed to be my best option if I wanted to keep on this path, unless I dropped to a really slow pace, lagging behind him and hoping he wouldn't see me, which felt weird and stalkerish.

It seemed like the best solution was just to turn around and run back the way I'd come from. I could do a mile or two nearer to my house, and it wasn't like this run had been going spectacularly anyway. Because while it had been really nice of Frank to help me with my car, it wasn't like I wanted to keep struggling to make conversation with him, or for him to feel like he had to run with me when he didn't want to. One interaction with Frank Porter per summer seemed like the right amount to me.

I turned around just as Frank stopped and knelt to tie his sneaker. He looked over and saw me, lifting his hand to cut the glare, then pulled his earphones out of his ears. "Emily?" he called.

I bit my lip. There was really no way to avoid this now without looking incredibly rude. I pulled my own earphones out and pressed Pause on my playlist. "Hey," I said, giving him a wave. I shifted my weight from foot to foot, hoping that maybe this had been enough and I could just start running again.

"I thought that was you," Frank said as he straightened up and headed toward me, dashing the last of these hopes. As he got closer, I could hear that he was a little winded, his breath sounding labored. His hair was dark red with sweat, and he was wearing a faded blue T-shirt that read *Tri-State Latin Decathlon . . . Decline if you dare!* He was wincing as he walked closer to me. "This is all your fault, you know."

I just blinked at him for a moment. I had no idea what I'd done, or what he was referring to. "Me?"

He ran his hand over his face and through his hair. "Yeah," he said. "I seem to remember you said you'd help me learn to run."

I opened my mouth and then closed it again, not sure what to say to this. It wasn't like he'd found me and asked me to do this. Was I supposed to have tracked him down and offered my running services, or something? "Sorry," I stammered, as I looked back to the lovely empty stretch of road behind me, wishing I'd turned away a second earlier, or that Frank had just tied his laces more tightly.

He smiled and shook his head, and it sounded like he was getting his breath back. "I'm kidding," he said. "I'm just so terrible at this."

I nodded and looked down at the road, at my sneakers on the asphalt, and took a breath. "Well, I should keep—"

"Are you going this way?" Frank asked, pointing in the direction I'd been heading. I didn't know if I could say no. If I did, I would pretty much be admitting that I was choosing not to run with him.

"Yeah," I finally said, aware that the answer didn't require nearly as much time to think about it as I'd given it.

"Me too," he said. He bent down to tighten his other shoe-lace and looked up at me. "Want to run together for a bit? Unless I'd slow you down," he added quickly.

"That's okay," I said, then wondered if this response had been rude. "I mean, I'm sure you won't. I'm not in the best shape myself."

"Excellent," Frank said. He nodded ahead, and I started running again, Frank falling into step next to me, groaning a little as he started to match my pace. We were running side by side, with me closer to the side of the road and Frank closer to the center line. We'd only been running for a few seconds before I noticed that he had started to drift nearer to me, so I moved over to the left to compensate. I thought this was just a one-time thing until Frank started to drift toward me again, and when I tried to move over this time, I was now running on the dirt.

"Um," I said, trying not to cough at the clouds that I was kicking up. "Frank?"

Frank glanced over at me and seemed to realize what was happening. "God, I'm sorry," he said. "Maybe we should switch places?"

"Sounds good," I said, as I jogged around to run on the outside of him. After we'd been running in silence for a few minutes, I looked over at him, then straight ahead again. I had no idea what the etiquette here was. Should we start listening to our own music again? Or maybe we should just keep running silently next to each other. But wasn't that kind of weird?

"*Bug Juice*?" Frank asked. I glanced over at him, surprised, and then I looked down and realized I was wearing the original Broadway cast T-shirt, the one that had been nightshirt-size on me when I'd first gotten it, but now fit me like a regular T-shirt.

"Oh," I said. "Um, yeah." I kept on running, Frank keeping pace next to me, and I heard, in the silence that stretched out, that I really needed to give him some kind of explanation; otherwise, it would just seem like I was a really big fan of a play that had closed years ago. "My, um, parents wrote it." I figured that was all he needed to know; I didn't have to tell him that the play had been inspired by my experiences, that Cecily, the lead, was based on me. At least, she was in the beginning of the play. She starts out shy, but over the course of it, she becomes confident and daring and brave, finally engineering the coup and takedown of Camp Greenleaf.

Frank's eyebrows shot up. "Really?" he asked. "That's so cool. I'm pretty sure I saw a production of it. I would have been like twelve or something. . . ." I nodded. This wasn't that surprising. Between the Broadway run and the endless regional and community theater productions, most people had at least some familiarity with the play. I braced myself for the inevitable follow-up question. "Have they written anything else?"

I looked to the road ahead for a moment before answering. This was the problem, I'd learned, with sudden and unexpected success. My parents had been writing plays for ten years before *Bug Juice* made it to Broadway, and they'd written plays since. But nothing had been as big a hit. It might have been partially my parents' fault for following up their crowd-pleaser about kids at summer camp with an incredibly depressing play about a suicidal country-and-western singer. "They're actually working on something now," I said, happy that I could answer like this, without having to go into details about their less-successful plays that very few people had heard of.

"Oh yeah?" he asked. He looked over at me, and I could hear that his breath was starting to get labored again.

I nodded. "It's about Tesla." Frank nodded, like this meant something to him. "You know who that is?" I asked, so surprised by this I didn't stop myself.

"Sure," Frank said, "He was a genius. Responsible for stuff like X-rays and radar. Way before his time." I nodded, realizing that for a moment I'd forgotten who I was talking to. He might have been red-faced and struggling to talk, but this was still Frank Porter, who was going to be in the running for valedictorian next year. "Can we," he gasped, and I could hear how ragged his breathing was. "Can we just maybe walk for a bit?"

"Sure," I said quickly. I had been feeling pretty winded

myself, and while I was in better running shape than Frank, I was still struggling. We slowed to a walk, Frank taking in big gulps of air.

"Sorry about that," he said when he'd gotten his breath back, wiping his sleeve across his face. "I'm probably holding you up. Feel free, if you need to go faster."

"It's okay," I said, then realized a moment later that I could have taken the out he was giving me and gone ahead on my own, with no hard feelings. But I could actually have used some walking time myself, even though I knew from experience how hard it was to start running again if you've been walking for too long. But right now, my legs felt like they were made of lead, and I knew it didn't seem likely I could start running again, not without a break.

Frank lifted up the bottom of his T-shirt and dried his face with it, and I felt my feet tangle. Frank Porter, for some reason, was in incredibly good shape—he was thin, but with really defined stomach muscles, his mesh shorts sitting low on his hips. I swallowed hard and looked away quickly, trying to concentrate on walking in a straight line. The second I got home, I *had* to tell Sloane—

Except, of course, that I couldn't. At least, not yet.

"Hey, can I ask you something?" Frank said after we'd been walking for a few minutes. I glanced over at him, trying to see the person he'd been not that long ago, Frank Porter, the nice class president, not the secretly ripped guy walking next to me.

Morgan Matson

I nodded, even though it had been my experience that when someone asks you if they can ask something—instead of just asking—it means it's going to be a hard question to answer. "The other night, at the Orchard," he said. He looked away from me and shook his head. "I'm really sorry if this is intruding," he said. "I just keep thinking about it, for some reason. But when I drove you to get gas . . ." He looked back at me, and I could tell he was trying to figure out how to put this. "Were you by yourself?"

I felt my cheeks flood with heat, and I knew it had nothing to do with the running. So Frank had noticed that I was there, all alone, like a huge loser. "Not that I wasn't happy to drive you," he added quickly. "Seriously, I didn't mind at all. I guess I was just wondering."

I gave him a tight smile, then looked ahead to the road, trying to figure out what to do, wishing with everything that I had that I'd just forced myself to keep running when he'd given me the opportunity to go. Could I just leave? Did I have to answer this question? What would happen if I just started running home? It wasn't like we were friends, after all. And then, suddenly, I realized that there was another option—I could tell him the truth.

Maybe it was because we *weren't* friends, or because I knew I would probably not see Frank Porter again this summer, but I found myself nodding. "Yeah," I said. "It was . . ." I let out a breath, trying to figure out how to put this. "Do you know Sloane Williams?"

"Of course I know Sloane," Frank said, which I'd been expecting. "You two are kind of a package deal, right?"

"Yeah," I said slowly. I realized I hadn't told anyone about this yet, and didn't have a practiced explanation. But for whatever reason, I had a feeling that Frank would be willing to wait until I figured it out—maybe because of all the open forums I'd seen him moderate, standing patiently in the auditorium with his microphone while some stoner stumbled through a grievance about the vending machines. "Well . . . she left at the beginning of the summer. I don't know where she went, or why. But she left me this list. It's . . ." I stopped again, trying to figure out how to describe it. "It's this list of thirteen things she wants me to do. And going to the Orchard was one of them." I glanced back at Frank, expecting him to look confused, or just nod politely before changing the subject. I didn't not expect him to look thrilled.

"That's *fantastic*," he enthused. "I mean, not that Sloane is gone," he added quickly. "I'm sorry about that. I just mean that she left you something like this. Do you have it with you?"

"No," I said, looking over at him, thinking that this should have been obvious, since I was *running*. "Why is it fantastic?"

"Because there has to be more to it than that, right?" he asked. "It can't just be the list. There has to be a code, or a secret message . . ."

"I don't think so," I said, thinking back to the thirteen items. They had seemed mysterious enough already to me without needing to go looking for extra meanings.

"Will you take a picture and send it to me?" he asked, and I saw he was serious. "If there's something else in there, I can tell you."

My first response was to say no—it was incredibly personal, and plus, there were things like *Kiss a stranger* and *Go skinny-dipping* on the list, and those seemed much too embarrassing to share with Frank Porter. But what if there was something else? I hadn't seen anything myself, but that didn't mean that there wasn't. Rather than telling him yes or no, I just said, "So I guess you really like puzzles."

Frank smiled, not seeming embarrassed about this. "Kind of obvious, huh?"

I nodded. "And at the gas station, you practically took over that guy's word search."

Frank laughed. "James!" he said. "Good man. I know, it's a little strange. I've been into them for years now—codes, puzzles, patterns. It's how my brain works, I guess." I nodded, thinking this was the end of it. I'd shared something, he'd shared something, and now we could go back to running. But a moment later, Frank went on, his voice a little hesitant, "I think it started with the Beatles. My cousin was listening to them a lot, and told me that they had secret codes in their lyrics. And I became obsessed."

"With codes?" I asked, looking over at him. We weren't even walking fast any longer. Strolling would probably be the word for what we were doing, just taking our time, walking side by side. "Or the Beatles?"

"Well . . . both," Frank acknowledged with a smile. "And I got Collins into them too. It was our music when we were kids." He nodded to the road ahead. "What do you think?" he asked. "Should we try running again?"

I nodded, a little surprised that he wanted to do this, since he'd really seemed to be struggling. But this was Frank Porter. He'd probably be training for a marathon by the end of the summer. We started to run, the pace only slightly slower than what it had been before.

"God," Frank gasped after we'd been running for another mile or so, "why do people do this? It's awful and it never gets any easier."

"Well," I managed, glancing over at him. I was glad to see that he was red-faced and sweaty, since I was sure I looked much the same. "How much have you been running?"

"Too much," he gasped.

"No," I said, taking in a breath while laughing, which made me sound, for an embarrassing moment, like I was choking on air. I tried to turn it into a cough, then asked, "I mean, how long?"

"Never this long," he said. "This—is too long."

"No, that's your problem," I said, wishing that this could have been a shorter explanation, as I was getting a stitch in my side that felt like someone was stabbing me. "Running actually gets easier the longer distances you cover."

Frank shook his head. "In a well-ordered universe, that

Morgan Matson

would not be the case." I looked over at him sharply. He'd said the first part of this with a funny accent, and I wondered if maybe we should stop, that maybe he'd pushed himself too hard for one day. Frank glanced back at me. "It's Curtis Anderson," he said.

This name meant nothing to me, and I shook my head. But then I remembered the CD that had slid out from under the passenger seat of his car. "Was that the CD you had the other night?" I asked.

"Yeah," he said. "The comedian. That's his catchphrase. . . ." Frank drew in a big, gasping breath. He pointed ahead of us, three houses down. "There's my house. Race you?"

"Ha ha," I said, sure that Frank was kidding, but to my surprise, a second later, he picked up his pace, clearly finding reserves of energy somewhere. Not wanting to be outdone—especially since I was supposed to be the expert here—I started to run faster as well. Even though every muscle in my body was protesting it, I started to sprint, catching up with Frank and then passing him, but just barely, stumbling to a stop in front of the house Frank had pointed at.

"Good . . . job," Frank gasped, bent double, his hands on his knees. Not having the breath to speak at the moment, I gave him a thumbs-up, and then realized what I was doing and lowered my hand immediately.

I straightened up, stretching my arms overhead, and got my first look at the house we'd stopped in front of. "This house is amazing,"

I said. It looked like something out of a design magazine—pale gray, and done in a modern style that was pretty unique for the area, which tended to favor traditional, especially colonial-style, houses.

"It's okay," Frank said with a shrug.

There was a small sign in front of the house that read, in stylized letters, *A Porter & Porter Concept*. I nodded to it. "Are those your parents?"

"Yeah," he said, a little shortly. "My dad's the architect, my mom decorates." He said this with a note of finality, and I wondered somehow if I'd overstepped.

"I didn't know you lived so close to me," I said. "I'm over on Driftway." The second I said this, I hoped it hadn't sounded creepy—like I made it my business to know where Frank Porter lived. But it was a little surprising—I thought I knew most of the kids who lived around me, if only through from the pre-license bus rides we'd all endured together.

"We've only been there about a year," he said with a shrug. "We move a lot." I just nodded—there was something in Frank's expression that told me he didn't want to go into this.

I nodded and unwrapped my earphones from where I'd wound them around my iPod. Frank was home, so clearly our run, unexpected as it was, had come to an end.

"Do it again soon?" Frank asked with a smile, but he was still breathing hard, and I could tell he was kidding.

"Totally," I said, smiling back at him, so he would know I got the joke. "Anytime."

I started to put my earbuds back in and noticed Frank was standing still, looking at me, not heading back inside. "Are you going to run back to Driftway?"

"It might be more like a walk," I admitted. "It's not that far."

"Want to come in?" he asked. "I'll buy you a water."

"That's okay," I said automatically. "Thank you, though."

Frank shook his head. "Oh, come on," he said, starting to walk toward the house. After a moment, I followed, falling into step next to him as we walked up the driveway. It was beautifully landscaped, with flowers planted at what seemed to be mathematically precise intervals. He walked around to a side door and reached under the mat for a key, then unlocked the door and held it open for me. I stepped inside a high-ceilinged, light-filled foyer, and had just turned to tell him how nice his house was when I heard the crash.

I froze, and Frank, standing just behind me, stopped as well, his expression wary. "Is—" I started, but that was as far as I got.

"Because this is my project!" I heard a woman screaming. "I was working on it night and day when you were spending all your time in Darien doing god *knows* what—"

"Don't talk to me like that!" a man screamed back, matching the woman in volume and intensity. "You would be nowhere without me, just riding on my success—" A woman stalked past us, her face red, before she disappeared from view again, followed by a man, red-faced as well, before he too passed out of view. I recognized them, just vaguely, as Frank's parents from pictures in the paper and school functions when they were usually standing behind their son, polite and composed and smiling proudly as he received yet another award.

I glanced over at Frank, whose face had turned white. He was looking down at his sneakers, and I felt like I was seeing something I absolutely shouldn't. And I somehow knew that, however bad this was for him, it was worse because I was there to witness it. "I'm going to go," I said, my voice barely above a whisper. Frank nodded without looking at me. I backed away, and as I reached the door, I could hear the voices being raised in the other room again.

I let myself out the door and started walking up the driveway, fast, wishing I had just gone home when I'd had the opportunity, and not had to see the expression on Frank's face as he listened to his parents screaming at each other. I started walking faster once I hit the street, and then broke into a run, despite the fact that every muscle in my body objected to this.

I ran all the way home and it wasn't until I'd almost reached my house that I noticed I'd been sticking to the outside, leaving enough room for someone to run next to me.

4
HUG
A
JAMIE

I stood behind the counter of Paradise Ice Cream and looked longingly at the door. In the four days that I'd been working at the ice cream parlor, I'd had exactly five customers. And one of them was just a guy who wanted change for the parking meter. If Sloane had been there, and we'd been working together, it would have been awesome, and the lack of customers would have been the job's biggest perk. But since it was just me, alone, all day, I found myself looking up hopefully whenever anyone walked by, crossing my fingers that they wanted some ice cream. But although people sometimes glanced in the window, they walked on, usually to the pizza parlor.

My customer-free and silent workplace wouldn't have been so bad, except when I left my job I had to go home, where my phone was still silent and I had nobody to hang out with.

I hadn't yet been able to cross anything else off the list, and two nights earlier, in a low moment, I'd taken a picture of it and e-mailed it to Frank's school address. I'd regretted it as soon as the e-mail had gone through, but since I hadn't heard anything from him, I figured that he was either not checking his school account over the summer, or that he'd forgotten all about our unexpected running conversation. Either way, I'd made no progress, and it was making me anxious.

Now, I looked away from the door and down at the napkin in front of me, where I'd compiled a list of all the Jamies from school I could think of. I didn't know any of them well, and I honestly didn't think I'd be capable of calling one of them up and asking if I could come to his house and hug him. I'd just remembered one more—I was pretty sure the guy who'd been in the mascot costume last year had been named Jamie—when the over-the-door bell jangled and a girl rushed into the shop.

I pushed the napkin to the side and tried to look professional. "Welcome to Paradise," I said, smiling at her.

She froze in the doorway and I realized why she looked familiar—she was the girl who worked two doors down at Captain Pizza. "Hi," she said in a shaky voice. I looked closer and realized that her face was blotchy and her eyes looked puffy. Aside from that, though, she was pretty—petite and curvy, with bright blond hair and bangs, and pale blue eyes that seemed to be about twice the size of normal people's eyes. She ran a hand through her hair and took a step closer to the counter. "I'm sorry," she said. "I actually don't want any ice cream." I sighed and nodded; at this point, I felt like this shouldn't even have surprised me. She took a big, shaky breath. "I just needed to get out of there for a moment. And if I went to my car, everyone would be able to see . . ." Her face crumpled and she held her hand up to her eyes. "I'm sorry," she said in a choked voice. "I'll be gone in a second."

"Um," I said as I looked around, like one of the signs about handwashing and checking freezer temperatures would help me in this situation. I came out from behind the counter and twisted my hands together. "Are you okay?"

The girl nodded and gave me an incredibly bad version of a smile, one that turned wobbly and collapsed after a few seconds. "No," she sobbed, starting to cry in earnest. I reached for one of the napkin holders on the counter and brought it over to her. She sank down onto one of the metal chairs and pressed a napkin to her face. "I just feel so stupid, you know. I should have seen it. It was right in front of my face. Like, literally. But my cousin Stephanie always *said* I was too trusting."

"Should have seen what?" I asked, taking a step closer to her. I couldn't decide if it would be rude or helpful to point out that, in the movies at least, people who were in emotional crises often got through it with some ice cream.

The girl wiped under her eyes, then blew her nose on the tissue and looked up at me. "That my boyfriend was cheating on me."

"Oh god," I said, pushing more napkins at her. "I'm so sorry—"

"With my best friend."

"Oh," I said, swallowing hard.

"And we all work together." She pointed in the direction of the pizza parlor. "Next door." Telling me all this information seemed to bring the gravity of the situation back again, and she burst into fresh tears.

"Um," I said, taking a step closer to the table, "is there a possibility that maybe you just misunderstood? Maybe your best friend didn't mean it, or maybe you saw something that wasn't . . ." My voice trailed off. A memory, one I didn't like to think about if I could avoid it, was suddenly intruding with full force—that night in May, Sam's house, the look on Sloane's face, the glass shattering at her feet.

"No," the girl said, her voice choked, as she shook her head. "I was out on delivery, and the last two were right near each other, so I got back super early." Her voice got quiet, and shaky. "And that's when I saw Bryan and Mandy, making out by the employee cubbies." She looked up at me and I saw her eyes were spilling over with tears. "That was *our* place. It was where *we* used to make out."

"I'm so sorry," I said, handing over another stack of napkins, realizing that I might have to get her another dispenser soon.

"And so I said, 'What is this supposed to mean?' I really was maybe willing to give them the benefit of the doubt. I swear," she said, pressing the napkin under her eyes again. "But then Bryan takes Mandy's hand and tells me that we need to talk. Can you believe it?" She started crying again, and I reached over and tentatively patted her on the back.

"I'm so sorry," I said. "I . . ." Something occurred to me, and I asked hopefully, "Your name isn't Jamie, by any chance?" After all, I was halfway to hugging her already.

"No," the girl said, straightening up. She pointed to her T-shirt, which was designed to look like a military uniform. On the shoulders, there were pizza toppings where medals would have gone—mushrooms and peppers and pepperoni slices. *DAWN* was printed on the shirt in military typeface, right over her heart. "Dawn Finley."

"Emily," I said. "Hughes."

"Nice to meet you," she said, giving me something that was closer to a real smile this time. "I'm really sorry about this," she said, pushing herself up to standing and scooping up her crumpled tissues. "Thanks for listening."

"Sure," I said, standing as well. "Are you sure you don't want any ice cream? On the house." Technically, I wasn't sure I was allowed to do this, but considering nobody had even come in to get any samples, I figured that a scoop or two wouldn't necessarily be missed.

"No, thank you, though," Dawn said. "Sorry again."

"It's fine," I said. "Really." Dawn gave me a half smile, then squared her shoulders and took a deep breath before pulling open the door and heading back toward the pizza parlor.

The bell chimed, then faded, and I was left alone again. And as I walked back to stand behind the counter, I realized that the silence somehow felt louder than it had before.

The afternoon passed with glacial slowness. I cleaned and then re-cleaned the glass cases, then re-organized the ice cream in the walk-in freezer, first by flavor grouping, then alphabetically. I wasn't in charge of locking up—that was Elise, the assistant manager, who came at closing every day. I had my eyes fixed on the back entrance, just waiting for Elise to show so that I could clock out and go home. I was trying not to think about the fact I had nothing to go home to, really, just parents who couldn't be disturbed and a little brother probably lurking in a doorway and no life whatsoever. I just wanted to get out. I was looking so intently at the back door that I didn't hear the bell jingle, and didn't notice there was someone in front of me until they cleared their throat.

"Sorry," I said, turning around quickly. Dawn was standing there, holding a pizza delivery carrier with a stack of tickets on top. "Oh, hi." She looked slightly better than she had earlier in the day, but her eyes were still red-rimmed and puffy.

"Hey," she said with an embarrassed smile. "I just wanted to thank you again, and apologize for earlier."

"It's really fine," I assured her. To my surprise, I realized I wanted to know what had happened when she'd gone back to work, what Bryan and Mandy had done. But I didn't actually know this girl, and now that she seemed embarrassed and slightly uncomfortable, I was starting to feel that way too.

"So if there's anything I can do, let me know," she said, shifting the carrier to her other hand, closer to the counter. "And I can get you a lunch special with my discount! Just come in any weekday, and . . ."

Dawn kept going, telling me about the pizza deals she could probably get for me, including a can of soda, my choice, but I was no longer hearing her. Instead, my eyes were fixed on the top delivery ticket. It was going to an address in Stanwich, to a Jamie Roarke.

I gasped. It felt like a sign. And if not a sign, at least an opportunity that I wasn't about to pass up. "Actually," I said, interrupting Dawn, "there is something you can do." She raised her eyebrows, and I took a breath, my eyes still fixed on the name on the delivery slip. "Can I deliver pizzas with you?"

★★★★

"And then Mandy started talking about how she felt like she never saw me anymore, and asked if I could get her a job at Captain Pizza too," Dawn said as she barreled down the road. I nodded and gripped on to the side of the car, feeling my foot press down on a phantom brake. I wasn't sure if Dawn was driving like this—fast, and a little distractedly—because she was reliving the Bryan and Mandy saga as she told me about it, or because she always drove like this, but either way, it was clear that we were definitely going to make Captain Pizza's promised delivery window. "And so I put in a good word for her and she got a job as a hostess, and it was so great for a while, and she and Bryan really got along, and I just thought everything was perfect, you know? I didn't even *suspect* anything else was going on."

"But you had no way of knowing," I said as Dawn screeched to a stop at a red, causing the figurines on her dashboard—including a shirtless male hula dancer who, I had learned, was named Stan—to bobble and shake. When I first asked to come along, I'd been surprised that she'd agreed so easily, but after I asked her where she went to school (Hartfield, going into senior year, like me) and she'd used the opportunity to fill me in on the drama, it was becoming clear to me that she'd just been glad to have someone to talk to, which I could more than understand.

"I know," Dawn said, as she glanced down at the directions on her phone, then jolted the car forward as soon as the light turned green. "But I feel like I should have, you know? Everything was going just perfect, and I was sure it was going to be just the best summer ever. It's like I jinxed it by believing that would happen." She made a hard left, flicking on her blinker for a second almost as an afterthought, sending Stan's hips swaying. "I just can't believe I've lost both of them," she said, shaking her head, still sounding a little dazed by this. "Like, in the same day. And all I want to do is talk to Mandy about this, but of course, I can't. . . ." Her voice trailed off and she glanced over at me. "Do you know what I mean?"

"Yeah," I said immediately, not even thinking about it first, just so glad to have someone verbalize what I'd been thinking for the last three weeks. "My best friend . . ." I hesitated. "She's away for the summer," I said, rationalizing, like I had with my mother, that this wasn't even really a lie. "And we used to hang out or talk every day, so it's just . . . hard to adjust to."

"*Yes*," Dawn said as she made a sharp right. She slowed slightly as she leaned forward, squinting at the numbers. "Why don't you just call her, though?"

"Because," I said, trying to think fast. "She's . . . you know . . . camping." Dawn glanced over at me, and I added, "In Europe."

"Oh," she said, looking impressed. "Really?"

"Yes," I said, already regretting this and wishing I'd chosen almost anything else, since I knew nothing about camping. Or Europe.

"Where?" she asked, and I tried to think fast.

"In . . . Paris," I said, wondering why I was continuing to do this, but realizing that it was probably too late to admit I'd made the whole thing up.

"I didn't know there was camping in Paris," Dawn said.

"Me neither," I said honestly. "But that's where she is," I added, just hoping that Dawn wouldn't ask any more questions, since I knew I wouldn't be able to keep this up for much longer.

Dawn took a breath, like she was about to ask something else, but then slammed on the brakes and leaned over to my side of the car. "Does that say thirty-one?" I nodded and Dawn pulled into the driveway, narrowly avoiding hitting the house's decorative mailbox. She put the car in park and then got out, tipping her seat forward so she could grab the carrier in the backseat. I got out as well, feeling my pulse start to pound in my throat. I'd been distracted on the ride over, both by Dawn's story and her driving, but now the reason that I was here—to hug one of Captain Pizza's customers—was unavoidable.

"So which house is this?" I asked, trying to keep my voice light and pleasantly curious. I knew she had four deliveries to make this round, but I had no idea where Jamie Roarke fell in that order.

Dawn picked up the ticket on top of the carrier and peered down at it. "Greg Milton," she read, then groaned. "He always orders like four kinds of meat toppings. I can barely lift his pizzas, they're so heavy. Did you want to come to the door?"

"No, that's okay," I said. I knew I was going to have to psych myself up to hug Jamie Roarke, whoever that was, and could use a moment of quiet. "I'll just wait here."

"Cool," Dawn said, heading toward the house. "Be right back."

As I watched Dawn walk up to the front door and ring the bell, I leaned back against her car, a green Volkswagen convertible

Morgan Matson

with a triangular Captain Pizza car topper. But rather than being on the roof, where I'd always seen them on pizza delivery cars, this was on the trunk of the car, like a shark fin.

She was walking back toward the car only a few moments later, tucking some cash into the front pocket of her shorts, and I let out a breath as I pulled the passenger-side door open and got in the car. I told myself that it didn't matter if Dawn thought I was weird, or if I scared this Jamie person, or if I would feel like I couldn't go back to Captain Pizza for the rest of the summer. I had to do this.

"So is this the last delivery?" I asked, twenty minutes and two other Jamie-free deliveries later, hoping I didn't sound as nervous as I felt as Dawn pulled down the driveway of a small, light-blue house.

"Yeah," Dawn said, shooting me a sympathetic look. "Has this just been so boring for you? It's for Jamie Roarke. She's the nicest, and she has the cutest puggle . . ."

Dawn got out of the car, and, hoping it sounded somewhat natural and spontaneous, I unbuckled my seat belt and said, "I think I'll come with you this time, if that's okay."

"Sure," Dawn said as she reached into the back and grabbed the carrier. "Come on."

I got out of the car, feeling my heart beating hard. I was grateful that this Jamie was a woman—it just seemed like it would make things easier. I followed behind Dawn, noticing for the first time that there was writing on the back of her shirt as well. *Captain Pizza—We're a MAJOR deal!* was emblazoned across her shoulder blades. I stood next to Dawn on the mat as she rang the bell, which chimed Pachelbel's canon. The door opened, and a woman who looked to be in her forties stood behind it, a dog peeking out from around her ankles.

"Hi," she said, fumbling in her wallet for some bills. "Sorry— you always get here so fast, I'm never quite sorted."

"No worries," Dawn said as she slid the pizza out of the carrier and dropped the now-empty bag at her feet.

I just stared at Jamie Roarke, my pulse pounding, willing her to come out from behind the door. She was still half hidden behind it. What was I supposed to do, pull the door open and hug her? What if she thought I was attacking her or something?

"I could have sworn I picked up some ones yesterday," she murmured as I swallowed hard and tried to get my courage up. I could do this. I could hug a total stranger. As though some-how sensing the direction my thoughts were going, the puggle at Jamie Roarke's feet started growling. "Quiet," she said as the dog bared his teeth—I was pretty sure—right at me. "Okay, got it," she said, looking up at Dawn and smiling as she handed over some bills. Her eyes landed on me, standing there in what was clearly not a Captain Pizza uniform, and her smile faded.

"That's Emily," Dawn said as she pocketed the bills and handed Jamie Roarke her pie. "She's just . . . observing."

Jamie Roarke gave me a nod, and I knew it was my moment. I just had to do this. Who cared what this woman or Dawn

Morgan Matson

thought? I just had to reach out and hug her. My opportunity was right in front of me. I tried to make myself do it, just take a step forward and give her a hug. But I couldn't seem to move. I just stood there, frozen, my heart slamming against my chest while I watched my opportunity slip away as Jamie Roarke thanked Dawn and then closed the door.

"So that's how it works," Dawn said as she picked up the empty carrier. She looked over at me in Jamie Roarke's porch light, where the moths were beginning to circle, drawn toward the brightness. "You okay?"

I nodded, and walked to Dawn's car without speaking, furious with myself. Who knew why Sloane had put this on the list, but she had—and it was one of the easier ones. And I couldn't even do it. The second things got hard, or I couldn't hide in the woods, I just gave up. I got into the passenger seat, slamming the door harder than I needed to, staring out the window, hating myself.

"Um," Dawn said as she started the car, glancing over at me. "You sure you're all right?"

"Fine," I said, hoping I didn't sound as upset as I currently felt. "I'm just . . . really tired."

"Oh my god, me too," Dawn said with a sigh. "I just feel like this has been the longest day ever. Do you ever feel that way? Like some days take five years, and others are over in like a minute?" Dawn talked on as we drove back, and didn't seem to notice that I wasn't saying much. I was happy to have her fill up the car with conversation, helping distract me from the truth of how I'd so decisively failed.

She parked crookedly in what I wasn't exactly sure was a spot, and as we both got out of the car, I saw Dawn bite her lip as she looked toward Captain Pizza. "It'll be okay," I said, without even thinking about it first. I wasn't sure I should have said it, since I had no way of knowing if it would be true. But Dawn shot me a smile that was much less trembly than the one she'd given me when she'd first shown up at Paradise that afternoon.

"I hope so," she said. "And thanks for coming with me tonight. The company really helped."

"Oh," I said. I felt myself smile at her, and I knew now wasn't the moment to tell her the real reason I'd wanted to come along. "I'm glad," I said truthfully. Dawn lifted her hand in a wave, then headed back up to the pizzeria, and I crossed the parking lot toward my car. I started to head home—after all, I didn't have anywhere else to go. But as I got closer, the thought of going back—to my quiet house and the hot, empty stillness of my room—started to make me feel claustrophobic. I turned off the road that would take me there and steered my car toward Stanwich's main downtown. There didn't seem to be a lot of activity going on—it was getting late, and this was, especially during the week, an early-to-bed town. The lights were still on in the diner, and I could see some booths that faced the windows were filled—the diner was pretty much the only place to eat after ten during the week. Most of the businesses downtown were closed, their lights off, and I could see, through the glass doors of the movie theater, a yawning employee cleaning the popcorn machine.

I knew I was just wasting gas at this point, but I kept on going. The mechanics of driving, plus the new mix playing on my iPod, helped me keep my mind off what I'd failed to do tonight, and the fact that I'd probably just blown my best chance to cross number eleven off the list.

I found myself driving farther and farther out, away from the main commercial districts, and it wasn't until the streetlights fell away and the stars took over the sky that I realized I was heading toward the Orchard. I slowed as I passed it—down the drive, I could see a few cars parked, but there were none on the side of the road, and had a feeling that whoever was hanging out there now was a pretty small group—nothing like the weekend parties. I kept on driving past, and when I saw the lights of Route 1 Fuel up ahead, I realized that it might not be the worst idea to fill up, especially since I'd been driving around aimlessly and had lost track of where I was with my gas levels.

As I stepped inside the mini-mart, I saw that it was the same guy who had been working behind the counter as the previous time I'd been there. He gave me a small smile, like maybe he remembered me as he set down the book he was reading and took my twenty. I was in better gas shape than I'd realized, and the car only took fifteen dollars. I headed inside for my change, and the guy set the book aside again, but this time it was faceup, and I read its title—*Beginning Sudoku: Tips and Tricks*.

Suddenly, it all came back to me. Frank, trying to get this guy to try it—I'd have to mention it, if I ever talked to him again—and him telling me that this guy's name was James. He handed me a five, and I took it, not quite able to believe I was going to do this. "You're, um, James, right?" I asked as I pocketed my change.

"Yeah," the guy said, sounding a little wary, probably wondering how I knew that, since he didn't have a name tag on.

"That's great," I said, speaking fast, and probably sounding insane, but not really caring. "Did, um, anyone ever call you Jamie? Like, ever?"

"My nana," he said after a pause, clearly confused as to why on earth I was asking this. "You know, when I was little."

That was good enough for me. That counted, right? It had to. "Okay," I said, nodding. I didn't let myself think about what I was about to do, because I knew I'd talk myself out of it. I just reached across the counter and gave him a quick hug, my arms just touching his back before I dropped them again. I took a step back from the counter and saw that he was staring at me, looking taken aback and more confused than ever. "Um, have a nice night," I said as I gave him a nod and hurried out to my car. I waited to feel incredibly embarrassed, but the feeling didn't come. It was more like a small victory, a secret to everyone else but me.

I started the Volvo and glanced back once at the gas station before I drove away. Through the window, I could see James still standing behind the counter, but not reading his book. Instead, he was looking down, off to the side, with a tiny smile on his face.

I pulled out into the dark night, feeling giddy, incredulous laughter starting to bubble up. I didn't try and keep it down, but just laughed out loud, alone in my car, not quite able to believe I'd just done that. "Jamie hugged," I said, in a *mission accomplished* voice to myself—or maybe to Sloane. I knew she would have loved that. If she could have seen me hugging the mini-mart guy, she wouldn't have stopped laughing for about two weeks. I felt the smile still on my face as I turned up my music, louder than normal, and drove home, tapping my fingers on the steering wheel.

★★★★

FEBRUARY

Four months earlier

I woke up with a start and blinked up at my bedroom ceiling and the inexactly placed glow-in-the-dark constellations that paraded across one side. I looked around, trying to figure out what had happened, why I was awake. I sat up and saw, at the foot of my bed, a pair of glowing yellow eyes staring back at me.

"Godot!" I hissed at him, flinging my pillow in his general direction. It wasn't that I particularly wanted to injure the cat—not right then, anyway—but he had startled me, and my heart was beating so hard I could feel it in my throat.

My aim was wide, and the cat didn't even flinch as the pillow sailed past him. He gave me a look that could only be described as contemptuous, then stretched and hopped off my bed, crossing to my door that was open a crack and squeezing himself through it. "Stupid cat," I muttered as I got out of bed to reclaim my pillow. As I did, I noticed that a pile of shirts on my dresser was lighting up intermittently.

I crossed to my dresser and quickly found the source of it—my cell, which had been buried under my clean laundry. I saw that I had four texts, all from Sloane.

> Hey are you awake?
> I'm downstairs
> Outside
> It's cold!!

I immediately typed a response back.

> Be right there!

Then I eased open my bedroom door and made my way down the stairs in the dark as quietly as I could. Even though I'd seen on my phone when I texted back that it was technically Saturday, we were still solidly in the middle of what my grandmother called the "wee smalls." My dad could be a notoriously light sleeper, and since he was teaching an eight a.m. class that semester, I didn't think he'd appreciate being woken up in the middle of the night on a day when he could normally sleep in. I'd only taken a few steps when I realized it had been a mistake to do this without shoes or something warm on. The house was incredibly drafty, especially in the winter, and my feet already felt half frozen. I kept pressing the button on my phone to light my way down to the front door, illuminating the picture that was on the home screen—me and Sloane at the Call Me Kevin concert we'd seen in August, my shirt turned inside out because I hadn't known until she'd told me, and made me change, that you weren't ever supposed to wear the T-shirt of the band to their concert.

I crept down to the first floor and no longer needed the cell phone light, thanks to the moonlight streaming in through the windows. I also didn't have to worry about being as quiet down here, and crossed to the mudroom as fast as I could. If I was freezing inside the house, I could only imagine what she was feeling outside of it.

I opened the front door wide and there was my best friend, her cheeks and nose pink, her shoulders sagging with relief when she saw me.

"Thank god!" Sloane gave me a tight, quick hug—one of her specialties; she somehow managed to make her hugs feel meaningful but also efficient—and crossed behind me into the mudroom. I could smell the perfume she always wore, more than usual tonight—woodsy notes mixed with gardenias. I pulled the door shut and she hustled into the house, rubbing her hands together. "I'm so glad you got my texts," she whispered. "I was *freezing* out there."

"What are you doing here?" I whispered back, even though we were in the kitchen now, a floor below where my parents were sleeping, and probably could have risked using something closer to full volume. I looked at her and took in, for the first time, what she was wearing. She was in a floor-length black gown with a neckline that dipped down and was gathered somewhere around her sternum with a rhine-stone brooch. Over this, she wore a little fur capelet that I had no doubt had been found in one of her grandmothers' extensive closets, or was from Twice Upon a Time, her favorite consignment shop, as it was clearly vintage. "Was there some dress code for tonight I wasn't told about?"

"No," she said, laughing. "I was at that party Milly and Anderson dragged me to, remember?"

"So how was it?" I asked. Something felt off, and I couldn't put my finger on what, until I noticed that we were almost eye-to-eye, since I was barefoot and Sloane was in heels.

"Can we go upstairs?" she asked, yawning and covering her mouth with her hand. "I'm exhausted."

I nodded and she turned and headed for the staircase, leading the way. She spent enough time in my house that she knew her way around and was finally comfortable enough to just reach into the fridge and take something if she was hungry. I followed a few steps behind, still not clear on why she'd come to my house after the party but happy to have her there nonetheless. She was walking a little more carefully than usual, her ankles wobbling just slightly in the heels, holding her dress out to the side so she wouldn't trip on it.

When she made it into my room, she kicked off her heels and went right to the drawer where I kept my pajamas. Sure enough, she pulled out one at the bottom of the stack, the crew T-shirt from the disastrous *Bug Juice* movie. It had been beset by problems the whole way through, starting with the fact that the producers had changed the ages of the kids from eleven to sixteen, and the lead actress had been shipped off to rehab mid-shoot. The shirt read *You Can't Handle the Juice*, a crew in-joke, and the first time Sloane had seen it, she had cracked up. She loved the shirt for some reason, and was always threatening to steal it.

"I swear," she said, yawning again as she pulled the shirt on over her head and then wriggled out of her dress, dropping it into a pile at her feet and stepping out of it, "one of these days. This shirt will just disappear, and you'll have no idea where it's gone to."

"I think I'll have some idea," I said. I went to the laundry pile on my dresser and saw my best pair of pajama pants was clean. "Want these?" I asked, holding them up. She nodded, I tossed them to her, and she pulled them on.

"Oh my *god*," she said, yawning again as she beelined for my bed. My bed was old and the mattress sagged in the middle, but it was queen-size, and there was enough room that we could face each other and still have enough space to see each other and talk. She took the side she always took when she stayed over, nestled down under the blankets, then hugged her pillow and smiled at me. I knew when she had something to say, and I could tell that she had been waiting for this moment—quiet, with my full attention—since I'd opened the front door. "So I met a boy tonight."

"You did?" I asked, getting into bed as well, pulling the blankets up and turning to her. "At the party?"

"Mmm-hmm," she said. "He was there with his parents too."

"Does he go to Stanwich?" I settled back, only to realize my pillow was still on the floor. I leaned half out of the bed to grab it, then plumped it once and settled into it, preparing to hear the story.

Boys had been besotted with Sloane since she'd shown up at Stanwich High, but she'd been picky. She'd dated a senior for a few weeks our sophomore year, then a fellow junior this past fall, and the summer before, had a brief fling with a guy who normally went to boarding school and was just in town for the summer. But none of these had lasted, and she hadn't seemed particularly devastated when they didn't—she was always the one who did the breaking up. But it had been a while since a guy had appeared on her radar—until tonight, apparently.

Morgan Matson

"No," she said. "Stanwich Academy." It was the private school in town, and while I vaguely knew some girls who went there, the two schools didn't really have much overlap socially. "His name's Sam. Sam Watkins." She pronounced the name carefully, like it was a foreign word she wasn't used to saying but nonetheless loved the sound of. She smiled, wide, and I saw in that moment that she really liked him.

"Oh my god," I said. "You're smitten already. I can tell." She didn't deny it, but buried her face in the pillow, so all I could see was her hair, the waves coaxed into curls for the evening. "So tell me about him."

She turned her head toward me, yawning, but didn't open up her eyes again when the yawn was finished. "He's great," she said, her words coming slower than before. "You'll see."

I waited for something else to come, an explanation of his greatness, when it occurred to me it was probably Sam who'd dropped Sloane at my house—Milly and Anderson would have just taken her back with them. Not because they would have cared if she slept over, but because they wouldn't have wanted to make an extra trip. I tried to recall if there had been a car there when I'd opened the door, some-one waiting to make sure she got in okay, but I just couldn't remember.

"Hey," I whispered. I nudged her ankle with my foot. "Did Sam—" I was about to ask her when I realized that she was breathing slow and regular, her mascaraed eyes firmly closed. Sloane could always drop off to sleep immediately, something she attributed to Milly and Anderson never giving her a set bedtime when she was little. "So you learn to sleep when you can," she'd explained to me. "None of this story-reading, glass-of-water nonsense. I was always the one falling asleep on the pile of coats at a party."

I waited to see if she was out for good, giving her one more gentle nudge. But she didn't stir, so I figured I'd just ask her in the morning. I closed my eyes, and felt myself drift off, somehow comforted by the knowledge that when I woke up in the morning, Sloane would be there.

****

I woke up with a start. I looked around, trying to figure out why I wasn't still sleeping. It wasn't that the cat had fallen asleep on my head again, or that either of my parents were yelling at me to wake up. Pieces of the night before came back—delivering pizza with Dawn, Jamie Roarke, hugging mini-mart James—and I realized, with some surprise, these weren't dream fragments. They had actually happened. I was about to try and go back to sleep, when the phone on my nightstand lit up.

A text.

I grabbed it and saw I had two—the first one must have been what woke me up. But despite the fact it wasn't even eight yet, as I looked down at the phone, I was wide awake. Both texts were from a number I didn't recognize. And as I held the phone in my hand, it buzzed with a third.

> Emily. You awake?
>
> I'm outside.
>
> Let's go.

It was like my brain short-circuited for a moment, then started working again, double-time. It was Sloane.

She was back.

I was out my door and down the stairs in a flash, not putting anything on over the T-shirt I'd been sleeping in, not trying to be quiet, not caring if I woke the whole house as my bare feet pounded down the stairs. Sloane was here, she was waiting for me, and she could tell me what had happened, where she'd gone—actually, I realized as I jumped down the last two steps to the first floor landing and launched myself into the mudroom, I didn't even care about that. All that mattered was that she was here, and things could go back to how they'd been.

I pulled open the front door and stopped short. Frank was sitting on the steps, wearing a T-shirt, shorts, and sneakers, iPod strapped to his arm, and he stood and smiled when he saw me. "Hey," he said. "Ready to go for a run?"

I opened my mouth, then closed it when I realized I wasn't exactly sure what to say. I just stared at him as I felt my heart rate start to slow, my hopes fall. It wasn't Sloane. She hadn't come back.

She was still gone.

"Uh," Frank said, and I noticed for the first time that he looked confused and a little uncomfortable.

I looked down at myself and suddenly realized that I had bigger problems. I was standing in front of Frank Porter—*Frank Porter*—in my nightshirt. Though it was slightly longer than a regular T-shirt, it wasn't by much, and I quickly tugged it down. I was barefoot, and—oh god—I still had on some of the zit cream I'd put on my face the night before. I wasn't wearing a bra. I quickly crossed my arms over my chest, then regretted this, as it caused the T-shirt to ride up higher.

"Sorry," Frank said, and while I had a feeling he was trying to sound contrite, this was undercut slightly by the fact that he also looked like he was on the verge of cracking up. "I got your cell number and address from the school directory. I didn't mean to wake you up—I guess I figured that if you weren't awake, you wouldn't . . . you know, come outside."

I nodded, like this was a normal conversation. But part of me was still reeling at the fact that this was happening at all. I honestly couldn't understand how I had gone, in the course of a week, from not speaking to Frank Porter, to knowing he had a sneaky hot body, to standing half naked in front of him.

"So," he said, glancing down at my feet with a smile, "is this the barefoot running trend I keep reading about?"

"Oh," I said. My face felt hot, like it was on fire, and I had a feeling it was bright red, which probably looked just fantastic with the white zit cream. "Um, no. Ha ha. I just . . ."

"Emily?" I turned and saw my dad standing behind me, wearing his robe and slippers and carrying his laptop, his glasses perched on top of his head. I truly hadn't thought this could get any worse. But apparently Frank Porter was going to see the entire Hughes family in their pajamas this morning.

"Dad," I said, hearing how strangled my voice sounded.

"Have you seen my glasses?" he asked, not, apparently, thinking anything was strange about the fact that his daughter was awake at eight a.m. and standing in the doorway in her pajamas, talking to a boy he'd never met.

"They're on your head, sir," Frank supplied from the porch.

My father reached up and patted his head, then nodded and put them on. Then he squinted out at Frank. "Do I know you?"

"That's Frank," I managed. It was possible to die of embarrassment, right? The expression had to have come from somewhere. "We were just, um, going running."

"Oh," my dad said. He stared at Frank a moment longer, then looked at me and frowned. "Well, be sure to put some shoes on." Then he continued on inside, no doubt heading to the dining room to start working.

"Okay," I managed. "I'll just go upstairs and put on something to run in. And then I'll be back."

"I'll be here," Frank said, and it looked like he was trying— though not very hard—to suppress a grin.

I nodded but, not wanting to turn around, backed up until I reached the doorway, then took a big step backward and shut the door. I leaned against it, closing my eyes, wondering for just a moment if I was actually in a nightmare. Surely this qualified.

Ten minutes later, I'd washed my face and put on a long-sleeved T-shirt and long leggings with my running shoes. It was already getting hot outside, but I felt that I needed to balance out the accidental half-nudity that had started my morning. "Ready to go?" I asked as I joined Frank outside, iPod in hand. I was hoping that if I was brusque and businesslike, he'd forget all about the state I'd shown up in.

"Sure," he said, walking to the end of the driveway with me. I could tell that he was trying to catch my eye, but I busied myself with selecting my new playlist and adjusting the volume, not putting in my earbuds yet or pressing play, since I still wasn't sure what the etiquette with that was.

"Ready?" I asked. Frank nodded, and we started running, me on the outside like before. I kept the pace slower, knowing that I certainly needed a warm-up, as my muscles were cold.

"So I guess I surprised you this morning?" Frank asked after a few minutes of silent running, and I got the feeling that he hadn't been able to keep this to himself any longer.

"A little bit," I said, realizing now that I was surprised—I hadn't expected him to want to keep running.

"I said we should do it again, and you said anytime," he said. "I remember you did."

"I thought you were kidding," I replied. "It didn't look like you'd really had a good time."

"Nothing worth doing is easy," Frank said. "Especially not in the beginning. But I'm not about to give up."

"Wow," I said, shaking my head. We ran in silence for a few steps, just the sound of our sneakers hitting the pavement, occasionally finding the same rhythm and landing in sequence, then falling out of it once more.

"Wow what?" Frank asked, a defensive note I hadn't heard before creeping into his voice.

"No," I said quickly, wishing I'd never said anything. "Nothing. Never mind." Frank nodded and looked straight ahead, his mouth set in a thin line and a dull flush of color in his cheeks. Oh god. Had I just insulted him? If Sloane were here, I could have asked her this question with my eyes, and she would have been able to answer me in the same way. But of course, if Sloane were here, I wouldn't be running with Frank Porter at all. "I didn't mean anything bad," I started, wondering even as I spoke if I should have just let this go. "I just meant that it makes sense."

There was a low-hanging branch in front of us, and we both ducked in unison to avoid it. "What does?"

"Just that you'd have that attitude," I said, trying to articulate what had been an instantaneous reaction. "It's understandable. I mean, because of who you are." Frank looked over at me, and from his expression, I hadn't cleared anything up, but had just made things worse.

"Who I am?" he repeated, his voice quiet.

"Yeah," I said, now really wishing I'd let things go and not tried to explain anything. I didn't even know Frank Porter; why was I attempting to tell him who he was? I had the distinct feeling like I was not awake enough to handle this conversation. "You're Frank Porter. You're good at everything."

"Not at running," he pointed out. "I'm *terrible* at that."

"But you're not giving up, like you said. So you probably will be soon."

Frank looked straight ahead, and we didn't speak for a few minutes, and I wondered if I'd overstepped, made things worse when I was trying to make them better. I was on the verge of trying to figure out how to apologize when Frank asked, "So how's the list coming?"

"You got my e-mail?" I asked, and he nodded. Even though I told myself it was a long shot, I could feel my hopes start to rise. Maybe there had been something in the list I'd just been overlooking, and the answer was right there, had been there all along. "Did you find anything?"

Frank shook his head, and I felt my hopes deflate. "But I've just started to look," he said, shooting me a quick smile. "And in the meantime, I had some ideas."

I looked over at him, then had to do an awkward skipping movement over a rock that had shown up in my path. But I was glad for the distraction; it allowed me to try and process how strange it was to hear Frank talking about my list like it was just ordinary, when it had been my secret, something I'd been

Morgan Matson

turning over and over in my head but not ever talking about. "What do you mean, ideas?"

"For finishing your list," he said, like this should have been obvious. "I can help you, if you want." I looked back at the road ahead, trying to sort through how I felt about this. It was one thing to go running twice with Frank Porter. This would be something else. "I'm seriously in need of a project," he went on. "I mean, even Collins has a summer project."

"He does?"

"He decided he's going to have a girlfriend by the end of the summer. Or, as he insists on putting it, a steady hang."

"And how's that going?"

Frank laughed. "About as well as you'd imagine. And I get to hear about it every day at work."

We ran in silence for a while then, but it didn't feel uncomfortable, and when I looked back at Frank, he held up his iPod, like asking if it was okay if we turned them on. I nodded and slipped my own earbuds in, listening to the same mix I had run to before. It was actually nice, running next to Frank but not feeling the pressure to say the right thing or keep the conversation going. It looked like he was occasionally laughing as he ran, which I didn't get, unless he was listening to someone like They Might Be Giants, which was about as far into the nineties as I ventured. We had gone farther this time, and we were almost at the entrance to the town beach. I pointed ahead at it, and Frank nodded, and maybe it was because we'd raced to the end before, but we both started sprinting. My muscles weren't protesting quite as loudly this time, but it was still a struggle to pick up my pace. I reached the carved wooden sign indicating the beach entrance before Frank did, but not by much. We both just gasped for breath for a few seconds, then Frank took his earbuds out and smiled at me. "Nicely done."

"You too," I said, as I pulled out my own earphones, bending over slightly, trying to take long, deep breaths and slow down my heart rate. I straightened up and we started to walk back, both of us grimacing, and I knew I'd be feeling this run tomorrow morning.

"Hey, what are you listening to?" Frank asked, and before I could stop him or even realize what was happening, he'd taken the iPod from my hands and was scrolling through my playlist.

"No, that's not—" I started. "I was just, um . . ."

Frank looked at me, and he was smiling now as he looked down at it. "You know there's a loop function, right?" he asked. "So you don't have to keep repeating the playlist?"

"I know," I muttered. "Mine's just broken because I left it in my car when it was raining. My roof doesn't work."

"I've never even heard of these songs," he said, frowning at it. "What's the Downeaster 'Alexa'?"

"It's Billy Joel," I said, and I could hear myself getting defensive, which was surprising, because I hadn't known I felt that strongly about him. "It's . . . about the plight of fishermen on Long Island." I had meant for that to bolster my argument that it was a good song, but as soon as I'd said it, I started to rethink this, especially when Frank started laughing.

"I honestly don't recognize half these artists," Frank said, shaking his head. "And why aren't there any *g*'s in any of these song titles?"

"It's nothing," I said, trying to grab it back from him. "Just . . ."

"You have a song on here called 'Aw Naw,'" he said. He turned to me, and I could see he looked incredulous. "Emily, is this *country*?"

"Well, what are *you* listening to?" I asked, feeling uncharacteristically bold as I grabbed his iPod, looking down at his playlist.

MIX #4

West Coast	Coconut Records
Heartbreak Yellow	Andy Davis
Our Deal	Best Coast
Dance for You	Dirty Projectors
We Can Work It Out	The Beatles
Crystallized	Young the Giant
Breaking It Up	Lykke Li
Airplanes	Curtis Anderson
Dreaming	Smallpools
Kiss Me Slowly	Parachute
Magic (feat. Rivers Cuomo)	B.o.B
Peggy-O	Among the Oak & Ash

Step Out	José González
City Living	Curtis Anderson
Golden Slumbers	The Beatles
No One Does It Like You	Department of Eagles
Gone, Gone, Gone	Phillip Phillips
Fallen	Imagine Dragons
Spitting Fire	The Boxer Rebellion
Yesterday	The Beatles
Simple Song	The Shins
Passenger Seat	Death Cab For Cutie
Thoughts at Arby's	Curtis Anderson
Midnight City	M83
About Today	The National
Wake Up	Arcade Fire

I didn't recognize most the songs, so I pressed Play on the song that had been paused, slipping one of his earphones in. I was confused at first, because I didn't hear music. There was just the sound of laughter, some people clapping, like I'd heard that first night in his truck. And then a guy with a Boston accent saying, "But seriously . . . in a well-ordered universe, we wouldn't have doormen, am I right? Like, we open doors for ourselves all day long. But in this one instance we become totally helpless?"

I looked up at Frank, who wasn't laughing anymore. "Is this that comedian?"

Morgan Matson

"Curtis Anderson," Frank said with a nod. "I don't know, I've always thought he was funny. Lissa thought he was really juvenile, but . . ." He shrugged.

"Is that what you've been running to?" I asked. Frank nodded, and I shook my head at him. "That's your problem. You need to make a mix with songs that will pump you up and get you through the run."

"I see," Frank said, nodding, his expression serious. "Like songs about fishermen?" I laughed at that without even thinking about it first and looked back down at his playlist.

"These aren't real bands," I said, as I scrolled through it. "Like, these have to be made-up names."

"You mean like the Beatles?" Frank asked, deadpan, as he tried to take his iPod back, and I pretended not to notice.

"Not like the Beatles," I said, as I finished scrolling through the songs. "But there *are* a lot of their songs on here."

"Told you I was obsessed."

"But 'Department of Eagles' is fake, right?" I said as I handed him back his iPod and he gave me mine. "That's not a real band."

Frank just looked surprised. "You've never heard them? They're great. I'll make you a mix."

He said this so easily, like he was sure we'd be seeing each other again, like these weren't just isolated incidents. But I suddenly realized I didn't want them to be. And so when we reached Frank's house and he said, "Do this again soon?" I nodded, hoping that it would be true.

"Got any big plans for the weekend?" he asked as he stretched out his quads, and I found myself watching, with more interest than I probably should have had, to see if he'd lift up his shirt to wipe his face again.

"Oh," I said, thinking fast. For a second, I thought about telling him the truth, but then immediately decided against it. "Not that much. You know."

"Well, hope it's good," Frank said, giving me a wave. I waved back and I started to walk toward home, telling myself that I'd done the right thing. Because even if he had offered to help me out with the list, I had a feeling that the student body president would not have been happy to learn that I was planning on crossing off number three on Saturday night. I was going to steal something.

5
SHARE SOME SECRETS IN THE DARK

I sat inside my car at the Hartfield drive-in and looked around, wishing I knew what, exactly, was involved in casing a joint. The heist movies I'd seen hadn't really been very specific. Luckily, though, it wasn't like this place was unknown to me. Sloane had introduced me to it after she'd only been in town for a month. I had never been to a drive-in before, but I'd loved it after the first movie—the big screen set up at one end of a field, the cars parked in slightly crooked rows, the speakers you could hang over the window of your car, the way they always played double features.

We went a few times every summer, the first year with my parents dropping us off, sitting on beach towels or blankets in front of the screen. But last summer, I'd driven us, and we'd been able to park with everyone else.

I let out a long breath, hoping that I didn't seem suspicious, and that I looked like I was just there, like everyone else, to see a Hitchcock double feature of *North by Northwest* and *The Lady Vanishes*, and not to commit my first crime.

Number three had been a question mark since I first read the list. It wasn't so much the stealing itself, but figuring out what to steal. But when, driving home from the gas station, I'd passed a billboard for the drive-in, I'd remembered a promise I'd made to Sloane two years earlier, and just like that, I'd known what it had to be.

****

JULY

Two Years Earlier

"The usual?" Sloane asked, and I nodded.

"Definitely." Sloane and I had only seen a handful of movies together so far, but we already worked out our routine, snack-wise. She was the one who had introduced me to the concept of shaking M&M's into the bag of buttered, salted popcorn and using Twizzlers as straws for Diet Coke. I had, in turn, gotten her hooked on the sour gummy candy that I never liked to see a movie without.

We pooled our cash as we made our way up to the concession stand, a tiny building that looked like it had been there forever, and when Sloane reached the front of the line, I took a step back to let her order. "Large popcorn," she said as I looked around the stand. There were vintage posters on the walls and framed pictures of the drive-in throughout the years. "M&M's, Twizzlers, two Diet Cokes." The guy behind the counter nodded and grabbed a bag for our popcorn, and I was happy to see that it looked like a fresh batch had just been made. I was about to remind Sloane to get extra butter when she grabbed my arm and pointed to a sign resting on one of the concession stand shelves, half tucked behind a display of Hartfield Drive-In T-shirts and mugs. "Look."

It was a small sign, the kind you put magnetized letters on, the kind I associated with bowling alley snack menus. But this one, instead of telling you how much the hot dogs were, read

> SLOANE
>
> LOVES
>
> FERRIS

I just stared at it for a moment until I realized that it was a reference to *Ferris Bueller's Day Off*. I didn't understand what it was doing behind the concession stand, but it had a very cool, vintage look to it. "Neat," I said as I reached for my phone. "Want me to take a picture?"

Someone else brought our snacks around to the side of the cash register, and Sloane paid without taking her eyes off the sign. "Is that for sale?" she asked as she handed our change over to me. I was in charge of the money when we were together. Sloane wasn't absentminded, but she seemed to have trouble to hanging on to money and was always finding bills in the pockets of her dresses and shorts, which she then treated as something to be celebrated, and would insist on buying both of us the biggest, most extravagant blended coffee drinks that Stanwich Coffee could make.

"Is what for sale?" the guy asked, already looking behind us to the next person in line, who was sighing loudly.

"The sign," she said, pointing to it. "The Sloane sign."

The guy looked at Sloane like she was crazy. "No," he said. "It's been here since the eighties."

"Are you *sure* it's not for sale?" she asked, giving him a big smile. But the guy seemed immune to this and let out a barking laugh.

"I'm sure," he said. "First time I've been asked that in twenty years, though. Next!"

Sloane's shoulders slumped and we headed back to our blanket. "Think I should have offered him something for it?"

I shrugged. I wasn't sure it would be helpful to point out that, after we'd bought the snacks, we had a grand total of $1.35 between us. "I'm not sure it would have made a difference."

"But it might have . . . ," Sloane said, glancing back toward the concession stand. It was getting dark; there were fireflies beginning to wink off and on in the grass, but the

Morgan Matson

sign, and the letters that formed her name, were still visible, catching the fading light and reflecting it back. She turned to me, and I could see her normal cheerfulness had returned. "Promise you'll help me get it," she said, leaning forward. "This is my new life goal." I laughed at that, and Sloane smiled too, but she didn't take her eyes from mine. "Promise, Em?"

"Sure," I said, easily. "We'll do what we have to. We'll come here every weekend and wear him down."

Sloane grinned and grabbed a handful of popcorn. "Awesome," she said. "We have a plan."

★★★★

So I would steal the sign for her. We'd never been able to get anyone to sell it to us, so this was the only option—and this way, I would get to cross something off the list and keep my promise to her, all at the same time. It was a perfect solution—unless, of course, I got arrested while trying to pull it off.

I didn't get in the concessions line right away, but circled around it, double-checking that the sign was still there. Luckily, it was off to the side where people picked up their food, not where they ordered it. So concession workers were dropping things off, then hurrying away to get other people's orders. I mentally walked through the mechanics of this, and I realized that I could make it look like I was just reaching for my order, grab the sign, and drop it into my bag. If someone caught me,

I could just pretend it had fallen in and I hadn't even noticed. I had brought my largest purse with me for this very reason, the better to conceal the evidence.

It wasn't the best plan, but at least it was a plan. I let out a breath and got in the line that was quickly filling up, feeling like everyone around me could tell what I was about to do.

"Emily?"

I felt my stomach plunge as I looked behind me and saw Frank, standing a few people back in line, with a surprised look on his face, raising one hand in a wave. I gave him a small smile in return, but then turned around to face the concession stand again, not caring if this seemed incredibly rude. What was Frank Porter doing at the drive-in?

"Hey."

I turned and saw that Frank had joined me in the line. He took a step closer to me and said in a low voice, "Mind if I jump the line?" He glanced behind him, at the older couple who were pursing their lips in disapproval, and said, too loudly, "Thank you for saving my place in line, Emily!"

I really wished he'd stop saying my name in front of potential witnesses. "You shouldn't—" I said, glancing ahead to the counter, and wishing that the line wasn't moving quite so fast. "I just . . ." I tried to get my head around how to explain that he couldn't wait in line with me because I was about to steal something. Even though he knew about the list, and this wouldn't seem *quite* so random, I didn't want to have to go into

Morgan Matson

an explanation with everyone in the line able to hear me talk about it. Also, what if Frank was still with me when I had to try and take it, and he tried to stop me? Or he got in trouble too?

"Crazy running into you here," Frank said, shaking his head. "This place is awesome. Have you ever been before?"

"Yeah," I murmured, feeling my heart racing ever faster in my chest, getting closer and closer to what I was pretty sure was a panic attack. The front of the line was just three people away, and I hadn't been able to get rid of Frank or properly psych myself up to commit my first crime. "A lot."

"I'm only here because of Collins," Frank went on, apparently thinking we were just having a nice conversation, not realizing that I was on the verge of an aneurysm. "He's got a thing for the girl who runs the projection booth. But now that I'm here, it's really—"

"You know what," I said, stepping out of line. "I actually . . . forgot something. So you order, and I'll get the thing I forgot, and, um . . . see you around, okay?" I stepped out of the line and walked in the direction of my car. I glanced back to see Frank looking at me, his brow furrowed, but then he stepped to the front of the line to order, and I went to the back of the line, which now seemed impossibly long. I was no longer sure if I'd even have enough time to do this before the concessions break was over.

I let out a breath and tried to get my thoughts in order. I could still do this. I just had to focus. The line moved forward quicker than I expected, and I realized, my stomach clenching, that there was only one other person in front of me, an older lady who was having trouble deciding between the Sno-Caps and the Junior Mints. I looked at the sign, then down into my huge, waiting bag.

"Next!" I looked ahead and saw that behind the counter was a concession worker I hadn't seen before, a guy who looked college-aged and bored—which was pretty much perfect.

"Hi," I said, stepping forward, hearing that my voice sounded about twice as high as normal. I didn't make eye contact with the guy as I said, "Small popcorn with butter and a Diet Coke."

"Eight even," the guy said, and I handed the cash I had ready over to him as the register drawer slid open with a *ding!* "Pickup's to your left. Next!"

I stepped to the side, letting my bag fall open slightly as I tried to look nonchalant. I pretended to yawn and stretched my arm out for the sign, my fingers just brushing the edge of it. I stretched farther out, almost off-balance, heart pounding, nearly grabbing it—

"Small popcorn and a Diet Coke." A girl had stepped up with my snacks, and I was so startled by this that I felt myself pitching forward, just barely catching myself before face-planting onto the counter. The sign wobbled and tipped forward, and the girl grabbed it, looking from the sign and then back to me with narrowed eyes. "What are you doing?"

"I . . . ," I started. I could feel the sweat beading on my upper lip and my heart wasn't pounding hard any longer, it now seemed to be pumping a lot slower than usual, which struck me as a bad sign. "I just . . ."

"Did you get that arm cramp again?" Suddenly, there was Frank, stepping up next to me. He slid his arm around my shoulders, and this was so startling that any excuse I might have been forming left my head entirely. "She gets those sometimes. Don't you?"

"I do," I said, nodding, trying to look as innocent as I could manage. "Yeah. Sometimes."

"Don't forget your snacks," Frank said, giving my shoulder a squeeze, keeping a trustworthy, class-president smile on his face. I picked them up and we both smiled brightly at the girl, who was watching us with a suspicious expression. She went to put the sign back, but then hesitated and moved it to the highest shelf of the concession counter, right behind the popcorn popper, meaning that it was basically now impossible to get.

Frank and I walked away, and when we'd gone almost back to the cars and it appeared the concessions police weren't going to give chase, I felt myself start to breathe again. I took a long drink of my soda, and it wasn't until I'd finished that I realized Frank still had his arm around me. He must have noticed this at the same time, because he dropped his arm and took a step away.

"So," I said, still a little surprised that he had been able to see just when I needed him. "Um, how did you—"

"I have *never* seen anyone look so suspicious," Frank said, shaking his head. "Ever. I figured I should probably stay close, just in case."

"Oh," I said, looking down at the ground. Even though rationally I knew that not being good at stealing was actually a positive thing, and not something to be ashamed of, it didn't currently change how I was feeling—like I'd just failed.

"So . . . uh, why were you trying to rob the concession stand?" Frank asked, sounding baffled.

"It's for the list," I said, raising one shoulder in a shrug. "Number three."

Frank glanced back at the sign, and I saw him reading Sloane's name, putting it together. He nodded and started to say something just as the loudspeakers crackled to life, announcing the movie's start in sixty seconds and the closing of the concession stand.

"I should go," I said. I knew that I should probably thank him for helping me, and that if he hadn't, I might be in serious trouble. But it really is humiliating to fail at something and then need to be rescued, even if that thing is committing a crime. I gave him a small smile and then headed to my own car, glancing over my shoulder to see Frank walking away as well.

I'd intended to make a getaway after grabbing the sign and not stay for the second movie. But it was clear as I got into my car that I wasn't going anywhere—the people in the rows behind me had pretty much boxed me in, and everyone was watching the movie, and I had a feeling that nobody was going to be happy to move if I tried to get out. So I put my drink into the cupholder and pushed my seat back, settling in. As I did so, I wondered if I was the only person at the whole drive-in who was watching the movie alone.

****

APRIL

Two months earlier

"How much did you offer this time?" I asked, as Sloane came back to the car, without the sign but holding an armful of our snacks.

"A hundred," she said with a sigh. "And they *still* wouldn't take it. I swear, at this rate, I'm going to need to bribe one of the employees."

"Or you could start working there," I suggested, as I took the popcorn from her and grabbed a handful off the top. "And get hired under a fake name. And it could be an inside job."

Sloane grinned at me. "I like the way you're thinking," she said. "What name?"

I thought about it, just enjoying the game. We were there to see a double feature of *Clueless* and *Troop Beverly Hills*, which meant that there were almost no guys in attendance at all. It seemed to be moms and daughters and groups of friends, like us. Since Sam had arrived on the scene, it felt like it had been a long time since just Sloane and I had hung out, and I'd been looking forward to this for weeks. "Alicia," I said, after thinking it over. "Alicia Paramount."

Sloane threw her head back and laughed. "I love it," she said. "I'll apply next week."

I started to walk around to the back of the Volvo. Once I'd gotten my license and we didn't have to watch on the grass any longer, we'd figured out the ideal movie-watching routine—my car turned around backward, the hatchback open, and both of us in the back, lying on pillows and blankets that would inevitably smell like popcorn for days afterward. "Coming?" I asked, when I realized that she was still standing outside the car, looking around.

"Yeah," she said, following behind me. But she didn't get into the back, just stood outside it, craning her neck like she was looking for something, fiddling with her keys—including the personalized SLOANE mini license plate keychain I'd special-ordered for her birthday—which was what she did when she was nervous.

"You okay?" I asked as I opened the Twizzlers and pulled one out, biting both ends off and then sticking it into my Diet Coke.

"Sure," she said. "I'm—" But she didn't finish this, as her phone beeped with a text. She pulled it out immediately and read it, smiling down at the screen as she typed a quick response back.

"Sam?" I guessed, taking a drink through the Twizzler.

"Yeah," she said, pocketing her phone and looking at me. There was a flush in her cheeks and I noticed how much more alive she now looked—happier, and more excited, like now things were actually happening, whereas before, they hadn't been. "So here's the thing," she said talking fast. "I told Sam we were going to be here, but I wasn't sure if he was going to come or not, but then—"

"Hey, you." There was Sam, sliding his arms around Sloane's waist and kissing her cheek.

"Hi," Sloane said, smiling wide as she turned to kiss him, and I could hear the happiness in her voice so clearly. "You're here! I wasn't sure if you were going to show."

"Of course I'm here," he said easily. He slung his arm around her neck, letting his fingertips rest on her arm. "Oh, hi, Emily," he said, as if he'd just noticed me.

"Hey, Sam," I said, trying to sound excited to see him, like I was happy he was here, not like I was disappointed that my night with Sloane had suddenly come to a crashing halt.

"Nice straw," he said with a short laugh, nodding at my cup with the Twizzler poking out of it. "Wow. God. I haven't seen that since I was, like, eleven."

"Yeah," I said, with an embarrassed laugh. "It's . . ." I wasn't sure how to finish this, so I just let my voice trail away. Sam was still looking at me, raising his eyebrows like he was challenging me to finish the sentence. He gave me a pitying smile, then squeezed Sloane's shoulder, threading his fingers through hers. "Come on," he said, nodding toward the far side of the field. "I've got a great spot."

"Oh," Sloane said, looking from me to Sam, some of the happiness fading from her expression. "I was thinking we could all watch together, maybe?"

Sam just laughed again, and I noticed, maybe for the first time, that he used his laughs to score points, like a punctuation mark, not because he found something funny. "I think Emily will be fine," he said, looking over at me, already starting to steer Sloane away from me. "Won't you, Em?"

There was absolutely no way to respond to this question except in the affirmative, and as I looked at Sloane's expression, I could see this was all she wanted—she wanted to be able to keep Sam happy, to go off with him, and for me to be okay with it. "Sure," I said, giving her a smile I didn't quite feel, wondering for a second if she'd be able to tell the difference. "You kids go have fun." I'd intended this to be funny, but it somehow didn't seem funny once I'd said it, Sam just looking at me quizzically, Sloane not laughing at my jokes like she normally did.

"Uh, okay," he said. He gave me a nod. "See you around, Em."

"Bye," I called as Sam started to walk away. Sloane turned back to look at me, and we had a fast and furious conversation as we mouthed our words—*Are you sure? Yes! Go have fun! Call you tomorrow? Yes!*

She shot me one last happy, excited smile, then turned back to Sam, already laughing at something he was saying.

I watched them go, feeling my own smile fade until it was gone. I climbed into the open back and took a sip from my soda. But the Twizzler suddenly made the soda too cloyingly sweet, and I pulled it out, replacing it with a regular straw instead. It was pretty childish, after all. I probably should have stopped doing it a while back.

I settled into the back, sticking to my side of the car even though there was no need to, trying to tell myself that things were fine, that I should be happy for Sloane. She'd met a guy she really liked, and what kind of best friend would I be if I couldn't be excited for her? Everything would be okay. And by the time the credits rolled, I'd even started to believe it.

****

Since I'd had no impending crime-committing to worry about, I'd actually been able to follow *The Lady Vanishes*, and I'd really liked it, though I did wonder why Hitchcock was so obsessed with trains—both of these movies had seemed to feature a *lot* of them.

I had stayed in my car for a bit, just looking at the darkened screen. The line leaving the drive-in was always epic, bottlenecks forming at the exit, and everyone honking, even though this accomplished absolutely nothing. Sloane and I had always just hung out in the car, lying back against the pillows and finishing the last of the snacks, discussing the movies or just talking.

When the silence got to be too much, I headed out with my trash and stuffed it into one of the overflowing cans. Now that the parking lot was emptying out, I could see Frank and Collins standing by Collins's minivan. Not feeling the need to keep humiliating myself in front of Frank—I figured that quota had pretty much been met tonight—I turned my head away and was halfway to my car when I heard Collins calling me.

"Emma!" he yelled, and then I saw Frank lean over and say something to him, and Collins nodded. "Emi*ly*!" he called, finally getting my name right. "Come here!" I just waved at him and continued over to my car, hoping that he would buy that I hadn't heard him. "*No*," Collins shouted, louder than ever, now incorporating large hand movements, pointing at me, then at him, and miming walking. "Come *over here*!" People were starting to turn and look, and I knew there was really no way I could keep pretending.

I let out a long breath and headed over to them. Frank and Collins were having what looked like an intense discussion that stopped abruptly when I reached the minivan. "Hello," Collins said, giving me a theatrical wink. "Don't you look lovely tonight. It would have been a fetching ensemble for a mugshot."

I could feel myself blush and looked over at Frank, who glared at Collins, who didn't seem to notice. I knew that I probably couldn't be mad at Frank for telling him. If the situation had been reversed and I'd been here with Sloane and caught Frank

Porter trying to steal something, I wouldn't even have waited until I saw her—I would have been calling her on the walk to the car. "Nothing to be ashamed of," Collins went on, smiling wisely at me. "Sometime, when the moment is right, remind me to tell you the story of my time in Disney jail." He lowered his voice and leaned closer to me. "Spoiler alert—*not* the happiest place on earth."

I just blinked at Collins. Had he called me over here so that he could make fun of me? I crossed my arms over my chest, and looked back at my car, wishing I hadn't stopped, just kept on walking. I would have been halfway home by now.

"Matt," Frank said. His voice was serious, and this—calling Collins by his real name—seemed to focus him.

"Right!" he said, clapping his hands together. "Okay. So I have managed to make plans with the lovely Miss Gwen for tonight," Collins said, and I noticed for the first time that a dark-haired girl was leaning against a sedan a few cars away, smoking a cigarette and talking on her phone.

"Oh," I said, remembering what Frank had said about Collins liking the projectionist. "Um, good for you."

"Why thank you." He straightened his neon-green polo and smoothed down his hair. Now that I'd seen him a few times this summer, I was beginning to understand that this was his summer uniform—a slightly too-tight bright-colored polo shirt, shorts, and beaten-up flip-flops, making him somehow always look like he'd just gotten off a poorly maintained boat. He smiled at me. "My charms, they're hard to resist."

"Dude, she's using you for a ride to this party," Frank said, shaking his head.

"I believe you mean she *invited* me to this party," Collins corrected. "And asked if I could drive her. Which, being a gentleman, I agreed to do."

Frank just sighed and looked down at the ground.

"Mike!" the projectionist yelled, stepping on her cigarette and lowering her phone. "Are we going, or what?"

"Coming," Collins yelled, not seeming to care she'd gotten his name wrong. "Anyway," he said, turning back to us, all business. "Emily. You can drive Porter home, right? Don't you guys live near each other?"

"Oh," I said, looking over at Frank, finally understanding why I'd been summoned. "Sure. No problem."

I had barely gotten the words out before Collins grinned, slapped Frank on the back, and clicked open the sliding minivan door with a flourish, motioning for Gwen to come over. She ignored the sliding door, got into the passenger side, still carrying on another conversation, and Collins got into the van through the side. The van peeled out of the lot with a screech of tires, leaving Frank and me alone.

"Sorry about this," Frank said, as we walked toward my Volvo, now one of the few cars left on the field.

"It's fine," I said. "I owe you anyway."

"Well, I appreciate it," he said. I unlocked the car and, when we were both inside, started the engine and headed toward the exit. I tightened my hands on the wheel, then released them, trying to figure out how to thank him for what he'd done for me. "Frank," I started, then I looked over to see that he was staring down at his phone.

"What?" he asked, looking over at me. "Sorry. I've been trying to get Lissa all night. I haven't been able to reach her, so I'm just going to shoot her a text. . . ."

"Right, of course," I said, looking back toward the road. "Sorry."

The faint tapping on his keypad filled the car, and I didn't want to turn on my iPod and disturb him—not to mention the fact that I also didn't want him to make fun of my music. Even when the texting sounds stopped, Frank was just looking down at the phone, like he was waiting for a response, and I wasn't sure it was the right moment to interrupt him. By the time I'd reached his house, though, he'd put the phone away, and I couldn't help but notice that I hadn't heard the cheerful *beep* sound that would have meant Frank had gotten a reply back.

"Thanks, Emily," Frank said as I pulled in the driveway.

"Sure," I said. "It was no—" Whatever I was about to say was lost, though, as I took in the view of Frank's house at night for the first time. The whole house was dark, but I could see that it was right on the water, something I hadn't been able to tell before from the road. Moonlight was shining down on the house and reflecting off its chrome and glass surfaces, seeming to light the whole thing up from the inside. "Are you right on the beach?"

"Yeah," Frank said. After a tiny pause, he added, "You want to see it?"

"Oh," I said, sitting back in my seat a little. I suddenly worried that I'd seemed too interested, and that he felt like he had to invite me in out of politeness. "No, that's okay. Plus, it looks like your parents are asleep."

"Nope," Frank said, and it sounded like he was trying to keep his voice light. I noticed this, and wondered when I'd started to be able to tell the difference. "Not home."

"Oh." I glanced at the clock on my iPod—the clock on my dashboard was forever stuck at 8:19. It was almost midnight, so this surprised me, but I certainly wasn't going to comment on it.

"Yeah," Frank said with a shrug. "My dad's in Darien, working on a house, and my mom has a decorating project in the city. And they're not supposed to be in the house together anyway, because . . ." He glanced at me, and suddenly I remembered his parents, red-faced and screaming at each other, Frank's expression as he listened to it. "So that's why nobody's there," Frank said in a quieter voice, and I suddenly understood what he was saying. That he was staying here alone. And even though my parents were still physically in our house, I knew what it was like to come home and have nobody be worried about you, or asking you about your day. All the stuff you can't wait to get away from, until it's not there anymore, and then you miss it like crazy.

"I'll come in," I said, surprising myself—and Frank, by the look of it. "Just for a little bit." With any other guy, I might have

Morgan Matson

been worried there was some sort of ulterior motive—asking me in, late at night, to an empty house. But that wasn't even anything I considered with Frank—long-term boyfriend and all-around good guy—except to realize it wasn't an issue.

"Great," Frank said, giving me a surprised, happy smile. "Let's go." I followed him around to the side door he'd gone in before. When he opened the door, a loud, persistent chime started, until Frank entered a code into a keypad I hadn't even noticed by the door. The beeping stopped and Frank moved forward, turning on lights as he went, and I followed, but then stopped short, looking around, really seeing his house for the first time, my jaw falling open.

It was beautiful. There were many other words for it, whole reams of adjectives, but at first glance, that was all I could come up with. The downstairs was open-plan, which meant I could see the entire bottom floor, the TV room blending into the study, which then became the dining area, and then an open-plan kitchen and breakfast nook. The house was light and airy, with high ceilings and lots and lots of windows, everything done in grays and blues and whites. Everything just fit together. There were tiny groupings of objects, arranged just so. I saw, on a bookshelf right by the front door, a big vase filled with long feathers. Which was arresting enough, but on the shelf above it, there was a medium vase filled with medium-size feathers. And at the top shelf was a tiny vase filled with the smallest feathers I'd ever seen. There was stuff like that, little details and perfect touches, everywhere I looked, and I suddenly wanted nothing more than to just stand there and take it all in.

"Emily?" Frank called, and I realized he had crossed the room and was standing by a glass door built into an entire wall of windows, all of which looked out onto the sand and the water.

"Yeah," I said, tearing myself away from the décor, knowing that there was a ton of stuff I wasn't catching. Frank opened the door, and we stepped out onto a wide wooden deck that looked out to the water, with four steps that led down to the sand. The only time I'd ever been to the beach at night was for the Fourth of July fireworks, when there were tons of people and everyone jockeying for space. But this stretch of moonlit beach was empty, and I realized that Frank and I would have the whole thing to ourselves.

I trailed Frank down the stairs and stepped onto the sand, then immediately kicked my flip-flops off so that I could feel it on my bare feet. I saw Frank do the same, pulling off his sneakers and then lining them up neatly by the deck's steps.

I walked toward the water, to where the sand got soft and more pliable, but where my feet would still be dry. There was just something about the beach at night. It was so quiet, without anyone else yelling or playing Frisbee or blasting their music. And maybe because of this, the sound of the water—even though we didn't even have real waves—seemed that much louder. And then there was the moon. It was huge tonight, in a sky that was filled with stars that reflected down on the surface of the water.

I expected that this would be it—I'd seen that Frank's house was, in fact, on the water, and now I'd leave and go home. But as I turned back, I saw Frank sitting on the sand looking out at the water, his legs extended in front of him. I hesitated for only a moment before I sat down as well, not too close to him, pulling my knees up and hugging them. "I like your backyard," I said, and Frank smiled.

"Well, I should enjoy it while I can," he said, picking up a handful of sand and letting it fall through his fingers. I sensed there was more to come, so I just looked at him, waiting, trying to be as patient with him as he'd been with me. "My parents are getting a divorce," he said. He let the rest of the sand fall and brushed his hands off. "That's what you saw the other morning." I could see the hunch in his shoulders. "It's gotten pretty messy."

I felt myself draw in a breath. It was what I'd guessed, given the screaming fight that I'd witnessed. "I'm really sorry, Frank."

He nodded and looked over at me, and it felt like in that moment, I was getting to see the real Frank Porter, like he was finally letting his walls down a little, not putting a good face on things. "Yeah," he said, giving a short, unhappy laugh. "They work together, so they're keeping it quiet, so they don't lose any jobs. But they're having trouble dividing assets, so they're not supposed to be in the house together without their lawyers present." His mouth was set in a sad, straight line, and though he was trying to sound like this wasn't bothering him, he wasn't really pulling it off.

"So," I said, leaning a little closer to him, trying to understand this, "I mean, who's living here with you?"

"Well, they're trading off," he said. "In theory. It seems to be easier for them to just stay near their other projects."

I nodded and looked down at the sand, smoothing out a patch of it, over and over again. Even though my parents weren't paying any attention to me or Beckett, they were still there. And I knew if I needed them, I could shake them out of their writing stupor.

"Anyway, that's why I'm here for the summer. I usually go to a program at Princeton. And I was going to go back again, but neither one could agree on who should pay for it, so . . ." He shrugged and gave me an attempt at a smile.

Even as I started to form the question, I knew I wouldn't have asked him if it hadn't been dark and I couldn't have looked down at the sand instead of at him. "Is your—I mean, is Lissa at the Princeton program?" It was what I'd been wondering since Frank had been trying to get in touch with her on the drive here. It had reminded me that, in all the times I'd seen Frank this summer, he'd never been with his girlfriend.

Frank nodded. "Yeah," he said. "We didn't think she should have to miss out just because I couldn't go." I waited for there to be more, but Frank just looked out to the water, and when he spoke again, his voice sounded like he was trying his best to be upbeat. "Anyway, Collins got me the job at IndoorXtreme, and here I am. It wasn't the summer I was expecting, that's for sure," he said. But then he smiled, a small smile, but a real one this time. "But it's turning out better than I imagined." He raised an eyebrow. "I mean, just tonight, I might have saved someone from getting arrested."

I smiled. "Thank you for that, by the way."

Frank waved this off. "All in a day's work."

"Does the offer still stand?" I asked, not knowing that I was going to, just blurting it out. "To help me with the list, I mean?"

"Of course," Frank said, turning to me. "Actually," he said with a smile, "I kind of already started."

I laughed, and knew that I really shouldn't have been surprised by this. "Of course you did."

"So," he said, and in his voice, I could hear Frank Porter, class president, beginning an assembly. "I've made a list of all the Jamies at our school, and divided them by gender, and—"

"Actually," I said, feeling myself start to smile as I leaned back on my hands, "that one's taken care of." Frank raised his eyebrows, and I extended my legs out in front of me, settling in for the story. "Okay, so the other night . . ."

I told Frank the story about delivering pizzas, and chickening out, but then going back to the gas station, remembering what he'd told me about the guy's name, and then we somehow moved on to other things. Before I knew it, the conversation was just flowing without me having to try and guide it, or be aware of its every twist and turn. I was no longer thinking about what I should say. I was just going with it, letting the conversation unfold.

****

"That makes no sense whatsoever." He just stared at me. "It's on the list because you're afraid of *horses*?"

"Yep."

Frank just tilted his head to the side, like he was trying to figure this out. "So, uh," he said after a moment. "Would these be, like, regular horses? Or possessed demon horses?"

"Regular horses," I admitted as Frank looked like he was trying very hard not to laugh. "I don't really know why."

"Well, for me it's heights," he said, shaking his head. Then he looked at me and I could see him start to blush a little. "As you probably saw the other day. My dad took me on a site visit when I was three, and I remember looking down and just freaking out. It's one of my earliest memories, and it involves sheer terror. And I tried to get over it last year, when we flew to Montreal for an academic decathlon . . ."

****

"It is not a good movie." Frank and I were now walking along the water's edge; as he'd been sifting through the sand, he'd come upon a rock and wanted to try skipping it. He also wanted to try and convince me that *Space Ninja*, the movie that had been playing at the multiplexes since Memorial Day, was an example of quality filmmaking.

"It is," he insisted, and when I raised my eyebrows at him,

he laughed. "Okay, maybe the fact that I saw it with Collins colored my appreciation of it. But you have to admit, it was way better than *Ninja Pirate*."

I just stared at him, wondering how he'd ever gotten a reputation for being one of the smartest people in school. "How is that proving your point?"

★★★★

"In a well-ordered universe," Frank said as we looked for more stones, since the first round of skipping hadn't gone as he'd hoped, "skipping stones would boomerang back to you, and wouldn't just be an exercise in futility."

"In a well-ordered universe," I countered, "people would stick to skipping stones on lakes and not, you know, Long Island Sound."

★★★★

"Can I ask about Lissa?" We had temporarily moved back to the steps after Frank had gone inside to get us both sweatshirts. "Do you miss her?"

He nodded and was silent for a moment before he said, "Yeah. I mean, we've never really spent this much time apart, so . . ." He shrugged. There was a long pause before he added, his voice quieter, "I think it's harder to be the one left behind." He looked over at me. "Do you?"

I knew he meant Sloane. "Yeah," I said. I thought about

telling him how it sometimes felt like I was only half there, without Sloane to talk to about what I was experiencing. How it felt like someone had chopped off my arm, and then for good measure taken my ID and sense of direction. How it was like I had no idea who I was, or where I was going, coupled with the fact that there was a piece of me missing that never seemed to stop hurting, never letting me forget, always reminding me I wasn't whole. But instead, I just looked at him, somehow understanding that he knew exactly what it was like to feel these things. "I do."

★★★★

"Oh, I meant to tell you," Frank said as I tried my own hand at skipping a stone. But I must have been missing some crucial component, because my stone just landed in the water and sank. "I checked with my mom. I saw *Bug Juice* when it was on Broadway—my first Broadway play."

I glanced over at him, and wondered if I'd been at the theater that day, as I usually was, hanging out with the merch girls and trying to score some peanut M&M's from concessions. I wondered what I would have thought of eleven-year-old Frank, if I would have known him back then. "It's based on me," I said. "Cecily is." Frank raised his eyebrows, looking impressed, and I went on. "I mean, in the beginning. She becomes less like me as the play goes on."

"What do you mean?" he asked as he picked up a stone,

tossing it in his hand a few times, like he was testing the weight.

"She becomes . . . brave," I finally said. "And really strong. Fearless." I dug my toes into the sand, then added, "Plus, there's the whole arson thing."

"Well, that too," Frank said, nodding. He sent his rock flying across the water, and it bounced off the surface five times before finally sinking.

I smiled. "Nicely done."

★★★★

"We've been friends since we were little," Frank said. We were back to sitting on the sand, and I was writing my name with my first finger, over and over, the looping E, the hook on the y. The conversation had turned to Collins, and the likelihood of him having any success with Gwen the Projectionist (slim to none) versus the likelihood of her ditching him for another guy as soon as they arrived at the party (high). "One of those friends you can't even remember making, you know?" I didn't, but I nodded anyway. "He was really excited I was staying in town this summer. We usually don't get to hang out this much."

"And plus, now he's got a wingman," I pointed out.

"Yeah," Frank said. "For all the good I'm doing him." He shook his head, but then smiled. "He's actually got some big camping trip planned for the two of us in August."

"In a well-ordered universe," I said, smoothing out my name and starting again, "camping would take place indoors."

****

The conversation started to slow around the time I began to feel the coldness of the sand through my jean shorts, and Frank started to yawn. We brushed off our hands and feet but tracked sand across the deck nonetheless. As we stepped inside, I waited for it to get strange, now that I could see him clearly again—his brown eyes, his reddish hair, his freckles.

But it didn't.

And I didn't understand why until I'd gotten back into the car and Frank had waved at me from the door and I'd turned in the direction of home. It seemed that somewhere between the arguments about the merits of ninja movies, he'd stopped being Frank Porter, class president, unknowable person. He'd stopped being a stranger, a *guy*, someone I didn't know how to talk to. That night, in the darkness, sharing our secrets and favorite pizza-topping preferences, he'd moved closer to just being Frank—maybe, possibly, even my friend.

6
KISS
A
STRANGER

I pulled my car through the gates at Saddleback Ranch, feeling my hands tighten on the steering wheel. This was what I'd been afraid of, ever since Frank told me that he had an idea for the list. Since he didn't know what Penelope meant, or which dress Sloane was talking about, and whenever he'd brought up the list, he'd avoided even mentioning the skinny-dipping or stranger-kissing, that only left a few options. And it seemed that Frank had decided today was the day I would finally ride a horse.

When I woke up the morning after our talk on the beach, I'd surprised myself by reaching for my phone and texting him, asking him if he wanted to run. And we'd been running every day since—usually mornings, but occasionally in the afternoons if neither of us had to work. It was the last thing I would have expected, becoming friends with Frank Porter, but it seemed like that was exactly what was happening. The downside to this, apparently, was that he did things like schedule horseback rides for me.

I parked in front—it looked like there was a small office and, across the parking lot, a barn and an outdoor riding ring where horses and riders were going through a jumps course, much nearer to me than I would have preferred. I got out of my car slowly, wanting to stay close to it in case one of the horses went rogue and charged at me or something. I could hear horses in the barn, and I tried not to think about how close they were, and how Frank expected me to ride one of them—horses that could kick you or step on you or fling you off their backs, if they so chose.

"Hey," Frank said, coming out of the office, looking relieved. "You came. I was worried you might have seen the sign and bolted."

"Ha ha," I said hollowly, suddenly wishing that Frank hadn't done this. It was one thing to share embarrassing stories with him; it was quite another to let him see me at my most pathetic and afraid.

"You doing okay?" Frank asked, taking a step closer to me. "You look kind of pale."

"I'm just . . . ," I started, looking toward the barn again. My heart was hammering violently, and I could feel that I was starting to sweat, and I wiped my palms on my jeans. "I'm not . . ."

"You here for the eleven o'clock?" I turned and saw a

woman in jeans and a Saddleback Ranch T-shirt leading out a horse that was so enormous, I almost had to tilt my head back to see the top of it. "Oh," she said, looking from me to Frank. "Were you here for the couples' ride?"

"No!" Frank and I said immediately, in unison.

"Just Emily," Frank said, nodding toward me.

"Okay then," the woman said, patting the horse hard on his flank, which made me wince.

What if he didn't like that, and took it out on me? Were horses one of those animals that could smell fear? It seemed likely, after all, their faces were practically all nose. Maybe sensing—or smelling—this, the gigantic horse snorted and stamped his feet, making me take a giant step back and bump into my car.

"Well, I've got Bucky all saddled up for you," she said.

"Why is he called that?" I asked, trying to take a step even farther back, not remembering that I was already pressed against my car. I could hear how high-pitched my voice sounded, but I also didn't think I was going to be able to do anything about it. "Is it because he throws people off?"

The woman frowned at me. "You okay, hon?"

"Do you maybe have a smaller horse?" I asked, trying to think of some way that this could maybe still be salvaged. "Like, something not so high?"

"Em, you okay?" Frank asked, taking a step toward me, his voice low.

"Like a pony?" the woman asked, looking confused.

"Maybe," I said, happy to have an option that would still be horseback riding, but just not quite so far off the ground. "Do you have any of those?" Before she could answer, my phone rang, and I grabbed for it, happy to delay the moment when someone would expect me to get on one of these horses and take my life into my hands. "Hello?"

"Hey," the voice on the other end said, and after a moment I recognized it was Dawn. "Are you at work?"

The day after my pizza ride-along, I'd stopped by Captain Pizza to say hi, making sure to glower at Bryan as I did so. I figured he deserved it—not only for what he'd done to Dawn, but also because he'd been wearing mirrored sunglasses indoors. We'd exchanged numbers, and Dawn would sometimes call me before she went into work, asking me to go into Captain Pizza and see what was happening with Bryan and Mandy.

"No," I said, then suddenly realized I might be able to turn this to my advantage. I would still be chickening out, but at least Frank wouldn't have to necessarily know I was chickening out. "Why, do you need me to come in to work?" *Work*, I mouthed to Frank, trying to ignore the woman holding the still-stamping Bucky by the reins.

"What?" Dawn asked, sounding confused. "No, I was just wondering if you could scout the Mandy and Bryan situation for me. I was trying to figure out how much time to put into my hair."

"Oh, I understand," I said, hoping that Dawn wouldn't think that I'd lost my mind—I figured I'd just explain things to her the next time I saw her. "Totally. I'll come in as soon as possible."

"Emily, what are you—" Dawn said, sounding more confused than ever. I hung up, then quickly switched the phone to silent in case she called back.

"I'm so sorry," I said to the woman, trying to make my voice match my words, but I could hear the relief creeping in. "I'll, um, have to reschedule."

"Trouble at Paradise?" Frank asked. His voice was light, but he was looking right at me, and I somehow had the feeling that he knew I was lying.

"Yeah," I said, tucking my phone into my pocket, looking down at the ground. "Really unexpected."

"I'm going to have to charge you for this since it's outside the cancel window," the woman said, leading the gigantic horse back to the barn. "But I'll give you half off your next ride, how about that?"

"Sure," Frank said. "We'll try again another time."

"I'm so sorry about the money," I said. "I can pay you back." But it was more than the money that was suddenly making me feel awful, now that the giddiness of getting out of this situation had subsided. I had the opportunity to cross something else off the list just handed to me, and I'd taken the first excuse to run away from it. And I'd wasted Frank's time, all because I wasn't brave enough to even try to get on a horse.

I gave Frank a half smile and got into my car, pulling out faster than was probably advisable when surrounded by giant horses, but I just wanted to get out of there. And as I turned down the street that would take me back home, I suddenly wondered if trying to ride a horse would have actually made me feel any worse than I did right now.

****

MIX #7

Don't You Worry Child	Swedish House Mafia
Jolene	The Weepies
King of Spain	The Tallest Man on Earth
She Doesn't Get It	The Format
Dirty Paws	Of Monsters and Men
Blackbird	The Beatles
High School Reunion	Curtis Anderson
The Gambler	fun.
Now Is the Start	A Fine Frenzy
5 Years Time	Noah and the Whale
I Will Wait	Mumford & Sons
Paperback Writer	The Beatles
Synesthesia	Andrew McMahon
Where Does This Door Go?	Mayer Hawthorne
House of Gold	Twenty One Pilots
Misadventures at the Laundromat	Curtis Anderson
Young Love	Mystery Jets

Morgan Matson

It Won't Be Long	The Beatles
Truth in the Dark	The Henry Gales
While My Guitar Gently Weeps	The Beatles
Re: Your Brains	Jonathan Coulton
Hannah	Freelance Whales
Mtn Tune	Trails and Ways
Home	Edward Sharpe & The Magnetic Zeros
Trojans	Atlas Genius
When They Fight, They Fight	Generationals
Take a Walk	Passion Pit

"I'm really sorry about that," Frank said as he looked over at me. It was two days later, and we were running. I'd shown up at his house that afternoon, ready to apologize, but Frank had just shaken off my apologies and then, to my surprise, had offered his own once we had gone about a mile into the five-mile loop I'd planned for us. "I never should have just sprung that on you. I keep thinking how I would have reacted if someone had just told me to go to the top of a skyscraper, with no warning. It wouldn't have been pretty."

"I am going to need to do it at some point, though," I pointed out.

"You will," Frank said, with such confidence, that I almost believed him. We ran for another mile before he looked over at me. "Music?" he asked.

I nodded and handed him my iPod. We'd been running

together three more times now and had worked out our routine. We talked for the first mile or so, while we were warming up. When breathing became more important than talking, we switched to music, which we would listen to for the rest of the run, and then we'd turn the iPods off as we'd cool down and walk to one of our houses—we alternated. But the run before, Frank had proposed that we switch iPods so that he could see if my "music, not observational comedy" theory was effective in terms of helping him run faster, and I could apparently learn all about some group called Freelance Whales which was, apparently, an actual band. I'd made him a mix of my favorite songs that hopefully weren't too alienating for someone who claimed he never listened to country and had no idea who the Cure was.

We fell into our running rhythm, and I noticed that our shadows were lengthening out in front of us in the late-afternoon sunlight, occasionally overlapping each other on the pavement. Even though it had been a hot day and was very humid out, I pushed us, keeping the pace up, and we both struggled to maintain it for the last three miles. As ever, we sprinted toward the finish. Frank was right next to me until the very last second, when I managed to spring forward, hitting our mailbox with an open palm, then bending double trying to catch my breath. I turned my head to the side and saw Frank doing the same.

"Would you think any less of me," he managed, "if I collapsed in that hedge?"

"Not at all," I said. "I might just join you." I straightened up and started shaking out my legs and hands, getting a fun pre-view of just how sore I'd be in the morning. We started walking in the other direction, cooling down, like my track coach was always yelling at us to do.

"I liked the mix," I said, handing him back his iPod. "But what was with all the handclapping songs?"

"That was Mumford," Frank pointed out, looking scandal-ized. "Do you know how many awards they've won?"

"Then you would think they'd be able to hire an actual drummer," I said, as Frank shook his head.

"Do you have any idea how many songs about trucks I just listened to?" he asked, as he handed me my iPod. "Five. Seriously. Not even just the country songs. What's that about?"

"You're the one with the actual truck," I pointed out. "So you'd think you'd be more in favor of them."

"If that logic made any sense—which it doesn't, by the way—you, with your Volvo, would have been way more into Swedish House Mafia."

"Which one was that?"

"Track one," Frank said, and I made a face. "Told you."

"Well," I said, trying to think back to what I'd just heard, "I'm sure the Beatles sang songs about trucks occasionally."

"Not that I can think of," Frank said immediately. "Unless you mean the fire truck in 'Penny Lane.'"

I shook my head and he lifted up his shirt to wipe his face, and I took a long look, then glanced away quickly, before he could catch me staring. "So what's with the Beatles?" Seeing the look of incredulity on Frank's face, I added quickly, "I mean, you told me why you started listening to them, because of the codes. But there were a *lot* of Beatles songs on that playlist."

"Do you not like the Beatles?" Frank asked, sounding shocked, as we finished our cool-down and started walking back toward my house. "Do you also not like sunshine and laughter and puppies?" I just stared at him, waiting for Frank Porter to reappear and realize he was being a little crazy, but apparently Frank was just getting started. "I don't think the Beatles get *enough* recognition," he said, speaking fast. "I mean, when you look at their body of work and how they changed music forever. I think there should be federal holidays and parades."

"Well, you can work on that," I said, as we arrived back in front of my house. "In case you need another summer project."

Frank laughed and looked toward the house, wiping his sleeve across his face. "Think you could spare a water?"

"Sure," I said automatically, not thinking about anything except how thirsty I was as we headed up the driveway together. I opened the front door and we stepped into the dark and cool of the mudroom, and it wasn't until the door was shut behind us that I suddenly realized what I had done—invited Frank Porter into my house.

He'd already seen my father in his robe, and I had just hoped—if he was going to come inside again—that I might be able to convince my parents to wear actual clothing. I suddenly realized I had no idea what Frank might be walking into.

I just crossed my fingers that the house wouldn't be too much of a disaster, that my parents would be quietly typing in the dining room, and that Beckett wouldn't be lurking in doorways, lying in wait to terrify us. "My parents are probably working," I said. "So we might need to keep it down—"

But as soon as we'd crossed through the mudroom and into the house, the sentence died on my lips. My parents were not only away from the dining room and their laptops, but they were in motion, pushing the sofa against the wall while Beckett skated around the TV room on his sneakers that turned into skates when he leaned back on his heels. Stacks of plays were balanced in his arms, and the cat seemed to be deliberately as underfoot as possible.

"Um," I said as I closed the door to the mudroom, causing everyone to stop for a moment and look over at me. I was very grateful to see that neither of my parents were wearing robes or sweatpants, but my mother had her hair in curlers and my dad was wearing two ties around his neck, so I wasn't sure this was *that* much of an improvement. "What's going on?"

"Emily, thank god you're home!" my mother said. She grabbed a stack of plays and papers from the ground and thrust them into my arms. "Go put these somewhere. And then could you see if we have anything to eat? Is there something in the freezer? Mini bagel micro whatsits?"

"I finished those last week," Beckett said, skating past me. "So no."

"I should probably go," Frank said to me quietly, but apparently not quietly enough because my dad straightened up from the couch and spotted him.

"A boy!" he said, relief in his voice. "Wonderful. Come help me lift this." He squinted at Frank through his glasses. "Hey, don't I know you?" he asked.

"Seriously, what is happening?" I asked, stepping slightly to the left to stop Frank from going to join my father. Both my parents looked at each other and then down at the floor and I suddenly worried that they'd really let the bills slide this summer while they'd been working, and everything in the house was about to be repossessed, or something.

"Living Room Theater," Beckett finally piped up when it became clear my parents weren't going to, as he skated deftly around the cat. "They forgot."

"Wait, here?" I asked, my stomach plunging, as I suddenly understood why everyone was running around. "*Tonight?*"

"Tonight," my mother said grimly, depositing another stack of plays into my arms. "We weren't exactly prepared."

"Living Room Theater?" I heard Frank echo behind me.

"Did someone cancel or something?" I asked.

"Well," my mother said, "we technically did volunteer to host it this year. But that was before we knew we would be writing. And your father thinks that e-mail is interfering

Morgan Matson

with his creative process, so he missed the reminders."

I closed my eyes for just a moment. "How soon?" I asked.

My dad looked at his watch and winced. "An hour."

"Um, what's Living Room Theater?" Frank asked me, as this information seemed to panic the rest of my family, who all sprang into motion again.

"Well, unless you leave now," I said, realizing it might even be too late as my mother dropped a stack of printer paper into his arms, "I think you're going to find out."

★★★★

JULY

One year earlier

"Explain this to me again," Sloane said as we—me, Sloane, my parents, and Beckett—walked up the driveway to Pamela Curry's house. "You guys don't get enough theater during the school year?"

My mother smiled and took a step closer to Sloane, linking her arm through hers. The two of them had gotten along right from the beginning, and a lot of times when she stayed over, I'd come downstairs in the morning to see Sloane and my mom sitting across the kitchen table from each other, talking, almost more like friends than anything else. "It started a few years back," she said. "At a theater/English department meeting about parking, of all things. We ended up talking about all the plays we loved, and how they had to be so carefully selected at the college—not to offend anyone, to cast as many students as possible, come in under budget, all the usual concerns. And then someone . . ."

"Harkins," my dad piped up from the other side of our group. "Remember? He got this thing going and then left when he got tenure at Williams."

"Anyway, Professor Harkins suggested that we get together once a summer—both the theater and English departments—and put up a play that would have been impossible to do during the school year. No props, no costumes, everyone holds the book."

"Sounds fun," Sloane said as we reached the front door, and my mother knocked once and then just pushed it open and stepped inside. Living Room Theater tended to make things a little more casual, and there was usually enough chaos going on before the show that people weren't bothering with details like answering the door.

We walked in and, sure enough, the downstairs was packed, mostly my parents' colleagues from both their respective departments, plus their kids. Kids were always invited to Living Room Theater, unless it was Mamet, in which case there was a strict thirteen-and-over rule. People were milling about, tonight's actors were walking around holding scripts and muttering, and everyone else was clustered around the food table.

I looked around, trying to be as subtle about it as possible, but apparently not succeeding, because Sloane leaned closer to me and whispered, "Seen him yet?" I felt myself blush as I shook my head. Pamela Curry and her two kids had moved here the year before, and she'd started working with my dad in the English department. Her son and daughter had been seniors when I was a sophomore, and I really only knew her daughter, Amy, because she'd shocked the whole school when she'd started getting all the leads in the plays, as a newcomer, right out of the gate. But I'd had an irrational and kind of gigantic crush on Charlie Curry, even though he went on to captain the tennis team and didn't seem particularly interested in dating non-tennis-playing underclassmen.

"Andrea! Scott!" Pamela Curry rushed up to my parents, giving me and Sloane a quick smile—Beckett had already disappeared in the direction of the food. "We're having a crisis."

"It wouldn't be Living Room Theater without one," my dad said sagely.

"We've lost our youngest sister," she said. "Susan Greene has the flu." Even though Susan, one of my mother's colleagues, was at least ten years older than my mom, Living Room Theater had always been cast age-blind.

"In *Crimes of the Heart*?" my dad asked, his eyes widening. "That *is* a crisis."

"I know." Pamela winced. "Babe is such a great part, too, but if it's not done well . . ."

"Why can't your thespian daughter do it?" my mother asked, and Pamela shook her head.

"She and her boyfriend are backpacking across Europe," she said. "Otherwise, I would have tapped her weeks ago." She looked suddenly to me and Sloane, her eyes lighting up. "Maybe one of you two?"

"Um," I said, trying to ignore my mother's encouraging smile, "not me." I looked at Sloane and raised my eyebrows. "Want to step in?"

"I'm happy to," she said, looking from Pamela to me, her brow slightly furrowed. "But Emily . . ."

"Wonderful!" Pamela said, almost collapsing with relief. "I thought I was going to have to do it, and believe me, that's something nobody wants to see. I'll get you a script."

A colleague called out to my parents, and they headed toward the other side of the room as Sloane turned to face me. "Why don't you do it?" she asked. "I'm pretty sure you know this play much better than I do, considering I've never heard of it."

"I didn't want to be in it," I said, even though this wasn't exactly true. And I couldn't blame it on not wanting to make a fool out of myself in front of Charlie, since he was nowhere to be seen. I just knew Sloane would do a much better job than I would.

****

"I'm not sure about this," Frank said as he peered around the dining room door and into the TV room, where the couch had been pushed aside to create enough space for a makeshift stage, and all the chairs we had in the house—and then pillows in front of them, once we'd run out of chairs—were lined up in front of it. We were both still in our running clothes and sneakers. I could have changed, of course, but since it was because of my parents that he was doing this, I didn't want him to be the only person there in athletic gear. It was five minutes to showtime, and Frank was looking a little pale. But given everything that had occurred in the last hour, I didn't exactly blame him.

"I tried to warn you," I pointed out, and Frank just nodded as he clutched his script. I had a feeling this was not particularly comforting at the moment.

When I had seen the tornado that was Living Room Theater approaching, I had pulled Frank aside before my dad could enlist him in any manual labor. "You need to leave," I said seriously. "Now."

Frank glanced into the living room, where my dad was yelping in pain. He had accidentally stepped on Godot, and the cat had wasted no time in enacting his revenge. "But it looks like your parents need help," he said.

I shook my head. "Seriously, get out while you can." Innocent bystanders had a tendency to get cast in these things, which was how two years ago, the plumber who'd come by to fix a leak had ended up playing Mercutio and had almost fainted.

"Em!" my mother said, rushing up to me and depositing a stack of plays in my arms. "Find something we can use, can you?"

"You haven't even picked a *play* yet?" I asked, aghast things were running this far behind.

"Hi," Frank said, holding out his free hand to my mother. "I'm Frank Porter, I'm a friend of Emily's." I looked over at him when he said this, and realized that it was true—he was a friend of mine, as much as I was still getting used to this.

"Oh," my mother said, raising her eyebrows at me and shooting me a smile before she shook Frank's hand. "*So* nice to meet you. You've been running with Em, right?" she asked, and I realized my dad hadn't been quite as distracted as I'd thought the morning he'd encountered Frank on the steps.

Frank nodded. "She's been getting me in shape."

"Hardly," I said. My mother gave me a significant smile, and I shook my head at her, not knowing how to convey nonverbally that he had a girlfriend and she had the wrong idea.

"Well, we're so glad you could join us for this," my mother said, and before I could tell her that he hadn't joined us, he'd just made the mistake of trying to come in for a water—which he still hadn't gotten—she was ushering him in the direction of the couch. "Do you have any back injuries?" my mother asked. "Might you be willing to lift some furniture?"

Go, I mouthed to Frank, but he was clearly much too well-mannered for this and was soon picking up one side of our couch, while I tore through as many plays as I could, counting speaking roles. As I tried to see if we could do *Noises Off!*, which had always been one of my favorites, I heard only snatches of the conversation that was going on as my dad and Frank tried to get the couch out of the TV room. "Your work . . . *Bug Juice* . . . Broadway . . ."

Then I heard a crash, and looked over to see my dad had dropped his end of the couch, leaving Frank struggling to hold one side of the couch aloft. "Andrea!" my dad yelled, as Frank lowered his end slowly, his face red. I had the feeling he was regretting that he hadn't just gone home when he had the chance. "Fred here had a great idea!"

"Frank," I corrected through gritted teeth. I couldn't help but wish for the parents I normally had—the ones who never would have forgotten about Living Room Theater, the ones who weren't bent on embarrassing me in every way they could.

"What's that?" my mother asked, emerging from the kitchen.

"*Bug Juice!*" my dad said. "Emily, stop looking for plays. We'll just put ours up. We have enough copies of the script."

"Wonderful," my mother said, her face relaxing. "I'll figure out some food and you can cast it."

My dad looked around, then pointed at Frank. "You can play Duncan," he said, and Frank shot me a look.

"Dad," I said, setting the pile of plays down and taking a step forward. Duncan was the second lead, after Cecily, and that was a lot to throw at someone who'd only come into the house in a futile attempt to get hydrated. "I'm not sure that—"

"And we need a Cecily," he went on, talking over me. "Andrea," he yelled in the general direction of the kitchen, "who can play Cecily?"

"Oh, god," my mother said, coming back into the room and trying to run her hand through her hair, apparently forgetting there were curlers in it. "I have no idea. Maybe Pamela's daughter?"

"If we don't have a good Cecily, the whole play falls apart," my dad said, shaking his head. "You remember what happened during that performance in Chicago."

"I know," my mother said. "Let's see. . . ."

"I'll do it." The words were out of my mouth before I realized I'd even thought them. My parents turned to me, both looking shocked. Frank, though, was giving me a smile from across the room.

"Seriously?" Beckett asked, sounding deeply skeptical.

"I think that seems very appropriate," my mother said, crossing past me to go back into the kitchen, giving my arm a squeeze as she went. "Thank you, Em."

"Yes," my dad said, after a small pause, still looking at me like he wasn't quite sure who I was. "That's . . . wonderful. Now let's move this couch."

This was how, an hour later, scripts in hand, Frank and I

ended up standing behind the doors of the dining room, looking out as the audience assembled. If I hadn't been so nervous about what was to come, I probably would have been much more embarrassed that Frank had been pulled so far into my parents' world and then forced to act against his will. I was beginning to feel dizzy, and it was becoming clear to me that it was much easier to volunteer to do the brave thing, and much harder to actually have to follow through with it.

I could see Dawn sitting in the back, and when she caught my eye, she gave me a wave and a thumbs-up. When it turned out we had almost no food in the house that we could serve, I'd proposed just getting pizza, and my mother had instantly agreed, putting me in charge of it while she tried to get the house in order. I'd called Dawn's cell, and told her we needed ten pies and assorted salads and breadsticks. Dawn then told me that she had just finished her shift, but if I called the actual restaurant and paid with a card, she could bring the order to me and then go home. When she'd arrived, she'd helped me set up the food, and when she'd found out what was about to happen, had asked if she could stay, and had ended up helping my mother do the last-minute cleaning.

The crowd suddenly seemed much bigger than it had in previous years. And why had I never considered how disconcerting it was to have a room full of people staring at you? I rolled my script in my hands. I was hanging on to it for dear life, even though I really didn't need it. *Bug Juice* had been such a part of our lives for so long that I had committed most of it to memory years ago, after seeing it performed over and over again.

"Two minutes," Beckett said, sticking his head into the dining room and then skating away again. He was in charge of reading the stage directions and holding the book. Even though all of us would have scripts in our hands, I'd been to a number of Living Room Theaters where people lost their place and then fumbled through their script for what felt like hours, trying to find their line.

"We should probably go stand with the rest of the cast," I said. The other main players were clustered in the kitchen, waiting for the play to start. The cast was big enough that people with one or two lines were just sitting in the audience and sharing scripts, and would make their way to the "stage" when it was time for their scenes. But the main actors—who included my mom's department secretary, the Elizabethan scholar in the English department, the assistant costume designer, three of the set guys, and a few of my father's grad students—had a green room for the night. Frank nodded but still looked nervous, and I suddenly realized that Frank Porter—who'd gotten up in front of the whole school, who was always making speeches, who seemed more together than anyone I knew—was nervous about performing a makeshift play in my TV room. It looked like he was much more nervous than I was—which for some reason made me feel brave.

"You're going to do great," I assured him.

Frank looked over at me, and gave me a half smile. "Thanks," he said quietly. I smiled back just as Beckett stuck his head into the kitchen again.

"Places!" he yelled.

An hour and a half later, the play was starting to wind down, and no major disasters had occurred. My first few lines had been rushed, the script shaking in my hand and my voice high and trembly. And it was a good thing I had the lines memorized—it didn't hurt that eleven-year-old me had pretty much written them—because in my first scene, my vision was too blurred and my script was vibrating too much for me to have read anything on the page anyway. But as the play continued, I could start to remember what it felt like to breathe normally again. And it wasn't like I was acting with Broadway's best, either—the Elizabethan scholar playing Camp Director Arnold said most of her lines with her back to the audience, and the grad student who played Tucker had lost his place four times in his first scene, which was impressive considering he'd only had three lines.

To my relief, Frank, as Duncan, had more than held his own. I wasn't sure I was going to encourage him to change direction and start auditioning for all the school plays, but he spoke his lines clearly, followed along with the script, and faced the right way. He also revealed an innate sense of comic timing I'd never guessed he had. So I was feeling like the evening hadn't been a total disaster, and had actually gone okay, as

Frank and I took the stage together for the final scene.

Duncan and Cecily had been on quite the whirlwind together, as they went from enemies to friends, until Cecily became convinced Duncan was only pretending to be her friend after it appeared he had turned against her during her court-martial after the color war. But it was just a misunderstanding, and in the final scene, on the last day of camp, the smoldering embers of what remained of Camp Greenleaf behind them, they finally cleared things up.

"I'm sorry," Frank-as-Duncan said to me.

"He crosses to her, stage right," Beckett intoned from his perch on the kitchen stool just offstage. He had been the true star of the night, always staying on top, reading the stage directions and jumping in with assistance when people lost their place.

"You should have told me what was happening," I said, as Cecily.

"I know," Frank said, glancing up at me and then looking down at his script again.

"I didn't think I could trust you," I said.

"But you can," Frank said. "I'm here."

"He takes her hand," Beckett read out from the stage directions. Both Frank and I looked over at him, but neither one of us moved. "He takes her hand," Beckett repeated, more loudly this time, and Frank glanced at me, then took a step closer.

I swallowed hard and could feel my heart start to pound. I

tried to tell myself that it was just acting. It wasn't a big deal. And it certainly didn't mean anything. I transferred my script into my left hand and met Frank's eye. He gave me a small, embarrassed smile, then reached out toward me. I met him halfway, our fingers awkwardly colliding until we got our palms lined up and he threaded his fingers through mine. His hand was cool, and I was suddenly aware how nicely our hands fit together, our fingers overlapping easily.

My heart was beating hard, and I could feel the blood pulsing in the tips of my fingers. How had this even happened? How was Frank Porter holding my hand?

"Cecily?" Beckett prompted, and I was jerked back to reality as I tried to turn to the last page of my script with only one hand.

"Sorry," I muttered, and there was low, polite laughter from the audience. I glanced up long enough to see my parents standing in the back, my dad's arms around my mom, both of them looking more present, and more relaxed, than I'd seen them in a while. I was just relieved that neither one of them seemed furious I had ruined their masterpiece. I flipped to the last page of the script, and there it was, in black and white, two lines away—*They kiss.*

I must have totally blocked out that this would be happening. I could feel my pulse start to race, and I worried my palm, still pressed against Frank's, was going to start to get sweaty very soon.

"Um," I said, struggling to find my place in the script. "And you'll always be here?" I asked him.

Now, just a bit too late, I remembered perfectly what came next. Duncan had the line that was always the last laugh of the play, about how he'd be there at least until his mom came to pick him up and take him back to Weehawken. And then Duncan and Cecily kissed while the rest of the campers filed onstage and sang the Camp Greenleaf song.

I didn't want Frank to feel like he had to kiss me, like he had clearly felt compelled to take my hand. I couldn't even imagine having to kiss Frank Porter, especially in front of all these people, and my parents and younger brother. Also, he had a girlfriend. And while real actors kissed other people all the time, this was different. This was—

". . . back to Weehawken," Frank said, finishing the line I hadn't heard him start, and there was laughter from the audience and I knew what was coming. I glanced, panicked, at my brother.

"They kiss," Beckett read, and I could practically feel Frank's shock and the expectant pause in the audience.

Frank and I looked at each other. We were still holding hands, but he still seemed impossibly far away from me, and I couldn't even imagine crossing that gulf to kiss him. Mostly because I couldn't even imagine kissing him. It was one thing to get to know him, and go running with him, but—

Keeping his eyes on me, Frank took a tiny step closer, and

it was like my brain was wiped clear of thoughts. It was like the world had started moving in slow motion as he moved a little closer to me still, and then started to tilt his head to the side.

"Lights down!" Beckett yelled, jerking me back to reality, and I blinked, trying to catch up with everything that had just happened—or almost happened. "Curtain!"

Everyone started clapping, and the rest of the cast filed out and we all joined hands—Frank and I hadn't stopped holding hands since Beckett told us to, I realized—and took a bow, and then people started getting up and putting the chairs away and drifting back into the kitchen to see if there was any food left.

Frank and I looked at each other, and after just a moment like that, we dropped hands. He stuck his hands in his shorts pockets and I grabbed the script with both of mine, twisting it into a tight roll, trying not to think about how cold my hand now felt.

"Hey!" Dawn said, coming up to us and giving me a smile. "That was really great."

"Thanks," I said, glancing at Frank, wondering what he was thinking about what had almost happened, but he was frowning down at his phone.

"Nice work, you two," my mother said with a smile as she passed me, giving me a quick hug as she went. I caught my dad's eye from across the room and he gave me a very dorky thumbs-up.

"Thanks," Frank said, glancing up from his phone for a

moment before typing a response into it, then looking up at me, his brow furrowed. "Hey," he said. "So here's the thing." He seemed to notice Dawn for the first time, and turned to her, holding out his hand in a manner that practically telegraphed *I'm the student body president.* "Sorry," he said, "I'm Frank Porter."

"Dawn Finley," she said as they shook. "You did a really good job."

"Well," Frank said, and he shot me a small smile. "I'm sure that was just due to my costar."

"What's the thing?" I asked, trying to change the subject.

Frank looked back down at his phone and said, a little doubtfully, "So apparently Collins is at my house. He wants me to come and hang out, and told me you had to come too." He looked up and shook his head. "Remind me to take his key away."

"Oh," I said, wondering why Collins had invited me specifically. But I had been seeing him more this summer than I ever would have predicted, so maybe he was just being nice, and inviting me to their hangout.

"And you're welcome to come too," Frank said to Dawn. "Unless you have other plans."

"Nope," said Dawn, looking thrilled by this invitation. "Sounds fun. You know, whatever it is."

"Emily?" Frank asked.

I looked around at the chaos that was still reigning in my house, all the people standing around and eating cold breadsticks.

I knew well how Living Room Theater nights ended up—the adults hanging out for far too long, exchanging department gossip for what always felt like hours. I had a feeling the house would be filled with people for a while, and if I did stay, I would undoubtedly be roped into cleaning up. "Sure," I said. "Why not?"

****

"This is a really nice house," Dawn said, her voice dropping to a whisper as she stepped inside, her expression looking much like I had a feeling mine had when I'd seen it for the first time. Since my car had been buried behind everyone who had parked in our driveway, Dawn had driven us all to Frank's in her convertible, her driving making me very glad that Frank lived so close to me.

"Thanks," Frank said easily, leading the way inside. "Collins!" he yelled, just as he slid around the corner in his socks.

"Hello," Collins said, a wink somewhere in his voice, smiling at me, stretching out the word more than usual, and giving it a few more *o*'s.

"Um, hi," I said, giving him a smile. "What's up?"

He looked behind me, saw Dawn and her shirt that read *Captain Pizza—A great COLONEL of an idea!* and brightened. "Did we order pizza?"

"No," Dawn said, looking down at her shirt. "I'm off the clock. I'm Dawn."

"Matthew Collins," he said. "Matthew with two *t*'s and Collins with two *l*'s. But call me Collins. Although," he said, raising an eyebrow, "let me be Frank." He cleared his throat and gave me an earnest, serious look. "Emily," he said, his voice both softer and deeper. "Is there anything—*anything*—I can do to help you? As soon as I finish saving the planet, I promise to get right on it."

"Collins," Frank said, walking past him and into the kitchen, but not before I saw that there were two dull red spots on his cheeks. "Will you stop it? That joke was old back in middle school."

"I'm just being Frank with them," he said, giving me an actual wink this time. "Want something to drink?" he asked as he followed Frank into the kitchen and pulled open the fridge, clearly as comfortable in Frank's house as Sloane had once been in mine.

"Sure," Dawn said, heading over to join him in the kitchen. As I watched her walk closer to him, I couldn't help but wish I'd had some way to warn her about Collins, and the fact that he'd probably be hitting on her relentlessly within seconds. But to my surprise, he just stood back respectfully to let her get a clearer view of the fridge, and didn't ask her if it hurt when she fell from heaven.

"Emily?" Frank called to me from the kitchen area, and I realized a moment too late that I was the only one still standing by the front door.

"Yeah," I said quickly, walking across the floor to join the group in the kitchen. Everyone was standing around the big island in the center that looked like it was made of granite or slate—some dark mineral, at any rate. There was a bag of tortilla chips on the counter that Collins opened as Frank grabbed a bottle of water from the fridge, and then handed one to Dawn.

"So," Collins said, rubbing his hands together and looking at me. "I was thinking about your list."

I stared at him in surprise, then looked over at Frank. The list hadn't been a secret, exactly, but I was just a little taken aback that Frank would have told Collins about it.

"What?" Collins said, picking up on this. "Porter will *not* stop talking about it. And I decided to help."

"What list?" Dawn asked, looking from Collins to me.

"The list from Sloane," Collins said, like he'd been involved with this from the beginning.

"Who's Sloane?" Dawn asked.

"Sloane's my best friend," I explained.

"The one who's camping in Paris?" she asked, and I gave her a quick nod, not meeting Frank's eye, even though I could sense he was looking at me.

"Anyway," Collins said. "I had a solution, so—"

"Which number?" I asked, really a little baffled as to what Collins could have come up with.

"Yeah, Matthew," Frank said, and his voice sounded measured, but I could also hear the irritation behind it. "Which number?"

"Hey."

I turned around, surprised, and saw a guy behind me, coming from the direction of the TV area—I supposed it wasn't really a room if there weren't any doors. I hadn't realized anyone else was there and I suddenly worried this perfect stranger had heard us talking about Sloane's list. He had close-cropped blond hair, and was wearing a T-shirt that read *Briarville Varsity Soccer*. Briarville was a boarding school an hour upstate, but while I'd heard of it, I'd never met anyone who went there.

"Perfect," Collins said, clapping his hands together. "We can get this going."

I felt myself frown. "Get what—" I started, when Collins interrupted, opening the fridge again.

"Want something to drink?" he asked the guy. "Water? Red Bull?"

"Agua," the guy said, coming to stand with us in the kitchen. "Thanks."

"Hey," Dawn said to him, crunching some chips and swallowing quickly. "I'm Dawn."

"'Sup," the guy said. "I'm—"

"*Shh!*" Collins yelled, so loudly that we all stopped and looked at him. He frowned at the guy. "What did we talk about?" The guy just raised his eyebrows, and Collins grinned at me, gesturing to the guy with a flourish, like he was presenting him on a game show. "So he's here for the first thing on your list. Enjoy."

I thought back to the list, and the first one, which was—

I drew in a shocked breath. I had a feeling I'd just turned bright red.

Kiss a stranger.

"Wait," I said faintly, looking at the guy. He wasn't bad-looking or anything, but that didn't mean I wanted to kiss him. Especially not here, in front of Collins and Dawn and Frank.

Collins smiled wide at me, and gave me another wink, this one bigger than before. "You're welcome," he said.

"Wait," Frank said, looking from the guy and back to me, then glaring at Collins, sounding more annoyed than I'd ever heard him. "Matt, I told you not to do this the first time you suggested it. But you go ahead and bring some random guy here to—"

"Hey," the guy said, lowering his water bottle, looking offended.

"What's going on?" Dawn whispered loudly to Frank.

"No," I said, taking a step away. Then, worried I might have insulted the guy, I said quickly, "Sorry. No offense. I'm just not . . . I mean . . ." I ran out of words and took a tortilla chip, just to have something to do with my hands.

"What?" Collins asked. "It's perfect. You don't know him, he doesn't know you. So get to it." He raised his eyebrows at us. "Chop-chop."

"Collins," Frank said, keeping his eyes on me, "if Emily doesn't want to do it—"

"Do what?" Dawn asked, crunching down on another chip, looking baffled but entertained, like this was a movie she'd walked into late.

"Kiss him," Collins said. Dawn looked surprised, but then she gave the guy a not-so-subtle once-over and shot me an approving thumbs-up. "It's on the list Emily's friend sent, the first one is 'Kiss a stranger,' so—"

"No," I said quickly, holding up my hands. There was no need to keep discussing this, because it was not going to happen. Ever. "I'm sorry. Um, thanks for the effort, but I'm not just going to go around kissing random—"

"You know," the guy said, setting down his water, starting to look annoyed, "my name's—"

"*Shh!*" Collins and Dawn yelled at him.

"No," I said again, shaking my head hard. "I don't even know him, and—"

"But isn't that the point?" It was Dawn who asked this. She turned to me, her eyebrows raised. "I mean, it wasn't 'Kiss someone you've already met,' right?"

Collins raised an eyebrow. I opened my mouth and then closed it again when I didn't have anything to say to this. It was true. It was also one of the main reasons I worried I'd never complete the list. And here a stranger was, being presented to me to kiss. I thought back to the night I hadn't hugged Jamie Roarke, and how frustrated I'd been with myself, how I was still mad at myself for chickening out on horseback riding. And

I really did need to get moving on the list, if I ever wanted to figure out where Sloane was. Would I get a better opportunity than this to kiss a stranger?

"Fine," I said, before I knew I'd made a decision. Frank looked over at me sharply, like he was surprised, but then looked back down at his water bottle, like he was suddenly very interested in where it had been sourced from.

"Cool," the guy said with a shrug. He took a purposeful step over to me, and without meaning to, I crushed the chip in my hand with a loud *crunch*.

"Um," I said, dropping the pieces onto the counter and brushing the crumbs off my hands. "Maybe we could go somewhere less . . . public?"

"There's a pantry," Collins said, nodding past the refrigerator, toward what looked like a narrow hallway.

"Okay," I said, mostly just to try and talk myself into this. Was I really going to do this? Furthermore, had I *volunteered* to do this? "Let's go."

"You could go outside," Frank called as I forced myself to cross the kitchen on legs that suddenly felt wobbly, pointedly avoiding looking at Dawn, who was shooting me an excited smile. "It's kind of tight in there."

"That's a good thing, Porter," I heard Collins say, but I just concentrated on looking straight ahead, suddenly worried about my breath.

Frank was right—the pantry was not particularly big. A

light went on automatically when I opened the door, and I could see that down the two steps, there were shelves of food on all sides, and in the middle, just enough room for two people. But that was about it.

I made myself put one foot in front of the other, walking down the steps to stand in the center of the room, surrounded by spices I could smell faintly and boxes of pasta and bags of rice and flour and sugar.

The guy followed, closing the door behind him and coming to stand in front of me. In the open-plan kitchen, I hadn't realized just how big he was. But now that we were in this tiny enclosed space together, it was very apparent. He had broad shoulders and big hands, and the already small space suddenly felt even more compressed. My heart was pounding, but I tried to make myself smile at the guy, like this was just normal, like I was always going around kissing people I didn't know in pantries.

I looked up at him and my heart started beating harder than ever. I tried to tell myself that I could do this. It was almost like, after not kissing Frank only an hour before, I was getting a second chance to try and be brave. I tried to tell myself that this was also just like a stage kiss, only without an audience. Just another kiss that didn't matter.

"Ready?" the guy asked. He didn't seem stressed by this at all, and I tried to take comfort in that. If it was no big deal to him, maybe it shouldn't have been such a big deal to me. I

Morgan Matson

swallowed hard and licked my lips quickly and took a tiny step toward him—really, all I could take in a space that small.

He gave me a lazy smile and put his hand on my shoulder, and started to lean down to me, just as the lights went out.

I took an instinctual step back, bumped into the shelf behind me, and heard something crash to the ground. I hadn't realized the lights were on a timer, but it made sense, since they'd gone on automatically. "Sorry," I said. "Um . . ." It was *dark* in there, since there were no windows and no light coming in anywhere. I didn't think I could see anything, not my own hand in front of my face, certainly not the guy.

"It's all right," he said, from somewhere in the darkness. I took a cautious step forward, and collided with something—him. I stretched my arm out and it hit his chest. Suddenly, I realized it might be easier this way, not having to see him. "Okay?" he asked.

I nodded, then realized what an idiotic move this was in a pitch-black room and said, "Yes." I took a quick breath and let it out just as his nose bonked mine. "Sorry," I said, reaching up and touching his face, trying to get my bearings. "I—" But I didn't get to say anything more, because a moment later, his lips were on mine.

We stayed that way for a few seconds, and I figured that Sloane's criteria had been met when the guy took a step closer to me, wrapped his arms around my waist, and started kissing me for real.

And under normal circumstances, it wouldn't have been something I would have reciprocated. But it had been two months since I'd been kissed. And in the darkness of the pantry, it didn't seem to matter that I didn't know his name and wasn't entirely sure he knew mine. It was like, because I couldn't see him, or myself, those distinctions didn't exist in the same way. It also didn't hurt that he was a really good kisser, and soon I was kissing him back, my pulse racing and my breath catching in my throat, his hands twined in my hair. It was only when his hands slipped under the hem of my shirt, moving towards my sports bra, that I came out of the make-out trance, snapped suddenly back to reality.

I broke away from him and took a step back, pulling down my shirt and feeling my way toward the steps. "Okay then," I said as I fumbled my way up the stairs in the darkness. I patted the wall until I found the light switch, and as it snapped on, we both flinched, the light seeming extra bright now. It was also disconcerting to suddenly see the guy, a whole person, not just lips and arms. I smoothed down my hair and opened the pantry door, the guy following behind me. "So," I said, when we were both in the hallway, before we had to join everyone else. I didn't feel embarrassed, exactly—it was more like I'd had an out-of-body experience in there and now was struggling to catch up. "Um. Thanks?"

"Sure," the guy said, giving me a quick smile. "That was fun."

I nodded and hurried back into the kitchen area. Frank was

leaning against the counter, typing on his phone, and Dawn and Collins were now sitting around the breakfast nook, Dawn laughing at something he was saying. "Hey," Collins called when he saw us. "Success?"

I ignored this question and turned toward Frank, trying not to look directly at him. "Is it okay if I grab a water?"

"Sure," he said, not looking up from his phone, and I assumed he was texting Lissa. "Help yourself."

I pulled open the fridge, grabbed a water, and, as I shut the door, caught Dawn's eye. She raised her eyebrows, and I gave her a tiny nod, and she grinned at me. Mostly so I wouldn't have to face the guy, or Collins, or watch Frank text his girlfriend, I turned my attention to the fridge door. Unlike the rest of the house, the collection of papers and magnets did not appear to be carefully curated. It looked kind of like our fridge door did—a mess of expired coupons, invitations, and reminders. I noticed an invite, slightly askew, toward the bottom of the fridge. *The Stanwich Architectural Society's Annual Gala!* it proclaimed in embossed lettering, *Honoring the work of Carol and Steve Porter.* Then it gave the date, about a month from now. Even though it was absolutely none of my business, I was bending down to see where it was being held—the bottom of the invitation blocked by some kind of color-coded calendar—when an alt-pop song started playing in the kitchen. I turned at the sound of it, and saw the guy, pulling his phone out of his pocket and answering it.

"'Sup," he said into the phone. "Yeah, okay. Just finishing

up here. I'm with Matthew." There was a pause, and he nodded. "Okay," he said. "See you in twenty." He hung up, put the phone back in his pocket and said, "Gotta bounce. The night is young."

"See you, Benji," Collins said, getting up and giving the guy what looked like an affectionate punch on the shoulder. I just blinked at him, trying to make the name fit. I had just kissed a guy named Benji?

"Ben," the guy said firmly, glaring at Collins. "Nobody calls me that anymore."

"I do," Collins said cheerfully. "Thanks for stopping by. See you on Sunday."

"Yeah," the guy said. "See you then." He took a step over to me and leaned down. I took a startled step back, wondering for a moment if he was trying to kiss me good-bye. But instead, he asked, in a low voice that I nonetheless had a feeling everyone in the kitchen could hear, "So can I get your number?"

"Oh," I said, thrown by this. I looked across the kitchen and saw Frank watching me, Dawn giving me a look that clearly said *Go for it.* "Um, thank you, but I'm kind of . . . I have this project this summer I'm working on, and . . ." He nodded and drew back from me. "Not that it wasn't good. It really was," I said quickly. "I mean . . ."

He gave me another lazy smile. "Just let Matt know if you change your mind," he said. "He's got my digits." With that, he turned and headed out, giving the people in the kitchen a wave as he left.

Morgan Matson

"So," I said to Collins, after I'd heard the door slam and I knew Benji was out of earshot. "How do you, um, know him?" I was suddenly incredibly relieved, remembering the Briarville T-shirt, that I wouldn't have to see him in the halls next year.

"Benji?" Collins asked, coming back to the kitchen island and reaching for the chips. "He's my cousin."

I nodded, like I was totally okay with all of this, with the fact that I had just kissed someone who was related to Collins, but my head was spinning. Collins took another handful of chips and headed back to the breakfast nook. I took a sip of my water, and realized it was just Frank and me together at the island, and that he was looking at me.

"Sorry that I told Collins about the list," he said in a quiet voice.

"It's fine," I said with a shrug. It had been more than fine, but I didn't think I wanted to tell Frank that. "And now I can cross that one off, so . . ."

Frank just looked at me for a second, then back down at his phone. "Yeah," he said. "Sure." He started typing again, not meeting my eye, so after a moment, I took my water and joined Dawn and Collins, though I started to regret this as soon as I approached and Collins waggled his eyebrows at me.

"So?" he asked, stretching the word out. "You and Benji? I see a future there."

"No," I said, taking a sip of my water. "No offense to your cousin, but . . . no."

"Surprising," Collins said, arching an eyebrow at me. "Because you were just in there a *long* time."

I coughed on my water. "We were?"

"You were," he said, raising an eyebrow at me.

I took another drink of water and shook my head. "Oh. Well. Um . . ." I looked over at him and saw he was still grinning. "Oh, shut up," I muttered, surprising myself—and Collins, by the look of it—as Dawn started to laugh.

Later, when I was walking home—after Dawn had left and the boys had started to play *Honour Quest*, a video game I had no interest in, despite Beckett always trying to get me to play with him—I found that I couldn't stop smiling. It was a warm, humid night, and I could see fireflies winking in the grass and hear the cicadas chirping. I headed home, my thoughts still turning over what had happened.

I had stood up in front of a crowd and performed, and it had gone fine. Nothing horrible had happened, and I'd gotten through it. But bigger than that, I had kissed a stranger. My pulse started to pick up a little as I flashed back to the pantry, to Benji's hands in my hair. I had *kissed* someone tonight, which I certainly had not been expecting to do. Not that I wanted to make a regular practice of kissing Collins's relatives in dark pantries, but for just a moment, it had made me feel brave.

And as I tilted my head back to look at the stars, I began to really understand, for the first time, just why Sloane sent me the list.

7
SLEEP
UNDER THE
STARS

The bell over the door jangled, and I stood up from where I was cleaning the ice cream case, taking a breath to welcome the customer to Paradise, but I stopped when I realized it was only Dawn.

"Hey," I said. "What's up?"

"Okay," she said, hurrying across the store and then leaning across the counter toward me, talking fast. "We have to discuss the fact that you made out with that dude for like *half an hour* in the pantry, and we have to talk about Matthew, because he seems awesome, and after all that, I have something for you."

"It wasn't half an hour," I protested, but Dawn just raised an eyebrow at me and I felt myself smile.

"I need details," she said, taking one of the perpetually empty metal seats and settling in. I noticed that today, her shirt read *Captain Pizza—We do PRIVATE parties!*

"Okay," I said, coming out from behind the counter, realizing that before we gossiped about my make-out session, I had to tell her the truth. "So . . . you know my best friend, Sloane? The one who sent the list?" Dawn nodded and I took a breath. "She's not camping in Europe. I don't know where she is. She just left, and all I have to go on is the list."

Dawn looked at me for a long moment. "Why didn't you just tell me that?"

"I don't know," I said, looking down at the black-and-white patterned floor. "It just . . ." I shrugged. I hadn't wanted to admit I had no idea where my best friend was. Now I knew that Dawn wouldn't have judged me for it, but I hadn't known that—or her—then.

"Wait a second," Dawn said, leaning forward. "Was that why you wanted to go on that delivery with me? To cross off 'Hug a Jamie'?" I nodded, realizing that while I'd been making out with Benji in the pantry, Collins must have been filling Dawn in on the rest of the list. "Well, I'm really glad you didn't," she said, her eyes wide. "Jamie Roarke's puggle is crazy. He would have freaked out if you'd tried it." She stood up and rummaged in her bag, then placed a pair of mirrored sunglasses on the counter in front of me.

"What are those?" I asked, picking them up. As I turned them over, I suddenly realized that they looked familiar—I was

Morgan Matson

pretty sure these were the ones I'd seen on Bryan. "Dawn," I said slowly. "What . . ."

"Number four on the list," she said. She grinned at me. "Want to break something?"

★★★★

MUSIC: BETTER FOR RUNNING THAN OBSERVATIONAL COMEDY

Make Me Lose Control	Eric Carmen
Let My Love Open the Door	Pete Townshend
Jolene	Dolly Parton
Springsteen	Eric Church
Badlands	Bruce Springsteen
Compass	Lady Antebellum
When You Were Mine	Cyndi Lauper
Let's Not Let It	Randy Houser
Sunny and 75	Joe Nichols
And We Danced	The Hooters
Don't Ya	Brett Eldredge
Anywhere with You	Jake Owen
867-5309 / Jenny	Tommy Tutone
Nashville	David Mead
Kiss on My List	Hall & Oates
Here We Go Again	Justin Townes Earle
Me and Emily	Rachel Proctor
We Were Us	Keith Urban & Miranda Lambert

Where I Come From	Montgomery Gentry
Delta Dawn	Tanya Tucker
Things Change	Tim McGraw
Mendocino County	Willie Nelson feat. Lee Ann Womack
The Longest Time	Billy Joel

The summer began to take shape. I had my largely customer-free job, I had early morning or late afternoon runs with Frank, and I had the list. But I was no longer, it was becoming very clear, on my own in trying to finish it. My friends were helping me.

"Want to go to a gala?" Frank asked, sliding something across the kitchen island at me. I'd been driving around with Dawn, keeping her company while she made deliveries, when Frank had called and invited me over, and he'd extended the invitation to her, so it was the four of us at his house. Dawn was out on the beach with Collins, and Frank and I had been tasked with bringing snacks outside. I looked at him over my armful of sodas, waters, popsicles, and the energy drink Collins loved and which I had a feeling would soon be banned by the FDA.

I glanced down and saw that it was the gala invitation I'd noticed when I'd been at his house the night I'd kissed Benji. Before I could read where it was being held, he put it back on the fridge with a Porter & Porter magnet. "It's for my parents," he said. "Collins is coming too, but since they're going to have to be in the same room together all night, pretending they

Morgan Matson

don't hate each other, I could use as many friends as possible."

"A gala, huh?" I asked, setting the waters down.

"And this way, we can cross off number eight."

I smiled at that—it had actually been my first thought. Though I realized that I hadn't checked on the dress in over a month, and it might have finally sold. "I'd love to."

"It's the last day in July," he said, giving me a level look. "Do you need to check your social calendar?"

I laughed at that, taking the rest of the drinks with me and leading the way outside.

The next day, I stepped into Twice Upon a Time, blinking at the dimness of the store, which was a stark contrast to the brightness outside. It was a consignment shop I'd been to many times with Sloane, but never alone. Maybe it was just that I had more time to pay attention now, but the store seemed some-how smaller than I remembered it seeming only a few months before, and a little more shabby.

"Hello there." Barbara, the owner, emerged from the back room with a vague, fixed smile, the kind she always seemed to give me. "Welcome to Twice Upon a Time. Have you shopped with us before?"

I swallowed hard and made myself smile at her. I wasn't sure why I was surprised that she hadn't remembered me, despite the fact I'd been in a dozen times at least over the years. "A few times," I said, already heading for the last place I remembered the dress hanging. It had never been a question in my mind which dress Sloane had meant. It was a dress I'd tried on purely for fun one afternoon when she seemed determined to try on every skirt in the store, twice. I tried it on as a lark, since I had no pressing need for formal wear.

But as soon as I put it on, I realized I didn't want to take it off. It was floor-length and black, with a high neck edged in gold and a plunging, open back. It was the most sophisticated thing I'd ever worn and I somehow felt different in it, like I was a person who had places to wear a dress like this, and exciting adventures to recount afterward.

Sloane had freaked out when she'd seen me in it, and insisted I buy it, right then and there, which was of course what she would have done. She even tried to buy it for me, sneaking it over to the register while I was getting dressed, and I had to wrench it away from her to get her to stop. Because the fact was, it was too fancy, too expensive, and I had no place to wear it.

Until now.

"I was actually looking for a black dress," I called to Barbara, as I looked around the store, beginning to panic because it wasn't hanging in any of the places I was used to seeing it. "I think I saw one in here, it had a low back . . ."

Barbara just blinked at me for a moment, but then recognition dawned. "Oh yes," she said. "I think I just moved it to the sale rack. Did you want to try it on, dear?"

"Nope," I said, as I plucked it from the rack and brought it up to a very surprised Barbara at the register. "I'll take it."

Morgan Matson

Getting through the list was apparently making me more bold in other aspects of my life—which was how I found myself sitting in a chair in front of Dawn's cousin Stephanie, at Visible Changes, the downtown salon where she was apprenticing.

"Are you sure?" Dawn asked from the chair by my side, looking at me through the mirror.

I brushed some droplets off my forehead and thought about it, about how this was the only way that I'd looked for the past few years. I picked up a lock of the hair that hung halfway down my back, then dropped it. "Anyone can have long hair." I nodded to Stephanie. "Let's do it."

An hour later I left the salon with sideswept bangs and hair in long layers that grazed my shoulders, feeling like someone else, but in the best way—like this was a me I hadn't known existed until that moment.

★★★★

PICK-UP YOUR PACE, PORTER! (EVEN MORE SONGS ABOUT TRUCKS)

Somethin' 'Bout a Truck	Kip Moore
Before He Cheats	Carrie Underwood
That Ain't My Truck	Rhett Akins
Cruise	Florida Georgia Line
Runnin' Outta Moonlight	Randy Houser
That's My Kind of Night	Luke Bryan
Dirt Road Anthem	Jason Aldean

Mud on the Tires	Brad Paisley
Drive	Alan Jackson
Papa Was a Good Man	Charlie Rich
Tim McGraw	Taylor Swift
Highway Don't Care	Tim McGraw
Barefoot Blue Jean Night	Jake Owen
Dirt Road Diary	Luke Bryan
You Lie	The Band Perry
Take a Little Ride	Jason Aldean

"In a well-ordered universe," I said to Frank, "there would be no mysteries."

He glanced over at me. We were doing a late-afternoon run, seven miles this time. He'd noticed my hair as soon as I'd stepped out of my house. This surprised me, because, well, he was a boy, but also because it was back in my usual running ponytail, so the change wasn't that obvious. But he'd told me that he liked it, which was more than I'd heard from my parents, who still hadn't noticed anything different. "What do you mean?" he asked. "Sloane?"

I nodded. "Yeah," I said. "You'd just know things. There wouldn't be these big, hanging questions."

Frank nodded, and we just ran for a while. "Lissa would argue with you about that," he said. "She got really into philosophy last year. So I'd have a feeling she'd say something like 'To know is not to know.'"

I glanced over at him. Frank didn't bring up Lissa very often, so I noticed whenever he did. "Is she having a good time at Princeton?"

Frank nodded, but then added, "I mean, I assume so. We've both done it before, so it's not like it's a new experience. And it's not really about fun. But she says the classes are great, really intense." We ran in silence for a few minutes, and I thought maybe we had moved on, when Frank said, "I would have seen her more, but they don't leave you a ton of time for socializing."

"Absolutely," I said, wondering why he felt the need to justify this to me.

"And she's coming for my birthday," Frank said, "so there's that."

"When's that?"

"July nineteenth," he said. He glanced over at me and raised his eyebrows. "Why? Are you going to get me a present?"

"No," I said with a shrug, as I picked up my pace. "I just thought maybe that was the day I'd let you finally beat me." I turned us down Longview, which had a hill that was going to be murder on the way up, but I'd been feeling that our runs had been a little too flat lately.

"Where are we going?" Frank asked, and he sounded worried, which I attributed to the fact that he'd just seen the hill. "Em?"

"Come on," I said, nodding ahead. I knew that I wouldn't

have enough breath to talk, so I slipped in my earbuds and turned on Frank's iPod. I'd scrolled through his list of band names, and I was pretty sure, at this point, that he didn't even *like* any of these bands, and was just doing this to mess with me.

I struggled up the hill, and when I turned to look at Frank, I noticed that he was looking straight ahead, not meeting my eye, probably concentrating on the run. We had just crested the top of the hill when a sign in front of a house caught my eye. *A Porter & Porter Concept*, it read, in the same font as the sign by Frank's house. I slowed as I looked at it. It was stunning, a beautiful three-story house done in a similar style to Frank's, but on a larger scale. The front was landscaped, and there was a bright-red mailbox by the end of the driveway, but the driveway was empty, so I took a tiny step closer to it. "Hey," I called to Frank, who was running in place, earbuds still in his ears. "This is one of your parents' houses."

"I know," Frank said shortly, nodding toward the road. "Come on."

"It's so cool," I said, taking a step closer, and then seeing what I'd missed before—there was a Realtor's sign on the lawn, a for-sale sign, with *Price Reduced!* across it.

"Emily," Frank called, and I walked away from the house, glancing back at it once before joining him and starting to run.

"Sorry," I said, when we'd made it down the other side of the hill and were cooling down. I wasn't even sure what I was apologizing for, but I somehow felt the need to say it.

"It's okay," Frank said. "I just try and avoid this place if I can." We walked in silence for a few moments, and I realized that Frank had more to say and was just figuring out how to say it—and then I realized that I could now tell this. "I hate that house," he finally said. "It's pretty much what ended my parents' marriage."

"What happened?" I asked after a moment, when Frank didn't go on.

He sighed. "It's a spec house. They built it with their own money, no buyer, all their own design, it was supposed to be their 'crown jewel.'" The way he put audible air quotes around the last two words made me think he'd heard this phrase a lot, and that he hadn't been the one to come up with it. "But they started having disagreements right from the beginning. Could they afford it, was it worth it, was it a good idea? They started arguing about the design, the direction, everything. It turns out they're really good working together when there's someone else in charge. When it's just them . . ." Frank's voice trailed off. "They fought a lot," he said quietly, and in that moment, I got a flash of what Frank must have been going through when this was happening, and how when I saw him at school, he just seemed so perfect, like everything in his life was working out.

"I'm really sorry," I said.

Frank shrugged and gave me a small smile. "Thanks," he said. "Anyway, it's done. It's empty inside, but it's done. And now that it's done, nobody's buying it." I thought back to the house, the cheerful red mailbox that now just seemed depressing. "They keep lowering the price, but nobody's even made an offer. It's not such a great situation."

We walked in silence, until Frank started to pick up the pace, moving into a jog. I started jogging along with him, keeping up even as we went faster, as he pushed our pace to the edge of where we'd gone, understanding that sometimes, you just needed to run.

****

The Fourth of July fell on a Wednesday, and with a stroke of good fortune, none of us had to work early the next day. So we'd all gone over to Frank's, and had watched the fireworks from the beach as they exploded over the water in a bright shower of sparks. Whenever I hung out at Frank's at night, we had the beach to ourselves, so it was strange to suddenly see other people sitting in front of their houses, on beach towels and blankets and lawn chairs, gazing up at the fireworks, bright against the dark sky.

Collins had decided a week before to take up the ukulele. He insisted on calling it his "uke," and was vehement that the ladies "loved a uke." To my surprise, he'd actually learned some chords, and as he played softly, I could almost tell what song it was. I leaned back on my hands and looked around, at Collins bent over his tiny instrument, and at Dawn leaning close to him, her eyes half closed as she listened to the music. Frank had his face turned up to the sky, and I watched him, rather than the

Morgan Matson

fireworks, as the light changed over his features, from red, to blue, to orange.

I looked back up at the sky myself before he caught me staring, and realized how peaceful I felt. I couldn't help but think about last year's Fourth, when I'd gone with Sloane to a party. She had been invited to it, but I hadn't, and even though she'd assured me it would be okay, I'd spent the entire night feeling like I was in the way, knowing I didn't really belong. I didn't feel that way now. And while I would have given anything to have Sloane there with me, it didn't change the fact that I was having a good time. And as I watched Collins play his last chord with a flourish and Dawn clap for him, as I watched the fireworks overhead bathe Frank's face in blue light, as I saw myself in the middle of it all, I realized that this was better. Even though Sloane had been there with me last year, this felt like I was where I belonged.

Hours later, I pulled into our driveway and then stepped hard on the brake. My mother was sitting on the porch steps, a mug in her hand. I glanced at the clock, even though it was pointless, and then down at the time on my phone. It was almost three a.m., which meant I was in big trouble. I'd avoided having the curfew conversation with my parents all summer, and had been coming home whenever I wanted, but I had the distinct feeling my luck had just run out on that front. I hadn't intended to stay at Frank's so long, but after the fireworks, none of us had wanted to stop hanging out. We'd played *Honour Quest*, Collins had attempted to make pancakes at midnight, and then we'd all ended up back on the beach.

I parked in my usual spot, trying to judge by my mother's expression in the moonlight just how much trouble I was in. I got out of the car, grabbing the striped beach towel that was going to let me cross off number three on the list. It had belonged to Frank's neighbor, but it had been forgotten on his deck post-fireworks, and with everyone cheering me on, at one a.m., I'd dashed across the sand to grab it. I knew I should probably feel bad about my first criminal act, but mostly I was just happy to get this one crossed off. It wasn't Sloane's sign, but it was something.

I took a big breath as I walked toward my mother, who smiled at me as I got closer, and braced myself for the worst.

"Late night?" she asked, taking a sip from her mug, and I could see how tired she looked.

"I guess," I said, not wanting to pretend it was an anomaly, just in case she had noticed me gone this late other nights. "You too?"

She shrugged. "Well, you know how the second act goes. Plus, there's a bit of a crisis with your brother."

"With Beckett?" I took a step closer to her, hoping that he hadn't finally fallen off something. "Is he okay?"

She nodded, but didn't look certain about this. "It's this camping trip. We're right in the middle of the play, so your dad had to tell him they weren't going to be able to go this summer."

I glanced up at Beckett's bedroom window, as though this would somehow give me some insight into how he was feeling. Of course, it showed me nothing, but I had a pretty good idea nevertheless. "How'd he take that?"

My mother bit her lip and looked down into her mug, cupping her hands around it. "Not well. Your dad told him there will always be next summer, but . . ." Her voice trailed off and I felt an acute pang of sympathy for my brother. I knew all too well what it felt like to have the summer you'd looked forward to taken away just like that. After a moment, my mom looked up at me and tapped the spot next to her on the porch. "Want to sit for a minute?"

Knowing this wasn't really a question I could say no to, I settled in next to my mother, setting my ill-gotten towel down next to me. She squinted at it. "Is that one of ours?"

"Kind of," I said, pushing it off to the side. "I got it at Frank's." This was, at least, slightly close to the truth.

"Ah," my mother said with a smile. "Frank. I like him."

I sighed. I'd gone through this with my mother the morning after Living Room Theater, but she still didn't seem to grasp it. "He has a girlfriend, Mom."

"I just said that I liked him," my mother said mildly, raising her eyebrows at me. "I think he's nice. And I'm glad you've been able to make some new friends this summer."

"Yeah," I said as I ran my hand along the wood of the porch, which had gotten so smooth over the years, you never had to worry about splinters. "Me too." My mother smiled at me and ran her hand over my head, smoothing my new bangs down. I saw that *FARRELLY* was written across the top of my new towel in big block letters, and I quickly folded the top of the towel over. "So what's the second act issue?" I asked, hoping my mother hadn't seen anything.

"Oh," my mother said, taking a long sip of what I could now smell was peppermint tea. "Your father and I have just come to a difference of opinion. He wants to focus on the rivalry aspect. But the fact is, Tesla and Edison were friends. That changed, of course, but they both got something from each other. And I don't think we should discount that."

I nodded, like I understood what she was saying. But mostly, I was thrilled that this conversation hadn't involved any lectures. "Well, I'm going to bed," I said, pushing myself to my feet, making sure the *FARRELLY* was hidden.

My mother smiled at me and waited until I was almost to the door before she added, "And, Em? Don't come in again at three a.m. and not expect any consequences."

"Right," I said with a sinking feeling, realizing I should have known this was probably too good to be true. "Um, got it. Night, Mom."

"Night, hon," my mom said. She stayed where she was, and for just a second, I thought about joining her. But I realized she had things to sort through—Edison and Tesla and friendships and rivalries. So I just looked at her for one more moment before turning and heading inside to bed.

****

"Wasn't that awesome, Em?" Beckett grinned at me from across the diner booth and I tried to smile back. My brother had been staying on the ground and barely speaking since he'd found out about the camping trip, so I'd taken him to the one place I was pretty sure would cheer him up. We'd met up with Dawn and gone to IndoorXtreme late, getting there just as they were closing, so Beckett could have the run of the place. He'd scaled the climbing wall with Collins, having races to see who could get down to the ground faster. Dawn and Frank had had an epic paintball fight, and I had somehow gotten stuck with Doug at the front counter, who had presented me with the first book in the series he was obsessed with, and then proceeded to tell me how it fit into the pop culture canon at large.

"And some people think," he'd said, as he flipped pages, and I looked longingly in the direction of the paintball area, where I could see Dawn slinking behind a hay bale, spy-style, "that Tamsin and the Elder are just rip-offs, so I don't want that to turn you off from the book."

"It won't," I assured him, hoping that this might wrap things up.

"Because that's a stupid argument," Doug said, clearly just warming to his theme. "Because that relationship exists every-where. Look at Obi-Wan and Luke. Look at Dumbledore and

Harry. Look at Gandalf and Frodo. They all have these people. They have to learn from them. But then they have to find their own strength and go it alone. So it's not derivative. Don't listen to the message boards." I had assured him that there would be very little chance of that, but by the time he'd started going into character backstory for me, Frank and Dawn, both paint-flecked, had called a truce, and Beckett was declared the victor, having beaten Collins in their last three races.

But despite the fact I hadn't had any fun, it was clear my brother had, and that was what I'd been aiming for, after all. I smiled back at him and then pulled out the laminated menu, wondering why diners always had the world's largest menus, and also if anyone had ever ordered the five-dollar lobster. We were all grabbing dinner before Dawn had to take over the evening delivery shift, and hoping nobody would want to know why one side of her hair was orange.

"So," Beckett said, looking up from where he was dripping water on his folded-up straw wrapper, turning it into a snake, "Frank and Collins and Dawn and everyone. They're your friends?"

"Yes," I said, a little surprised by the question. "Why?"

Beckett shrugged. "I don't know. It's just different. You never used to have this many friends."

I opened my mouth to say something to that, when the diner's glass door opened and Dawn, Collins, and Frank all came inside, Dawn shaking her head at me. "Oh no," I sighed, as I slid to the end of the booth so that Frank could sit next to me. Collins slid in next to Beckett, and Dawn next to him, and she nodded at me.

"They're back to it," she confirmed.

"Don't let me down," Frank said to Collins, pointing across the table. "You said you'd pay this time."

"In my life, have I ever lied to you?" Collins asked, sounding affronted.

"Let it be," Frank said, shaking his head. "We don't need to go into that."

"Please stop this," I said, but Frank and Collins just shook their heads without even looking at me. For the last three days, they had been starting their sentences with only the titles of Beatles songs. They were allowed to speak normally to everyone else—and they'd put the game on hold when they were at work—but with each other, they were locked in, trying to prove who was the bigger fan.

"What's going on?" Beckett asked, looking from Frank to Collins.

"I wish you guys would just declare a winner," Dawn said, then frowned. "Actually, 'winner' might be the wrong word in this situation."

"Bucket," Collins said, turning to my brother, "how well-versed are you in the Beatles?"

"I'm looking through you," Frank said, shaking his head, and Collins pointed to my brother.

"With a little help from my friends," he said, defensively. "Since when is that not allowed?"

"*Anyway*," Dawn said, turning toward me. "I want to set you up with someone." This was surprising enough that I just blinked at her, and saw Frank turn his head sharply to look at Dawn.

"I'm so tired," Collins was saying as he flipped through the menu. "Maybe I'll get some coffee."

"I don't . . . ," I started. I was about to tell Dawn that I wasn't interested, even though I really couldn't have said why. It wasn't like I still wasn't over Gideon, or anything like that. "Um, who is it?"

Collins was snapping his fingers at Frank, who said, sounding distracted, "Right. Um . . ." A moment later, he seemed to realize what he'd done. "Wait," he said quickly. "Help. You can't do that. . . ."

"I just totally won!" Collins yelled, pumping his fist in the air. "There is not, to the best of my knowledge, a Beatles song called 'Right Um.'" He drummed his hands on the table excitedly, then leaned back against the booth, like he was settling in. "Bucket, let me tell you a story. Once upon a time, there was a place called Liverpool . . ."

I looked at Frank. "Sorry you lost," I said, even though I couldn't be happier this game had ended.

Frank just shrugged. "I'm sure we'll do it again at some point," he said. "Every few years, we seem to need to try and prove who's a bigger fan. But listen," he said, suddenly looking serious, the way he did when we were strategizing about my list. "I have the perfect solution for number thirteen."

Thirteen was "Sleep under the stars," and I looked across the table at my brother, who seemed absorbed in learning about how Paul and John met. While I appreciated Frank's initiative, I'd had an idea for this brewing ever since I'd talked to my mother on the porch. "I've got that one taken care of."

"You do?" he asked, sounding surprised. "Oh. Okay. What is it? And when?"

I just looked at him, suddenly knowing the exact right way to answer this. "It won't be long," I said, and was rewarded when Frank smiled, suddenly, like I'd just surprised him.

That night, I tiptoed into my brother's room, trying not to make any noise, but finding it difficult when I kept impaling my feet on the toys that seemed to cover his floor more evenly than his carpet. "Beckett," I whispered when I got close to his bed. "Hey. Beck. *Ow.*" I tried to take a step closer, and felt something small and plastic lodge itself in my foot.

"Em?" Beckett sat up in bed, blinking at me in the faint glow of his nightlight, which he always swore he didn't need. "What's wrong?"

"Nothing," I said, trying to shake what turned out to be a Lego from my foot as I limped over to him.

"Then why are you here?" he asked, sitting up farther.

"I had an idea," I said, crouching by the side of his bed,

trying not to put my feet any new places. "Want to go camping?"

Beckett sat all the way up, pushing his curls out of his face. "What do you mean?"

"I mean, let's sleep outside. I have the whole thing set up. Mom and Dad won't care."

Beckett just looked at me for a long moment, like he was weighing whether I was being serious, or maybe if this was just a very realistic dream. "But how?" he finally asked, which was how I knew he was getting on board. "We don't have any camping stuff. Dad and I were supposed to get it together."

"I think I've figured it out," I said, crossing my fingers in the dark that I had. "Meet you in the backyard in ten."

Ten minutes later, almost exactly, Beckett stepped outside in his pajamas, still looking dubious. "Ta-da," I said, hoping that he wouldn't think it was stupid, or turn around and head back in. I had set up a mini campsite, in the very center of the yard. Since we didn't have a tent, I'd just laid out two sleeping bags and pillows head to head.

"Really?" Beckett asked, taking a small step forward, beginning to smile.

"Put this on first," I said, tossing the bottle of bug spray at him. It was the one thing I was worried about—since we would be sleeping out in the open, I had a feeling that unless we took precautionary measures, we were going to get eaten alive by mosquitos.

Beckett sprayed himself until he was coughing, then ran

Morgan Matson

over to the sleeping bags, tossing the spray in my direction. I doused myself in it, then crawled into my own sleeping bag.

I settled back into my pillow and looked up. I was glad that these sleeping bags were the crazy insulated you-can-take-them-on-mountains kind, because despite the fact the evening was still warm, it felt cooler at ground level, and a little damp. I looked straight up and just took in the stars shining above us, with nothing blocking their view, and suddenly regretted all the nights I'd slept with anything between me and the sky.

"This is cool," Beckett said, and I turned my head to see him looking up, his arms folded behind his head. Neither of us knew any constellations, so we found our own, groupings of stars like Crooked Necktie and Angry Penguin, and made up the corresponding stories that went with them. Beckett's voice had started to slow down halfway through the origin of Basket of Fries. I had a feeling he was about to fall asleep, and I knew I wasn't going to be far behind him. I closed my eyes only to open them once more, and make sure it was all still there—the riot of stars above me, this whole other world existing just out of reach.

"Can we do this again?" Beckett asked.

"Sure," I said, as I let my eyes stay closed this time. "We'll do it next month."

"Okay," Beckett said. After a stretch of silence in which I was sure he had fallen asleep, he asked, "What about Sloane?"

I opened my eyes and pushed myself up on one elbow to get a better look at him. "What do you mean?"

"I mean . . . we won't do this when she comes back, right?" My brother's voice was small. "You'll probably be too busy."

It was my first instinct to deny this, to assure him that nothing would change. But a second later, I knew that I wouldn't be here, now, with my brother, if Sloane was still in town. I would either be hanging out with her or waiting to hang out with her. "It won't matter," I finally said. I could hear the certainty in my voice, and just hoped Beckett could too. "You and me. Next month. I promise."

"Awesome," Beckett said around a yawn. "Night."

A moment later, I heard his breathing get longer and more even—it was a running joke in our family how quickly Beckett could fall asleep, and apparently being outside wasn't impeding that.

I rolled onto my back and looked up at the stars. Beckett's words were reverberating in my head, but for some reason, I didn't want to think about what would happen when Sloane came back, how things might change. Instead, I looked over at my brother, already fast asleep, before letting my own eyes drift closed, feeling like maybe I'd been able to set something right.

8
PENELOPE

Just because I knew what Sloane had intended with some of the items on the list didn't necessarily mean that I wanted to do them. The next day I'd stood at my dresser, my neck itching from where the mosquitos had gotten me, staring down at number five. I knew what she meant by "Penelope," and I also knew what she wanted me to do. Even though I knew it hadn't moved, I reached into my top drawer and pulled it out, staring down at it, my picture and the unfamiliar name, realizing that this was probably the one I needed to do next.

★★★★

MAY

Two months earlier

"Okay!" Sloane said as she got into my car, slamming the door behind her and turning to smile at me. "Are you ready?"

"I guess," I said with a laugh. "I'm just not sure what I'm supposed to be ready *for*."

Sloane had arranged for us to hang out on this Friday night a whole week in advance, which was unusual, but I was grateful for it. She was always with Sam, and while usually one night a weekend it would be me and Sloane and Sam and Gideon, it wasn't enough, especially since her attention was focused on her boyfriend when we were all together. There was also the fact that she was different around him. It was nothing I'd been able to put my finger on for the first few times we'd hung out together. But I'd come to realize I didn't like the way Sam treated her, and I hated the way Sloane acted around him.

I had really tried for the first month. Sloane obviously liked him, and saw something really special in him, so I'd done my best to do the same. But the more time I spent with him, the harder it got. To start with, he didn't like me. He was alternately possessive and dismissive of Sloane—something I really didn't like to see—but from the beginning, he had seen me as some sort of threat. He always seemed to be trying to stir up trouble in subtle, hard-to-define ways. He would look at me a little too long when I came into a room,

Morgan Matson

or stand a little too close to me and just smile blandly as he did it, as though daring me to call him on it, or say something about it. He corrected me whenever he got the chance. And on the occasions when Sloane—or Gideon—would say something about it, he would just shoot me a big smile and say, "I'm just messing around. Emily can take a joke, right?"

"It's just his sense of humor," Sloane would say the few times I'd tried to broach the subject with her. "He's actually really shy, and that's how he compensates."

And even though I didn't see this, I figured that my best friend knew him better than I, and so I'd let it drop, not wanting things to be strained between us, any more than they already were. So the possibility of a night that was just the two of us was something I'd been looking forward to all week.

She had told me to "dress to impress" and then we'd spent a full hour on the phone as she went through my outfit options with me. We didn't even need to video chat, since Sloane knew my wardrobe as well as her own. When we'd selected an outfit that worked, I'd put it on and wondered just what was going to happen tonight. I was wearing the shortest skirt I owned—it was actually a skirt of Sloane's that she'd given to me, and you could tell, since I had several inches on her. She'd paired this with a gauzy white one-shouldered top, and told me she would bring a red lipstick for me to wear that would make the whole thing pop.

Sloane was dressed much the same, in a tight-fitting dress, her hair long and a little wilder than usual, her eyes done smoky in a way that I could somehow never pull off without looking like I'd been injured.

"I'll give you directions," she promised, clapping her hands together. I pulled to the end of her driveway and looked at her expectantly. "Left," she said with great authority, as she cranked the music—her mix—and I headed away from Stanwich, and toward Hartfield.

I hadn't spent much time at all in downtown Hartfield, and was glad that Sloane was providing directions. Considering it was also a weekend night, the main strip of bars and restaurants was packed, crowds of people walking along the sidewalks and spilling into the street, the slow-moving parade of cars trying to edge past them.

"We should try and find parking," she said, as I passed a lot where the prices had been raised to ten dollars for the night, and guys with glowsticks and flags were trying to direct people in.

"So we're doing something around here, then," I said, glad to have some indication of what was going to be happening tonight.

"Maybe," Sloane said, raising an eyebrow. "Maybe not. Just—there!" she pointed ahead, where the car in front of me was, miracle of miracles, pulling out of its parking spot.

I put on my blinker and turned quickly into the spot, and

it was a good thing, because three other cars had zoomed forward toward it, one from the opposite side of the street, and were currently blocking traffic. "You know what?" Sloane said, as I killed the engine and handed her my iPod to lock in the glove compartment. "I think that's a good sign. I think it means tonight's going to be the best ever."

"So?" I asked as I unbuckled my seat belt and turned to face her. "Do I finally get details?"

Sloane pointed across the street. "McKenzie's," she said with a grin.

I turned to look, not quite understanding how this was going to happen. McKenzie's was a straight-up bar, with no all-ages dining area, which bugged Sloane to no end, since there was also a stage at the back and great bands were always performing there, and we could never get in to see them. "Did they change their policy or something?"

"Nope," she said. She pulled something out of her bag with a flourish, then took my hand, opened my palm, and dropped something into it. I picked it up and held it up to the light from the streetlights to get a better look. It was a Nevada state ID card, with my picture, an address I didn't recognize, and the name Penelope Entwhistle. "What is this?" I asked, looking closer at it and seeing a birthday that was five years earlier than mine.

"Your first fake ID," she said, leaning over to look at it. "Want to see mine?" She dropped it into my palm, and I could see that hers was from Utah and her name read *Alicia Paramount.*

I smiled at that. "Nice name."

"Thanks," she said, taking it back. "Ready to go?"

It hit me, much later than it should have, that we were going to use these IDs to get into a bar. And we were going to do it now, before I'd had any time to wrap my head around the idea. "Wait," I said, as Sloane's hand was already on the door handle. "We're going to use these for McKenzie's?"

"That's the best part," she said with a smile. "Call Me Kevin is playing there tonight. Totally not advertised. We're going to get to see them in a crowd of, like, fifty. Isn't that amazing?" She grinned at me and got out of the car, leaving me to scramble out behind her, locking my door and then hurrying to join her as she crossed the street, darting across the traffic rather than waiting for the light to change.

"Sloane," I said, as she got into the line that led to McKenzie's entrance. I saw that the door was guarded by a hulking guy in a black leather jacket, who was shining a flashlight down on the IDs people were handing to him.

"Alicia," she corrected.

"I don't think we should do this." I lowered my voice as I looked forward in the line. Everyone around us seemed much older than we were, and I was sure they—and the door guy—would all be able to tell that we were high schoolers attempting to get in somewhere we weren't allowed.

"There's nothing to worry about," Sloane said, lowering her voice as well. "I had the guy who made Sam's do these for us. And he never has a problem with his."

I could feel panic start to rise up, and I didn't even know why, exactly. "I just . . . ," I said as I looked down at the ID. In the glare of the streetlight, it looked incredibly fake, like it had been made at home on someone's computer. "Why Penelope?"

Sloane laughed. "I don't know, I just thought it sounded right. Oh," she said, leaning closer to me as the line moved forward and my heart started beating double-time, "don't forget to memorize your address and birthday. Just in case they ask."

"Are they going to?" I asked, and I could hear my voice coming out high and stressed.

"I don't know," Sloane said, starting to sound exasperated. "It's my first time."

"I don't think . . . ," I said, even as I took a step forward. "I don't think that this is a good idea."

"Emily, come on," Sloane said. We were just one person away from the door guy, who now seemed twice as big up close. "Just relax, okay? It'll be fine."

"No," I said, not joining her as she took another step forward. "I don't want to."

She looked at me, and I could see the confusion on her face. "It's okay," she said with a smile, but glancing back behind her at the door guy. The people behind me in line were starting to shift, and I knew that I was holding things up by not moving forward. "Come on."

"I'm not going in," I said, taking a step out of the line, and the couple behind me immediately filled my place.

"Why are you—" Sloane started, then let out a breath and shook her head. It felt like we were in uncharted territory, like we suddenly had to use a language neither of us was fluent in, because Sloane and I didn't fight, not ever. She told the couple behind her to go ahead, and they took her place eagerly. "I want to go in," Sloane said, and I could see that she didn't understand why I wasn't just agreeing with her.

"I don't," I said quietly. I didn't know how else to explain it.

"Okay," she said, glancing at the door guy, then back at me. She looked at me for a moment, and it was like I could feel her waiting for me to change my mind, go along with her like I always did. After a long moment she said, "I guess I'll see you later."

I drew in a breath; it honestly felt like someone had punched me. I'd just assumed that Sloane would leave with me, that we were in this together. The vagueness of her *later* was terrifying to me. "Sure," I said, not telling her any of this, not telling her what I was feeling, just making myself give her a trembling smile. "See you." I turned to head back to the car, my ankles wobbling in the heels she'd picked out for me, the clothes she'd chosen for me feeling too tight and itchy.

"Emily," Sloane called after me, half pleading, half annoyed. I didn't let myself look back right away, just concentrated on walking away from my best friend, even though it was the last thing I wanted to be doing. After a moment, I turned back, and saw her smile as she pocketed her ID and stepped past the door guy into the darkness of the bar.

I sat in my car, and when the sedan outside my window slowed, I shook my head for what felt like the hundredth time that night. When people saw me in the driver's seat, parked in an ideal spot, they all got really excited and turned on their blinkers, thinking I was leaving, any minute now. I would shake my head, and motion for them to go around me, but still they seemed wildly optimistic, sitting there with the lights flashing, waiting for me to give up the spot and go.

I had thought about it when I first got back to the car alone. I was just going to head home and let Sloane find her own way back, since she wanted to go to this bar so badly. I had even put the keys in the ignition, but hadn't started the car, sat back against the seat and tried to sort through everything that had just happened, and so quickly. I realized there was a piece of me that had been waiting for this to happen ever since we'd become friends—the moment when Sloane would realize I wasn't cool enough, or daring enough, to be her best friend. I knew at some point she would figure it out, and of course, tonight I'd given her ample proof.

I stayed in my car for two hours, occasionally playing games on my phone, then worrying about the battery, wanting to keep some juice in it in case she texted. Even though I'd put the keys in the ignition, I'd never really intended to leave. I didn't at all trust Sam to come and get her, Milly and Anderson weren't reliable enough, and I couldn't even calculate how much a cab from Hartfield to Sloane's house in backcountry would be. More than either of us had, that was for sure.

There was a knock on the passenger side window, and I shook my head without looking up from my phone. "I'm not leaving," I called.

"Good to know," Sloane said through the glass. I looked up and saw her standing by the passenger side door, and I reached over to unlock the car, and she got in. "Hey," she said.

"Hi," I said, sitting up straighter and setting my phone down. Things felt strange and tentative between us, in a way they never had, not even when we'd first met.

"Thanks for waiting," Sloane said. She leaned forward, not meeting my eye, and pulled my iPod out of the glove compartment, hooking it up to the line in.

"Sure," I said, hating how stiff and formal this seemed, wishing we could just go back to being us again. "Did you . . . have fun?"

"Yeah," she said, glancing out the window. "It was okay. You know."

I nodded and started the car, even though I *didn't* know, and that was apparently the whole problem. We drove in silence, Sloane's face lit up by my iPod screen as she flipped through the mixes she'd put on it, all her music. I swallowed hard as I turned the car onto I-95. I didn't know how to fix this, what to say—I just wanted things to go back to how they'd been a few hours ago. "So what was it like?" I asked when I couldn't stand the silence any longer. I could hear how high and forced my voice sounded, like my mother when she was trying to get Beckett to tell her about his day at school.

Sloane sighed and looked out the window. "Just don't," she finally said.

"Don't?" I repeated, feeling my stomach sink.

"If you'd wanted to know what it was like, you should have come in with me," she said, shaking her head as she spun the track wheel, going too fast now to even see any of the song names. "I mean, I put a lot of work into tonight. I bought our IDs, I planned the outfits, I arranged all this, because I wanted to see the band with *you*. Not by myself."

I glanced away from the highway and at my best friend for just a moment. "Then why didn't you tell me?"

"Because I knew you wouldn't have come!" Sloane almost yelled this, and I think it surprised us both, as silence descended in the car for a moment. "And I was right, wasn't I?" I tightened my hands on the steering wheel, gripping ten and two as hard as I could, willing myself not to cry. "You're so scared of things sometimes, and for no reason," Sloane said, her voice quieter now. "And sometimes, I wish . . ." She didn't finish the sentence, just let it hang in the car between us.

I wished it too—whatever it was that in that moment Sloane wanted me to be, that I was falling short of. I took a shaky breath and said, "I'm really sorry."

"It's okay," she said immediately, easily, and I knew she meant it. It was something that still amazed me about her— how quickly she was willing to forgive. Since everyone in my family—including the cat—was a grudge-holder, I couldn't quite believe it sometimes.

"Next time, right?" I gave her a quick smile, and I could hear how I was forcing my voice to be cheerful. But Sloane just smiled back at me.

"Sure," she said easily. She spun the track wheel once again and then clicked the center button, and "With You," her favorite Call Me Kevin song, began to play.

"Did they play it?" I asked, nodding toward the stereo.

"Third song," she said, as she smiled at me and settled back into her seat, tucking her legs up underneath her. "And I think it must not have been on the set list, because the drummer was totally off until the bridge. . . ."

She started talking me through the night, moment by moment, the adventure she'd had without me, pausing only to sing along to the refrain. And by the time the last chorus played, I had joined in.

★★★★

"Penelope Entwhistle," I muttered under my breath. I hadn't had the same good luck this time, and I'd had to park in one of the ten-dollar lots. I'd gotten cash out of the ATM on the way over, when I'd realized halfway there that I couldn't use my debit card, since the name printed on it wouldn't match my ID. And I had a feeling that leaving a paper trail was not the best idea, considering that I was about to break the law. "Penelope Entwhistle," I said as I walked down the street on shaky legs toward McKenzie's, trying to make it sound like it was a name I'd said for years and years. "Twenty-one Miller's Crossing, Reno, Nevada. Eight nine five one five."

I'd checked McKenzie's website, and tonight was the only night they had a band playing. It wasn't Call Me Kevin, of course—it was some band I didn't recognize called the Henry Gales. But it had forced me into doing this tonight, since if there was a band, at least there would be something to do, and I wouldn't just be at a bar . . . and what? I had no idea. I couldn't even finish the sentence, as I'd never been in a bar that was only a bar. But if there was a band, even if it turned out to be a terrible band, it somehow made this feel more okay, like I was just seeing a concert. While pretending to be someone named Penelope.

After our run that morning, Frank had asked me if I wanted to hang out that night, and I'd said no. I didn't want to tell him I was trying to do this, just in case it all went horribly wrong. I had launched into a series of excuses that didn't even sound believable to me by the end—something about babysitting Beckett and catching up on reading for next year and helping my mother clean out the fridge. He'd just listened with raised eyebrows, then nodded. "If you're organizing my surprise party, Emily, you can just tell me." His birthday was in three days, and it had started coming up in conversation more and more.

"Right," I said, trying to laugh this off. "Totally." I would have worried that, after that, he'd expected me to do something for him, but I knew Collins had been planning something.

"Penelope," I said to myself, as I noticed I was getting very close to the door guy. It was the same guy from two months earlier, although now he appeared even bigger, somehow, his phone looking tiny in his hand. I wondered if it was there so that he could call the police immediately when underage people tried to get into his bar. "Penelope Entwhistle. Twenty-one Miller's Crossing . . ." I smoothed down my dress. I was wearing a similar version of what Sloane had picked out for me to wear, and as I put on makeup and high heels, it hit me that it had been a very long time since I'd dressed up. I'd gotten so used to spending my days in flip-flops and sneakers that my ankles were wobbling dangerously, no longer used to this.

There was no line at the door tonight, probably because it

was a Thursday and there was no major band playing a secret show. Just the door guy. I made myself walk closer to him on legs that were shaking. *Penelope*, I said over and over in my head. *Reno. Eight nine five one five.*

"Hello," I said as I got close to the guy. I was clutching my bag in one hand and my ID in the other, so tightly that I could feel the plastic cutting into my fingers.

"ID?" the guy asked, sounding utterly bored.

"Here you are," I said, handing it over to him, hoping it wasn't damp, as my palms had begun to sweat the closer I'd gotten to him. He shined his flashlight on it, then glanced at me, then nodded inside. "I can go?" I asked, not sure that we had finished our interaction.

"Yeah," he said, handing me back my ID. "Have fun."

"Thank you very much," I said as I pulled open the door, unable to believe it had been that simple. I walked inside and looked around. I suddenly felt like I had a giant *UNDERAGE* sign above me, that it was clear to everyone there that I'd never been in a bar before and didn't know what I was doing.

I took a few tentative steps in. I could see a small stage— more like a raised platform than anything else—along the back wall. There were booths on both sides of the room, and wait-resses walking around with trays. And opposite the stage was a bar, with stools surrounding it, only half full. This wasn't like the bar that was part of the country club where I'd worked, where I could grab the soda gun and refill the Cokes and Sprites my tables ordered. That had pretty much been a long counter with a harried guy named Marty working behind it, making what seemed like an endless stream of gin and tonics. This was different. The surface was polished metal, and the shelves of liquor stretched up almost to the ceiling, and each shelf seemed to be lit with its own blue light.

I drifted a little closer to the bar, not sure what to do. Since the band wasn't on yet, I felt like I had to do something—I couldn't keep standing in the doorway all night, especially if I wanted to be inconspicuous. But the bar was so much more intimidating than I'd realized it would be. And did I even order from it? Or was I supposed to flag down one of the waitresses with trays?

"Watch yourself, hon," one of the waitresses said as she passed me, and I stepped quickly out of the way. I let out a shaky breath and walked up to the side of the bar that had the fewest people sitting around it, then climbed up onto a stool and rested my purse on my lap. I wasn't sure what happened now, but at least I wasn't standing in the way.

"What can I get you?" asked the bartender, who had floppy blond hair and a V-neck T-shirt with an extremely deep V.

"Oh," I said, glancing up at the blue shelves of liquor, like I was actually considering getting something up there. "Diet Coke, please?"

"Sure thing," he said. "With rum?"

"No!" I said, more vehemently than I meant to. "I mean,

just, you know. Neat. Straight. Plain." I was just tossing around words I'd heard people use in movies when they were in bars, hoping one of them would make sense to this guy.

"Sure thing," he said, grabbing a glass, filling it up with a soda gun, and sliding it across the bar to me. "That's five."

I blinked at this, surprised, since I'd never paid that much for a Diet Coke in my life. I slid a five across the bar at him, but a moment later had another mini panic. You were supposed to tip bartenders, weren't you? I had no idea how much. After a moment, I slid another five across the bar, and he picked it up.

"Thanks, love," he said, pocketing it with a smile. "I'm Jared, by the way. You live around here?"

"I'm Penelope Entwhistle," I said immediately, and probably too fast, since he looked a little taken aback. "I'm from Reno?"

The guy nodded. "Nice," he said. "The Biggest Little City in the World."

I smiled like this meant something to me, wishing I'd done my Reno research before trying to pose as a native. I took a sip of my five-dollar Coke and pulled out my phone, wondering when I could leave, when this would have met Sloane's criteria and satisfied her list. Surely she didn't expect me to be here all night, did she? I wasn't sure I was going to be able to afford it, if every drink was going to cost me ten dollars.

A blast of reverb sounded from the other end of the bar, and I saw three skinny guys had taken the stage, dragging on their amps and looking winded. "Hey," one of them said, wincing at the microphone's feedback. He had curly blond hair and a guitar slung around his neck. "We're the Henry Gales. Thanks so much for having us." The drummer counted off "One, two, three, four," and they launched into a somewhat shaky first few chords before they found their rhythm.

I realized after half a verse that I knew the lyrics, could anticipate what was coming next. It took until the chorus for me to recognize that they were playing "Truth in the Dark," a song that had been on Frank's last running mix. And though I hadn't admitted it to Frank, I actually really liked the song, and found myself mouthing the words of the chorus along with the band. I picked up my phone and took a picture to show Frank later. I knew I could have texted it to him, but I had a feeling that would lead to lots of questions I didn't really want to answer at the moment, questions like *Why are you in a bar?*

I felt myself lean back into my chair, taking a sip of my Diet Coke, realizing with some surprise that this might actually be fun.

An hour later, the band had announced the end of their set after a drum solo that had gone on just a little too long, and I felt like I'd be more than able to cross Penelope off the list. I nodded at Jared as I slid off my stool and headed toward the door, the last song they'd played—I was pretty sure it was about Kansas, though the lead singer could really have worked on his enunciation—repeating in my head. I was making my way toward the exit when I noticed a blond girl near the doorway, talking to one of the waitresses. They were both looking at me. I glanced away, figuring that maybe their eyes had just landed on me for a second, but when I looked back, they were both still staring. And now the waitress was pointing directly at me.

My heart started to thud, and it was like all the other times I'd been scared in my life had just been for practice, because this was the real thing. Somehow, someone had found out that I was underage, and I was going to get hauled into jail. It would go on my permanent record, and then I'd never get into college—

The blond woman nodded and started walking right toward me, and I realized that I only had a tiny window to make it to the door, so I hustled across the room as fast as I could in my dress and heels. I had just stepped outside, the bouncer looking up at me, when I heard someone yell, "Hey! Penelope!"

Even though I probably should have just kept walking, I turned around and saw the girl was standing right behind me. This was actually happening. This was real.

She was petite, with long hair and a heart-shaped face, which didn't seem to fit with the angry scowl she was currently directing right at me. "You thought you'd get away with it, didn't you?"

"Look," I said, taking another step away, feeling how wobbly my ankles were in the heels. "I'm really sorry. I just didn't—"

"You didn't think I'd find out?" She was suddenly right there, in my face.

"Find out what?" the bouncer asked, standing up, suddenly seeming more huge than ever. I braced myself for it, for her to tell him that I was underage, that they should call the cops.

"This is the skank who's been hooking up with Jared." I was so relieved to hear this that I felt myself smile, which I realized a second later, had really not been the right reaction. "You think something's funny?" she asked.

"No," I said quickly. "Nothing. I'm just—that's not me."

"Jared has been cheating on me with some *skank* named Penelope," the girl yelled. "I know it. I've checked his phone, you know."

"Not that Penelope," the bouncer said, surprising me— and the girl, judging by her reaction. "That Penelope's got, like, really big hair."

"Carl," the girl said, sounding crestfallen. "You *knew* about this?"

I took my opportunity to leave and hurried down the street, my heart still pounding hard, but not with fear this time. It was more like I could feel adrenaline coursing through my body as I headed toward my car. I had done it. I had gone to a bar and ordered drinks and been mistaken for a skank and almost gotten into a fight. It all felt strangely triumphant, and the only thing I wanted to do was tell someone about it. I pulled out my phone as I crossed the lot to the Volvo, texting as I walked.

> Hungry? Diner in 15? I just
> crossed off #5.

Frank was already there when I walked in, sitting in a booth facing the door, a plate of fries for us to share in the center of the table. I'd texted Dawn, too, but she was out on a delivery and I found I didn't mind that it was just me and Frank. As I got closer, he saw me and his eyebrows flew up. I caught my reflection in the glass window that faced the street, and understood why. I was wearing a short, tight dress and heels, too much makeup, and my hair carefully styled, when most other people in the diner were in jeans.

"Hey," I said casually, sliding into the booth across from him and helping myself to a fry, like this was just a totally normal evening, like this was what I wore to help my mother clean out the fridge.

Frank was still staring at me, a smile playing around the corners of his mouth. "And just what are you supposed to be?"

I gave him a pleased-to-meet-you smile. "Penelope Entwhistle," I said. "Twenty-one Miller's Crossing, Reno. It's a pleasure."

I saw understanding begin to dawn on his face, and I pulled out my phone and slid it across the table toward him, the screen showing the Henry Gales rocking out. Frank looked down at it and then back at me, his jaw falling open. "Okay," he said. "Talk."

"So," I began, "I was at McKenzie's—"

"The *bar*?" Frank asked, looking surprised.

"Yeah," I said, blasé, like this was no big deal. Frank just looked at me evenly, and I felt myself break, laughing, knowing I wouldn't be able to keep it up around him. "I know," I said. "And I was terrified I was going to get kicked out. . . ." I took another fry, then leaned across the table and started to tell him the story.

9
BREAK
SOMETHING

"How long is this going to take?" Beckett whined, kicking one sneaker against the other.

"It might take a while," I admitted, trying at least to be honest with him. Beckett and I were standing outside the office of My Pretty Pony, where I was scheduled for a four o'clock ride. Even though Frank had been trying to schedule my makeup ride, I kept putting him off. I figured as long as there were giant horses, and I was expected to ride them, I couldn't imagine a different outcome than before. So like the Saddleback Ranch woman had suggested, I had looked into the pony ride option, and found there were quite a few. They admittedly were mostly geared toward small children, but there was nothing on this place's website that said adults couldn't have a pony ride too. I'd checked.

"Aggh," Beckett groaned, slumping onto a nearby bench.

"Hey," I said. "I just bought you ice cream, remember?"

Beckett just looked at me, unimpressed. "It was free, Em." I had to concede this was true. We'd come from Paradise, where Kerry was working. She had just waved me off when I'd gone to pay, which was a nice surprise for me, but apparently wasn't going very far to win over my brother. I had hoped it would work to basically bribe him into coming with me, since this way we could spend time together when he didn't have camp, but also because I didn't want to do this alone, and was way too embarrassed to admit to anyone else where I was.

"Hi, are you here for your four p.m. ride?" A woman wearing jeans and a pink T-shirt came out, bending down to smile at Beckett, who pointed at me, stone-faced.

"Um, that's me," I said, waving at her. "I'm Emily."

"Oh," she said, just staring at me for a moment. Then she seemed to regroup, and nodded a little too vigorously. "Well . . . okay. We should be able to accommodate you." She glanced at my brother and then back at me, still obviously very confused as to what was happening here. "Are you two riding together? Or did you want to try it out first and show him it's not scary?" She mouthed the last word to me, and Beckett rolled his eyes hugely at this.

"No," I said, wishing that either one of these explanations

was true. But when I'd offered Beckett his own pony ride, he'd looked at me like I was crazy, making me think that maybe I should have invited Dawn instead. "I just . . . wanted to take a pony ride."

"Okay," she said, after waiting a moment, clearly expecting something more rational to come after this. "Well, I'll get you all set up then." She headed back into the barn that was adjacent to the office, and I was about to try again to sell Beckett on the idea of joining me when my phone buzzed. I saw that it was Collins, which was unusual. Collins would sometimes text me, and he was always sending me links to what he assured me were hilarious videos, but he almost never called.

"Hey," I said, answering the call.

"Emily!" he said, and I could hear that his voice was high and stressed. "Where are you?"

"Um," I said. I looked around, and my eyes landed on the very pink My Pretty Pony sign, written in elaborate cursive. "Why would you need to know that?"

"Because I am *freaking out*," he said, his voice getting even higher. "Do you even know it's Frank's birthday?"

"Yes," I said slowly, walking a few steps away from my brother, who seemed far too interested in this conversation. "We went running this morning, stopped for donuts afterward, and everyone at the donut shop sang to him." I didn't get the sense that this was something they normally did, but by the time I'd pulled out the pack of birthday candles I'd brought from home, and then had to ask the staff if they had any matches, everyone had gotten into it (it probably didn't hurt that we were the only customers) and had sung, and then clapped when Frank blew out the candle in his bear claw. When we'd traded iPods that morning, I'd also made sure to assemble a mix of all Happy Birthday songs for him—starting with the Beatles, of course. I had a present for him as well but I'd figured I'd just give it to him the next time we went running, since I knew Lissa was coming into town today to celebrate with him.

"Well," Collins huffed, "everything is falling apart and I need your help."

"Sure," I said, glancing back quickly to my brother, to make sure he hadn't decided to start scaling the barn, but he was still in the same spot on the bench. "What's going on?"

"What's *going on*," he said, "is that Lissa can't get up here from Princeton, for some reason. And Frank's at lunch with his mom and then going to dinner with his dad, and I'm stuck at work and can't leave to get the party set up, because Frank has the day off, and if I left Doug in charge of more than just shoe rental, the whole place could burn down and he'd still just be reading about gnomes."

"They're not gnomes," I heard Doug say in the background, his voice heavy with disdain. *"Please."*

"So what can I do?"

"I need you to go get Lissa." I drew in a breath, and Collins must have heard, because he started speaking fast. "I know it's a long drive, and I'm sorry to ask. But there's nothing else to be done."

"Um," I said. It wasn't the two hours down—and back—that was giving me pause. I didn't know what was. I thought as fast as I could, frantically casting about for another option. Maybe Dawn? She had never met Lissa, but I could always text her a picture or something. "The thing is . . ." I felt someone tugging at my sleeve, and looked down and saw Beckett.

"What's going on?" he asked, my distressed expression clearly giving him hope. "Can we leave?"

"The thing is," I said again, "I actually have a lot of stuff going on this afternoon. Important stuff. And—"

"Emily?" I looked over, and saw the woman in the pink shirt smiling at me. "Your pony is ready, whenever you want to take your ride."

I clamped my hand over the microphone, but clearly not fast enough, because Collins said, his voice heavy with disbelief, "Em, seriously?"

"Fine," I said, realizing I was caught. "Text me the address."

Since I'd already prepaid, I got a coupon for another pony ride, and it didn't escape my notice that I was starting to accumulate riding credits all over town. I dropped a thrilled Beckett off at home, then yelled to my parents that I was going out for a few hours and taking the car, and while my mother nodded distractedly, my dad barely looked at me. They both had the rumpled, exhausted look they got when they'd been working for hours. I headed for my car, getting in and then doubling back to the garage to put the wooden piece that fitted over the roof into the trunk. Because while I was pretty sure it wasn't going to rain, the last thing I wanted was for Lissa Young to get rained on in my car. Then I let out a breath and headed out of the driveway, putting on some music, loud, aiming for the highway, telling myself that I was just doing Collins—and Frank—a favor, and there was no need to be this nervous. But despite this, even just the prospect of Lissa being in my car suddenly made me want to change everything about it.

As I pulled onto I-95 and skipped through on my playlist to what had become my favorite Eric Church song, I realized that there was something else that was bothering me about having to spend time with her. Lissa seemed to belong to a different world, the school world where Frank was Frank Porter, this impossibly perfect guy, the one who was nothing like the one I'd gotten to know this summer, the Frank who tripped over his own feet occasionally and was scared of heights and who sometimes had flecks of orange paintball paint in his hair. Someone who could speak in Beatles lyrics for two days, and who I'd watched have a nacho fight with Collins.

I'd been driving for about an hour when my phone started to ring from the passenger seat. My car was old enough that I couldn't use any hands-free devices with it, so I jabbed at the screen, trying to hit the button that activated the speaker. Sloane had told me once that when she talked to me like this, it sounded like I was at the bottom of a cave with bad cell reception, but I figured it was better than getting a cell phone ticket, like Collins had gotten the week before.

"Hello?" I called in the phone's general direction. It hadn't looked like it had been a call from any of my saved contacts, but I didn't want to look away from the road long enough to really investigate this.

"Hello?" I looked at the phone and saw, to my shock, that Lissa had appeared on my screen—I must have pressed the button to do a video call.

"Oh," I said, trying to lean a little more into the frame. "I didn't mean to—just hold on a second." I signaled, glad to see that I was almost at a rest stop. I didn't know what the cell phone laws were regarding video calls, but I also didn't want to risk finding out. I pulled off the highway and into the rest stop. It was a small one, just bathrooms and some vending machines. But it was pretty crowded, several minivans filled with families, exhausted-looking parents and kids running around in the late afternoon sun. I pulled into a space away from the noise of the families and put the car in park, holding up the phone, wishing that I'd brushed my hair recently, or that I'd put on more makeup this morning than just a swipe of lip balm. "Hi," I said. "Sorry—I was just trying to put it on speaker, I didn't mean to select video."

"Hi," Lissa said, giving me a small smile. "It's fine." She looked the same as she did in school, maybe a little more tan.

But I couldn't help notice that her eyes looked red and a little puffy. "How are you, Emily?"

There was something about Lissa that made me want to sit up straighter, and made me wish I'd read a newspaper recently. "Fine," I said, straightening my posture. "I think I'm about an hour away right now. I have the address, so—"

"That's what I'm . . . well . . . ," Lissa said, looking away, and pressing her lips together. After a pause, she turned back to me. "I just wanted to talk to you before you got too far. I hope it's okay that I'm calling. Collins gave me your number."

"It's fine," I said. "Like I said, I should be there in an hour. I drive slow." I smiled, but she didn't smile back, just looked a little bit stricken and I suddenly realized why. "Slow*ly*," I added quickly. "I drive *slowly*. But if I get back on the road, I should—"

"I'm not coming," she said, interrupting me. "I . . ." She looked down and let out a breath before she looked at me again. "I know I should have been planning on it, but there's just too much going on here."

I just looked at her for a second. I didn't know this girl at all, but I could tell that something wasn't right. I just sat there in silence, hoping that it wasn't obvious I didn't believe her.

"I thought I'd be able to get away," she continued, still not looking at me. "I'm sorry that you've had to drive all this way for nothing."

"Oh," I said. "Um . . ." I suddenly thought about Frank, about how disappointed he'd would be, and what this would do to the party that Collins had been organizing.

"I'll call Collins and tell him about the change in plans," she said, sounding more businesslike now, like this was one more thing to be checked off her to-do list. "And Frank," she added after a moment, "of course."

"Okay," I said. "Um . . . all right." Lissa nodded. I realized I wasn't sure how to wrap up this conversation.

"So you've gotten pretty close with Collins, I guess?" she asked, looking right at me. "I was a little surprised when he told me that you were coming to get me, but I guess if you two are—"

"No!" I said, more vehemently than I meant to. Not that I couldn't understand the appeal, in theory—Dawn had been going on and on the other day about how he looked just like the astronaut's cute sidekick in *Space Ninja*, and I could kind of see it—but I just wasn't interested in him like that. "Um, no," I said, a little more quietly. "We're just friends. Frank, too," I added. If Frank hadn't told her, I wasn't sure I should be the one to let her know that I'd been hanging out with her boyfriend. But I also didn't want to let her think that I was just Collins's friend. It seemed too much like lying, somehow, or like Frank and I had been sneaking around.

"Good," she said after a moment. "That's . . . good. I'm glad." We just looked at each other for another moment, then she glanced away. When she looked back at me, the vulnerability that I'd seen a moment before was gone, and she looked somehow distant, her voice all business. "I shouldn't keep you," she said. "I'm sorry, again, about not reaching you sooner."

"No problem," I said, and then a moment later immediately regretted not saying something more impressive. "I'll . . . um . . . see you around?"

She gave me a quick smile. "Absolutely," she said. "Thank you, Emily." And with that, my screen went dark, and I was staring back at my own confused expression.

My phone rang again an hour later—but an hour in which I'd only moved a few miles. There was something going on—I figured it had to be some sort of accident, and I'd been trying to scan through the radio stations, looking for some answers, but somehow only getting ads and weather. Because I wasn't moving very fast, I could see that it was Collins calling me, and I was able to answer without accidentally starting a video call with him. "Hey," I said, as I answered. "Did Lissa call you?"

"She did," he said, and let out a long breath. "Sorry to send you all that way."

"Don't worry about it," I said. "Um . . . how's Frank?"

"I'm trying to make the best of things over here," Collins said, which, it occurred to me, wasn't exactly an answer to the question. "Plans are in flux, so just text me when you get back to town, okay?"

"Sure," I said. "There's some weird traffic thing going on, though, so I might be a while."

"Not a problem," he said. "I'll—" I lost what Collins was

saying, though, because the car in front of me slammed on their brakes. And even though we were crawling, I still had to slam on my own, and then hold my breath, hoping the car behind me saw this and wouldn't rear-end me. After a few seconds, I relaxed—I was fine, but all the stuff that had been congregating under the passenger seat had been jostled loose, and there was now a pile of junk on the floor.

"Collins?" I called into the speaker. But whether the phone had gotten turned off when I'd stopped, or he'd given up, either way, he was no longer there. I put the phone aside and glanced down at the mess. There was a tube of Sloane's mascara, a cracked pair of sunglasses, a half-filled water bottle, and the book I swore up and down to the Stanwich High librarian that I'd returned. There was something else, too. I glanced away from the road for a moment and bent down for it. It was a disposable camera.

HOW EMILY SEES THE WORLD was written across the back of it in Sharpie, in Sloane's handwriting. She had given it to me sometime last year, and it was almost full, just a few pictures remaining. Even though it was getting dark fast, I held up the disposable and took a picture of the highway and the hood of my car and the seemingly endless red ribbon of brake lights—capturing, at that particular moment, how I saw the world.

****

I parked my car in the Orchard's lot, then killed the engine and just sat for a moment, looking out into the night. It had taken me much longer than should have been rationally possible to get back to Stanwich. I'd been getting text updates from Collins along the way. People were meeting up at the Orchard, and I should come by when I made it back into town.

I had hesitated before responding to this, once I'd made it back home and into the sanctuary of my room. Presumably, a lot of the people who were hanging out were Frank's other friends—like the ones that I'd encountered the first night with him, when he'd taken me to get gas. I hadn't been back to the Orchard since, and I really wasn't sure how I would fit in with those people. I was preparing to write Collins another text about how bad the traffic was, begging off, when I got another text.

> Hey are you coming? At the
> Orchard. See you soon?

It was from Frank, and I texted back without a second thought that I'd be there soon. Then I reached for a Sloane-chosen outfit—a vintage dress from Twice that I'd worn a lot last summer. But after I put it on, I found myself pulling at the straps, tugging at the hem, not liking what I saw in the mirror. For some reason, it didn't feel like me any longer. I took it off and changed into the denim skirt I'd bought with Dawn last week and a white eyelet tank top. Feeling more like myself somehow, I dabbed some makeup on, and made sure to get Frank's present before grabbing my flip-flops and heading back to the car.

Now that I was there, though, the present suddenly seemed stupid, and I didn't want Frank to feel like he had to open it in front of people—which was actually the last thing that I wanted. I carefully placed it behind my seat and got out, straightening my skirt as I went.

As I walked, I couldn't help but remember the last time I'd been to the Orchard. When I'd been all alone, miserable, looking down at my phone and trying to pretend that I was meeting someone, that there were people there waiting for me. And now, I realized with a shock, both of those things were true. And unless things went really wrong, there was no way I could picture myself spending tonight hiding behind a tree. It hit me just how much could happen in two months, how, since the last time I'd been at the Orchard, everything had changed.

Maybe not everything. I slowed as I realized Gideon was sitting on top of one of the picnic tables, at the very edge of the clearing, his head turned away from me. I immediately looked around for Sam, but didn't see him, which I was glad about. I knew I could have just taken the long way to the center of the clearing, where I was pretty sure I could see Collins—I couldn't imagine who else would be wearing a plum-colored polo shirt, at any rate. But I somehow found I didn't want to skulk around and hide from Gideon, or have things be awkward all evening. And so, before I could talk myself out of it, I was walking up to Gideon and touching him on the shoulder.

He turned around to look at me, almost losing his beer bottle in the process. "Hey," I said, giving him a smile. "How's it going?"

He just blinked at me for a moment, like he was trying to make sense of the fact that I was standing in front of him—or that I was going up to him to say hi, and not the other way around. "Hi," he finally said.

"I just wanted to say hello," I said, after a slightly strained pause. I'd kind of forgotten just how painful conversations with Gideon could sometimes be, and I was beginning to regret starting this one.

He nodded and rolled the bottle between his palms, and when nothing followed, I finally got the hint that he really didn't want to talk to me. I took a breath to tell him that it was great to see him, and that my friends were waiting—one of which was true—when he looked up at me. "Have you had a good summer?"

"Oh," I said, gathering my thoughts, and not just replying with a standard "Great!" Gideon didn't ask these questions just to be polite, and never wanted to hear that everything was fine when it wasn't. "It's not what I expected," I said. As I did, I realized we'd all had summers we hadn't been expecting—Frank, Dawn, me, Collins, even Beckett and my parents. "But it's been good. I've been having fun."

He looked at me for a moment, then nodded. "I'm glad," he said, in that slow, careful way of his. "Have you been . . ."

"Well, hello there." There was suddenly someone next to me, sliding his arm around my shoulders. I turned, expecting to see Collins or a Stanwich College freshman pushing his luck, but took a tiny, startled step back when I realized that it was Benji.

"Oh," I said. I took another step away, extricating myself from his arm. "Um, hi there."

Gideon had stood up and was frowning down at Benji—no small feat, since Benji was pretty tall himself. "Emily, you know this guy?"

"Oh yeah, she does," Benji said, with a wink at me—maybe it was a Collins family trait—clearly not reading the room very well and taking another step toward me. "How've you been?"

"Oh, fine," I said, a little too brightly.

"Em," Gideon said, and I could hear the hurt in his voice, though he was clearly trying to cover it up. "Are you two—"

"What am I thinking?" I babbled, mostly so Gideon wouldn't ask his question and I wouldn't have to answer it. "This is Gideon," I said, making the introductions. "And that's Benji."

"Ben," Benji said, his smile fading.

"Right, of course," I said quickly. "Well, this was fun, but I should probably—"

"So what have you been up to?" Benji asked, smiling at me again. "I haven't seen you around."

"Well, no," I said, wondering what he was getting at, since the only place I'd ever seen him before had been in Frank's pantry.

"So you guys . . . ," Gideon said, looking from me to Benji, his expression hard.

"No," I said quickly, just as Benji replied, "Well, this *one* time . . ."

"Emily," Gideon said, now just looking confused.

"There you are." I turned and saw Frank, a bottle of water in his hand, walking up to me.

"Hi," I said, smiling at him, happy to see him even though I'd just seen him that morning. Now that he was in front of me, I couldn't believe I'd ever thought about not coming here.

"What's going on?" Frank asked, looking slightly confused as he glanced from Gideon, to Benji, to me.

"Nothing," I said quickly, realizing this might be my opportunity to make an exit and leave unscathed. "We should go, right? To celebrate your birthday? Now?" I widened my eyes at him, hoping that he would get the hint.

He seemed to, because he gave me a smile that was clearly concealing a laugh and said, "Yes. My birthday. Absolutely."

"Bye," I said to Gideon as Benji wandered away toward the keg guy. Gideon was now looking from Frank to me, his expression crestfallen. "I'll see you around?" I asked him. But Gideon had never made things like this easier when he didn't have to, and he didn't say anything, just steadily looked back at me for a long moment.

"Okay," Frank said brightly after a moment, morphing into the student body president, capable of organizing large groups of people and doing it smoothly. "Have a great night. Emily, if you want to follow me, we're set up over this way . . ." He steered me toward the far picnic table, where there was what looked like a supermarket cake, Collins talking to a girl entirely out of his league, and Doug standing awkwardly next to some of Frank's school friends.

I could sense the question that Frank wanted to ask, but I didn't want to answer it, and just looked straight ahead, not meeting his eye as we walked toward the party.

★★★★

MAY

Two months earlier

"You have to let me see it," Gideon said, trying to twist around to see his arm and the Sharpie tattoo I was currently working on.

"No," I said, turning his head away. "Not until I'm finished. You know how bad I am at this."

He reached over and brushed one of his big hands over my hair, smoothing a piece of it behind my ear. "You're not bad at it," he said.

"Ha," I said. "It'll be worse if you don't hold still."

"Holding," Gideon said, shooting me one of his small, rare smiles. In the two months that the four of us had been hanging out, Sharpie tattoos had become a thing we did. While we started the evenings together, Sloane and Sam

SINCE YOU'VE BEEN GONE

would inevitably break off on their own, and then it would be me and Gideon and a Sharpie, passing the time. It had started that first night we'd gone to the Orchard, and had just become a tradition, though it had taken me a while to build up the courage to draw one on him. I had less than no artistic talent, and Gideon was a natural and gifted artist, though he denied this and insisted it was just something stupid he did for fun. I'd started to really look forward to mine, even though I knew as it was being drawn on that it was temporary. The tattoos faded over time and with every shower until there was just a faint suggestion of whatever it was that had been adorning my hand or arm or ankle.

Sloane clearly thought that Gideon would be the perfect solution to my problems with Sam. This way, we could all hang out, but she could spend time with Sam as well. And it wasn't that I didn't like Gideon. He was a really nice guy, a good kisser, and had a sly sense of humor that only came out once you got to know him. But I was still left with the lingering, nagging thought that I hadn't chosen him, he'd been presented to me. And I couldn't help but wonder what would have happened if we'd just met, without the expectations of both our best friends pushing us together.

But it was nice with him now, in Sam's TV room, sitting next to each other on the couch. The movie we'd all been watching was on pause, the TV having long switched over to the screensaver of generic pictures—a butterfly on a leaf, an

Morgan Matson

African vista, a lighthouse. We'd all been watching together when Sam had gotten a text. Sloane had seen it and said something to him I couldn't hear. Sam had stormed into the kitchen in a huff, and Sloane had followed. That had been over twenty minutes ago, and when it had become clear they weren't reappearing any time soon, Gideon had paused the movie and procured the Sharpie, raising an eyebrow at me. It was my turn, and since you couldn't erase marker, I had planned out this design and was working very carefully on it. It was a series of ocean waves that wrapped around the front of his arm. I could draw waves, they were pretty easy, just a continual scrolling pattern. And then atop one of the waves, I'd drawn a bear on a surfboard. I knew it didn't make much sense, but cartoony bears were one of the few things I could draw well, so I just hoped Gideon wouldn't question it too much. I put the final details on the bear's ears and leaned back a little, looking at my handiwork. I realized I was actually pretty happy with this one. Gideon was still turning his head away, and impulsively I scrawled *Emily xoxo* on his arm, then sat back and capped the marker. "Done," I said.

He turned his head, looked at it, and smiled. "That's awesome," he said. "The best one yet." He squinted down at his arm. "Is that a bear?"

"Um," I said. It didn't seem like such a great sign that he had to ask this. "It's supposed to be."

"I love it," he said. "It's great." He looked at me for a

moment, then leaned forward and kissed me. After hesitating for just a second, I kissed him back, and I felt the Sharpie fall from my hand. He pulled me closer, wrapping his arms around me.

"Whoa." I pulled away and sat up slightly, seeing Sam standing in the doorway of the TV room, a sour expression on his face. "I didn't mean to interrupt."

"Didn't see you there," Gideon said, sitting up straighter, his face flushed red.

"Clearly," Sam said, with one of his smiles that never seemed to have all that much humor in it.

"Where's Sloane?" I asked, looking behind him, but not seeing my best friend.

"Kitchen," he said with a shrug, like it didn't concern him all that much. He nodded at the TV. "We watching this?"

"Sure," I said, moving closer to Gideon to make some more room on the couch. Sam crossed to sit against one end of it, grabbed the remote and pointed it at the TV just as Gideon picked up his phone, resting on the coffee table, and groaned.

"I have to go," he said quietly to me as he set the phone back down. "Curfew." I had never been to Gideon's house or met his parents, but from the little he'd told me, I had gotten the distinct impression that they were very strict. His curfew was a full two hours earlier than mine. I nodded, and he leaned over and gave me a quick kiss on the cheek, while I felt Sam watching us. "Call you tomorrow," he said, pushing himself up off the couch. He and Sam did the thing they always did—it was half a high-five and half a handshake. "Say good-bye to Sloane for me?" he asked as he headed toward the front door, and I nodded.

"Sure thing," I said. He smiled at me, and a moment later, I heard the door slam and the sound of his car engine starting up.

"You know," Sam said from his side of the couch. I suddenly wished I could move to sit at the other end of it—or even leave the couch entirely—without it being incredibly obvious that I wanted to get away from him. "I think that was directed to me."

I just looked at him for a moment. "What was?"

"When he asked about saying good-bye to Sloane. I think that was to me, not you."

"Oh," I said. I couldn't believe that this mattered to him, but apparently it did. "Um, sorry about that." I glanced back toward the kitchen, wondering if my best friend needed me. I was actually feeling a little uncomfortable about it being the three of us here; I usually left around the same time Gideon did. "I think I'll go find Sloane," I said, starting to get up.

"And leave me all alone?" Sam asked. If he'd been smiling, or joking, I might have laughed at this, but he was just looking at me, his face serious.

"Ha," I said, glancing back to the kitchen again. I knew

I should just get up, go find Sloane, and tell her good-bye.

"So you and Gideon are getting close," he said, moving a little nearer to me on the couch.

"I guess so," I said, feeling distinctly uncomfortable. And Sam moved closer still, his expression almost carefully blank, like he knew he was making me nervous, and he liked it.

Sam leaned closer and lowered his voice. "You want to know what he told me about you?"

"I really don't," I said, forcing a laugh that even I could hear fell flat. "Want to watch the movie?"

"Nope," Sam said, still looking right at me. "We should be friends, Emily."

"We are," I said lightly, just wanting this strange exchange to be over as quickly as possible. It was underscoring for me that I was never alone with Sam; I was beginning to realize that I preferred it that way.

"Really?" he asked, leaning even closer to me.

Two things happened then, very quickly, the kind of quick where you don't have time to think anything through, you just react and hope for the best. Sam leaned in to kiss me and I saw Sloane rounding the corner, coming in from the kitchen, carrying two glasses in her hands.

And I could have just ducked or turned away from Sam. But I didn't. I let him kiss me, and I waited just a second more before I broke away, pushed him away from me and said, loudly, "What are you *doing*?"

Morgan Matson

There was the sound of glass breaking, and I looked over to see Sloane, her blue eyes wide, shattered glass at her feet and what looked like Coke spilling onto her shoes, the new white pony-skin ones she'd saved a month to buy.

Sam's head snapped around, and he looked from Sloane to me, shaking his head. "It isn't . . . ," he said, talking fast, his voice high. "Emily was totally throwing herself at me after Gideon left, and . . ."

Sloane looked at me, like she was looking for the answer. I looked right back at her and shook my head. There was a fraction of a second where I wondered if she would pick Sam, his version of things, their three months over our two years. But this worry faded when I saw in her eyes how completely she believed me. "Em, would you mind waiting by the car?" she asked, her voice quiet and breaking. "I'll be there in just a minute."

I nodded, scrambled to my feet, and grabbed my purse. As I headed to the front door, I saw that Sam's expression was equal parts shocked and angry. "Wait, you don't even believe me?" he asked, his voice rising.

"Nope," I heard Sloane say, still quiet, before I stepped out into the night and pulled the door shut behind me.

I just stood on the *Welcome, Friends!* mat for a moment, trying to put everything that had just happened into some kind of order. Deep down, I knew I could have stopped it. But if Sam was going to try and kiss me anyway, shouldn't Sloane have seen it? So she could finally see what kind of guy he was?

I knew I was justifying something that I shouldn't have done, but before I could continue to talk myself into it, an SUV pulled into the driveway. Through the windshield, I recognized Gideon, who was already smiling at me as he killed the engine and got out of the car. I walked down Sam's front steps and over to my car, and we met halfway.

"Hey," he said. "Leaving already?"

I glanced back toward the house. I knew I didn't have a ton of time, if Sloane did go through with ending it, like I was fairly sure she was going to. Sloane didn't fight with people, ever, so even if Sam wanted a long, drawn-out breakup, he wasn't about to get one. "I am," I said slowly. I had no idea what—if anything—I should tell him. I had no doubt that Sam would soon spin this story whatever way suited him.

"I forgot my phone," he said, nodding toward the house.

"Listen," I said quickly. Between his curfew and the fact that I had a feeling that Sloane wasn't going to want to linger, I had to make this fast and get it over with. Because Gideon and I were done. I felt a small pang as I realized this, but I pushed on past it. We had always been the add-ons to our best friends' relationship, and it wouldn't make much sense for us to continue, just the two of us. There probably wasn't enough there to last on its own. Better to get out now, before we'd had the chance to try and preserve something that wouldn't have worked. "I think Sloane and Sam are breaking up," I said, glancing back toward the house.

"No," Gideon said, his face falling. "Are you sure they're not just fighting? Because—"

"So I just . . . ," I started, then stopped when I realized I didn't know how to finish the sentence. I'd never had to break up with anyone before. "This has been really great," I said after a moment. "But . . ."

Gideon just looked at me, and I saw understanding slowly dawn on his face. "Wait," he said. "Emily. What are you saying?"

"Just that I think it would be too hard now," I said, realizing as I did that there had been very few actual nouns or verbs in that sentence. "I just do." The door opened, and Sloane came out barefoot, carrying her ruined flats. "So . . . take care, okay?" I asked, hating myself even as I asked it, but telling myself that this was for the best. It would be better to end it right then, rather than drawing it out.

Gideon was still looking at me like he was hoping that at any moment, I might tell him this had all been an elaborate joke. But I made myself turn away from him and headed to my car, but not before I got a glimpse of the *xoxo* I'd drawn on his skin not very long ago.

★★★★

Two hours later, the cake had been eaten, the birthday song had been sung, and most of the guests had departed.

And I was tipsy.

It wasn't something that I had planned on, at all. But when I arrived at the picnic table, Collins had given me a red cup of beer and a fork—he hadn't remembered to get plates for the cake. He'd gotten the cake at a discount, since someone hadn't picked it up, which was also the reason it read *You Did It, Wanda!* There was no indication of what, exactly, Wanda had done, just a few lopsided red sugar roses on the corners. The cake was sickly sweet, and at first, I'd just sipped at my beer to balance out the taste. But as I'd had more, I found it made my strained conversations with Frank's other friends a little easier to get through. None of them could understand why I was there, most of them appeared to think I worked with Frank and Collins, and the remainder seemed to be convinced that I was dating Doug. And it wasn't until I'd finished my second cup that I realized I was officially tipsy. I was baffled as to why until I realized I hadn't had anything to eat that day except for birthday donuts with Frank, hours and hours before.

Which explained my current state, but didn't help me do much about it. I ended up sitting on a picnic table with Collins, who was finishing up the last bites of the cake and bemoaning his romantic woes to me. It was perfect, because it seemed like he was more interested in a monologue than a dialogue, and whenever I had too much to drink I got oddly honest and told people things I never would have otherwise.

"And I'm a catch, right, Emily?" he asked, waving his fork

in his general direction. "I mean, the C-dawg's got style. He's got panache, you know? And he knows how to please the ladies."

I started to feel slightly sick, and I wasn't sure it was the beer. "Um . . ."

"And yet all these girls just passing up their ride on the C train! Their loss, though. Am I right or am I right?" He took a big bite of cake and ended up with frosting on his nose.

I reached over, held his face steady, and wiped it off while Collins blinked at me, surprised. It was another thing that I did when I'd had a bit to drink—I acted without thinking first, without running through possibilities and outcomes, and just did. "I don't know," I said, thinking back to the girl he'd been hitting on earlier that night, and all the girls he was forever making a spectacle of himself in front of at school. "Did you ever think about asking out someone maybe a little less . . ." I paused. I had a feeling that I was going to insult him if I kept going and said something along the lines of "on your level." But my brain at the moment wasn't coming up with any other alternatives. "You know," I finally said. "Someone that you're maybe already friends with."

Collins shook his head. "Dawn said the same thing last week," he said dismissively. "But you can't help who you fall for. The heart wants what it wants." I didn't feel up to arguing with that at the moment, and just looked around at the dwindling crowd.

"Too bad she couldn't make it," I said.

"Yeah," Collins agreed. "I tried my best, but apparently she had to 'work.'" He put air quotes around the last word, shaking his head dismissively. Dawn had been invited, but her manager apparently had been calling into question how long she was taking with her deliveries ever since she'd started hanging out with us, and so she didn't want to push her luck.

"I think that was the last of them," Frank said, coming to join us as he waved at two guys—they'd been convinced I worked at IndoorXtreme and seemed insulted when I'd said I couldn't get them free passes—as they headed to the cars.

"Did you have fun?" Collins asked, like he couldn't have cared less what the answer was, but I knew him well enough by now not to believe it.

"It was great, man," Frank said, hitting him on the back as I rolled my eyes. I had no idea why boys, when they became affectionate, got violent. "Thanks a lot."

"Yes," I said, carefully standing up, but still somehow managing to lose my balance and catching myself on the table. "Really . . . great."

Frank looked at me, levelly. "Keys," he said, holding out his hand for them.

"Have you had anything?" I asked, even as I was digging in my purse for them.

"Just a month's worth of sugar," he said, glancing at the remains of the cake. "Nothing to drink, only water." I handed Frank my keys, very relieved I hadn't had to call Dawn or my parents or a taxi—the possibilities I'd been running through in my head, none of which I'd particularly liked. "I'll meet you by your car," he said. "Collins and I are just going to clean this up."

Collins turned to him, looking surprised. "We are? I mean, I am?" He sighed and gestured to the picnic table with the remains of the cake and empty red cups scattered on the ground. "But I organized all this!"

"I'll help," I said, bending down to get a cup, but losing my balance halfway and having to brace myself on the picnic table.

"Car," Frank said, placing his hands on my shoulders and turning me in the direction of the parking lot. "I'll be there in five minutes."

"This is going to take *five minutes*?" Collins grumbled as he bent down to pick up a cup.

"I'll see you there," I said, somehow not even feeling embarrassed that this was happening. I knew I would probably feel it in the morning—along with a splitting headache—but for the moment, I was just vaguely relieved that things were working out.

I focused on making my way back to the car, wondering why I never normally had to concentrate this hard on walking, since it was actually very challenging. It wasn't until I reached the Volvo that I realized I couldn't get in—I'd given Frank the keys. So I carefully pushed myself up to sit on the trunk, feet resting on my back bumper. I leaned back to look up at the stars, amazed at how they were taking over the whole sky. "Emily?"

I sat up more cautiously than usual to see Gideon standing by the driver's side of an SUV parked a car away from me. He must have unlocked the car, because the interior lights flared on, suddenly very bright against the darkness. "You okay?"

"Fine," I said, pronouncing the word carefully enough that I might have undercut my intention. "I mean, I'm not driving or anything," I assured him. "But it's being handled."

"Do you need a ride?" he asked, his brow furrowed, and I could see why he was confused—when someone is sitting on the trunk of a parked car, it would seem to indicate they're having some transportation issues.

"No," I said, shaking my head once to each side—things started to get a little spinny if I did more than that. "My—Frank is driving me."

"Frank," Gideon said, shaking his head as he looked down at the keys in his hands. "You sure didn't waste any time."

"What's that supposed to mean?" I asked, but not in the sarcastic way people generally asked it—I honestly didn't know what he meant. A moment later, though, I caught up and felt my jaw drop. "No, no," I said. "No. We're not—he has a girlfriend. A really serious one. And I was supposed to pick her up this afternoon, but . . ." I trailed off when I realized Gideon probably didn't need to hear about the details of my day. "Where's Sam?" I asked. Not that I wanted to see him, but seeing Gideon twice without Sam's presence was just surprising.

He gestured back to the Orchard. "He wanted to stay

a little longer." He looked at me for a long moment, his expression unreadable. "Where's Sloane?"

I shrugged, feeling how loose my shoulders were. "She . . . left," I said. "At the beginning of the summer."

"Where?" Gideon asked, and the force of that simple word—and the fact that I still didn't have an answer—hit me hard.

"I don't know," I said, hating that I had to, that I didn't have any other answers. "But I'm working on it."

Gideon just shook his head, looking down at his keys. "The two of you," he said. "You just leave people behind, no explanations, don't care if—"

"Wait," I said, getting down from the car. "I don't—" Gideon ran his hand over his close-cropped hair, and it was then that I saw something peeking out of his T-shirt sleeve. It was something I never would have done if I hadn't had two beers on an empty stomach. But without thinking it through, I was crossing to him and pushing up his shirtsleeve to see what I knew would be there.

It was the last Sharpie tattoo I'd given him, the night everything had fallen apart with the four of us. And though I'd given it to him in May, months ago, it looked freshly done, the waves still endlessly cresting. And since Gideon didn't smell terrible, he'd obviously been bathing, which meant . . .

I looked up at him, and he took a step away, but not before I saw where I'd signed my name just to the side of his tricep—*Emily xoxo*. He'd been coloring it in ever since—those lines I'd drawn without any real thought to them, just to kill some time. It felt like someone had just punched me, and I felt dizzy in a way that had nothing to do with the beer.

He slowly rolled his sleeve down, and I finally let myself see it—the pain I'd caused him, the damage I'd left behind. "Gideon," I started. "I'm sorry—" But he was already turning away from me.

"Sure," he said, his voice flat and sarcastic.

"I am," I said, taking an unsteady step closer to him, resting my hand on the hood of his car. I wished that I was more sober for this, because getting my thoughts in line was a struggle, but I knew I had to at least try. "Listen. I shouldn't have ended things like that." As soon as I said it, I realized that I probably also shouldn't have been dating him in the first place, but wasn't sure that would be helpful to say. "I never meant to hurt you. Really." I searched his face, trying to see if this had gotten through, these words I should have said months ago.

Gideon looked at me for just a moment before shaking his head, pulling open his door, and getting in his car. "See you," he said, not looking at me. Then he pulled out of the Orchard, his lights briefly lighting up the old faded sign, with its ever-hopeful, twinned cherries.

I watched his taillights until they got more and more distant and then faded from view entirely. I realized, in that moment, that I hadn't needed to destroy Bryan's sunglasses in the Paradise parking lot. Because it was clear to me now that I'd already broken something.

Frank arrived at the car a few minutes later and unlocked the doors. I got into my passenger seat, where I wasn't sure I'd ever sat before. I looked at him as he adjusted the seat, pushing himself back from the steering wheel, then starting my car and pulling out into the night.

"So who was that guy earlier?" Frank asked after a moment, glancing over at me. "The one you clearly wanted to get away from?"

"Gideon," I said. "My . . . ex, I guess." I wasn't sure I had the right to call him that, since we'd never been official. But he was really the closest thing I had to one.

"Oh yeah?" Frank asked, looking away from the road for longer than I would have advised. But somehow, in my slightly fuzzy state, it didn't seem to bother me that much. "What happened?"

I shrugged, really not wanting to go into the whole thing—and not only because I had behaved in a way I wasn't proud of. "We weren't right for each other," I said, realizing as I said it that it was true. I took a breath. I was starting to talk again before I'd even worked out what I was going to say. "You wouldn't do that," I said, shaking my head. "Not without asking me." Frank glanced over at me, baffled, but I didn't stop to explain. "Of course you wouldn't." I could feel myself start to laugh at the thought of it. Frank wanting me to date someone like Sloane had was crazy, but if he did, I knew he'd be checking with me constantly, making sure I was okay with it. Frank drove me home when I had too much to drink, and scheduled horseback rides for me, and had seemed really alarmed that I'd never heard of a band called the Format, and made me a mix to correct it. He looked out for me. "But I wouldn't do it now, either," I said. I wouldn't agree to it now. The fact that I'd just let Sloane set me up with Gideon, barely asking any questions, seemed like it had happened a long time ago now.

"You know I have no idea what you're talking about, right?" Frank asked as he made the left onto the street that would take me home.

"I know," I said. I thought about trying to explain it to him, but then just decided to let it go. "I'm sorry about Lissa."

Frank glanced over at me, then back at the road again. He leaned forward slightly, and moonlight from the open roof spilled across his face, lighting him up. "It was okay," he said slowly, like he was trying out these words, in this order, for the first time. "It turned out fine. And I had a great birthday."

"Really?" I asked, a little doubtfully, thinking of Lissa bailing, of Wanda's cake, of having to drive me home.

"Really," he said firmly. "I mean, I started off the day being serenaded by donut shop employees, so it was pretty fantastic."

"I'm still just sorry about this—making you drive me on my birthday." He glanced over at me, one eyebrow raised, and it occurred to me after a moment this wasn't quite right. "Your birthday," I said, trying to get my thoughts in line. "Drive me on your birthday."

"It's really not a big deal," he said. "It's the least I could do after you trekked down to New Jersey to get Lissa."

"Not all the way," I said. "She called me about halfway there." Frank nodded, and I leaned back against the passenger-side door, curling my legs under me. I stretched my hand up through the open roof, feeling the warm night air rush around and through my fingers, looking up at all the stars that were visible tonight. In the dark car, with only the dashboard light, it looked like I could maybe reach them, if only I tried hard enough.

I leaned my head back against the window. My neck felt liquid and relaxed; despite what had just happened with Gideon, I was feeling somehow peaceful as I watched Frank driving me home. "You're driving my car," I said, shaking my head. "Nobody ever drives my car but me. It feels like I'm always driving other people around."

"How am I doing?"

"Good," I concluded after a moment. "It's acceptable."

Frank smiled at that, and when we reached my house, he pulled the car into the spot I always parked in, and as he killed the engine and handed my keys to me, it hit me that he knew where I parked my car. He knew where I lived, and didn't need directions to bring me home.

We just sat in the car for a moment, looking ahead at my house, which was dark and quiet. Even all the cicadas seemed to have signed off for the night, and it was like the whole world was sleeping, the moon above out in full force and lighting everything up.

"Wait," I said suddenly, turning to him.

He smiled. "I'm not going anywhere, Em."

"No," I said, shaking my head. "I mean, how are you going to get home?"

"I'll walk," he said. "It's not that far. I do it every day, after all."

"But that's during the day," I pointed out. "It's nighttime now. There could be vagrants. Or coyotes."

Frank just shook his head, still smiling. "I think I'll be okay." He got out of the driver's seat, and I scrambled out of the passenger side to follow him.

"Well, then I'll walk with you," I said, and Frank stopped in the driveway and shook his head, turning to me.

"That doesn't make any sense," he said, his voice patient. "Because then *you'd* have to walk back here, and I'm not letting you do that in your present state."

"Oh my god!" I said, maybe more loudly than I should have, since it seemed particularly loud against the quiet of the night, and Frank glanced toward my sleeping house. "*Present!* I forgot to give it to you! Hold on."

"Still not going anywhere," he pointed out, and I could hear a laugh somewhere in his voice. I walked back to the car and yanked the wrapped package out from where I'd hidden it behind the front seat.

"Here," I said, walking back to him and holding it out.

"You really didn't have to do this," he said, shaking his head.

"Of course I did," I said, reaching out and giving his arm a small push. But it didn't quite work out like I'd hoped, and my hand lingered a little too long on his arm before I got my thoughts working and pulled it back again. Somewhere in the more lucid part of my brain, I knew that was something I would have not ordinarily done, but it had already happened before that part of my brain could catch up to things.

Frank unwrapped the package slowly and carefully, and as he got closer to seeing what it was, I suddenly wondered if I'd chosen the wrong thing, or if he would think this was stupid. "No way," he said as he pulled back the final corner and held up the CD I'd had to track down online. *Curtis Anderson—Bootlegs and B-Sides.* It was a comedy CD that had a tiny printing and hadn't done well, but from everything I'd been able to glean, it was considered his best. I'd had to bid against anderfan2020 on eBay in a heated auction, but I'd gotten it in the end.

"I just thought," I said, wishing I wasn't so worried about his reaction, "that, you know, in a well-ordered universe, you would already have this. So . . ."

Frank shook his head and looked up at me. "I can't believe you did this."

"You can return it if you want," I said, even as I said it, wondering if that would be possible. But I was pretty sure at the very least, I could probably sell it to anderfan2020.

"Are you kidding?" he said, turning it over to read the back. "This is fantastic. Thank you."

I felt myself start to yawn, and Frank tucked the CD under his arm. "You should get some sleep," he said, starting to head toward the road.

"I'll walk you," I insisted, falling into step next to him.

"Then I'm just going to have to walk you back," he pointed out.

"Stop halfway?"

Frank looked at me for a moment, then nodded. "Deal," he said, and we walked together down the driveway, and turned left onto the road. Since it was totally deserted out, we could walk down the middle of the road, each of us taking one side of the center yellow line. The moonlight was so bright that it was casting our shadows onto the asphalt, and we walked in silence that felt totally comfortable, like maybe we didn't need to talk just then.

I yawned again, and Frank stopped walking. "I'm walking you home now," he said, changing direction.

"What happened to halfway?" I asked, even as I turned around as well and started walking back toward my house.

"I was never going to actually do that," he said. "I mean, there could be coyotes out here. Or vagrants."

"Good point," I said, trying to stop myself from smiling but not really succeeding. "Hey," I said, suddenly thinking of something that I'd been wondering all night. "What do you think

Wanda did?" When Frank just stared at me, looking baffled, I added, "Cake Wanda?"

"Oh," he said, as understanding dawned. "I was wondering about that, myself. Maybe she broke out of prison."

"Or she won the lottery," I suggested. "And her friends realized she could afford a *much* better cake."

He laughed. "She rid the town of its chronic vagrants-and-coyotes problem."

I smiled at that, and we walked in silence for a moment before I said, "Maybe she didn't do something big. Maybe she just told someone something."

Frank looked over at me, more serious now. "Like what?"

I shrugged. "Something they'd been needing to hear," I said. I thought it over for a moment, then added, "I don't think you have to do something so big to be brave. And it's the little things that are harder anyway."

"And you usually don't get cakes for doing them," Frank pointed out. He stopped walking, and I realized we'd made it back to my house. I was about to protest, to offer to walk him halfway back, when I was suddenly hit with another wave of fatigue, and I yawned hugely.

"Thanks for walking me home," I said, looking across the road at him. "And for, um, driving me home as well."

"Of course," he said. He lifted his CD. "Thank you for this."

I just looked at him in the moonlight for a long moment— something I knew, even as I was doing it, that I never would have done if I'd been stone-cold sober. "Happy birthday, Frank."

He smiled at me, looking tired but happy. "Good night, Emily."

I walked down the driveway to my house, and I knew without looking back to check that Frank was still there, waiting to see that I got in okay. And sure enough, after I'd unlocked the door, I turned around and saw him, alone in the road, CD under his arm, moon shadow stretching out behind him. From the doorway, I raised a hand in a wave, and Frank waved back, then turned and started walking home himself.

10
RIDE A DERN HORSE, YA COWPOKE

"You've got this," Frank assured me as I stared at the riding ring in front of me and tried to remember how to breathe.

"Totally," Dawn said, giving my shoulders a squeeze. Collins's mouth was full, but he gave me a thumbs-up.

I was back at Saddleback Ranch, figuring that at this point, so close to the end, I should follow Sloane's list to the letter. And it *didn't* say pony ride. When I'd told Frank I was ready to give it another shot, he'd booked the time, and then everyone else had decided to come along. They claimed it was for moral support, but I had a feeling it was to stop me from bailing again. And since Dawn was here—wielding my How Emily Sees the World disposable camera—it wasn't like

I'd be able to take a call from her and pretend it was urgent.

The horse that I was going to be riding was named Butterscotch, which seemed much better to me than Bucky, and Frank had assured me that he'd requested their smallest non-pony horse. The woman in charge had told me what to expect before she went to get the horse from the stables. She'd offered me a trail ride, which I had immediately turned down. When she finally seemed to get that I was only doing this to conquer a fear, she'd proposed just having the horse walk with me around the ring a few times.

"Aw, it's so cute!" Dawn said. I turned to see where she was looking, and saw the Saddleback Ranch woman leading out a lumbering horse who looked half asleep. It didn't put me at ease—it was still a horse, after all—but it was about half the size of Bucky, and the very sight of it didn't terrify me.

"Not at all evil or scary," Frank said, giving me a smile.

"Do you want to go make friends with it first?" Dawn asked. "Matthew, give Emily the snacks."

Collins swallowed, looking alarmed. "Um . . . what do you mean?"

Dawn smiled at him. "So we can give them to the horse! The carrot sticks?"

"Oh," Collins said, after a pause. "You see, you should have told me we were bringing snacks for the horse. I thought they were for us. My bad."

"Wait, you ate all of them?" Dawn asked, taking her canvas

bag back from Collins and peering inside. "The apple too? And where are the sugar cubes?"

"You're telling me we brought the sugar for a *horse*?" Collins asked, incredulous. "What does a horse need sugar for?"

"I can't believe you just ate raw sugar cubes," Dawn said, shaking her head.

"They're sugar cubes!" Collins said, his voice rising. "What else are you supposed to do with them? And since when do horses get snacks?"

"It's okay," I said. "Really." While I appreciated the thought, I didn't want to put my hand anywhere near the horse's mouth and give it an opportunity to bite me.

"Ready?" the woman called from the center of the ring.

I felt everyone's eyes swivel over to me, and I nodded, and made myself walk toward the horse, even though the only thing I wanted to do was turn and run back to my car. The woman helped me get one foot into the stirrup, and I swung my other leg over the horse's back. Once I was in the saddle, I gripped the reins, bracing myself for the worst—the horse would throw me off, or start running at a gallop, or drop to the ground and roll over me. But none of that happened. Butterscotch just stood there, her sides expanding slightly under my legs as she breathed in and out.

"You look great!" Dawn called, giving me a thumbs-up.

"Oh, you know what? It looks like Butterscotch fell asleep," the woman said. "Just give her a gentle kick."

That sounded like a terrible idea to me, but once I nudged her a little, Butterscotch woke up, shaking her head in a way that made me grab onto the saddle. But that was about as violent as she got. She started to lumber around the ring, and I didn't have to do anything. It was like she'd done this hundreds of times and knew just where to go. I would occasionally feel myself start to panic as I felt the horse moving beneath me, but I tried just to keep breathing. After all, I had hugged gas station employees and almost gotten in fights and kissed strangers in pantries. I could do this.

And as she walked around the ring, not seeming at all like she had any desire to knock me off her back and make a run for it—and truly, if she did, it wasn't *that* far to fall—I started to breathe a little easier. This wasn't so bad. It wasn't something I was going to start doing on a regular basis, but it was okay. I was okay.

"Smile!" Dawn yelled from the side of the ring, holding up my disposable camera. I gave her what I was sure was more like a grimace, but I was actually glad that she was documenting this. And as Butterscotch and I went around the ring one last time, I even felt myself relaxing just a little bit, trying to enjoy, if I could, what was left of the ride.

"So where are you with the list?" Collins asked as we all congregated around our cars. I think the woman had seemed surprised that I had only wanted to be on the horse for five minutes, but helped me down anyway, and I'd even given

Butterscotch a tentative—*very* gentle—pat as she went back to the stables.

We'd taken four separate cars there, which probably wasn't great for our carbon footprints, but when I'd asked Frank if he wanted to carpool, he'd told me that he had to get ready for something right after, and was vague when I asked him for details.

"Three left," Dawn said, her brow furrowed. "Or four. Right?"

Before I could answer, Frank jumped in. "Three. Dancing, the dress, and skinny-dipping."

I nodded, all too aware that I'd left two of the hardest ones for last. Whereas the dress thing had been taken care of with Frank's invitation, and I supposed I could always just dance all night in my room with my iPod playing, the skinny-dipping was still one that I wasn't sure how I was going to manage. But even despite that, the fact that I'd crossed off most of the list was still surprising to me. It had seemed so impossible when it had first showed up—and now it was almost over.

"Oh," Dawn said, looking down at her phone, her eyes widening. "I should get going."

"Deliveries?" Collins asked, handing her back the empty canvas bag.

"I wish," she sighed. "We're catering a wedding tonight at the Stanwich Country Club, and I have to help serve."

"You are?" Frank asked, sounding surprised.

SINCE YOU'VE BEEN GONE   *329*

"Yeah," Dawn said, with a shrug. "Sometimes people have different stations, for the food, you know, like sushi or whatever. And these people wanted an Italian station, so . . ."

Frank looked at Dawn a moment longer, then turned to me. "You should crash the wedding."

"What?" I asked, just as Collins asked, "She should?"

"Yeah," Frank said, nodding. "Dance until dawn!"

"I'm sorry," Collins said, shaking his head. "Who are you and what have you done with Frank Porter?"

"I can sneak you in!" Dawn said, clapping her hands together. "And we can hang out. I'm always so bored at those things, and everyone always pretends they can't see you. What are you going to wear?"

I turned to Frank, who was looking at me with a small smile, a challenge in his eyes. It *would* be a great opportunity to cross one off. And since I'd worked there last summer, I was pretty sure I knew the Stanwich Country Club well enough to navigate my way around without getting caught. "Okay," I said to Frank, then nodded at Dawn. "Let's do this."

11
DANCE
UNTIL
DAWN

In my cupholder, my phone buzzed and I pulled it out. "The man with the umbrella does not see the sunset," I said, keeping my voice low.

On the other end, I could hear Dawn doing the same. "In Rome, the fountains all face north." When we'd decided to do this, Frank had given us a crash course in spy codes, but I'd already forgotten what most of them meant, and had the distinct feeling Dawn had as well, and that we were both still using them because it was fun.

"Jenga," I whispered as I looked around, slouching low in my seat. I still couldn't quite believe I was about to do this. There was silence on Dawn's end, and I added, "I mean, I just parked."

I'd gotten ready up in my room, putting on the dress I'd worn to last year's prom. It was pale gold, strapless, and tea-length, fitted at the waist with just a slight flare in the skirt. As I got ready, I had my fingers crossed that this wedding wasn't themed, and that I wasn't going to show up wearing the completely wrong thing. I'd curled my hair so the layers framed my face and put on much more makeup than usual, and by the time I'd finished my best attempt at a smoky eye, Dawn had texted.

Dancing getting started! See you soon?

I texted back, and then grabbed the tiny beaded clutch I'd borrowed from my mother without asking. I wasn't sure how late the wedding was going to go, and after my mother's lecture on the porch, I didn't want to push my luck, so I'd asked if I could sleep over at Dawn's house. My mom had agreed—she remembered Dawn from when she'd met her briefly at Living Room Theater. And even if I didn't end up sleeping over, I knew this would let me come home late without anyone waiting up for me. But even so, as I crossed to the door, I was glad that it was late enough at night that my parents were locked in their study. I think even in their close-to-the-end brain fog, they might have had some questions about why I was attending a sleepover in formal wear.

I still had last summer's employee parking sticker on my car, and I hoped nobody would be looking at it too closely tonight. But as I pulled into the parking lot, I didn't feel as nervous as

I'd expected to. I was even hoping it might be fun. I felt myself smile as I walked, thinking about how nervous I'd been just to go into Paradise and talk to Mona—and what a difference a summer could make. Dawn had texted me the location, and I hurried around from the employee parking lot to the main grounds, slowing down once I saw other wedding guests, just trying to look like I was out for a stroll.

"Open sesame," I said into my phone. "I'm on my way."

"Copy that," Dawn said, "over and out."

She hung up and I crossed toward the reception, which was set up under a big tent on the lawn. I could hear music coming from it as I got closer. I took a big breath and stepped under the tent. It looked like everyone had abandoned the tables, because the dance floor was packed. There was a live band playing, not a DJ, and even though I didn't have much experience with wedding bands, I could tell they were good, the lead singer belting out a song that had been overplayed on the radio all summer, but somehow making it soulful and her own.

I edged along the side of the tent, where the food stations were set up, and tried to keep from laughing as Dawn approached me, a platter in her hand. "Can I get you anything?" she asked with a grin. "Bruschetta, perhaps?"

"No, I'm okay," I said, pressing my lips together to keep from smiling.

"Then go dance," Dawn said, bumping me with her hip in the direction of the dance floor. "That's why you're here, right?"

It was. I took a step toward the dance floor, just as the band launched into their rendition of "Cupid Shuffle." Sloane, on principle, hated songs where everyone danced together. It was the source of one of our biggest disagreements, about movie musicals—I loved them; she wasn't a fan. But I really liked when there was a pattern to follow, and you weren't just dancing on your own, trying to hope you didn't look like an idiot. So it was with some relief that I could start Cupid Shuffling along with all these people I didn't know, as we slowly turned in a circle as the song directed us to.

When they segued into "Footloose," I felt myself start to move to the beat without even thinking about it. I looked around, waiting for one of these strangers to point at me, to start whispering that nobody had seen me before, that someone should throw me out. But by the time the song was into the second chorus, it became clear to me that everyone there was much more interested in having a good time than in cataloging wedding guests. It was a fun group, too, people cheering or booing when they didn't like the song choice, everyone dancing enthusiastically if not with a great deal of skill. And even though I was on my own, even though I didn't have anyone to jump up and down and yell with when a favorite song came on, I felt myself getting into the music, finding freedom in the fact that these people didn't know me, nobody did, and so it didn't matter if I looked like an idiot.

Two songs later, I was hot and sweaty and having fun. The

Morgan Matson

music was loud, and I had my eyes closed as I swung my hips from side to side, letting my hair whip around my face. I hadn't been dancing since the prom, and I'd forgotten just how much I loved it. And when there was nobody to try and impress, no moves you have to edit for the sake of trying to look cool, it was that much more freeing. I tipped my head back and sang along when I knew the words, and when I didn't, I just danced, my hands up and swaying in the warm night air, not caring if anyone was watching or what they thought of me. My feet were hurting in my heels, and I had a feeling I had mascara all over my face, but I didn't care. I was having a good time. "You Shook Me All Night Long" came to a dramatic end, and I played air drums along with the drummer, feeling like if I couldn't dance until dawn, I could at least dance until the band called it a night, and Sloane would just have to be okay with that.

The band launched into their rendition of "Jack and Diane," and I brushed my sweaty hair out of my face. I looked around to see if I could see Dawn, and maybe get a water from her. I was scanning the crowd for her when I realized I recognized some-one in it—it was Frank, and he was looking right at me.

I felt my jaw fall open, and then closed it quickly. He walked across the dance floor to me, hands in the pockets of his suit, taking his time, like he was enjoying the fact that he'd just thrown me for a loop. "What are you doing here?" I asked, my voice low, once he reached me.

"I think I could ask you the same question," he said. "I

mean, you didn't think I was going to let you do this without me, did you?" He nodded toward the center table, where the happy couple was feeding each other cake. "The bride's my cousin."

"Why didn't you just tell me?" I asked.

"And miss the look on your face?" Frank asked, shaking his head. "Never." The band started playing their version of "I Gotta Feeling" and I found myself moving without even thinking about it, the pounding beat making it easier to forget that Frank was now watching me, that I didn't have quite the same freedom as before.

And five songs later, I'd totally forgotten it. Frank had taken off his jacket, and we were dancing up a storm, so much so that people were starting to give us a wide berth. He would twirl me in, then send me spinning, and I'd almost bonked my head twice on a centerpiece when he'd dipped me and I'd lost my balance. He wasn't the best dancer, but neither was I, and after a song or two we had found our groove and were dancing together as easily as we ran together. The band had just played a cover of "Sweet Caroline" that had everyone on their feet, and Frank and I had been yelling the *bum-bum-bum*s at each other. When the song ended, everyone clapped, and I felt myself laughing, not for any specific reason, just that I was flushed and tired and happy.

The bandleader announced that they were slowing it down, and they started playing "You Send Me," a song I'd always loved.

I looked around, still trying to see if I could find a water, about to suggest to Frank we sit this one out, when I saw that he had extended his hand to me.

I was on the verge of starting to make a joke, but whatever I'd been about to say left me as I saw Frank's serious expression. I met his eyes and reached out my hand to his. His fingers clasped around mine, and he pulled me close to him, gently, like he was making sure it was okay. I slid one of my arms around his neck, and he had one hand on my waist. Somehow, we were still holding hands, his fingers lightly wrapped around mine as we moved slowly to the music together.

He laughed softly and shook his head, and I leaned back to be able to look at his face, which was close to mine, closer than it had ever been. "What?"

"Just . . . you," he said after a moment, with a faint smile. "Crashing a wedding."

"Your idea."

"I know," Frank said. "But I was just thinking about that first night at the Orchard."

"What about it?" I asked. I was trying to focus on having a conversation with Frank, and trying not to think about how close together we were, that he was touching my waist, that he was holding my hand.

"You just seemed so . . . diminished," he said after a moment. "Like you were hoping nobody would see you."

I kept my eyes on his, not letting myself look away. "And now?"

He looked right back at me as he gave me a half smile. "You're the brightest thing in the room," he said. He lifted his hand from my waist, and slowly, carefully brushed a stray lock of hair from my cheek. "You shine."

My breath caught in my throat. People said those kinds of things about Sloane—not about me.

"What?" Frank asked, his eyes on mine.

"Just . . ." I took a shaky breath. "Nobody's ever said something like that to me."

"Then they don't see what I see," he said. I looked into Frank's eyes and knew, without a doubt, that he meant every word. I started to say something when the chorus kicked in and Frank moved closer to me.

He was tall enough, even in my heels, that I could have rested my head on his shoulder. I swallowed hard, feeling the need to try and freeze the moment and sort through everything that was happening, and figure out just what I was feeling. Our faces were close enough that I could see the constellation of his freckles, his dark eyelashes, and smell that he was wearing some kind of cologne for the occasion—it smelled like cedar, like early mornings, and it made me want to step even closer and breathe him in.

Frank's hand tightened on my waist, just a little bit, and it could have been just him moving with the music. But even though we weren't looking at each other—even though we both seemed to be working very hard *not* to look at each other—I had a feeling

No

338   *Morgan Matson*

he'd done it on purpose, and a moment later, he unclasped his hand from around mine and threaded my fingers through his.

I felt my heart pounding as I concentrated on staying upright and moving to the music, on the song that I knew was ending, any minute now, and I couldn't tell if I wanted it to end right then, or keep playing on for days. I looked up at him, realizing again just how close we were, when the song ended and "Pour Some Sugar on Me" started. He dropped my hand and took a step away, and I looked away, pretending to straighten my dress, not exactly sure what had just happened.

"Hey!" Dawn was approaching us, a half empty water bottle in her hand, smiling at Frank. "When did you get here?" She looked around hopefully. "Is Matthew here too?"

"No," Frank said, pointing at me. "I figured that one wedding crasher was enough."

I nodded at Dawn's water bottle. "Is there any way I could have some of that?"

"Sure," she said, handing it over. "All yours." She yawned and stretched her arms over her head. "I swear, I am never doing one of these again. It's much better to be on the road and actually getting tips. Thank god this is finally over."

"You're done?" I asked as I lowered her bottle, realizing I'd just drunk all of it. Dawn nodded.

"You guys want to come to my place and hang out?" Frank asked, as he pulled out his phone. "I'm not sure if Collins had plans, but I can text him . . ."

"Cool," Dawn said. "Sounds good."

"Em?" Frank asked, looking over at me as he texted.

"Actually," I said. I took a breath before speaking again, not quite able to believe I was about to suggest this. But I couldn't think of a better time, or one when I'd be so willing to take a risk. "I had an idea . . ."

12
GO
SKINNY-
DIPPING

"I can't believe this," Collins said as we stood in a line on the sand, still fully dressed, and looked out at the water. "And this was Emily's idea?"

"Yep," I said, still getting my head around that fact myself. "It's for the list."

"Please," Collins said, waving this away. "This is all just a grand scheme to check out my bod. You can admit it."

"So, um," Dawn said, twisting her hands together, sounding more nervous than I'd ever heard her, "do we have a plan? Like, are we going to go in one at a time while everyone else looks away? Or all at once? Or . . ."

"Emily?" Frank said, looking over at me with a smile, even

though I could see he was blushing—which he really hadn't stopped doing since I'd proposed this, back at the wedding.

Maybe it had been the hours of dancing, or the slow-dancing with Frank, or the fact that I'd been dehydrated, but skinny-dipping had sounded like such a good, easy option back then. But now, actually standing in front of the water and contemplating swimming in it naked—with my friends—things were no longer seeming quite so simple.

"Okay," I said after a minute, when I realized that since I had proposed this thing, I couldn't back down, and I needed to be the one to try and figure something out. I glanced up and wished, for the first time all summer, that the moon wasn't quite so full. It was like having a giant spotlight shining down on us. I looked at the stack of four beach towels that Frank had brought out from the house and tried to sound more confident than I felt. "Okay. I think we should all put on the towels, and then we can go with the towels down to the water, and then throw them aside and jump in." It seemed like the best plan I could think of for limiting out-of-the-water nudity.

"When did she get so bossy?" Collins muttered to Frank, shaking his head.

"I just think," I started, "this way, we'll all feel comfortable, and—"

"To heck with that," Collins said as he kicked off his flip-flops and yanked off his polo shirt, getting it stuck briefly on his head. When he started to drop his shorts, I realized where this was going and turned away, and after a noticeable pause, Dawn did too. "Here I go!" I heard Collins yell, and I looked a second too soon, seeing Collins's bare butt as he dove into the water. "Agh! That's cold!" he yelled, then held his nose and ducked under. But he was grinning when he surfaced again, and waved us in. "Come on," he called.

"I think I'm going to do the towel thing," Dawn said, grabbing hers, and I took one as well.

"Me too," I said.

I glanced at Frank's neighbors' houses, to make sure they were all staying dark, but it didn't seem like we'd woken anybody up. Dawn and I walked a little bit up the beach, and I held up my towel for her, blocking her from view while she took everything off and wrapped herself in the towel, and then she did the same for me. I knew this was ridiculous, since we were going skinny-dipping, but I just didn't think I was ready to run full-out buck naked toward the water Collins-style. By the time we headed back to the water, clutching our towels, Frank had gotten in as well, and was next to Collins in the water. I could just see their bare chests, and tried to tell myself I would have seen them anyway if we'd all been swimming, that it wasn't a big deal. But I still felt my heart pound as the boys turned away so that Dawn and I could run in.

"Ready?" I asked, looking at her.

"I don't know," she said, shifting from foot to foot. She

looked toward the water, biting her lip. "I'm not sure . . ."

"Come on." I smiled at her. "It'll be fun." And without waiting, without thinking about it, I dropped my towel and ran toward the water, feeling the cool night air on my skin, feeling utterly free, my hair streaming out behind me, as I splashed into the water and then extended my arms above my head and dove under.

When I surfaced, I saw Dawn plunging into the water as well, doing more of a belly-flop than a dive, emerging with her hair plastered down. "That *is* cold!" she gasped, grinning at me. "Oh my god."

But cold or not, the water felt amazing, and I realized just how different it was from swimming with a bathing suit on. It reminded me of sleeping under the stars—with nothing between you and the elements.

Soon, it just felt normal to be swimming together like this—you couldn't really see anything under the water, anyway. The four of us would swim on our own and then come back together, and even when we were just treading water or standing with our feet touching the sand, talking, it felt that much more exciting, because I knew that under the water, we were all naked.

After we'd been in the water for a while, I swam apart from the group, out of view, so that I could just float on my back and look up at the sky. I was aware of Collins calling to us, saying that the C-dawg was getting out, and then the sound of splashing as he presumably made his way up to the beach. I let myself float there for just a little while, feeling really content and at peace. I was still a little amazed that this was happening. That this, the thing that had seemed so impossible, so terrifying, so utterly beyond me, was happening. I was having fun. And that I was the one who made it happen. "I did it," I said out loud, sending my voice up to the stars above me, not really caring if the others heard me.

"Guys?" Dawn called, her voice sounding worried. I ducked under the water and surfaced again, smoothing my hair down and swimming over to her. "Where are our towels?"

I looked toward the beach as well, and saw what she meant. The towels that she and I had left there were nowhere to be seen. I could see my clothes, in a pile way up the beach, but the thought of running across that expanse of sand, naked, did not seem that appealing.

"Collins!" I yelled, as Frank swam over toward us.

"What's the problem?" he asked.

"Our towels are gone," I said, still scanning the sand for them.

"What?" Collins asked, emerging on Frank's deck, dressed in shorts and an oversized sweater. I realized after a moment that I could tell they were Frank's clothes.

"Are you wearing my clothes?" Frank yelled, and Collins shrugged.

"I was cold," he called back. "Is there some sort of problem?"

"What did you do with the towels, Collins?"

"Me?" he asked, looking offended. "Nothing. Why would you presume it was me?"

"Who else would it be?" Dawn asked.

"I don't know," Collins said with a shrug. "Beach hobos? See you guys inside." He gave us all a grin and disappeared back in the house.

"I'm going to kill him," Frank muttered as he looked over at me. I hadn't realized he'd come quite so close, and especially after we'd danced together, it was disconcerting to realize that Frank Porter was naked, right next to me. And that I was naked right next to him, with nothing separating us but water.

"I see them!" Dawn said, pointing. The towels were neatly folded, almost at the top of the beach by Frank's steps. "Should we go one by one, or . . . ?"

"On the count of three, maybe?" Frank suggested.

"Let's just go!" I yelled, as I splashed out of the water, running toward the beach. I was half yelling and half laughing as I went, feeling the warm night air on my skin. I heard splashing behind me and figured that Frank and Dawn had started running as well.

Someone crashed into me—it was Dawn, running with her eyes closed. "God! Sorry!" she yelped as she changed direction, and started running toward Frank's neighbor's house.

"Dawn," I called. I looked around, just to try and see if I was heading in the right direction, and saw Frank's bare back in the moonlight, then immediately looked away again. I ran faster, then realized I was reaching the towels at the same time as Frank. "Sorry," I said as we both turned away, but not before I saw a full view of those abs that I'd only gotten glimpses of before.

Some part of me realized how absurd this was, Frank and I standing next to each other—naked—neither of us sure where to look or who was going to get a towel first. I kept looking over at him, then immediately looking away, trying not to see too much, but getting quick flashes—Frank's chest, his jawline, his hipbone . . .

I crossed my arms over my chest and turned my head just slightly to see that Frank was looking away. "I'll get a towel first?" I asked, and he nodded. I grabbed one from the pile and wrapped it around me. I took another for Dawn, who was still running in the wrong direction, weaving up the beach.

"Got it," I said to Frank, and then turned my head away before I saw anything else. "Dawn!" I yelled to her, holding out the towel in front of my face. "Come toward my voice!"

"Thank you," Dawn said as she hurried over to me and took the towel. "I couldn't see where I was going!"

"Who knows, the Farrellys probably wouldn't have minded," Frank said as he came over to us, his towel riding low on his hips. I felt myself swallow hard, thinking of the full glimpse I'd just gotten, and also wondering if there was a way I could suggest that he maybe stop wearing a shirt on our runs.

"I've got your clothes," Dawn said, snapping me out of this and making me realize I was still staring at Frank's bare chest.

"Right," I said, suddenly feeling very warm, despite the fact the water had been cold and I'd been shivering a few minutes ago. We headed up to the deck, where Collins was now standing, a mug in his hand and a satisfied smile on his face.

"I'm going to kill you," Frank told him matter-of-factly.

"Oh, come on. Admit it, that was much more fun," Collins said. "The real skinny-dipping experience. You're all welcome. Now, who wants hot chocolate?"

By the time I pulled into my driveway, it was almost light out. Frank had found clothes for me, since I really didn't want to attempt to get back into a formal dress after an ocean swim—a soft pair of gray sweatpants, and the academic decathlon shirt he'd worn the first day we'd gone running together. We ended up just sitting around Frank's kitchen island, drinking the hot chocolate Collins had made, and then finally just eating all the marshmallows, until it was almost five. Then Dawn and I headed home, Collins crashed on Frank's couch, and Frank waved good night to us from his doorway.

I killed the engine and caught my reflection in the rearview mirror. My hair was in tangles, and the wedding makeup I'd worn was half washed off, half smeared under my eyes. But my cheeks were flushed and even though I looked like a mess, I looked happy. I looked like someone who'd had a night, and had a story to tell about it. Which was, I realized as I collected my dress and heels in my arms and made my way, yawning, to the front door in the cool early light, exactly what had happened.

13
THE BACKLESS DRESS. AND SOMEWHERE TO WEAR IT

"Hello?" I answered my phone without opening my eyes. It was two days after we'd gone skinny-dipping, and far too early to be awake if I wasn't going to be out running. And since Frank had gone camping with Collins, I wasn't running—which meant I should still be sleeping.

"Morning," Frank said, far too cheerful in the morning as usual, and I rolled onto my side, eyes still closed, holding my phone up to my ear.

"Hey," I said, smiling. "How's the camping trip?"

"Uh," Frank said. "Have you looked outside yet?" I suddenly became aware of a steady, rhythmic sound hitting the window and roof. I opened my eyes and pushed my bedroom curtains aside. The sky was gray and there was rain beating down against my window.

"Oh," I said, leaning back against my pillows. "So I take it the camping trip is off?" I asked.

"Off," Frank confirmed. "And Collins is really upset about it, for some reason."

"Well," I said, glancing out to the rain again. Even if they put it off for a day, I had a feeling the ground might be too wet to camp successfully. "Maybe you guys can reschedule?"

"I was thinking the same thing," he said, and even though I couldn't see him, I was pretty sure he was smiling. "Are you busy tonight?"

"No," I said slowly, not sure what I would be letting myself in for by admitting this. "Why?"

"I'm going to text you an address," he said. "And see if Dawn's free too."

"Okay," I said, and waited for some more information, but apparently none was going to be forthcoming. "What is this?" I finally asked.

"You'll see," he said, and he was definitely smiling now, I was sure of it. "Be there at nine. And you might want to bring a sleeping bag."

"You're sleeping over at Dawn's again?" my mother asked, blinking at me. She and my father both had the bleary-eyed look of people who had spent too much time in front of their computer screens.

"Yeah," I said, trying to tell myself that this was only a slight tweaking of the facts. I still didn't even know what Frank had invited me to, but like the night of the wedding and skinny-dipping, I knew that telling my mother I had a sleepover would at least buy me a late night out, no questions asked. Or so I had thought. "Is that okay?"

"Fine with me," my dad said, pushing his glasses up on top of his head and rubbing the bridge of his nose. "Just make sure you have her over here too, to thank her. Okay?"

I nodded, thrilled that this had been so easy. "Sure," I said. "Great."

I started to go when I realized my mother was still looking at me, her head tilted slightly to the side. "When's Sloane back, Em?"

"Oh," I said, surprised by the question. "I—I'm not exactly sure."

"Sloane," my dad said, leaning back in his chair and shaking his head. "Is she doing okay?"

I looked at him, completely confused by this. "Why wouldn't she be?"

"She just always seemed a little . . . lost to me," he said. I was about to take a breath, try and refute this, since it was the opposite of everything I'd ever thought about her, but my dad was putting his glasses back on and squinting at the computer. "Do we really have to have the death scene with the pigeon?" he asked with a sigh.

"You know we do," my mother said, shaking her head and leaning closer to her own monitor. "I'm as happy about it as you are."

Normally, I stayed out of my parents' writing process. They either told me far more than I wanted to know, or got defensive if I asked the simplest questions. But I was not about to let this one slide. "Pigeon?"

My dad was already typing with one hand, and used the other one to point at my mom. "As Tesla was dying," she started.

"In a hotel room," my dad interrupted. "Can you think of anything sadder?"

My mom went on. "As he was dying, he kept telling people that he was in love with a pigeon outside his window."

I just stared at them. "A pigeon."

She nodded. "He said it was the most beautiful thing he'd ever seen. That it could see into his soul. That it was special." She started to type again as well, and I knew that I could go now, having secured my permission to go, and that my parents were a few seconds away from not even being able to tell if I was still in the room. But I didn't think I could leave it like that. "And?" I asked. "Was it? Special, I mean?"

My mother glanced over at me and gave me a sad smile. "No," she said. "It was just a pigeon." They both started typing again, their keyboards making a kind of music together. I listened for just a moment before I backed out of the dining room and closed the door quietly behind me.

Morgan Matson

"Any idea what this is about?" Dawn asked me as we both got out of our cars and walked toward the front door. I had a sleeping bag rolled under my arm, and I saw that Dawn did as well—and that she'd also been smart enough to bring along a pillow, which I now realized I'd forgotten. It had stopped raining an hour or so before, but everything was still chilly and damp, and there was the feeling in the air like the rain could start up again at any moment.

"None," I said. Frank had texted me an address that hadn't meant anything to me, but as soon as I'd pulled into the driveway, I'd recognized it. It was the spec house, the one that was sitting empty, the one we'd passed while running.

Frank pulled open the door before we'd even had the chance to knock, and stood on the threshold, smiling at us. "Hey," he said, holding the door open. "Welcome to indoor camping."

"Indoor what?" Dawn asked as we stepped inside. I immediately took off my flip-flops and put them next to Frank and Collins's shoes, and Dawn followed my lead. The walls of the foyer were bright white and the wooden floors were pristine, and the last thing I wanted to do was to track mud all over the place.

"Indoor camping," Frank repeated. He gave me a look. "Someone once told me that in a well-ordered universe it's the only way to camp." He smiled and then led us into the main room, and I saw what he meant. The room—the whole house—was totally empty, no furniture anywhere, not a single decoration or knickknack cluttering up the place. Except, that is, for two round camping tents that had been erected in the middle of the room. There was an entire camp set up in the empty room, including folding chairs and a Coleman lantern. "It seemed like the next best thing."

"And plus, no bugs," Dawn said. She rolled out her sleeping bag next to one of the tents. "This is awesome."

"Is it okay we're here?" I asked Frank in a low voice.

He shrugged. "It's not like anyone's bought it," he said, a bitter note in his voice that I hated to hear. "So as long as we don't wreck the place, I think it'll be fine."

Since there was no electricity—or any lights or appliances that ran on electricity—it was actually more like real camping than I'd been anticipating. When it got dark outside, it got dark inside the house as well, the only light coming from the flickering lantern we'd set up in the center of the "camp."

Collins, for some reason, had been withdrawn all night, not really participating or hanging out with us, and he'd retired to his tent pretty early and zipped the flap closed. I could see that Dawn looked hurt by this, but kept up a brave face anyway, trying her best to join in when Frank decided we should tell ghost stories, despite the fact that all she could seem to contribute was a recap of the last slasher film she'd seen. She decided to call it a night pretty soon after that, moving her sleeping bag so that it was next to Collins's tent, and zipping it up around her shoulders.

And then it was just me and Frank and a flickering lantern throwing huge shadows against the unadorned white walls. He headed into his round orange tent, and I spread out my sleeping bag on the floor, now really regretting not bringing a pillow along with me. I had balled my sweatshirt up under my head, and was trying to find a place where my face wasn't hitting the zipper, when Frank stuck his head out of his tent.

"Night, Emily," he called, reaching over to turn off the lantern.

"Night," I called back, giving him a smile and trying not to wince as some of my hair got caught in the zipper.

"What are you doing?" he asked, keeping his voice low.

"Nothing," I said, a little defensively. "Just . . . you know, sleeping."

"Where's your pillow?" he asked. There was a loud sigh and the sound of someone turning over in Collins's tent, and Frank glanced over at it, then walked closer to me, kneeling down in front of my sleeping bag. "Where's your pillow?" he asked, more softly.

The light from the lantern was playing over his features, lighting them up and then throwing them into darkness again. I registered that he was now dressed for bed, wearing a light gray T-shirt that looked soft and a pair of long shorts. Since I hadn't known I'd be staying over—which I really should have, given the fact he'd told me to bring a sleeping bag—I was still in the T-shirt and leggings I'd come in, which happily could double as sleep clothes. But I'd wriggled my way out of my bra under the sleeping bag, and so made sure to keep holding the sleeping bag up high as Frank knelt next to me.

"I didn't bring one," I said, with a shrug. "But I'm fine. I have a sweatshirt. And it's just as good."

"It's not," Frank said, a note of finality in his voice, and I suddenly wondered if he wanted me to go home. "It's ridiculous to sleep like that all night."

"Oh," I said, feeling more disappointed by this thought than I should have been. But it was like my heart just plunged into the bottom of my sleeping bag. "Well. I can go, then, I guess."

Frank smiled and shook his head. "Don't be stupid," he said. "Come share mine. It's big enough for two."

"But—" I started, but Frank had already taken the lantern with him and headed for his tent. "Frank!" I shout-whispered, but a second later, the light from the lantern went out. Collins sighed loudly from his tent again, and I realized I had limited options. I could stay out here, using my very uncomfortable sweatshirt as a pillow, and probably wake up with a zipper scar across my face that would make me look like a pirate; or I could share Frank's tent with him. Would it seem weird if I didn't?

And even though *Sleep next to Frank Porter* hadn't been on Sloane's list, the thought of it still felt incredibly scary. But there was no other real option, unless I wanted to draw attention to the fact that I thought it might mean something when he obviously didn't. And the fact was, I wanted to. I didn't know what that meant, and didn't really want to think about what it meant just now. I spent a futile few minutes trying to get my bra back on in the dark, then gave up and just stuffed it into the bottom of my sleeping bag, then crawled out of it and walked over to Frank's tent, pulling my sleeping bag behind me.

The flap was half down and I unzipped it all the way. My eyes had adjusted to the dark enough that I could see Frank sit up and smile at me. "Hey," he said, his voice quiet but suddenly seeming loud in this small, enclosed space.

"Hi," I murmured as I pulled my sleeping bag inside. Though I couldn't see much, the interior of the tent seemed smaller than it had from the outside. But it was a two-person tent, and Frank's sleeping bag was on one side that seemed demarcated by the seam that ran over the top. I turned away from him as I got into the sleeping bag, then pulled it up in front of me.

"See?" Frank asked, moving his pillow so that it was right in the center of the seam, and between our two sleeping bags. "More than enough room. Much better than a sweatshirt."

I lay down slowly, mostly sticking to my edge of the pillow—though it did actually seem to be an extra wide one, and it wasn't like Frank and I were forced to lie right next to each other.

I was aware of how *quiet* it was in the tent—just the sound of Frank's breathing and the occasional crinkle of one of our sleeping bags and, from the roof far above, the sound of the rain that must have started up again. I felt my eyes start to get heavy, and could hear that Frank's breathing was growing slow and even. And though I couldn't see details—he was just a nearby shape in the dark—I knew I could have reached out and touched his face without extending my arm. "Good night," I whispered into the darkness.

"Night, Em," Frank said, his voice slow and peaceful, like he could drop off at any moment and not be sure if this conversation had just been part of his dream.

I curled up on my side, facing him, and felt myself relax into the pillow we were sharing. And before I dropped off to sleep myself, I registered that our breath was now rising and falling together.

****

Before I was even fully awake, I could sense that something was different. I opened my eyes and realized after a second that I wasn't in my bed at home. I realized another second later that I was lying in a tent with Frank, and that his arm was around my shoulders.

I felt myself freeze as I tried to assess the sleeping arrangement we had moved into sometime during the night. I was lying on my side, and so was Frank, both of us facing the same way. We were still in our respective sleeping bags, but we had moved nearer during the night, and we were now lying close together, fitted next to each other like two spoons. Our heads were close on the pillow, and Frank's arm was over my shoulders and resting by my elbow.

Morgan Matson

I didn't move for what felt like at least a minute or two, reminding myself to keep breathing in and out. When I'd gotten the hang of respiring again, I turned, a millimeter at a time, pausing every time it seemed like there was a hitch in Frank's breath, until I was lying on my other side, and we were facing each other. The light was cool—it must have been early still—but I could see Frank perfectly. He had a crease running down the side of his face and his normally neat hair was sticking up.

And as I lay there next to him, his arm still around me, as we shared a pillow, I realized that I liked him.

Of course, I liked him as a friend. But this was different. This was more than that. This was wanting to reach over and touch his cheek, lightly, so as not to wake him. This was what had been bouncing around somewhere in my mind ever since the night of his birthday when I'd looked at him just a little too long in the moonlight. It was what I'd felt when we'd danced at the wedding. It was why I'd felt so awkward, going to pick up Lissa. It was why I wanted to stay exactly where I was, but why I also knew I needed to go.

I closed my eyes again for just a minute, even though I knew I wasn't going to be able to get back to sleep, or stop these revelations from crashing down on me. It was like hitting the snooze button on your alarm—your sleep in that window is never very good, since you know it's borrowed time, and that it will be over all too soon.

I let myself look at him a moment longer, knowing I'd never

be this close to him again, then feeling sick when I wondered if he and Lissa had ever shared this tent, too. And, really, what was I doing there? I needed to leave.

I eased myself out from under Frank's arm and then out of my sleeping bag. I didn't want to wake him, didn't want to have an awkward conversation. I just left my sleeping bag where it was rather than deal with how disruptive it would be to try and get it out of the tent. I unzipped the flap as slowly as possible, checking in with Frank to make sure this wasn't waking him, then crawled out of it and zipped it back up. I tiptoed across the floor, shook out my sweatshirt, and then pulled it on. It was chilly outside the tent, in an unheated house with no rugs, and I rubbed my hands together and turned back to the tent as I looked around for my purse.

I stopped short when I realized Collins was awake, sitting at the edge of his tent flap, looking out across the room. For just a moment, it was like I could picture him in the woods some-where, in that same position, looking out to a sunrise and not just a blank wall. He glanced over at me, and I felt even colder as I saw his expression. I knew then that he'd seen me come out of Frank's tent. Probably he assumed the worst, even though nothing had happened.

I took a breath, to try and whisper-explain myself, but Collins just looked away from me, moved back into his tent, and zipped himself in without a word.

★★★★

Morgan Matson

> Hey, you okay?
> We're not running AGAIN? Finally
> ready to admit my superiority? ☺
> Breakfast? Meet you at the
> diner?
> Em, what's going on?
> Are you still coming tonight?

In the three days that had passed since the indoor camping,
I'd been avoiding Frank. I was still trying to get my head around
the fact that I liked him as more than a friend. And I had a
feeling that if we were on a long run together, some or all of
this would come pouring out, probably in an incredibly embarrassing way. So for the moment, I was being a coward, texting
him vague replies about being sick and having twisted my ankle
and being busy with Paradise. The last text I'd gotten from him,
though, I couldn't ignore. I'd committed to the gala, I'd spent
a lot of money on a dress, I needed to cross it off the list, and I
was going to go. He needed me for support and as his friend; I
knew I had to be there for him.

> Still coming. Text me the
> address?

But getting ready for it didn't feel like the fun, exciting time
that I'd been imagining. I couldn't help but think back to the
last time Sloane and I had gotten ready for an event. We'd always
tried to get ready together, even if only one of us was going
out. It was just more fun to have someone there, helping with

makeup, strategizing about the night, weighing in with wardrobe decisions. The last time we'd done this had been for junior prom, in her room, since her parents were out of town. She had worn an amazing vintage dress from Twice, a long beaded caftan, and she had done her makeup sixties-style, all cat eye and false lashes, but had kept her hair modern and flowing down her back.

"Finishing touch," she'd said when we were coiffed and made up and ready to go. She'd lifted the throw rug in her bedroom and pressed down on the loose floorboard. I'd seen her do this before; it was where she kept her precious things, the things she didn't want to get lost or go missing, two things that seemed to happen with regularity around her house. She reached down into the space and pulled up a tiny bottle of perfume and dabbed it on her wrists and throat. "Milly would use up the whole bottle otherwise," she said, offering it to me as I shook my head. "And this stuff's expensive. It was a gift from my aunt." She put it back under the floorboard, and smoothed down the rug. Then she smiled at me and said what she always did before we went out. "Let's go have the best night ever."

I was thinking about this as I spritzed on some perfume myself. I capped the bottle and looked at my reflection in the mirror. The backless dress was just as striking as it had been all those times I'd tried it on at the store, but I wasn't sure I liked it now. I wanted Frank to notice me in it, but at the same time, that felt like the last thing I should want.

"Okay," I said, as I looked in the mirror, pulling my shoulders back and making myself say it since Sloane wasn't here to. "Go have the best night ever."

I headed down the stairs carefully, holding up the hem of my dress, calling good-bye to my parents. I'd told them about the gala, and my mother had offered to loan me her beaded clutch I'd already taken for the wedding. I'd thanked her, deciding she didn't need to know I'd already used it once this summer.

I was heading to my car when I realized I still hadn't gotten the address. I pulled out my phone, and saw I had a text from Frank that I must have missed when I was in the shower.

> 21 Randolph Farms Lane, see you
> soon!

I just stared at it for a moment, even checking my text log, but there was no other texts from him saying that he was kidding, or that he'd gotten the address wrong. But there was nothing else. Which meant, I realized as I pulled open the driver's side door, that I was going to a party tonight at Sloane's house.

****

APRIL

Three months earlier

"Another one?" Sloane raised an eyebrow at me.

Despite the fact that my eyes were starting to burn, I nodded immediately. "Let's do it." We were five hours into a marathon of *Psychic Vet Tech*, a show that neither of us had paid attention to when it had first come on this year, but that we'd started binge-watching that night, thinking it would be fun to mock it, only to find ourselves getting drawn in very quickly. I was sleeping over at Sloane's, which was always much more fun than sleeping over at my house. When we slept over at mine, my mother was always around, wanting to know if we needed anything, checking up on us. When I slept over at Sloane's, most of the time, her parents weren't even there, and tonight was no exception. Milly and Anderson were out for the night—or maybe the weekend, Sloane hadn't been sure—and Sloane had taken over as hostess, getting us both Diet Cokes with lemon slices in wine glasses, and cooking dinner for us in the kitchen.

"It's my specialty," she said, tasting something from one of the pots on the stove, frowning, and then adding more pepper. "And I mean that literally. It's the one and only thing I can make. It's my penne arrabbiata. But we didn't have any penne. So it's spaghetti arrabbiata."

"How did you learn to make this?" I asked, leaning against the kitchen counter, sipping my Diet Coke. I knew I could have probably offered to help, but there was something about the whole situation that felt so glamorous—so *adult*—that I just wanted to take it in.

Sloane frowned down at the piece of paper she was working from and pulled the pencil out of her hair, which fell down around her shoulders. She pushed it impatiently

Morgan Matson

out of her face and scribbled something on the paper, then twisted her hair up again and stuck the pencil through it. "The arrabbiata?" she asked. "My aunt taught me. And I know I took a picture of her recipe, but I didn't write it down. And now I can't find what camera it was on, so I'm just trying to remember . . ." She stirred something that was bubbling on the back burner. "So this might be terrible," she said, not sounding too bothered by this. "Just warning you."

But the pasta had been delicious, and we'd eaten it in Anderson's study, both of us perched on the leather couches with our plates, getting more and more involved with Willa, the heroine, who worked at an animal clinic and could communicate with the animals in her care, using their knowledge to help her solve crimes.

"Awesome," Sloane said now, as she stretched. "I think I've got two more in me tonight, how about you?"

"Absolutely," I said, though I had a feeling we were going to end up watching the whole first season and falling asleep sometime when the sun started to rise. We'd done it before. I stood up and gathered the plates, noticing that both our glasses were empty. "You want a refill?"

"Sure," she said, as she curled up on the couch, cuing up the next episode. "Or why don't you grab the wine that's in the fridge?"

"Okay," I said, hoping I didn't sound thrown by this. Sloane always insisted her parents didn't care if we drank—even if they were home—but it was so different from how I'd grown up, I still had trouble getting my head around it.

I walked across the downstairs to the kitchen, a little slower than I needed to, trying to take it all in. Sloane's house couldn't have been more different from mine, with its antiques and rugs and oil paintings with individual lights. I crossed into the kitchen without turning on the light, and put the plates in the sink. Unlike my house, where the kitchen was the hub and everyone gathered there, it seemed mostly unused in Sloane's house. The first time I'd opened her refrigerator, I'd been shocked to see there were only some take-out containers, a bottle of champagne, and a few ketchup packets. I honestly hadn't known that it was possible to have a refrigerator without a bottle of ketchup in it. I pulled open the fridge and reached for the bottle of white wine.

"Having a nice time?" I whirled around, my heart hammering, and saw Milly sitting at the kitchen table in the dark, a glass of red wine in her hand. I hadn't known that Sloane's parents had come back but realized they had, as usual, come back from someplace fancy—Milly was wearing a floor-length beaded dress that pooled at her bare feet.

"Oh," I said. I looked down at the bottle of wine I was holding in my hand and realized how this must look. It was one thing for Sloane to tell me her parents were fine with us drinking; it was quite another for her mom to catch me taking her chardonnay. "Yeah. Um . . ."

"Close the door, would you, dear?" Milly asked, holding her hand up to block the weak refrigerator light. I closed it, and the kitchen fell into darkness again.

"Um," I said, trying to decide what I should do. Hide the wine? Put it back? Pretend like I was cool with this too? "Thanks so much for letting me stay over."

"Of course, Amanda," she said, giving me a smile as she took a sip. "It's our pleasure."

I just kept the smile on my face, not sure if I should correct an adult, Sloane's mother, about this. It seemed less embarrassing for both of us if I just let it slide. But there must have been something in my expression, even in the darkness, that gave it away, because Milly lowered her glass and squinted at me. "Not *Amanda*," she said, shaking her head. "My goodness, where is my mind?"

"It's Emily," I said, with a laugh I hoped didn't sound too forced.

"Yes, of course," Milly said, with a laugh of her own. "I'd forget my own head if it wasn't attached to my neck." I nodded at that, and was about to say something else on some safe topic, like the weather, when Milly went on, thoughtfully, "No, Amanda was Sloane's best friend in Palm Beach."

She sipped her wine again, like nothing was wrong, and I tried not to let it show just how shocked I was. Sloane had never mentioned an Amanda.

"And then it was . . . What was that girl's name in South

Carolina?" Milly asked, drumming her nails on the table, now seeming to be talking more to herself than to me. "When we were with my sister Laney . . ." I realized, all at once, that this was definitely not the first drink she'd had tonight. There was a looseness in her voice that I wasn't used to hearing, and it made me feel nervous. Between that and the fact that I was holding a bottle of wine in front of an adult who wasn't lecturing me, it suddenly felt like there was nobody in charge. "Charlotte!" Milly said triumphantly, taking a sip of her wine.

I gave her a weak laugh in return, though my head was spinning. And it hit me that I probably couldn't ask Sloane, demand she tell me about other friends she had. Or if I did, she would probably just tell me about them, girls I'd never thought to inquire after since I'd never until this moment imagined they existed. I knew, rationally, that this was no big deal and I was getting bothered by nothing. But still.

"Em!" I turned in the direction of Sloane's voice, and realized she was probably wondering what had happened to me. "Come on! This next episode is called 'The Diamond and the Dachshund,' so you know it's going to be amazing."

"I should . . . ," I said, taking a step toward the door.

"Of course," Milly said, giving me a vague smile. She wasn't demanding her wine back, so I just took it with me. "So nice to see you again, dear."

I made myself smile back at her. "You too." I couldn't have said why, but I had the feeling that she had already forgotten my name. I walked straight back into the library, not stopping to look around this time, and took my spot next to Sloane on the couch.

"Finally," she said, as she took the wine from me and poured us each a glass. "I was getting worried you'd gotten lost or something."

I was on the verge of telling Sloane her parents were here, and her mother was in the kitchen, when I realized I had no idea how long they'd been back for. But the fact was, they hadn't come in to say hi to their daughter. And suddenly, I missed my mother, her constant popping in whenever I had a sleepover, her presence that I knew I could depend on, no matter what. "Just moving slowly," I said, as I grabbed the remote and pointed it at the TV, making myself smile at her. "I ate too much pasta. Ready?"

Sloane clapped her hands together and grinned at me. "Always."

14
STEAL
SOMETHING

I stood against the wall of what had been Sloane's living room, clutching a glass of sparkling water I'd gotten from a passing waiter. I was gulping it, hoping that the cold would wake me up, so I could try and understand what was happening. Because it felt a little like I'd just been dropped into a nightmare, or one of my parents' experimental plays, where everything is designed to make you feel off-balance.

I was standing in Sloane's living room, and it was still Sloane's living room. Everything was still there. The furniture, the rugs, the oil paintings with their little lights, the books on the shelves bound in leather. None of it made any sense to me. Why had the Williamses left all their stuff behind? For just a moment, I wondered if it meant they were coming back. But even I couldn't seem to get myself to believe it, and another explanation had started to circle around in my mind—maybe they had left it behind because it wasn't theirs to take.

The house was packed, mostly people who seemed around my parents' age, in tuxedos and gowns, with waiters passing around trays. Frank had waved across the room to me when I'd come in, but he was clearly being monopolized by his parents' friends. I was okay with that, because I still wasn't sure what I was going to say to him, or what it was going to be like between us. Frank's parents, standing in the center of the room, seemed to be pulling off the illusion that things were still fine with them, unless you chose to notice how far apart they were standing, and how they never seemed to talk to each other.

I looked around at the familiar room, one I thought I'd never see again—and certainly not looking just like it always had. I crunched down on an ice cube and it made my back teeth ache. Now that I was in her house, I felt a sudden, surprise rush of missing Sloane intensely.

But I'd been missing her all along. Hadn't I?

As I shook my glass, just to hear the ice cubes clink, I realized that I hadn't, not recently. That her list had become less about Sloane, and more about me. And Frank and Dawn and Collins, too. I wasn't sure what that meant. I wasn't sure what I wanted it to mean. I sipped at my water, wondering how much longer I had to stay. I was feeling jittery and out of sorts, like even being in Sloane's house was making me think about things I hadn't had to face in a while. And all I really wanted was to go home and not leave until things made sense again.

I saw Collins across the room, and waved to him. He met my eye, but then looked away, and I could see him sigh before he turned and headed toward me, expertly navigating his way through the crowd, his hands stuffed in his tuxedo pockets. He had dressed to the nines for the occasion, wearing a maroon bow tie and matching cummerbund, along with a pocket square.

"You're looking very dapper tonight," I told him as soon as he was close to me.

"Thanks," he said a little shortly. He looked at me, then flicked his eyes away. "Nice dress." The way he said it, I could tell it wasn't exactly a compliment. Even though it was over-heated in the house, far too many people and not enough air, I suddenly felt chilled. And I remembered the look Collins had given me as I'd left Frank's tent.

As though sensing this thought, Frank looked over at me and Collins, grimacing and shooting us a *Sorry about this* expression.

"Look," I said, turning to Collins. I took a breath and decided to jump right in and not bother with the segue. "About the other morning, what you saw. Me in Frank's tent? Nothing happened. I just didn't bring a pillow."

"I didn't think that anything happened," Collins said, his voice flat.

"Oh," I said, a little thrown by this. I'd expected this,

somehow, to be a much longer conversation. "I just didn't want you to think I'd do something like that."

"Emily, I don't," Collins said, now sounding annoyed. "Come on. We're friends." I just looked at him for a moment, and maybe something of what I was thinking was in my expression because he frowned. "What?"

"I just . . . ," I started. I really hadn't expected to have this conversation with him, but we were there, so I might as well tell him what had been bothering me, just a little bit, all summer. "It's just sometimes . . . it seems like you don't want me around. That's all. Sometimes I think you do," I added quickly. "But it's just a little confusing."

Collins just looked at me for a moment, then tipped his head in the direction of the side porch. I nodded, and he led the way outside, as though he was the one who knew this house well, like he'd been the one to sit on this porch with Sloane on the Adirondack chairs, feet propped on the railing, looking up at the stars, talking for hours.

The porch was empty, maybe because the air was humid and damp, and there was a charged, heavy feeling, like the sky could open and it could storm at any moment. "Are we actually talking about this?" he asked, when we were both outside. "We have our honesty hats on?"

"Um," I said. "Okay. Hats on."

Collins looked away for a minute, out to the rolling hills that had been Sloane's backyard, then turned to me. "Frank's my best friend. Has been since we were kids. But most of the time, I only get to hang out with him when he's not with Lissa, or student government, or the newest species of frog that needs saving."

"Collins," I started, but he waved this away.

"It's okay," he said, "it is what it is and I've accepted that. But this summer, when she was away, when he wasn't trying to save the world or get the most polished transcript in history, I thought it was going to be the summer of Frank and Collins. Working together, hanging out . . ."

"And that's happened," I said, hearing how defensive my voice was, since I thought I knew where this was going.

"For about a week. And then you showed up."

I swallowed hard. Even though I'd agreed to the honesty, that didn't mean I necessarily liked this conversation. "But . . . ," I started.

"And I'd been planning this camping trip forever, and when it gets rained out, Frank tell me he has this great idea for how to make up for it. And he invites you and Dawn." He let out a breath and stared down at the scuffed wooden floor, his shoulders hunched.

"I didn't mean to get in between you guys," I finally said, hoping he knew it hadn't been anything deliberate. "I'm sorry."

"I know," Collins said, shaking his head, sounding frustrated. "And I'm sure Frank doesn't even know he's doing it. It just gets hard, always being someone's second choice."

I took in Collins's expression and realized why it was so

familiar. It was the same one I'd had when Sloane had started choosing Sam over me. It was the reason I'd started skipping meets and cross-country practices, since I wanted to hang out with her whenever I could. "I know," I said quietly.

"I think you do," Collins said. He shrugged. "Or at any rate, you will soon enough."

"What do you mean?" I asked. Collins just looked at me for a long moment, and I got the impression that he was weighing how much to tell me. "Hat," I reminded him.

"Okay," he said, folding his arms. "What do you think is going to happen when Lissa gets back?"

This question, on top of what I'd realized in the tent, hit me with what felt like physical force. "I . . . What do you mean?"

"I mean, do you think he's still going to keep hanging out? And are you going to keep hanging out with Dawn when she's back to school at Hartfield?" He gave me a measured look, and I realized Collins had been paying much more attention this summer than I had given him credit for. "September's coming soon, Emily. And I know you lost your friend, but you didn't do a great job picking replacements."

I took a step back; it felt like Collins had slapped me. "That wasn't . . . ," I started. "I didn't do that." But the words had hit a nerve; they wouldn't be affecting me this way if they hadn't. It was pretty much what I'd just thought, after all.

"Okay," Collins said with a shrug, clearly willing to let it go.

"And are *we* not going to be friends?" I asked, a little

combatively. I was still trying to get my head around the fact that apparently everything I thought had been building this summer was going to disappear in a few weeks' time.

"We'll be friends," he said to me. "But," he said, and in that word, it was like the old Collins persona came back; his very posture seemed to change. "When I start dating the very lucky lady who'll be my steady hang, maybe not so much." He winked at me. "You understand."

"Do you want to hear the truth?" I asked. I didn't even think about it, just suddenly wanted to be as direct with him as he'd been with me. "Are our hats still on?" Collins nodded, looking wary, and I said, "You ask out the prom queens because you know they'll say no." It had just been a theory, but when he flushed a dull red, I realized that it had been correct. "Why don't you try asking someone who might actually say yes?"

Collins just shook his head. "I don't expect you to understand this, Emily," he said after a pause. "But who's going to want to go out with me?" His voice was shaky, and after a summer of bravado and theatrical winks and neon polos, I felt like I was finally seeing him, hat on and guard down. Not the guy who tried the week before to get everyone to call him LL Cool C—Ladies Love Cool Collins—even though it only seemed to stick with Doug from work. This was the real Collins. And the real Collins just looked sad and disappointed. He gave a short laugh and gestured to himself. "I'm not exactly a catch."

"Of course you are," I said, surprised and a little mad that he couldn't see this. "And you should ask Dawn." As I said this, I just hoped that I'd understood her offhand comments about him, not to mention how long it had taken her to look away when he was skinny-dipping.

Collins just looked at me for a long moment, then down at the ground. "You think she'd say yes?" he finally asked, sounding more nervous than I'd ever heard him.

I wanted to be able to tell him yes, definitively, but I didn't really feel sure about anything anymore. "What's the worst that could happen?" I asked, doing my best to give him a smile. He gave me a tentative one back just as the porch door opened.

"Matthew!" an older woman, half of a couple who had been talking to Frank for most of the night, motioned for him to join them inside. Collins glanced at me, but the woman seemed pretty insistent, making large *Come here* movements with jewel-encrusted hands that caught the light and reflected it onto the walls.

"Sorry," Collins said to me. "Uh . . ."

"Go," I said, giving him a smile. "I'll be fine." He nodded and made his way back into the house, and I followed a minute later. As I passed the living room, I sensed Frank trying to catch my eye, but I looked away, into my glass. I could hear fragments of conversations as I walked, architectural terms I didn't understand, but also snatches of discussions that baffled me.

Yes, the house is stunning isn't it? All the original Harrison furnishings . . . in trust . . . some fight over a will . . . I don't know, some tenants, I think? Well, not any longer . . .

Every room I stepped into, I saw Sloane. There was the couch where we'd mainlined whole seasons of TV shows; there was the table we'd sat on top of, sharing a pint of ice cream while she told me all about her first kiss with Sam, there was the counter where she'd laid out every eye shadow she owned, trying to get my eyes to turn the same color.

I had just given my empty glass to a bored-looking cater-waiter when I spotted the back stairs at the end of the hallway. There was a ribbon tied across them, clearly indicating that the upstairs rooms were off-limits.

I headed toward the stairs, already coming up with my alibi if I needed one. *I was just looking for the bathroom. I didn't see the ribbon. I got lost.* I looked quickly over each shoulder, then lifted the ribbon, ducked under it, and hurried upstairs.

Like the downstairs, everything upstairs was still the same. The hall table, the oil paintings, the framed maps. I looked for a long moment at the window at the end of the hall, the one with the beige curtains, the one that I had helped Sloane tumble into on the day we met, the day she told me that she'd been waiting for me—or someone like me.

I looked away from the window and walked on, down the hall to the room that had been Sloane's. I paused for a moment outside of it, praying that it wouldn't be locked. But the old glass doorknob turned easily in my hand, and I looked around again once more before slipping inside.

All the furniture was the same—but everything about it was

Morgan Matson

different. When the room had been Sloane's, there had been stuff everywhere, makeup and clothing and the British fashion magazines she special-ordered taking up the surface of every dresser and most of the floor. She'd twined twinkle lights around her four-poster bed and had covered the mirror with pictures—me and her, her and Sam, ripped-out pages from magazines. But now, every trace of her was gone. It was just an anonymous room, one that could have belonged to anyone.

It was worse, somehow, being up here than being in any other room of the house. I started to go when I suddenly turned back, remembering something.

The throw rug was still there, and I lifted it up, folding it back and trying to remember where the loose board was. When I found it, it just creaked open a little, and I pressed on it harder, easing it up. When Sloane had been using it, there had usually been a collection of things, rotating as their importance changed. But now, there was only one of her disposable cameras and a thin layer of dust. I pulled up the camera, wiping it off. There was nothing written on it, and it looked like all the pictures had been taken.

I don't know what I'd been expecting. I put the board back where it was supposed to be, folded down the rug, and left Sloane's room, not letting myself look back, closing the door behind me and hurrying downstairs, even though the last thing I wanted to do was go back to the party.

I made it back to the living room without being stopped,

and saw that Frank's parents were now standing even farther apart from each other, fixed smiles on both their faces, and Frank was nowhere to be seen. I tried to fit the camera into my clutch, but it was one of the tiny, useless ones, and was barely big enough to fit my keys and ID, so there was no getting a disposable camera into it. I headed toward the front door, glad for an excuse to get away from the party for a bit, figuring I'd just leave it in my car.

"Hey." I turned, my hand on the doorknob, and saw Frank. His hair was slightly askew, like he'd been running his hands through it. He was wearing a tux, and the sight of him in it made me feel off-balance. He looked so handsome, I had to look away from him, or I knew I wouldn't be able to stop staring.

"Hey," I said, mostly to my shoes. "How's it going?"

He looked toward the center of the room, where his parents were now standing on opposite sides. "It's going," he said grimly. "Were you leaving?"

"Well," I said, looking down at the camera in my hand. "I was just going to my car—"

"Because if you are," Frank said, overlapping with me, "I'd love a ride home. I have to get out of here."

"Oh," I said. "Um, sure." I was more than happy to leave, I just didn't know if Frank was supposed to. But he just nodded and held open the door for me. I stepped through it and heard him draw in a breath.

"That's really quite a dress," he said, and I realized he must have just seen the back—or lack thereof.

We walked down the steps together, the steps that I had sat on next to Sloane while we read stacks of magazines and worked on our tans, the steps I'd sat on when I was desperate to find her. "In a good way?" I asked. Frank opened his mouth to answer as thunder rumbled somewhere in the distance. "We'd better go," I said, picking up my pace. "The roof's open."

We walked together across Sloane's driveway. I'd avoided the valet guys and just parked at the end of the long line of cars on the side of the road, so we had a bit of a hike to the car. "Thanks," Frank said as we walked.

"Sure," I said, glancing over at him. His hands were deep in his pockets, and I knew him well enough to see that he was upset about something. "Is it okay for you to leave?"

"It's fine," he said shortly. "I really shouldn't have come in the first place. Sorry to drag you out here."

"It's okay—" I started, as thunder rumbled again and we both picked up our pace, hurrying for my car as the wind started to blow, and I realized we were in our usual running spots, just wearing evening clothes, and not T-shirts and shorts. There was something strange between us tonight, some weird tension that hadn't been there before, and I didn't think it was just coming from me. I unlocked my car, and we both got in. I didn't bother with music, just turned around and passed Sloane's house again on the way up the road. As I did, I saw the house all lit up, and through the windows, the crowd, in their tuxes and gowns. It was how I'd always imagined the house, and tonight, I'd been a part of it. But it wasn't how I'd thought it would feel. It just felt sad.

I turned down the road that would take me to Frank's, and started to drive a little faster than I normally would have, worried about the rain I had a feeling was coming. I couldn't help thinking about both the tarp and the wooden piece resting, warm and dry, in the garage. When we'd driven nearly halfway to Frank's without a word, I glanced over at him. His jaw was set as he looked out the window, and I knew something was wrong. "Are you okay?" I finally asked.

"I don't know," he said, looking over at me. I suddenly saw this wasn't just about his parents—he was mad at me. "What happened to you? You disappear from camping without saying good-bye, you won't answer any of my texts, then you show up tonight in that dress . . ."

"What's wrong with the dress?" I asked, adjusting the neckline, suddenly feeling self-conscious.

"Nothing," Frank said, letting out a breath and shaking his head. "I was just worried, that's all."

"I'm sorry," I said. "I was just . . . thinking about some things."

He looked over at me for a moment. "Me too." I nodded, but was suddenly afraid to ask him what they were. What if Collins was right, and what he'd been thinking about was that we couldn't be friends anymore? "Emily," he said, but just then, rain started to hit my windshield—and come in through my sunroof.

"Oh my god," I said, speeding up. "I'm so sorry. Just . . . um . . ." The rain was coming down harder, and I turned up my wipers. I was starting to get wet as the rain poured in through the roof. Even though I wasn't directly under it, it was hitting the console and splashing me, and coming in sideways when the wind blew. I reached into the side of the door where I'd put Sloane's disposable and held it out to Frank. "Would you put that in the glove compartment?" I asked, raising my voice to be heard over the wind that had started to pick up.

He took it from me, glancing over with a question in his eyes. But I looked straight ahead, just concentrating on getting him home before he got too wet or either one of us said something we shouldn't.

I pulled into his driveway and put the car in park, expecting him to get out and run for it while he was at least partly dry. But he just looked at me across the car, through the rain that was pouring down into my cupholders.

"What were you thinking about?" he asked, his expression serious and searching. "You haven't been talking to me this whole week. What was it?"

"Nothing," I said, looking away from him. "I told you, I'm sorry. You should go inside, you're getting soaked—"

"I don't care," he said, leaning forward. "Tell me what it was."

"Nothing," I said again, trying to brush this off, trying to go back to something that felt more like solid ground. I reached for the game we'd been playing all summer, the phrase I knew by heart. "You know, in an well-ordered universe . . ." But I looked at him, at the rain running down his face, his white tuxedo shirt getting soaked, and realized I couldn't finish it this time.

Or maybe I could, because I leaned forward, into the rain, and kissed him.

He kissed me back. It lasted just a moment, but he kissed me back, right away, without hesitation, as though we'd always been doing it.

But then he pulled away and looked at me. We were both leaning forward, which was ridiculous, since that meant we were directly underneath where the water was coming into the car.

I looked back at him through the rain that was pouring down between us and took a breath to try and say something, when he leaned forward, cupping my cheek with his hand, and kissed me again.

And it was a kiss that felt like it could stop time. The rain was falling on us, but I didn't even feel or notice or care about it. We were kissing like it was a long-forgotten language that we'd once been fluent in and were finding again, kissing like it was the only thing either of us had wanted to do for a long, long time, kissing with the urgency of the rain that was pounding down all around us and onto the hood of the car. His hands were tangled in my hair, then touching my bare back, and I was shivering in a way that didn't have anything to do with the cold. His face was wet as I ran my hands under his jaw and over his cheeks, as I pulled him closer to me, feeling my heart beating against his, feeling that despite the rain, despite everything, I could have happily stayed like that forever.

Until, abruptly, Frank stopped.

He broke away and dropped his hands from my hair. He sat back heavily against the side of the car. "Oh my god," he said quietly.

I sat back as well, trying to catch my breath, which was coming shallowly. "Frank . . . ," I started, even though I didn't have anything to follow this.

"Don't," he said quickly. He looked over at me, and I could see how unhappy he suddenly looked—because of me. I had done this. Reality came crashing down on me in a horrible wave. He had a *girlfriend*. He had a very serious girlfriend and I knew it and I had gone ahead and kissed him anyway. I suddenly felt sick, and looked down at my hands, which were shaking.

"I'm sorry," I whispered, hearing how scratchy my voice sounded. "I shouldn't have—"

"I have to go," he said. "I—" He looked over at me, but nothing followed this. After a moment, he opened the door and got out, closing it hard behind him and walking up the steps to his house, not running, his shoulders hunched, just letting the rain beat down over him. I waited until I saw that he had gone inside. And then I waited a moment more, to make sure he wasn't going to come back out and somehow make things okay again.

When it was clear that wasn't going to happen, I put the car in gear and headed home.

And when I started to cry as I pulled into my driveway, it was coming down hard enough that I could pretend that it was only the rain hitting my face, and not the fact that I'd just lost another friend.

****

"Em?" my mother knocked on the doorframe and stuck her head into my room, her expression worried. "You okay, hon?"

I looked up from the floor, where, in an effort to try and deny the fact that everything in my life was falling apart, I'd been cleaning out my closet.

The morning after the kiss, I'd texted Frank, but had gotten no response. I'd spent the day staring at my phone, waiting to hear from him, glad for once that Paradise was totally deserted, since I would have been useless to anyone who wanted ice cream. I'd finally run out of willpower that night and had called him, but it had gone right to his voice mail. I still hadn't heard from him the next day, and I finally told Beckett to hide my phone somewhere high so I'd stop staring at it. On the third day, trying to pretend I wasn't stalking him, just getting some exercise, I'd walked past his house, and saw that his truck was gone. I figured maybe he was at work, but it was still gone at night when I drove past. It was that night, when I'd begun to think I really was never going to hear from him again, that I got a text.

> Hey, can't talk right now.
> Sorting through things. More
> soon.

As someone who had been raised by two playwrights, I understood subtext. And this text, coupled with the fact I hadn't heard from him in three days, meant Frank was brushing me off, acting like I was a stranger. He clearly wanted to forget what had happened, and act like the kiss had never taken place—as though that would make it go away.

I'd been dodging Dawn's calls, not wanting to tell her what happened until I spoke to Frank. But since I no longer felt like I owed him anything, the next day, when Dawn called, I picked up.

"Oh my god," she said, before I even said hello, her voice high and excited. "I'm so glad you're finally around! Have you been sick or something?"

"Well—" I started, but she was already continuing on.

"I have a date tonight! With Matthew! He asked me yesterday. We're going to the movies, isn't that great?"

"Yes," I said, feeling myself smile for the first time in days, beyond glad that Collins had taken my advice. "That's fantastic."

"So you have to help me figure out what to wear," she said. "But maybe later tonight? I'm at work now anyway, and it'll help to be in front of my closet." She took what sounded like a much-needed breath. "What's up with you? Are you okay?"

"Frank and I kissed," I blurted out. I knew I wouldn't be

able to make small talk about anything else with that on my mind, since it was pretty much the only thing I had thought about for the last three days. "I kissed him," I admitted. There was just silence on Dawn's end, and I went on, in a rush, "And now I don't know what's going on. He texted me back, but it doesn't seem like he really wants to talk to me. And I just want things to go back to how they were. . . ." Even as I said this, I knew it wasn't true. I didn't really want that at all. But I would have preferred that over whatever we were doing now.

"Emily," Dawn said, and her voice was colder than I had ever heard it. "He has a girlfriend."

I blinked, a little startled by Dawn's change of tone. "I know," I said slowly. "And I feel terrible about this. I—"

"Do you?" she asked. "Because you knew he had a girl-friend when you went ahead and kissed him, didn't you?"

"Dawn," I said, trying to regroup. I had actually hoped to talk to her about this, to get her take on things, and instead, it felt like I was being attacked. "I—"

"Did you honestly think I would be on board with this?" she asked, her voice rising. "After what Mandy did to me? After what Bryan did?"

I closed my eyes for just a second and rested the phone against my head. "No," I said. "I'm sorry. I just don't know what to do, and—"

"Look, I can't really talk right now," she said, her voice clipped and cold. "I'm at work."

"Okay," I said, a little confused, since Dawn had never exactly been committed to her job. "Should I call you later?"

"I have to go," she said, not really sounding angry any longer, just sounding sad. "I have to work, and then I have this date to get ready for, so . . ."

A moment too late, the penny dropped. Dawn didn't want to talk to me anymore. She didn't want to be friends with me, not after what I'd done. We said stilted good-byes and I hung up the phone, feeling like everything in my life was suddenly breaking apart and floating away just when I needed it most.

After I hung up with Dawn, I called Collins. When he answered the phone, he sounded wary, and I hadn't gotten far in my halting explanation when he cut me off.

"I know what happened," he said, letting out a long breath. "This isn't good, Emily."

"I know that," I said. Any last hopes I was holding on to that Frank might want to still be friends again, or that we might be able to move past this, ended when I heard the resigned tone in Collins's voice. "But I just wanted to—"

"You know I can't do this, right?" he asked, not sounding angry, mostly just tired. "I can't take your side. He's my best friend."

"I know he is," I said, "But if you could just talk to him—"

"I can't," Collins said. "Even if I wanted to, which I *really* don't. He's in New—" Collins stopped abruptly, but I'd heard enough to put it together. I hadn't realized that I could feel worse, but I did. I now understood why Frank's truck hadn't been at his house. He was gone. He had gone to Princeton. He had chosen his girlfriend. Of *course* he had; it wasn't even a question. And he'd slept there, with her.

I knew I had no right to feel mad about this, but even so, I had to fight back the tears that were threatening to escape—for what Frank and I had had, and for what we would never have, and for what I'd broken.

"I'm sorry, Em," Collins said, and I could hear that he meant it.

"Yeah," I whispered, not trusting myself to say much more, trying to keep my voice steady so that he wouldn't hear that I was about to burst into tears. It was suddenly becoming clear to me that I had nobody on my side. "Have a good time tonight."

"Thanks," he said, and his voice was gentle when he added, "Take care, okay?"

And I'd nodded, even though Collins couldn't see me do it, and hung up, realizing that he had just told me good-bye. So I'd lost Dawn, and Collins, and of course, Frank. With one stupid action, I'd just wrecked everything that I'd built over the course of the summer.

And now my mother was standing in my doorway, because even she had noticed that something was wrong. "Hi," I said, setting down the pair of shoes Sloane had bought for me the last time we'd been at a flea market together. I squinted at my mother, and noticed that she was wearing actual clothing, and that her hair was washed. "Did you guys finish your play?"

My mother gave me a smile that was equal parts thrilled and tired. "Late last night," she said.

"Wow," I said, making myself smile at her. "That's great. Congrats."

"Thanks," she said, her smile fading as she took a step closer into my room. "I'm just a little worried about you."

"I'm fine," I said quickly, automatically. And if my mother had still been deep in writing mode, she would have left it at that. But she just looked at me a moment longer, the kind of look that let me know that she was back, and the slack I'd been able to have all summer was pretty much over.

"We'll talk later," she said, her tone leaving open no real discussion of this. "But right now, Frank's downstairs."

I stared at her. "He is?"

She nodded as she headed out of my room. "And you might want to rescue him," she added. "I think Beckett's down there with him."

That was all I needed to hear. I pushed myself off the bed, and glanced at the mirror briefly before taking the steps downstairs two at a time. I didn't look my best, but Frank had seen me, for so many mornings, right after I'd rolled out of bed. And since I had a feeling that he was only there to tell me what I already knew—that we weren't friends anymore—I wasn't sure I necessarily needed to look great for that.

I found him and Beckett on the front porch, Beckett

showing off his ninja kicks, all of which were getting distressingly close to Frank's face. Just seeing Frank again was enough to make it feel like one of Beckett's kicks had landed right in my stomach, and I hated how much I'd missed him. "Beck," I said, looking away from Frank, not sure I was really up to talking directly to him just yet. "Be careful."

My little brother looked at me scornfully. "I'm always careful," he said, before attempting a roundhouse kick that landed him flat on his back on the porch. "Ow," he muttered.

"Can we talk?" Frank asked me.

Since Beckett was showing no signs of moving from the porch, I nodded toward the driveway. "Want to take a walk?"

"Sure," he said easily. I looked at him and realized that for some reason he looked *happy*. Clearly, he had not had the same few days that I had. He had just rolled with it, and probably everything in his life was still going wonderfully.

I could feel my anger start to build as he followed me up the driveway, toward the mailbox. As we walked, I noticed there were only our cars parked there. "Did you walk here?"

He nodded, and smiled at me, like life was just so great. "I kind of felt like it."

I nodded, swallowing hard, wishing he would just get this over with. When I hadn't heard from him after his text, I'd assumed that this would be our new status quo—we'd just never speak again, and forget about everything we'd shared over the course of the summer. But I'd forgotten I was dealing with

Frank Porter, who probably wanted to make sure that I was fine with pretending that we'd never been friends, so he could cross this issue off, one more thing neatly and successfully resolved.

We had only gone a few steps down the road when he stopped and looked at me. "Listen," he said. He was smiling again, like he was just so happy he couldn't hide it, even as he was preparing to break my heart. "Emily. I just wanted to—"

"You know, we don't have to do this," I said, cutting him off. I couldn't do much about this situation, but I could limit the number of times this week that people told me they were done with me forever. "I get it, okay?"

He just looked at me for a moment, his brow furrowed. "You do?"

"I do," I said, crossing my arms over my chest. "I got the message."

Now he looked very confused, his head tilting to the side. "What message?"

"That we're not friends anymore," I said, and even though I was trying to keep my voice steady, it broke on the last word. "And you know what, maybe we never were. And it's not like we're going to be friends when school starts, so it's probably just better this way."

Frank shook his head. "What are you talking about? I wanted to—"

"I just don't need to hear it, okay?" I could hear how high and shaky my voice sounded. "We don't have to do this."

Frank looked at me, and I could see some of his sureness—his confidence—begin to ebb. "We don't?"

I shook my head. I just didn't want to go along with it. Maybe for once, Frank Porter didn't get to have everything neatly resolved. "I get that you were trying to be the good guy and come here so we could put it behind us. But I don't need it." And then, because I didn't think I could stay there and look at him anymore, I turned and walked away, back toward my house.

I heard Frank call my name, but I didn't turn around, and when he called it again, I broke into a run, aware as I did so that it was the first time all summer that I was running alone.

15

The summer had come full circle.

Once again, I was all alone. I had no friends, and nobody to hang out with, but this time, it was all my fault. Once again, I was having trouble grasping how I'd gone from having people to talk to, plans, some semblance of a life—to nothing, all in a moment.

I was going to work and avoiding Captain Pizza, though I had once passed Dawn while she was talking on her phone as I headed into Paradise and she sat outside the pizza parlor. We'd made brief eye contact before we both looked away and she went back to her conversation. I only caught the occasional word, but I could hear how happy she sounded—her voice was suffused with it, and she kept calling the person on the other end "Matty"—which seemed to indicate that the movie date had gone well. I hated that I didn't know more, that I hadn't heard the recap, moment by moment. And while I was happy for both of them, it made me feel all that much more alone.

I'd started taking long runs by myself, in neighborhoods I'd never run with Frank, going out of my way to avoid bumping into him. I hadn't heard from him since the morning I ran away from him. And while I didn't regret what I'd done, there were still moments when I wondered what would have happened if I'd just let him finish, heard him out. But then I would tell myself, firmly, that I'd done the right thing—Frank, as junior class president, had once convinced me that school really *should* start fifteen minutes earlier. He was that talented a speaker. And I hadn't wanted to hear him talk his way out of our friendship, talk his way around the fact he'd kissed me back, talk me into agreeing with him that it had just been a huge, terrible mistake.

Because while it had been a mistake—all the proof I needed was in my current total lack of friends—I wasn't willing to deny that it had happened, or the fact that it had meant something. I found myself thinking, more than I really should have, of Frank's hands on my bare back, of his fingers tangled in my hair, of his mouth on mine, of the way he'd run his thumb over my cheek, of the fact that it had been, without question, the best kiss I'd ever gotten.

But none of this changed the fact that I missed him in my

Morgan Matson

life. I hadn't realized how much I'd come to rely on him, how often I'd text him throughout the day, how much I needed his perspective on things, how boring my iPod seemed without his music.

With all the time I had on my suddenly friendless hands, I tried to be productive. I had dropped off both of the disposable cameras to be developed. I'd organized my closet, taken Beckett for a haircut, and finally read the first book in the series Doug was always going on about.

And every so often, I would go to my dresser and pull out the list. I had done it—every single one.

1. ~~Kiss a stranger.~~

2. ~~Go skinny-dipping.~~

3. ~~Steal something.~~

4. ~~Break something.~~

5. ~~Penelope.~~

6. ~~Ride a dern horse, ya cowpoke.~~

7. ~~55 S. Ave. Ask for Mona.~~

8. ~~The backless dress. And somewhere to wear it.~~

9. ~~Dance until dawn.~~

10. ~~Share some secrets in the dark.~~

11. ~~Hug a Jamie.~~

12. ~~Apple picking at night.~~

13. ~~Sleep under the stars.~~

All these things that had shaped my summer. I'd finished her list. I was done.

So where the hell was Sloane?

I'd started this believing that, somehow, when I finished, I would have the answers I needed. I would know what had happened to her. But now that I looked at it, I wondered if this had just been a distraction. I'd been avoiding questions like *why* my best friend had just left me without a word. I'd been thinking, hoping, that this would lead to something. But maybe it was like all her other lists, full of things she must have known, deep down, I would be too scared to attempt.

As I looked down at it, at her careful handwriting, at all my flaws that were exposed on the page, I found myself getting furious. I crumpled the list into a tiny ball, and for good measure, picked up the envelope and crumpled that too. Then I grabbed my keys and took the stairs two at a time, throwing the list and the envelope into the kitchen trash, yelling to my parents in the TV room—my dad scratching his new beard, my mom working on her macramé project—that I was going out.

I drove around town for hours, until the sun went down and the first stars began to shine. I wasn't going anywhere in particular; I just felt the need to be in motion. I was driving past places I'd gone with Sloane, places I'd gone with Frank, and feeling the loss of both of them so sharply. How was I supposed to keep living in this town when everything I saw reminded me of someone I'd lost?

There was a party going on at the Orchard—I could tell from the cars lining the road. I pulled in, but left my car running,

Morgan Matson

looking at all the people there with their friends—and remembering that, not so long ago, I'd been among them. I turned the car around and left, realizing I should probably stop in for gas, since in my aimless driving I'd lost sense of where my car was with fuel. There was also the fact that I no longer knew who I could call to help me if it died again.

I stopped by Route 1 Fuel, and when I walked into the mini-mart, saw that James was behind the register once again. He was leaning against the back counter, reading a thick book entitled *Mastering Sudoku—For the Advanced Player*. I hadn't seen him since I'd hugged him, and hoped this wouldn't be awkward as I handed over twenty dollars. But he just smiled at me as he put my bill in the register, then nodded out at the Volvo. "Check your oil?"

"Oh," I said. I wasn't sure he would have offered if I hadn't hugged him, but I wasn't going to turn this down—especially since I had no recollection of the last time it had been checked. "Sure," I said. I walked outside and he followed, then waited while I tried to figure out how to pop my hood.

"So when were you in South Carolina?" he asked, wiping off the end of the dipstick with a rag and then dipping it into my oil gauge.

I looked over at him and realized he had been reading the bumper stickers along the side of the car. I scanned them, trying to see what he'd seen. "Why do you ask?"

He tapped one I'd hardly noticed, a dark-red sticker, half

peeling off and mostly faded. *Save the SC Sea Turtles!* it read. Next to this was an image that looked familiar—a palm tree and a crescent moon.

"I wasn't," I said, turning my attention back to him. "The stickers came with the car. I've never been."

He nodded. "Too bad. It's really pretty down there." He closed the hood and patted it once. "You should be okay for another few hundred miles."

"Great," I said. "Thanks a lot." He nodded, gave me a quick smile, and headed back into the store.

I looked at the bumper sticker until a car pulled up behind me, engine idling, clearly desperate to get this specific pump. I pulled out of the gas station and headed for home, trying to sort through why I was sure I'd seen it before. It was in my mind, but just out of reach, until I paused at a stop sign and remembered.

The envelope.

I sped home, barely pausing at stoplights, screeching into the driveway and parking at an angle, not even locking my car as I ran inside and straight to the kitchen. I went directly to the trash, and started digging through it.

It was still there, only halfway down, and thankfully not covered in anything disgusting. I smoothed out Sloane's list and then the envelope, feeling my heart thud in my chest as I looked at it. There, where the return address was supposed to be, was the same image on my bumper sticker. The image that meant South Carolina.

I took the list and envelope with me as I headed up to my room, needing space and quiet to try and figure this out, not wanting to have to answer any questions. I sat on my bed and stared at the envelope until my eyes burned, trying to make it make sense.

I couldn't sleep that night. I felt like I was too close to something. Sloane had an aunt in South Carolina. I knew that. But I couldn't exactly go knocking on every door in the state, could I? I closed my eyes, trying to think. The answer was there—somewhere—I just had to adjust my eyes to see it properly.

★★★★

I was waiting outside the CVS when a tired-looking employee holding a to-go coffee unlocked the doors at six a.m. It was likely there wasn't anything to be found in either of the cameras. But I was all out of other options, and around five, I'd woken up with this, the closest thing I had to a plan.

The photo department wasn't even open yet, but after the night I'd had, I knew I wasn't going to be able to wait until ten, and I convinced the employee to get my pictures for me. I suspected he did it mostly so that I'd leave the store, and him, in peace, but he rang me up, and I left the store clutching the two photo envelopes.

I waited until I got back inside my car before opening them. The first envelope had the picture Dawn had taken of me riding Butterscotch, so I knew this was the one that had come from my car. There were the horse pictures, and the picture I'd snapped of the highway on Frank's birthday, but all the rest of the pictures were of Sloane.

Sloane at the drive-in, drinking Diet Coke out of a Twizzler straw, looking at the screen, her expression rapt. Sloane bargaining for a vintage leather jacket at a flea market upstate, looking determined—and then one of her triumphant, modeling the jacket for the camera. Sloane sitting on the roof of my car, wearing her vintage heart sunglasses, extending a bag of chips toward the camera, laughing. Sloane on the picnic table at the Orchard, the Thursday we'd cut class and shared an entire pizza. Sloane at the beach, smiling over her sunglasses at me. Sloane in the morning after a sleepover, yawning, her hair undone and wild.

I looked at the last image for a long moment, then tucked the pictures back in the envelope. They hadn't shown me anything I hadn't known before. Nothing that helped with where Sloane was now. Just my best friend, the center of my world for the last two years.

I opened up Sloane's envelope and started looking through the pictures, and felt my eyes widen.

The first one was of me and Sloane, a selfie that we'd taken the first day of junior year, me carefully dressed, my outfit looking brand-new and stiff, Sloane looking much more relaxed in a vintage romper, smiling at me, not the camera. There was one of a recipe, then one of me, cross-legged on the couch in Stanwich Coffee, hunched over my history textbook. There was one of me and

Beckett watching TV. Me and Sloane, almost out of frame, totally out of focus, both of us bent double laughing. Me, my head bent, lacing up my running shoes. Me giving Sloane a cheesy thumbs-up after a race. The front seat of my car, with the pile of snacks for a flea market road trip. Me and my mother in the kitchen, sitting at the table, discussing something, my mother gesturing big while I listened. Beckett, grinning down at the camera from the top of the doorway. The two of us, carrying dripping ice cream cones, both covered with rainbow sprinkles. Me, dressed for the prom, fixing my hair in front of the mirror. Me and Sloane sitting on a picnic table at the Orchard, barely visible in the falling darkness. Me, laughing, holding my hand in front of the camera. Me, driving, hands a blur as I drummed on the steering wheel. Me, smiling at her through the camera, my expression relaxed and happy.

I set the stack down and wiped my hands under my eyes, even though it didn't do much to stop the tears that had started to fall. All this time, I had just assumed that I'd been the one who cared more. That Sloane had floated above it, not missing me, which was why she'd been able to leave me behind. But this . . .

I picked up the pictures again, looking through the images— some carefully composed, some clearly shot in the spur of the moment. Sloane had seen me. She had taken these pictures of me, of us, many of which I hadn't seen her take. She had needed me as much as I'd needed her. I could see that now, and it made me ashamed that I'd ever thought anything else.

I wiped at my eyes again and ran my fingers through my

hair, trying to pull myself together, flipping through the pictures one last time. I stopped on the recipe photo, squinting at it. It was out of focus, but I could see that it was her aunt's arrabbiata recipe, the picture Sloane had taken but then hadn't been able to find. Now it made sense, since she'd never gotten the camera developed. I felt my heart pound as I stared down at it.

The recipe was handwritten, but it was written on a personalized recipe card. And the top of the card read *From the Kitchen of Laney Alden*. In smaller letters underneath that, it read *River Port*.

Alden was Milly's maiden name, I knew that much. I could picture the tote that Sloane had hauled to the beach all last summer, emblazoned with her mother's initials. And Sloane had told me it was her aunt who had given her the arrabbiata recipe. The aunt who lived in South Carolina.

I grabbed my phone and looked up *Laney Alden South Carolina*. I got seven results, all from people who seemed to live on opposite ends of the state. I typed in *Laney Alden South Carolina River Port*, and one listing came up—with an address. I looked down at my phone and realized I finally had my answer. It was where Sloane was. I could feel it.

It was seven by the time I got back home. I'd worked out my plan on the drive over—I'd make my parents coffee before they got up, get them in a good mood before I told them the truth—that Sloane was in South Carolina, and they needed to let me go see her.

I'd expected the house to still be quiet, but all the lights were on, Beckett was outside walking along the porch railing, and there were three suitcases lined up by the steps.

I walked over to Beckett, trying to make sure he saw me, so he wouldn't get startled and go plunging onto the driveway. "Hey," I said, and he glanced over at me, hardly bothered.

"Hey," he said, then started walking backward.

"What's going on?"

Beckett sighed deeply. "Dad's making me go to a baseball museum. Cooperstown."

"Oh," I said sympathetically. My father was emphatic about the fact that he loved baseball, and that Beckett did too, but neither of them were true fans. My mother's theory was that my dad had watched *Field of Dreams* a few too many times and become convinced that the only way to really bond with your son was through baseball. "Sorry about that."

"Sorry about what?" my dad asked as he came out to the porch, wearing a Stanwich College baseball cap and looking far too cheerful, considering it wasn't even eight yet. "Em, were you gone this morning? We looked for the car."

"Yes," I said, thinking fast. "I was just . . . scouting a new run. I wanted to see how long it was."

"Oh," my dad said. He didn't look convinced, but he shrugged and said, "Well, I'm glad you're up. Both your mom and I are heading out, and we wanted to talk to you first."

I glanced down and realized that explained the third suitcase. "Mom's going to Cooperstown too?"

"Nope," my mother said as she came out of the house and down the steps, holding an overstuffed purse. "Thank god." She smoothed my hair down with her hand. "You're up early, hon. Everything okay?"

"Where are you going?" I asked as I watched, with increasing alarm, as my mother headed over to my car and slung her bag into the driver's seat.

"New Haven," she said. "I'm giving notes on a tech rehearsal for a friend today, and staying to watch the dress on Sunday."

"And how long is Dad going to be gone?" I asked, as my father picked up his suitcase and Beckett's duffel and headed for the car my parents used.

"He'll be back Sunday night too," my mom said as she rummaged in her purse, coming up with her sunglasses and pushing them through her hair like a headband.

"Wait," I said, as I watched my dad shut the back of his car and yell at my brother to get a move on, feeling like things were moving far too quickly. "So you guys are leaving me for the weekend?"

"Did you want to come?" my mother asked, brightening. "I'm sure you could sleep on the couch."

"Or you could come to Cooperstown," my dad called cheerfully, walking away from his car and back to the house. "It's the birthplace of baseball, you know."

"No, thanks," I said, looking between the two cars. It wasn't so much that my parents were leaving me; it was that they were

Morgan Matson

leaving me with no transportation. "But what am I supposed to do about getting around?"

My mom raised her eyebrows. "I didn't think it'd be a problem for the weekend," she said. "I thought that Frank or Dawn could drive you if you needed to go somewhere. There's food in the fridge, so you shouldn't need to go out for that."

"But—" I started, feeling panicky. I realized that if I'd confided in either of my parents, they would have known that Frank and Dawn weren't options at the moment, but that didn't change the fact that I was going to be stranded.

"If you really need to go somewhere, there's money in the conch for a taxi," my dad said, maybe seeing something of what I was feeling in my expression. "But if you're not comfortable staying alone . . ."

"No, no," I said quickly, trying to get in front of this before I found myself being hauled along to a baseball museum or stuck in some drafty theater watching lighting cues change. I made myself smile at them. "I'll be fine."

My parents headed out shortly after that, both of them trying to beat the traffic that they were convinced would grow exponentially by the hour. I watched my mother, driving my car, make the right turn out of the driveway, her hand waving out the window at me, then I walked back and sat down on the front steps in the sudden silence of the driveway, thinking.

All I had wanted to do, ever since I saw Laney Alden's address on my phone, was get in my car and drive down there. It would be a longer trip than I'd ever taken before, but it wasn't undoable.

I pulled up the address again and called the number listed. It rang and rang, then a cheerful-sounding woman came on the machine, telling me I'd reached the Alden residence, asking me to please leave a message after the tone. I hung up before the beep, not even that disappointed. I hadn't really expected to get Sloane—if she wasn't answering her cell, she probably wasn't answering her aunt's landline.

I stared down at the address. I had finally found her and now I couldn't even go? I had known my parents weren't going to be thrilled with the idea of me driving down to South Carolina. Since they were gone, though, they'd given me a two-day window in which to do this. Unfortunately, they'd also taken away my means of transportation. In a well-ordered universe, you would have been able to rent a car at seventeen. But . . .

Just like that, a possible solution occurred to me. It was so scary, and so potentially awkward that it really seemed like it should have been number fourteen on Sloane's list. I pulled out my phone and looked at the time. I had no idea if he was still running. But if he was, the timing would work out.

I stood up and walked down the porch steps. I was still in my flip-flops, and I kicked them off. I left them at the end of the driveway, took a breath, and started to run.

I reached his house and sat down at the end of his driveway to wait for him. If he was still running, he'd be coming home around now.

The birds were out in full force, and it was already really hot out, which didn't seem like a good sign, considering how early it still was. I felt the warm breeze blow my hair forward, over my face, not sure what I was more scared of—that he would show up, or that he wouldn't.

I heard the sound before I saw him, the sound of sneakers hitting pavement at a steady pace. And then there he was, coming around the curve of the road, headphones in and iPod strapped to his arm. He was staying far over to the inside of the road, like he was leaving room for me. I had a flash of pride as I took in his pace and the fact that he didn't even look winded, realizing that he probably wouldn't have been doing that well without me, without all our mornings together. I wondered what he was listening to, if it was a mix I knew.

He saw me, and even from twenty feet away, I saw his expression of surprise as he slowed to a jog, then a walk, pulling his earbuds out. It felt like my legs were shaking, but I made myself stand up, not letting myself look away from him, even though this became harder the closer he got. This was the most familiar Frank to me, the Frank I'd spent my summer running next to, trading stories and songs, pushing each other on. I felt a pang of missing him twist my stomach as I looked at his hair brushed back from his forehead, at his left shoelace that was threatening to come untied. We stood there, by the side of the road, just looking at each other.

"Hi," I finally said, making myself speak, feeling like I

should start since I was the one who'd shown up unannounced in his driveway.

"Hey," Frank said. His voice was cautious, and he seemed to be looking at me closely, searching my face like he was looking for an answer—to what, though, I had no idea. He broke eye contact and looked at the ground, and at my feet.

"It's, um, that barefoot running trend I keep hearing about," I said, and Frank gave me a half smile. "I found Sloane," I said, all in a rush, to stop myself from saying anything else to him, things I really shouldn't. "She's living down in South Carolina."

"Oh," Frank said, and I could tell that this wasn't what he'd expected me to say. He nodded. "That's good, right?"

"I need to go there," I said, still speaking fast, like I might be able to rush past whether this was actually a good idea or not. "I want to find her. But my parents are gone for the weekend and they took both of the cars." Frank just looked at me, waiting for me to go on, and I knew I probably wasn't making much sense. I took a breath before asking, realizing that he very probably would say no, and then not only would I not be going to find Sloane, but I would have made a fool of myself to boot. But I was standing barefoot in his driveway to ask him this—there was nothing to do but say it. "Would you be willing to drive me? I'd ask to borrow your car, but I can't drive a stick shift."

Frank just looked at me, his head tilted slightly to the side. He wasn't jumping in to agree to this, but he also wasn't saying no.

"I'll pay for gas and everything," I said quickly. "And it won't be that long. I have to be back by tomorrow night."

He just looked at me, still not speaking. He took a breath like he was about to say something, but then just let it out slowly, and I had a feeling I knew what his answer would be, could tell in that silence how ridiculous he thought this was.

"I know it's stupid," I said, breaking eye contact with him, and looking up to the tree above me as a bird alighted on the uppermost branch. "But I wouldn't ask if it wasn't important."

"You want to drive to South Carolina and back by tomorrow night," he said, finally breaking his silence. He didn't phrase it like a question, more like he was just trying to get a grasp of the facts. I nodded and Frank looked away for a long moment.

When he looked back at me, though, he had a ghost of a smile on his face. "Then I guess we'd better get going."

16
TAKE
A ROAD
TRIP

An hour later, we were on the road.

I had gone home to take a shower and try and get my head around the fact that we were actually going to do this.

I'd gotten dressed but hadn't put on any more makeup than usual, or attempted to do anything special with my hair. The last thing I wanted, after kissing him in my car, was for Frank to think that this was some kind of plot to get him alone so I could seduce him or something. I thought for a moment of wearing a high-necked, long-sleeved shirt, but the fact was, it was simply too hot out. I'd looked at my pajamas for a long moment, doing the math. According to the directions I'd found, it seemed like the drive down there was going to take around ten hours, which would also mean ten hours back. Which meant that, at some point, we'd have to get some sleep.

But I headed out of my room without packing my pajamas, or anything I would normally bring for an overnight stay. I couldn't even begin to picture where we would be tonight, or what it would look like, so it was like I couldn't make the leap to prepare for it. I somehow still couldn't understand that I might be seeing Sloane in just a few hours.

I'd closed the blinds and poured some extra food in the cat's bowl, despite the fact he hadn't been inside for a week or so. And as I'd left the kitchen, I'd grabbed the emergency cash from the conch shell even though I was pretty sure my Paradise wages would cover all our food and gas. Then I'd locked up and headed outside just as Frank pulled his truck into the driveway.

I got in the passenger seat and buckled up while Frank turned around and headed down the driveway to the road. "Ninety-five South?" he asked, at the end of the driveway, and I nodded. I had directions on my phone, and I'd also printed them out, in case my phone died on the return trip. "Here we go," he said quietly, turning right, in the direction that would take us to the highway.

We drove for maybe half an hour in silence before I fully grasped the impact of what I'd just gotten us into. Not the trip itself—though I was well aware that it was crazy in its own right. But I hadn't thought through the fact I was putting myself in a confined space with someone I hadn't really spoken to in over a week. And we were going to have to be together for twenty hours, at least. This somehow hadn't been factored in to my earlier decision to ask Frank, and as we crossed into New York, and then New Jersey, I started to regret not investigating how much it would have been to take a cab, or a bus. Because our conversation on this road trip so far had been limited to only the most basic driving talk—*Can I get over to that lane? How are we on gas? Take the left exit*. And I was realizing that it was pretty terrible to be sitting in silence with someone who you always used to have something to say to.

"Music?" I asked, after we'd been driving in New Jersey for a good twenty minutes and I just couldn't stand the silence any longer. Frank glanced over at me and shrugged, nodding down at his iPod on the console.

"Sure," he said, politely, like I was a stranger. "Whatever you want."

I could feel myself getting mad at him, which wasn't really fair, since he was currently in the middle of doing me a huge favor. I bit back saying something to him, and reached forward to the radio. I scrolled through until I found something not-terrible, a station that seemed to mostly be playing music that had been popular five years ago. "This okay?"

"Whatever you want," Frank repeated, with the same inflection, irritating me even further.

"Fine," I said, turning the volume up slightly, so that the

silence in the truck wouldn't be quite so apparent. We'd only passed two exits, though, before I reached forward and turned it down again. "Thank you for doing this," I said, when I realized I hadn't told him this yet. "I really appreciate it."

Frank looked away from the road and glanced at me, then turned back to the highway that still seemed pretty clear, despite my parents' worries. "Sure," he said, in the same overly polite and formal voice that was currently driving me crazy. "It's what *friends* do, right?"

He put a spin on the word, like he was saying it sarcastically. I wasn't even sure what to make of that, so I just gave him a tight smile, turned the volume back up, and looked out the window again.

Maybe Frank had been feeling as annoyed as me, because by the time we crossed into Pennsylvania—the Keystone State—the tension between us was palpable, and rising, like the shimmering heat coming off the asphalt in the distance. And in contrast to the occasional license plates I saw, it was becoming clear by the charged silence between us that neither of us currently had a friend in Pennsylvania.

We'd long since lost the somewhat decent radio station, and while I'd tried to scan through them to find something else, I kept getting commercials and what sounded like polka. So I'd finally just turned off the radio, but the quiet in the truck felt oppressive, and I couldn't help but wonder if we would have been better off with the accordions.

"We need gas," Frank announced four exits later, breaking what felt like hours of silence.

I leaned forward to look at the signs that were posted by every exit, letting you know what you could find at that turnoff—usually just food, gas, and lodging, but I had seen the occasional ones for camping and swimming. Once we had gotten out of the tangle of the tri-state area and cleared New Jersey, things had opened up, and now I could see across the horizon, as this stretch of the state was pretty flat—blue sky stretching out endlessly in front of us, and bright-green grass on either side of the highway. It wasn't congested, and Frank had mostly been staying in the left lane, driving fast but always within shouting distance of the speed limit. "It looks like there will be some in three miles," I said as we passed the sign, and he moved a lane over.

Frank nodded but didn't say anything, and I just looked at him, long enough that he noticed as he shifted and glanced over at me with raised eyebrows. "What?"

"Nothing," I said, turning to look out the window. Frank took the exit—in addition to gas and food (no lodging) there was fishing at this location, as well. If we'd been talking, I had a feeling we would have been joking about the sign's fish symbol, which was comically oversized and about to bite down on a tiny hook. I would have made some remark about how this exit apparently had giant mutant fish, in addition to a Chevron, or Frank would have. But instead, we just passed the sign in silence and headed to the gas station, which happened to be part of an enormous travel mart.

"I'm happy to get the gas," Frank said as he pulled up next to the pump, but I shook my head.

"I insist." It was one thing I knew I wasn't going to budge on. If Frank was driving me, in his car, down to South Carolina, I was not going to let him pay for gas as well.

He handed me the keys and said, "It takes regular. Do you need some help?" I just shook my head, and Frank headed inside to the travel mart. I used my debit card to fill up the tank—I didn't want to use the conch money until we had to. As I watched the numbers go up—it appeared that the truck had a very large tank, which meant I was paying more for gas than I ever had in my life—I felt myself getting more and more frustrated. It wasn't that there was anything wrong with what Frank had said; it was the tone—so blandly polite. It occurred to me that maybe the only reason he'd agreed to come on this trip was because he was Frank Porter, ever the Boy Scout. And if that was the case, maybe he was fine with us just not talking for the next twenty hours. I suddenly thought back to Frank's parents at the gala, standing next to each other but not speaking, not once throughout the course of the night. Frank might have been okay with it, but I wasn't. The pump clicked off, and I winced at the amount and returned the nozzle. Not stopping to get my receipt, letting the wind take it and bear it away, I marched into the travel mart.

I found Frank by the cold drinks case, grabbing a water and a Coke.

"Hey," I said. Frank looked over at me, letting the glass refrigerator door swing shut, giving me a little blast of cool air.

"All filled up?" he asked in that same bland, maddening tone.

"Listen, I don't think it's fair for you to be mad at me." I was speaking without thinking about it first, not hesitating, just saying what I felt.

He just blinked at me for a moment, then looked down at the bottles in his hands, wiping the condensation off his water bottle's label—Lancaster Blue, a brand I'd never heard of before. "Let's not do this," he said, his voice tight. "We have a long drive ahead."

"So we're just supposed to sit there in silence?"

Frank looked back at me, and I saw frustration pass over his features. "Look, I'm here, aren't I? I'm helping you out. Let's leave it at that." He turned and headed to the chips aisle, and I followed, after grabbing myself a water and a Diet Coke.

"No," I said, more loudly than I intended to, and a woman who'd been reaching for a bag of Fritos glanced up at me. I took a step closer to him and lowered my voice. "If you're mad at me, just be mad at me. Don't pretend you're not." Somewhere in all this was getting lost the fact that I was mad at *him*, but I was no longer sure who was in the right, since we'd both behaved badly—me by kissing him, him by ignoring me for a week.

The woman with the Fritos was still looking at us, and Frank must have seen this, because he retreated to the candy aisle, and I followed. "*If* I am mad at you?" he asked, stopping in front of the chocolate section, like it was a rhetorical question, like the answer was obvious. "You ran away from me, Emily. Literally. You left me standing in the middle of the road because you wouldn't even hear me out."

I stared at him for a moment. I hadn't realized he would be mad about this; I'd assumed it was because of the kiss. "Well," I said, feeling a little off-balance, "maybe I didn't want to listen to you tell me we couldn't be friends anymore."

Frank just looked at me. "And what if that's not what I was going to say?"

"'Scuse me." I turned around and saw what looked like a bleary-eyed trucker reaching for the Reese's Pieces, which I was currently standing in front of.

I stepped aside, and Frank turned and walked up to the register. I followed, placing my items next to his on the counter, my thoughts spinning. I glanced over at him as I reached into my bag for my wallet. I was so sure I'd known what he'd come to my house to say; it was like I'd never allowed for another possibility.

"Um," I said, as the woman behind the counter started to scan our items, "So what were—"

"Four eighty," the woman said. Frank reached into his pocket, but I pushed a five across the counter to her before he could pay.

I took my change, and we picked up our respective drinks. Frank headed out of the mini-mart, into the sun, and I hurried to follow him. I realized, as we walked to the truck, that I had the keys, and could refuse to let him in until he told me, but I didn't think this would be the best way to go about things. I handed him the keys and walked around to the passenger side. I made myself wait until we were back on the highway before asking him again.

"So," I said, playing with the cap on my water bottle. "What was it that you were going to say?"

Frank let out a breath, and I saw his hands tighten on the steering wheel. "This is why I'm mad," he finally said, still looking straight ahead at the horizon. "I go to speak to you. I get my courage up, and you won't even listen to me. But now, a week later, only when we're stuck in a car together, you want to know."

Just like that, I felt myself get mad again. "You disappeared for days. You weren't texting me back."

"But then I came to your house," Frank said, as he changed lanes, his voice rising. "And you wouldn't give me a chance to explain."

"Well, I'm sorry if I'd had enough of people vanishing on me this summer!" I was yelling this before I knew I was going to say it, before I was really even aware it was what I felt.

"Oh," Frank said after a moment. He glanced over at me, and I thought I saw something in his expression soften. "I guess I didn't think about that."

We drove in silence, and I kicked off my flip-flops and

curled my legs up under me. I noticed the silence didn't feel quite so charged any longer. It wasn't the easy quiet that had been between us before, but it no longer felt uncomfortable. "So do you want to tell me now?" I finally asked.

Frank shook his head, but then said, "Maybe later." He reached forward and turned on the radio, starting to scan for a station, and I let it go for the moment, unrolling my window and letting the warm air whip my hair around my face.

I wasn't sure if it was the heat, or the fact that we'd landed on a station that seemed to be mostly easy listening, all soft wailing saxophones, or the fact that I'd gotten almost no sleep the night before, but as we crossed into Virginia, I felt myself yawning, my eyes getting heavy. I rested my head against the window and felt my eyes close.

I half expected I would dream about Sloane, if I dreamed at all. But when I opened my eyes again, I realized that I'd been dreaming about Frank. We'd been back together in his tent, where it was warm and peaceful, and he wanted to tell me something, something important.

I sat up and looked around. At first, all I could see was green. The truck was parked, I was alone in it, and all around me was green—brilliantly colored trees and grass. After a moment, I realized we were parked at a scenic overlook, and that Frank was standing a few feet away, taking pictures with his phone.

From the light, it looked like it was getting to be later in the afternoon, and when I pulled out my phone, I saw that it was almost six. It no longer felt quite so oppressively hot out, though it was hard to tell inside the truck. I stretched my legs in front of me, and rolled my shoulders back. Even though I could see the highway, you couldn't hear it here, just the low drone of cicadas and the occasional birdcall.

I wasn't sure how long Frank was going to be, so mostly to occupy myself, I reached for his iPod and started scrolling through it. He never titled his playlists—this had been one of our bones of contention as we exchanged music, since I always titled mine, titles that he'd liked to make fun of—so I just went to "Mix 14," which I assumed was the newest one, and scrolled through the songs.

MIX # 14

Entertainment	Phoenix
My Racing Thoughts	Jack's Mannequin
I Need My Girl	The National
Let's Not Let It	Randy Houser
Yesterday	The Beatles
Each Coming Night	Iron & Wine
Magnolia	The Hush Sound
I Always Knew	The Vaccines
Little Talks	Of Monsters and Men
You Came Around	Nico Stai
Everybody Talks	Neon Trees
Makes Me Lose Control	Eric Carmen

In My Life	The Beatles
Let's Go Surfing	The Drums
Young Love	Mystery Jets
Emmylou	First Aid Kit
Moth's Wings (stripped down version)	Passion Pit
It's a Hit	Rilo Kiley
Lights & Music	Cut Copy
You and Me	Parachute
Eleanor Rigby	The Beatles
Man/Bag of Sand	Frightened Rabbit
Isn't It a Lovely Night?	The December
Look at Us Now	Math & Physics Club
You Send Me	Sam Cooke

At first I was just looking through them, noticing with a bittersweet satisfaction that there was Eric Carmen on the list, which I'd introduced him to, and that Frank had even allowed some country on his precious iPod. But as I looked at it a little longer, I realized there was something else.

There was a code.

I wondered if he'd even known he was doing it. But there was my name in the song titles, over and over again. I felt myself smile as I looked down at the tiny, glowing screen, wondering when he'd done this. I wasn't sure what it meant, but it felt like he'd just given me a present.

Frank lowered his phone and turned around, and I hurriedly

dropped the iPod back in the console where I'd found it. I smiled when I saw him coming toward me. I wasn't thinking about the fact that things were strange between us at the moment; it was just my automatic reaction to seeing him. He smiled back at me, though this faded a moment later, like maybe he'd also forgotten for just a second.

"Where are we?" I asked, as he settled himself back behind the wheel.

"North Carolina," he said. "We're getting close."

I nodded, expecting to feel nervous or anxious about seeing Sloane, but I didn't. I just felt a kind of calm certainty, like we were heading in the right direction.

We got back onto the highway, and I'd only just managed to find a decent radio station before we were crossing into South Carolina. I looked at the state sign as we passed it, decorated with the palm tree and crescent moon that I now knew well. Even though it looked like we wouldn't get to the exit for River Port for an hour, I found myself sitting up straight, not just letting the scenery and exit signs pass me by, but paying attention to them, to each mile that was bringing me closer to Sloane.

We'd been driving for about an hour after the rest stop when Frank turned the radio off and looked over at me, like he was going to say something. Then he reached over and turned it back on again, but only for a moment before he snapped it off, the silence filling the car.

"So," he said.

Morgan Matson

I waited for more, but when nothing came after a few moments, just Frank looking straight ahead, at the highway, I prompted, "So?"

"The thing I was going to tell you," he said slowly, like he was finding the words as he was speaking them. "You said you wanted to know what it was."

"Yes," I made myself say, even though I was now more scared of the answer than I had been when I was pushing Frank to tell me outside the travel mart.

He looked over at me, long enough that my heart started to beat harder. "Lissa and I broke up," he said, then turned the radio back on again.

I stared him. We were still on the highway. I was holding the directions and looking for 14A, the exit that would take us to River Port. But nothing else was the same. It was like the very air in the truck had changed.

Frank was looking straight ahead, like he had no idea he'd just made it harder for me to breathe. "When," I started, finally, realizing that I had to say something, and that I wasn't up to asking him what I really wanted to know. "When did this happen?"

"A few days after the gala," he said. "I drove down to Princeton to talk to her."

I'd known that he'd gone to her, but I that thought it was to *be* with her—not to break up with her. A new, terrible fear crept in—was I responsible for this? Had Frank broken up with his long-term girlfriend because I'd kissed him?

He let out a long breath, then went on, "Things hadn't been right with us for months," he said. "I was really trying, this summer. I didn't think that it would matter, being apart. But it wasn't just the distance. It was more than that. It had been going on for a while."

I just nodded. I had dozens of questions, but none that I felt I could ask him. Maybe Frank sensed this, because he went on, "We didn't really have all that much in common anymore. It was more like . . . we were just used to each other."

"So . . . ," I started, hoping this wasn't the exact wrong question to ask. "It wasn't because of me?"

"No," Frank said, shaking his head. "I mean, when we first started hanging out this summer, I wasn't thinking that way," he said. "At all. I was committed to Lissa. And you and I were friends. But then . . ." Frank glanced over at me for just a second, but that was all that it took. It suddenly felt like the truck was a good ten degrees warmer than it had been just seconds ago. He cleared his throat before speaking. "I don't know. Maybe it was the night of my birthday. But at some point, I started . . . thinking about you," he said, a little haltingly, "more than I knew I should. Much more." Without even leaning over to look in my side mirror, I could tell that I was blushing. "But I wasn't sure . . . I didn't know how you might be feeling until you drove me home."

"Right," I murmured, thinking about the way I had kissed him, not the other way around, making my feelings pretty clear.

"And it wasn't fair to her," Frank said, glancing quickly into the rearview mirror and changing lanes. "Or you. So I drove down to see her."

"What happened?" I asked, wishing I could seem impartial, detached, and not like someone who was desperate to know how things had turned out.

Frank took a breath and let it out. "She was feeling the same way," he said. "It was why she didn't come in July. She knew if she saw me, she'd have to break up with me, and she didn't want to do that to me on my birthday. And as soon as I started to tell her what I was feeling, she was pretty quick to end it."

"I'm really sorry."

Frank nodded, and paused for a long moment before he said, "I think we're going to be fine. I don't think we'll ever be great friends, but it's okay."

"Good," I said, trying to sound cheerful about this when my thoughts were spinning. I remembered when Frank came to my house, and how happy he had seemed. He'd wanted to tell me then that they'd broken up. And I hadn't even let him finish, and had run away from him. I suddenly wished, more than anything, that I'd let Frank tell me when he'd wanted to. Because I was no longer sure what any of this meant.

"So, um," Frank said, sounding more nervous than I'd ever heard him, "what do you—"

"Oh my god," I said, loudly, pointing out of my side of the car as 14A approached with worrying swiftness. "There's our exit." Frank glanced at the mirror, then cut across the two lanes that were thankfully free of cars, to take the exit for River Port. "Sorry," I said, when we were off the interstate and winding around the ramp. "I didn't mean to interrupt you." In fact, I really, *really* hadn't wanted to interrupt him then, because it had seemed like he was about to ask me something important.

"It's okay," he said, stopping at a red and glancing over at me. "I was just . . ." The car behind us honked and Frank looked around. "Do I take a right here?"

I fumbled for the directions, and realized that this might be the worst possible moment to have an important conversation. "Right," I confirmed, and Frank made the turn. I looked down at the directions, which got much more complicated than they previously had been, then over at Frank.

"We don't have to talk about this now," he said. He nodded to the directions in my hand. "Let's just get there first."

"Okay," I said, nodding a few too many times. I was actually grateful to have a moment to try and process everything I'd just learned in the past few minutes. And following the instructions to get to 4 Brookside Lane, with their clear steps to a known outcome, seemed preferable to trying to sort through my tangle of thoughts.

I rolled down my window, and Frank did the same, and the warm, early evening air blew through the truck, ruffling the directions in my hand. We drove through a one-street down-town, drug stores and clothing shops, but also a lot of empty storefronts, for-sale signs in the windows. We turned down a side road that took us through a neighborhood that looked grand but fading, with mansions on either side of the road, most separated by long stretches of land. We'd been driving for a few miles when I realized we were getting close.

"We should be coming up to Brookside," I said, leaning forward to look for it. "On the left." A moment later, I saw the sign, half hidden by an overgrown tree. "There."

"They don't make this place easy to find," Frank murmured as he made the turn. We were looking for number four, but this didn't appear to be an ordinary road, where that would have been a simple thing to find. We passed the drive for the first house, but it wasn't until several minutes later that we saw the second one. The road was long, with trees on either side, so overgrown they almost met above us and formed a canopy.

I glanced at my phone as Frank drove slowly down Brookside and we passed the third house. It was almost eight, and night was falling, the shadows of the trees lengthening and stretching out all around us.

"Are you sure this is right?" Frank asked. He turned on the headlights, which were suddenly bright against the falling darkness and squinted out in front of him. "Because I don't think—"

"It's there," I said, pointing to the driveway. You would have missed it unless you'd been searching for it. There was a brick pillar on either side of the drive, and they both had brass plaques on them that read *4 Brookside*, but the bricks were crumbling and it looked like the brass hadn't been polished in a while.

Frank turned down the driveway and I felt my heart start to beat faster. When a house came into view, I took off my seat belt and leaned forward to look closer.

The house was big and white and sprawling, and you could tell it had once been impressive, but the paint was peeling, and the lawn looked overgrown. But I barely noticed this, because there was a girl sitting on the mansion's steps in the falling darkness, reading a magazine and sipping a Diet Coke.

Frank had only just stopped the car before I was getting out of it, closing my door behind me and walking toward the house and my best friend.

Sloane looked up from her magazine and her jaw dropped open. She stared at me as I walked closer in the fading light and looked up at her.

I smiled at her before I spoke. "Hi."

17
FIND
WHAT'S
LOST

"Emily?" Sloane dropped the magazine and stood up, stumbling once as she took the steps down to the driveway. She stood in front of me, her eyes wide and shocked, like she wasn't entirely sure this was actually happening.

"Hey," I whispered, feeling tears come to my eyes.

"Oh my god," she said, still looking stunned, shaking her head. But then she smiled, and I saw that her blue eyes were shiny with tears as well. "Oh my *god*," she said again, and reached out and hugged me close. I hugged back, and couldn't tell if I was laughing or crying, or both, but whatever it was, it sounded like Sloane was doing the same. "What are you doing here?" she asked when we broke apart. "How did you find it? I mean . . ."

"It's a long story," I said, still looking at Sloane, trying to take her in. I'd expected to see the Sloane I remembered—wearing some fabulous vintage dress, with red lipstick on and earrings that jangled when she turned her head. But she was dressed in a pair of jean shorts and an old T-shirt that she'd only ever worn before as a pajama top. Her hair was back in a messy ponytail, and her pink toenail polish was chipped almost to the point of no longer existing. She was still Sloane, of course . . . but not a version I was familiar with.

I took a breath to begin to explain when the truck door slammed and we both looked in its direction. Frank was walking around to the hood and leaning against it. Anyone else would have probably stayed put—or at least looked deeply uncomfortable, but Frank seemed like he was taking this in stride, like helping to reunite friends was just a normal thing he did. "Hi," he called, raising a hand in a wave.

Sloane squinted through the darkness. "Emily, I might be hallucinating," she said calmly, as she turned to me. "Because I could almost swear that was Frank Porter."

I nodded and motioned Frank over. "Like I said," I told her as she turned to me, jaw dropping once again. "It's a long story."

Twenty minutes later, it was just the two of us, sitting on the house's back porch.

The porch was wide, with a screened area just off it, and a swing, flowerpots, and wicker chairs with patched and sun-faded cushions. It looked out on the brook that the street was named for, that I could now hear better than I could see, as night was falling, a blue night with fireflies already lighting up intermittently from all sides. Sloane was on her own in the house—Milly and Anderson and her aunt Laney had gone to Charleston for the weekend. Because it seemed that they lived with her aunt now—they'd been living here the whole time.

Frank had claimed that he was exhausted, and asked if he could crash on the couch for a while. I wasn't sure if this was because he was giving Sloane and me some time to talk, or if he was actually tired. As I thought back on the day, and the fact that he'd been driving in the sun for hours—and hadn't taken a nap, like I had—I realized it might have been some of each.

Sloane had gotten us both Diet Cokes, and was walking around the porch barefoot, lighting citronella candles and plugging in the twinkle lights that she'd told me her aunt absolutely hated, but that she'd gone ahead and covered the porch with anyway.

When the lights had been lit, she came and sat next to me, and we looked at each other. It suddenly seemed like there was so much to say—so much to get through—that it was hard to even begin.

"I can't believe you're here," she said, tucking her legs up underneath her and shaking her head. "I keep thinking this is a dream, and I'm going to wake up at any moment." She studied me, tilting her head to the side. "I *love* the hair," she said. "It looks amazing."

I smiled and brushed my bangs back. There was a piece of me that wanted, so badly, to just jump back into being Sloane-and-Emily again, for as long as I was here. I could see it would be easy; she'd already been giving me several *We need to talk about this* looks in terms of Frank, and I could feel the pull to keep things light, just have fun and let things go back to how they were. But I needed answers, and I hadn't come all this way to leave without them.

I reached into my bag and pulled out the list, the paper deeply creased from a summer of folding and refolding. "I got your list," I said. "I did them."

Her head snapped up. "All of them?"

"All of them," I said, handing it to her.

"Really?" she asked. She looked shocked—and a little skeptical. "Even the skinny-dipping?"

"You just left," I said, hearing my voice shake, remembering her disappearance, the weeks of silence, and then what it had been like to get the list and nothing else, no explanation. "I had no idea where you were or why. Just this."

Sloane just looked at me for a moment, and I could practically feel the part of her that hated confrontations shrinking away. But, surprising me, she nodded. "I know," she said. "And I'm sorry. I just thought it was for the best."

"How could it be for the best?" I asked. "I've spent the whole summer wondering what happened to you, and why you somehow didn't care enough to tell me."

"It's not that," she said quickly, her voice hurt and a little sharp. "Are you kidding me?"

"Then what?"

Sloane glanced out to the brook, where I swore I could hear what sounded like frogs somewhere in the distance. As I waited for her response, there was a piece of me that still couldn't believe that I was here, with Sloane again, on a humid night on a porch in South Carolina, finally getting my answers.

"When you move as much as I have," she finally said, still not looking back at me, "you know how it ends. You promise to stay in touch with people, but it doesn't work out. It never does. And you forget about what the friendship used to be like, why you liked that person. And I hated it. And I just didn't want to do it again. Not with you."

I looked at her, her head still turned away from me, but I knew her well enough to hear the tremble in her voice, the one she was trying to hide. "So what, then?" I asked, trying to keep my voice gentle. "You just leave without an explanation?"

"I just thought it would be better," she said, running her hand over her face and turning back to me. "To remember it as it was. As really great. Not anything else. Just the best friend I've ever had."

I felt my lip start to tremble and bit down on it, trying to marshal my thoughts. I could see where she was coming from, in theory. But only in theory. And before I'd worked it all out, I was speaking, my words coming out in a jumble. "No," I said, shaking my head. My honesty hat was on, and I was calling her out on this. Sloane glanced over at me, and I could see this had surprised her. "You can't just leave people behind because you think it's going to be too hard to commit to a friendship. You can't live your life that way."

"You don't understand," Sloane said, her voice quiet. She looked out to the water for a second, and I knew that the role I'd played in our friendship before—the one I could feel her wanting me to move back into, like the way you try and force your feet into a favorite pair of shoes even after they've gotten too tight—would be to let this go, not push her, smooth it over, go on to other things.

"So help me understand," I asked, looking right at her, not letting her off easily.

Sloane let out a long breath that had a hitch somewhere in the middle. "You know why we move so much?" she finally asked. She was looking at the ground, not meeting my eye. "Because my parents blew through their trust funds and have never had real jobs. So we just go wherever people or relatives will let us stay in their summerhouses or second homes. And sometimes Anderson actually makes a good investment, and we have a little money, but of course, it's gone immediately. . . ." Her voice trailed off, and I heard in that moment, just how tired she sounded.

I just looked at her for a moment. Suddenly, it was like I didn't even recognize the person sitting next to me, the person

I'd thought I'd known better than anyone. While I'd been sharing all my secrets with her, she'd been keeping huge ones from me.

"So you lied," I said, and I could feel my anger start to come back again, and my voice begin to rise. I thought about how dazzled I'd been by Sloane since the first day, how much I'd wanted to be like her—and it hadn't even been real. None of it had. "Why would you—"

"Because it's embarrassing!" Sloane's voice broke on the last word, and I could see her hands were shaking. "You have this perfect family. And I've got Milly and Anderson." She let out a short, unhappy laugh. "You were always telling me how great you thought my parents were, how glamorous our lives were, how wonderful the house was. . . ." She shook her head. "You know it wasn't even our house? The heirs were fighting over it, and Milly's a second cousin or something, so she talked them into letting us be the 'caretakers.' And when the will was settled, of course, we were out of there." She looked at me, then back down at her hands again. "I'm sorry," she whispered. "I just . . . wanted you to like me."

I sat back against the step, trying to process all this. And I thought, for some reason, of the spec house—the structure that was perfect only from the outside. I looked at Sloane, and saw the hunch in her shoulders, and suddenly understood how hard it must have been for her, not letting anyone—even me—know any of this. And I realized it didn't matter.

"I don't care," I said. She looked up at me, and I shook my

head. "I mean, I wish you would have told me. But the house? None of that stuff's important."

Sloane looked at me, and I saw her eyes were wet. "Really?" she said. It was more like a whisper than a question. I nodded, and she wiped her fingers beneath her eyes.

We sat in silence for a minute, and it felt a little bit like the start of something. She was telling me the truth, and I had refused to just go along with her. It felt new. It felt like maybe now we could start the next chapter of our friendship—whatever that ended up looking like.

Sloane leaned against me, and I leaned back, until, after a few moments, you couldn't tell who was holding up who.

"So," Sloane said after a long moment. I saw, to my surprise, that she was looking down at the list and smiling. "Skinny-dipping," she said, sitting up and turning to face me. "Spill."

I laughed. "It was your idea," I said, thinking back to the night on the beach, how I knew it was a great story, one she'd never believe.

"Emily," she said, "*I've* never even gone skinny-dipping!"

"I can give you some pointers, if you want," I said, with a grin. "Like . . . always keep an eye on your towels."

She was still just looking at me like she wasn't entirely sure who I was. "And you really used Penelope? And you kissed someone? Oh my god. Who?"

"I tried to steal your sign from the drive-in," I said. "But it fell and I almost got caught. Frank bailed me out." Sloane

Morgan Matson

looked at me, alarmed, and I added, "Not literally. He just covered for me."

"I really can't believe you did all these," she said, still sounding a little awed. "You actually rode a horse?"

"I guess I thought they would lead me to you," I said, "somehow."

Sloane looked at the list for a long moment, then smiled. "Maybe they did."

I thought of how I'd gotten here—and how I probably wouldn't have spent the summer with Frank if I hadn't gone to the Orchard that first night. Or become friends with Dawn on my quest to hug a Jamie. I thought about all the things her list had given me over the course of the summer, and everything that had happened because of it. "Maybe you're right."

When the mosquitos started attacking us, we went inside to find Frank waking up from his nap. Sloane heated up a frozen pizza, bemoaning the lack of delivery options in River Port. We ate standing around her kitchen counter, and after Frank polished off three slices, he headed to bed in the guest room that Sloane had made up for him. We discussed—but I was trying not to think about—the fact that we were going to have to be on the road again by seven. I needed to get back before my parents, so they wouldn't realize I'd left to travel over many state lines with a boy.

Sloane lent me sleep clothes and a toothbrush, and when I unfolded the T-shirt, I realized it was actually mine—the *Bug Juice* movie shirt.

We were sleeping on the screened-in porch, where she'd set up an ad hoc bedroom during the heat wave that River Port was currently going through. Sloane was on the porch's couch, and she dragged in a foldaway bed for me, and we pushed them close enough so that we wouldn't have to raise our voices to hear each other when we talked.

"Okay," she said, when we'd turned out the last of the lights and I could only see her by the moonlight coming in from outside. "Frank. Start talking."

I smiled against my pillow and filled her in on the broad outlines—our friendship, my crush, the kiss, the Lissa-breakup bombshell. And us, together, here. Now.

"Oh my god," she said, once I'd finished. She had reacted just as I'd hoped she would throughout. She'd been responding at the right moments, making me realize how much I'd missed telling her things—her enthusiasm, her complete lack of judgment, the way that, even when you were wrong, she was on your side. "I mean," she went on without waiting for me to answer, and though I couldn't see it, I could hear the smile in her voice, "what are you thinking?"

"I don't know," I said slowly. If Frank and I tried to be something, it would be *real*, in a way that was scary—but also really exciting.

"He did just get out of a really long relationship," Sloane pointed out. "Is this going to be a rebound thing?"

"No," I said automatically, without even having to think

Morgan Matson

about it. And I realized as I did that Sloane didn't know Frank. And she didn't know the me I was with him. "It's more than that."

"But . . ." She propped herself up on one elbow. "Frank Porter is like the most serious guy we know. If you're going out with him—you're *committed*."

"But that's what I want," I said, again without thinking about it.

"Really?" Sloane asked. Not skeptically, just with surprise.

"I know things might not work," I said. "And I know it's scary, but the things that are worth it are. It feels right."

"What is that like?" Sloane asked, her voice quiet, genuinely curious.

I knew the answer to that immediately. It was like swimming under the stars, like sleeping outside, like climbing a tree in the dark and seeing the view. It was scary and safe and peaceful and exciting, all at the same time. It was the way I felt when I was with him. "Like a well-ordered universe."

We were silent for a few minutes, and I realized it was okay. Maybe we didn't have to share every single feeling we were having, and analyze it. "Em," Sloane finally said. "I'm only asking because I don't want you to get hurt. But what if it doesn't work out?"

When I answered her, I could hear the hope in my voice. "But what if it does?"

I woke up when it was still dark out, and reached underneath my cot to check the time on my phone, cupping my hand over the screen to shield the light from Sloane, who I could tell was still asleep, her breath coming slow and even. It was five-thirty in the morning, and I was amazed I was awake, considering that Sloane and I had talked for hours.

There had just been too much to cover, and every time one of us would mention that we should probably stop talking and get some rest, something else would come up that had to be addressed. As we talked, trying to fit three months' worth of conversations into a few hours, it felt like we were fighting against the dawn that was coming, and if we just kept talking, and filling up the hours, maybe we could hold it off.

But then the pauses had gotten longer, until there was just silence between us, and I drifted off with the knowledge that if I thought of something else I needed to say to Sloane, she would be right there to hear it.

But as I climbed out of bed now, I was trying my best not to wake her as I walked onto the back porch. It was still dark out, but the stars were fading, and I had a feeling the sun was going to be up before too long. I looked over and saw my list, folded up, where we'd anchored it under one of the candles. I picked it up, planning on putting it back in my purse for safekeeping, when I had an idea. I ducked back into the screened porch, retrieved my purse, and brought it back outside with me. I found a pen and my schedule for next week at Paradise in my bag. I turned it over to the blank sheet on the back, lit one of the candles so that my handwriting wouldn't be too illegible, and started to write.

1. Call your best friend twice a week.

2. When your phone rings, answer it.

3. If you meet someone you like, wait two weeks before kissing him.

3a. (Okay, one week.)

4. Date someone who'll wait to make sure you get inside before driving away.

5. If you're mad at someone, <u>tell them</u>. I promise nothing bad will happen.

6. Get your license. (This way, you can drive me when I come and visit.)

7. Hug a Carl.

I kept on writing, filling the list out, trying to do for Sloane what she'd done for me. When I'd finished, I added at the bottom, *When you finish this list, find me and tell me all about it.*

I heard the door from the screened porch slam, and I turned around to see Sloane, in her vintage silk pajama set—I'd been with her when she bought it—crossing the porch and sitting next to me on the top step.

"Hey," she said, around a yawn. "I woke up and you weren't there."

"Yeah," I said, raising my eyebrows at her. "That's really awful, isn't it?"

Sloane laughed and I saw she'd understood me. She nodded at the paper in my lap. "What's that?"

"It's for you," I said, handing it to her. She unfolded it and

I watched her expression change as she read it. "I just thought I should give you something to start on," I said. "You know, since I've finished all of mine."

Sloane smiled and bumped her shoulder into mine, but then left it there, and I leaned into her as well. "You should probably get going, right?" she asked after a few minutes, her voice soft and sad.

"I should," I said. But neither of us moved, despite the fact that across the brook I could see the first ribbon of dawn at the bottom of the horizon, and the day that had come after all.

By seven thirty, Frank and I were ready to head out. I'd showered and borrowed one of Sloane's dresses—she'd admitted she owed me after taking the *Bug Juice* T-shirt. As I came outside with my purse, Frank and Sloane were talking, and they stopped as I approached. This worried me slightly, especially coupled with the fact that when I raised my eyebrows at her, Sloane shot me a tiny wink.

Frank was wearing a Hilton Head Golf Tournament T-shirt that confused me until I realized that Sloane had probably taken it from Anderson and given it to him. Frank said good-bye to Sloane, and then he headed over to the truck, and I knew that he was giving Sloane and me a chance to say our farewells alone.

"So," Sloane said as we stood together by the front steps. "We'll talk tonight?"

I nodded. It was one of the things we'd discussed last night in the dark—we would talk twice a week at least, without fail.

Morgan Matson

She wasn't allowed to disappear on me, nor I on her. "I'll call you as soon as I'm back," I promised.

Sloane looked at me and shook her head. "I can't believe you came here," she said. She let out a shaky breath, and her lower lip was trembling, just like I could feel mine was. "I just . . . ," she started.

I nodded. "Me too," I said. She hugged me tight, and I hugged her back. I was going to miss her—I knew it. But somehow, I had the feeling that we were going to be okay. I didn't know what would happen with us. Maybe we'd find a way to attend the same college and be roommates and have the most amazingly decorated dorm room ever. Maybe we'd end up being pen pals, sending lists back and forth. Or we'd just stick to talking twice a week, or we'd video chat, or else just spend all our money traveling to hang out with each other on weekends. I somehow knew that the particulars didn't matter. She was my heart, she was half of me, and nothing, certainly not a few measly hundred miles, was ever going to change that.

We broke apart and Sloane wiped under her eyes. "I'm sorry," she whispered.

I gave her a trembly smile back. "It's okay," I said.

"We'll talk tonight," she said. It wasn't a question. It was the plan, and I nodded.

"Tonight," I said. We just looked at each other for a moment longer. There was nothing to do now but leave, and we both knew it. I made myself turn and walk away from her, back toward the truck, and Sloane stayed where she was, by the steps.

I got into the passenger seat, and looked across at Frank. "You okay?" he asked, as I buckled myself in and rolled down my window while he started the engine.

I looked back at Sloane, who was still standing by the steps, not making any move to go inside. "Yeah," I said. "I am."

Frank pulled the truck down the driveway, and I turned in my seat to look back. Sloane was walking behind us, holding one hand up in a wave. I waved back, and she followed behind us until we turned onto the main road. I leaned half out the window to wave back at her, and I saw her see this and smile. And she kept following the truck, like we were a very small parade, waving and waving, until Frank took the curve in the road and then she was gone.

Morgan Matson

18
TAKE
A
CHANCE

We didn't have the radio on this time, but I didn't want it. Both our windows were unrolled and the warm air was blowing through the truck ruffling Frank's hair, which had dried funny, with pieces sticking up here and there. It was all I could do not to reach over and run my hands through it.

He took his eyes off the road and looked over at me, and I didn't blush or look away. I just looked right back at him. There was tension between us again, but it wasn't the simmering, angry kind that had been there the day before. This felt like the way you get nervous right before something exciting happens—the moment when you're balanced on the top of the roller coaster, the hush before the surprise party, the second after the diving board but before the water, when you can close your eyes and imagine, for just a second, that you're flying. The feeling that good things were coming, almost here, any moment now.

Frank was driving with one hand on the wheel, the other resting on the seat between us. Without knowing I was going to, without thinking about it first, I slid as close to him as my seat belt would allow and rested my hand on his.

He smiled without taking his eyes off the road, turned his palm up, and threaded his fingers through mine. My heart started beating double-time, but it only lasted a moment, as Frank took his hand back, put on his turn signal, and took the next exit off the highway.

I glanced over at him, surprised. "Where are we going?"

He smiled at me. "You'll see."

I leaned forward to try and see where he was headed, but we were only off the highway for a few minutes before he turned down a narrow, unmarked dirt path. "How did you even know about this?" The sun hadn't yet totally risen, but the path was so dense with trees that it almost looked like we were going into night again as he drove through them.

"Sloane may have mentioned something about one of her favorite spots," he said, making another turn.

The dense trees opened up and there was a clearing that he pulled the truck into. He put it in park and turned off the engine and, like we'd discussed it beforehand, we both got out. The clearing provided a scenic viewpoint of its own, though

Morgan Matson

this one wasn't marked for tourists, and we were the only ones seeing it. All around us was the view of a gorgeous valley, slowly being lit up by the rising sun.

Frank turned to look down at me, and he was right there, so close. "Hi," he said.

I looked up at him. Now that the moment was here, it didn't feel scary. What would happen would happen, and I couldn't know or control it. But I was ready for it to begin. "Hey," I said.

"In a well-ordered universe," he said, and I could hear how nervous he was, "I'd be able to do this." He leaned his head down and kissed me softly, then pulled back, making sure this was okay.

I smiled at him. "Then we must be in one," I said. And as the sun rose behind us and he bent his head down to kiss me again, I leaned forward.

Toward him, and to whatever came next.

IF YOU ENJOYED THIS, TURN OVER TO READ THE
BEGINNING OF MORGAN'S FIRST BOOK . . .

Amy & Roger's EPIC Detour

Morgan MATSON

RAVEN ROCK HIGH SCHOOL
Raven Rock, CA

FINAL REPORT CARD

Student

AMELIA E. CURRY   JUNIOR/500 TRACK

Class	Final Grade
American Literature	A
American History	A
Chemistry	B-
French	B+
Physical Education	B
Honors Theater	A

Notes

This student's academic record will be transferred to STANWICH HIGH SCHOOL, Stanwich, Connecticut. Student will be matriculating as a senior in the fall.

Absences

1—Excused (A)
5—Excused (D)

Excused Absences

A Illness
B School-Sponsored Event
C Vacation
D Bereavement
E Other

Eureka [I have found it]
—California state motto

I sat on the front steps of my house and watched the beige Subaru station wagon swing too quickly around the cul-de-sac. This was a rookie mistake, one made by countless FedEx guys. There were only three houses on Raven Crescent, and most people had reached the end before they'd realized it. Charlie's stoner friends had never remembered and would always just swing around the circle again before pulling into our driveway. Rather than using this technique, the Subaru stopped, brake lights flashing red, then white as it backed around the circle and stopped in front of the house. Our driveway was short enough that I could read the car's bumper stickers: MY SON WAS RANDOLPH HALL'S STUDENT OF THE MONTH and MY KID AND MY $$$ GO TO COLORADO COLLEGE. There were two people in the car talking, doing the awkward car-conversation thing where you still have seat belts on, so you can't fully turn and face the other person.

Halfway up the now overgrown lawn was the sign that had been there for the last three months, the inanimate object I'd grown to hate with a depth of feeling that worried me sometimes. It was a Realtor's sign, featuring a picture of a smiling, overly hairsprayed blond woman. FOR SALE, the sign read, and then in bigger letters underneath that, WELCOME HOME.

I had puzzled over the capitalization ever since the sign went up and still hadn't come up with an explanation. All I could determine was that it must have been a nice thing to see if it was a house you were thinking about moving into. But not so nice if it was the house you were moving out from. I could practically hear Mr. Collins, who had taught my fifth-grade English class and was still the most intimidating teacher I'd ever had, yelling at me. "Amy Curry," I could still hear him intoning, "*never* end a sentence with a preposition!" Irked that after six years he was still mentally correcting me, I told the Mr. Collins in my head to off fuck.

I had never thought I'd see a Realtor's sign on our lawn. Until three months ago, my life had seemed boringly settled. We lived in Raven Rock, a suburb of Los Angeles, where my parents were both professors at College of the West, a small school that was a ten-minute drive from our house. It was close enough for an easy commute, but far enough away that you couldn't hear the frat party noise on Saturday nights. My father taught history (The Civil War and Reconstruction), my mother English literature (Modernism).

My twin brother, Charlie—three minutes younger—had gotten a perfect verbal score on his PSAT and had just barely escaped a possession charge when he'd managed to convince the cop who'd busted him that the ounce of pot in his backpack was, in fact, a rare California herb blend known as Humboldt, and that he was actually an apprentice at the Pasadena Culinary Institute.

I had just started to get leads in the plays at our high school and had made out three times with Michael Young, college freshman, major undecided. Things weren't perfect—my BFF, Julia Andersen, had moved to Florida in January—but in retrospect, I could see that they had actually been pretty wonderful. I just hadn't realized it at the time. I'd always assumed things would stay pretty much the same.

I looked out at the strange Subaru and the strangers inside still talking and thought, not for the first time, what an idiot I'd been. And there was a piece of me—one that never seemed to appear until it was late and I was maybe finally about to get some sleep—that wondered if I'd somehow caused it all, by simply counting on the fact that things wouldn't change. In addition, of course, to all the other ways I'd caused it.

My mother decided to put the house on the market almost immediately after the accident. Charlie and I hadn't been consulted, just informed. Not that it would have done any good at that point to ask Charlie anyway. Since it happened, he had been almost constantly high. People at the funeral had murmured sympathetic things when they'd seen him, assuming that his bloodshot eyes were a result of crying. But apparently, these people had no olfactory senses, as anyone downwind of Charlie could smell the real reason. He'd had been partying on a semiregular basis since seventh grade, but had gotten more into it this past year. And after the accident happened, it got much, *much* worse, to the point where not-high Charlie became something of a mythic figure, dimly remembered, like the yeti.

The solution to our problems, my mother had decided, was to move. "A fresh start," she'd told us one night at dinner. "A place without so many memories." The Realtor's sign had gone up the next day.

We were moving to Connecticut, a state I'd never been to and harbored no real desire to move to. Or, as Mr. Collins would no doubt prefer, a state to which I harbored no real desire to move. My grandmother lived there, but she had always come to visit us, since, well, we lived in Southern California and she lived in Connecticut. But my mother had been offered a position with Stanwich College's English department. And nearby there was, apparently, a great local high school that she was sure we'd just love. The college had helped her find an available house for rent, and as soon as Charlie and I finished up our junior year, we would all move out there, while the WELCOME HOME Realtor sold our house here.

At least, that had been the plan. But a month after the sign had appeared on the lawn, even my mother hadn't been able to keep pretending she didn't see what was going on with Charlie. The next thing I knew, she'd pulled him out of school and installed him in a teen rehab facility in North Carolina. And then she'd gone straight on to Connecticut to teach some summer courses at the college and to "get things settled." At least, that's why she said she had to leave. But I had a pretty strong suspicion that she wanted to get away from me. After all, it seemed like she could barely stand to look at me. Not that I blamed her. I could barely stand to look at myself most days.

So I'd spent the last month alone in our house, except for Hildy the Realtor popping in with prospective house buyers, almost always when I was just out of the shower, and my aunt, who came down occasionally from Santa Barbara to make sure I was managing to feed myself and hadn't started making meth in the backyard. The plan was simple: I'd finish up the school year, then head to Connecticut. It was just the car that caused the problem.

The people in the Subaru were still talking, but it looked like they'd taken off their seat belts and were facing each other. I looked at our two-car garage that now had only one car parked in it, the only one we still had. It was my mother's car, a red Jeep Liberty. She needed the car in Connecticut, since it was getting complicated to keep borrowing my grandmother's ancient Coupe deVille. Apparently, my grandmother was missing a lot of bridge games and didn't care that my mother kept needing to go to Bed Bath & Beyond. My mother had told me her solution to the car problem a week ago, last Thursday night.

It had been the opening night of the spring musical, *Candide*, and for the first time after a show, there hadn't been anyone waiting for me in the lobby. In the past, I'd always shrugged my parents and Charlie off quickly, accepting their bouquets of flowers and compliments, but already thinking about the cast party. I hadn't realized, until I walked into the lobby with the rest of the cast, what it would be like not to have anyone there waiting for me, to tell me "Good show." I'd taken a cab home almost immediately, not even sure where the cast party was going to be held. The rest of the cast—the people who'd been my closest friends only three months ago—were laughing and talking together as I packed up my show bag and waited outside the school for my cab. I'd told them repeatedly I wanted to be left alone, and clearly they had listened. It shouldn't have come as a surprise. I'd found out that if you pushed people away hard enough, they tended to go.

I'd been standing in the kitchen, my Cunégonde makeup heavy on my skin, my false eyelashes beginning to irritate my eyes, and the "Best of All Possible Worlds" song running through my head, when the phone rang.

"Hi, hon," my mother said with a yawn when I answered the phone. I looked at the clock and realized it was nearing one a.m. in Connecticut. "How are you?"

I thought about telling her the truth. But since I hadn't done that in almost three months, and she hadn't seemed to notice, there didn't seem to be any point in starting now. "Fine," I said, which was my go-to answer. I put some of last night's dinner—Casa Bianca pizza—in the microwave and set it to reheat.

"So listen," my mother said, causing my guard to go up. That was how she usually prefaced any information she was about to give me that I wasn't going to like. And she was speaking too quickly, another giveaway. "It's about the car."

"The car?" I set the pizza on the plate to cool. Without my noticing, it had stopped being a plate and had become *the* plate. I was pretty much just using, then washing, the one plate. It was as though all the rest of the dishes had become superfluous.

"Yes," she said, stifling another yawn. "I've been looking at the cost to have it shipped on a car carrier, along with the cost of your plane fare, and well . . ." She paused. "I'm afraid it's just not possible right now. With the house still not sold, and the cost of your brother's facility . . ."

"What do you mean?" I asked, not following. I took a tentative bite of pizza.

"We can't afford both," she said. "And I need the car. So I'm going to need it driven out here."

The pizza was still too hot, but I swallowed it anyway, and felt my throat burn and my eyes water. "I can't drive," I said, when I felt I could speak again. I hadn't driven since the accident, and had no plans to start again any time soon. Or ever. I could feel my throat constrict at the thought, but I forced the words out. "You know that. I won't."

"Oh, you won't have to drive!" She was speaking too brightly for someone who'd been yawning a moment before. "Marilyn's son is going to drive. He needs to come East anyway, to spend the summer with his father in Philadelphia, so it all works out."

There were so many things wrong with that sentence I wasn't sure where to begin. "Marilyn?" I asked, starting at the beginning.

"Marilyn Sullivan," she said. "Or I suppose it's Marilyn Harper now. I keep forgetting she changed it back after the divorce. Anyway, you know my friend Marilyn. The Sullivans used to live over on Holloway, until the divorce, then she moved to Pasadena. But you and Roger were always playing that game. What's it called? Potato? Yam?"

"Spud," I said automatically. "Who's Roger?"

She let out one of her long sighs, the kind designed to let me know that I was trying her patience. "Marilyn's son," she said. "Roger Sullivan. You remember him."

My mother was always telling me what I remembered, as if that would make it true. "No, I don't."

"Of course you do. You just said you used to play that game."

"I remember Spud," I said. I wondered, not for the first time, why every conversation I had with my mother had to be so difficult. "I don't remember anyone named Roger. Or Marilyn, for that matter."

"Well," she said, and I could hear her voice straining to stay upbeat, "you'll have a chance to get to know him now. I've mapped out an itinerary for you two. It should take you four days."

Questions about who remembered what now seemed unimportant. "Wait a second," I said, holding on to the kitchen counter for support. "You want me to spend four days in a car with someone I've never met?"

"I told you, you've met," my mother said, clearly ready to be finished with this conversation. "And Marilyn says he's a lovely boy. He's doing us a big favor, so please be appreciative."

"But Mom," I started, "I . . ." I didn't know what was going to follow. Maybe something about how I hated being in cars now. I'd been okay taking the bus to and from school, but my cab ride home that night had made my pulse pound hard enough that I could feel it in my throat. Also, I'd gotten used to being by myself and I liked it that way. The thought of spending that much time in a car, with a stranger, lovely or not, was making me feel like I might hyperventilate.

"Amy," my mother said with a deep sigh. "Please don't be difficult."

Of course I wasn't going to be difficult. That was Charlie's job. I was never difficult, and clearly my mother was counting on that. "Okay," I said in a small voice. I was hoping that she'd pick up on how much I didn't want to do this. But if she did, she ignored it.

"Good," she said, briskness coming back into her voice. "Once I make your hotel reservations, I'll e-mail you the itinerary. And I ordered you a gift for the trip. It should be there before you leave."

I realized my mother hadn't actually been asking. I looked down at the pizza on the counter, but I had lost my appetite.

"Oh, by the way," she added, remembering. "How was the show?"

And now the show had closed, finals were over, and at the end of the driveway was a Subaru with Roger the Spud Player inside. Over the past week, I'd tried to think back to see if I could recall a Roger. And I had remembered one of the neighborhood kids, one with blond hair and ears that stuck out too far, clutching a maroon superball and calling for me and Charlie, trying to get a game together. Charlie would have remembered more details—despite his extracurriculars, he had a memory like an elephant—but Charlie wasn't exactly around to ask.

Both doors of the Subaru opened, and a woman who looked around my mother's age—presumably Marilyn—got out, followed by a tall, lanky guy. His back was to me as Marilyn opened the hatchback and took out a stuffed army-style duffel and a backpack. She set them on the ground, and the two of them hugged. The guy—presumably Roger—was at least a head taller than she was, and ducked a little bit to hug her back. I expected to hear good-byes, but all I heard him say was "Don't be a stranger." Marilyn laughed, as though she'd been expecting this. As they stepped apart, she met my gaze and smiled at me. I nodded back, and she got into the car. It pulled around the cul-de-sac, and Roger stood staring after it, raising one hand in a wave.

When the car had vanished from sight, he shouldered his bags and began walking toward the house. As soon as he turned toward me, I blinked in surprise. The sticking-out ears were gone. The guy coming toward me was shockingly good-looking. He had broad shoulders, light brown hair, dark eyes, and he was already smiling at me.

I knew in that instant the trip had suddenly gotten a lot more complicated.

*But I think it only fair to warn you, all those
songs about California lied.*
—*The Lucksmiths*

I stood up and walked down the steps to meet him in the driveway. I was suddenly very conscious that I was barefoot, in old jeans
and the show T-shirt from last year's musical. This had become
my de facto outfit, and I'd put it on that morning automatically,
without considering the possibility that this Roger guy might be
disarmingly cute.

And he really was, I saw now that he was closer. He had wide
hazel eyes and unfairly long lashes, a scattering of freckles, and
an air of easy confidence. I felt myself shrinking in a little in his
presence.

"Hey," he said, dropping his bags and holding out his hand to
me. I paused for a second—nobody I knew shook hands—but
then extended my hand to him, and we shook quickly. "I'm
Roger Sullivan. You're Amy, right?"

I nodded. "Yeah," I said. The word stuck in my throat a little, and I cleared it and swallowed. "I mean, yes. Hi." I twisted
my hands together and looked at the ground. I could feel my

heart pounding and wondered when a simple introduction had changed to something unfamiliar and scary.

"You look different," Roger said after a moment, and I looked up at him to see him studying me. What he mean by that? Different from what he'd been expecting? What had he been expecting? "Different than you used to look," he clarified, as though he'd just read my thoughts. "I remember you from when we were kids, you and your brother. But you still have the red hair."

I touched it self-consciously. Charlie and I both had it, and when we were younger, and together all the time, people were always stopping us to point it out, as though we'd never noticed ourselves. Charlie's had darkened over time to auburn, whereas mine stayed vividly red. I hadn't minded it until recently. Lately it seemed to attract attention, when that was the last thing I wanted. I tucked it behind my ears, trying not to pull on it. It had started falling out about a month ago, a fact that was worrying me, but I was trying not to think about it too much. I told myself that it was the stress of finals, or the lack of iron in my mostly pizza diet. But usually, I tried not to brush my hair too hard, hoping it would just stop on its own.

"Oh," I said, realizing that Roger was waiting for me to say something. It was like even the basic rules of conversation had deserted me. "Um, yeah. I still have it. Charlie's is actually darker now, but he's ... um ... not here." My mother hadn't told anyone about Charlie's rehab and had asked me to tell people the cover she made up. "He's in North Carolina," I said. "At an academic enrichment program." I pressed my lips together and looked away, wishing that he would leave and I could go back inside and shut the door, where nobody would try and talk to me and I could be alone with my routine. I was out of practice talking to cute guys. I was out of practice talking to anyone.

Right after it happened, I hadn't said much. I didn't want to talk about it and didn't want to open the door for people to ask me how I was feeling about things. And it wasn't like my mother or Charlie even tried. Maybe the two of them had talked to each other, but neither of them talked to me. But that was understandable—I was sure both of them blamed me. And I blamed myself, so it made sense that we weren't exactly sharing our feelings around the kitchen table. Dinners were mostly silent, with Charlie either sweaty and jumpy or swaying slightly, eyes glazed, as my mother focused on her plate. The passing back and forth of dishes and condiments, and then the cutting and chewing and swallowing process, seemed to take up so much time and focus that it was really amazing to think we'd once had conversations around the dinner table. And even if I did think about saying something occasionally, the silence of the empty chair to my left killed that impulse.

At school my teachers had left me alone, not calling on me for the first month afterward. And then after that, I guess it just became habit that they didn't. It seemed like people could revise who you were very quickly, and they seemed to have forgotten that I once used to raise my hand and give my opinions, that I once had something to say about the Boxer Rebellion or symbolism in *The Great Gatsby*.

My friends had gotten the message pretty quickly that I didn't want to talk to them about it. And without talking about it, it became clear that then we really couldn't talk about anything. After not very long, we just stopped trying, and soon I couldn't tell if I was avoiding them or they were avoiding me.

Julia was the one exception. I hadn't told her what had happened. I knew that if I told her, she wasn't going to let me off the hook. She wasn't going to go away easily. And she didn't. She'd found out, of course, and had called me constantly right after, calls I let go to voice mail. The calls had tapered off, but she'd started e-mailing instead. They came every few days now, with subjects like "Checking In" and "Worried About You" and "For God's Sake, Amy." I let them pile up in my in-box, unread. I wasn't exactly sure why I was doing it, but I knew that if I talked to Julia about it, it would become real in some way I couldn't quite handle.

But as I looked at Roger, I also realized that it had been awhile since I'd had an interaction with a guy. Not since the night of the funeral, when I'd invited myself to Michael's dorm room, knowing exactly what was going to happen. When I left an hour later, I was disappointed, even though I'd gotten exactly what I thought I wanted.

"It's not true, you know," said Roger. I looked at him, trying to figure out what he meant. "Your shirt," he said, pointing. I glanced down at the faded blue cotton, emblazoned with ANYONE CAN WHIS-TLE. "I can't," he continued cheerfully. "Never have been able to."

"It's a musical," I said shortly. He nodded, and silence fell, and I couldn't think of anything else to say on the subject. "I should get my things," I said, turning to the house, wondering how the hell we were ever going to get through four days.

"Sure," he said. "I'll load my stuff in. Do you need a hand?"

"No," I said, heading up the stairs. "The car's open." Then I escaped inside, where it was blessedly cool and dark and quiet and I was alone. I took a breath, savoring the silence, then continued into the kitchen.

The gift my mother had sent was sitting on the kitchen table. It had arrived a few days ago, but I hadn't opened it. If I opened it, it meant that the trip was actually going to happen. But there was no denying it now—the proof was making comments about my T-shirt and putting his duffel bag in the car. I tore open the package and shook out a book. It was heavy and spiral-bound, with a dark blue cover. *AWAY YOU GO!* was printed in white fifties-style script. And underneath that, *Traveler's Companion. Journal / Scrapbook / Helpful Hints*.

I picked it up and flipped through it. It seemed to be mostly blank pages, with a scrapbook section for preserving "Your Lasting Memories" and a journal section for recording "Your Wandering Thoughts." There also seemed to be quizzes, packing lists, and traveling tips. I shut the book and looked at it incredulously. This was the "present" my mother sent me for the trip? Seriously?

I tossed it on the counter. I wasn't about to be tricked into thinking this was some sort of fun, exciting adventure. It was a purely functional trip that I was being forced to take. So I didn't see any reason to make sure I'd always remember it. People didn't buy souvenirs from airports they'd had layovers in.

I walked through the rooms on the first floor of the house, making sure that everything was in order. And everything was—Hildy the Realtor had made sure of that. All our furniture was still there—she preferred not to sell empty houses—but it no longer even felt like ours. Ever since my mother hired her, she'd taken over our house to the point where I sometimes had trouble remembering what it used to feel like when we were all just living in it, and it wasn't being sold to people as the place where they'd always be happy. It had started to feel more like a set than a house. Too many deluded young marrieds had traipsed through it, seeing only the square footage and ventilation, polluting it with their furniture dreams and imagined Christmases. Every time Hildy finished a showing and I was allowed to come back from walking around the neighborhood with my iPod blasting Sondheim, I could always sense the house moving further away from what it had been when it was ours. Strange perfume lingered in the air, things were put in the wrong place, and a few more of the memories that resided in the walls seemed to have vanished.

I climbed the stairs to my room, which no longer resembled the place I'd lived my whole life. Instead it looked like the ideal teen girl's room, with everything just so—meticulously arranged stacks of books, alphabetized CDs, and carefully folded piles of clothing. It now looked like "Amy!'s" room. It was neat, orderly, and devoid of personality—probably much like the imaginary shiny-haired girl who lived in it. Amy! was probably someone who baked goods for various sports teams and cheered wholeheartedly at pep rallies without contemplating the utter pointlessness of sports or wanting to liven things up with a little torch song medley. Amy! probably babysat adorable moppets up the street and smiled sweetly in class pictures and was the kind of teen that any parent would want. She probably would have giggled and flirted with the cute guy in her driveway, rather than failing miserably at a simple conversation and running away. Amy! had not, in all probability, killed anyone recently.

My gaze fell to my nightstand, which had on it only my alarm clock and a thin paperback, *Food, Gas, and Lodging*. It was my father's favorite book, and he'd given me his battered copy for Christmas. When I'd opened it, I'd been disappointed—I'd been hoping for a new cell phone. And it had probably been totally obvious to him that I hadn't been excited about the present. It was thoughts like that, wondering if I had hurt his feelings, that ran through my head at three a.m., ensuring that I wouldn't get any sleep.

When he'd given it to me, I hadn't gotten any further than the title page. I'd read his inscription: *To my Amy—this book has seen me through many journeys. Hoping you enjoy it as much as I have. With love, Benjamin Curry (your father)*. But then I'd stuck it on my nightstand and hadn't opened it again until a few weeks ago, when I'd finally started reading it. As I read, I found myself wondering with every turn of the page why I couldn't have done this months ago. I'd read to page sixty-one and stopped. Marking page sixty-two was a note card with my father's writing on it, some notes about Lincoln's secretary, part of the research he'd been doing for a book. But it was in the novel as a bookmark. Page sixty-one was the place he'd gotten to when he'd last read it, and somehow I couldn't bring myself to turn the page and read beyond that.

slam without saying good-bye or leaving a note. In the paper sack Walter had packed a change of clothes, a paperback John D. MacDonald and the postcard that Nancy had sent with a picture of Central Park on the front. There was an address on it, an address in New York City, and that's where he was headed.

He had seventy-six dollars of his own and fifty-five dollars of his father's that he'd taken off the dresser that morning while his father was down the hall shaving. He figured that the money would be missed sooner, and for longer afterward, than he would be.

He walked to the car, the car that had been his ever since his grandfather had left it to him in the will that had been read forty-eight hours before. He was going to get on the highway and just drive, like all those songs and books and movies had urged him to do. And at the end of it, after all those miles passed, there would be Nancy waiting at the end of it.

You got one chance to take a trip like this, he thought as he put his grandfather's keys into the ignition, dice keychain dangling, coming up snake eyes. You had to do it when you were young and had the energy to drive all night and didn't care about the quality of the motel and it didn't even really matter where you ended up. This is what he'd thought about, working in that museum every day, surrounded by the artifacts carefully labeled, everything that the young braves had taken on their spirit quests. He just figured that this would be his. He started the car, pressed his foot down on the gas, and drove away, resolving not to look back but breaking it immediately, seeing his own eyes in the rearview mirror, seeing his

I still had no idea what Walter saw. I wasn't sure I was ever going to know. But I wasn't about to leave the book behind. I picked it up and tucked it carefully in my purse. I gave the room a last look, turned out the light, dragged my rolling suitcase out into the hall, and closed the door behind me. It was actually a relief not to see the room anymore. In the past month, I'd spent almost no time in it, crashing downstairs on the couch most nights and just heading up to get clothes. It was too stark a reminder of my life Before. And it still didn't make any sense to me that absolutely everything in my life could have changed, that it all could have become After, but the pictures on my walls and the junk in the back of my closet remained the same. And after Hildy's Amy! makeover, it seemed like the room had become a version of myself that I would never live up to.

I was about to drag my suitcase downstairs, but I stopped and looked down the hall to my parents' bedroom. I hadn't been in it since the morning of the funeral, when I'd stood in the doorway so my mother could see if the black dress I'd chosen was appropriate.

I walked down the hall, passing Charlie's bedroom, which was adjacent to mine. The door to Charlie's room had been closed ever since my mother slammed it behind her after she had literally yanked him out of it one month earlier. I opened the door to the master bedroom and stood on the threshold. Though tidier than it once had been, this room was at least still recognizable, with its neatly made king-size bed and stacks of books on each nightstand. I noticed that the books on my father's side, thick historical biographies alternating with thin paperback mysteries, were beginning to gather dust. I looked away quickly, reminding myself to breathe. It felt like I was underwater and running out of oxygen, and I knew I wasn't going to be able to stay there much longer. The door to my father's closet was ajar, and I could see inside it the tie rack Charlie had made for him in fifth-grade woodshop with his ties still hanging on it, all preknotted to save him time in the morning.

Trying to quash the panicky feeling that was beginning to rise, I turned away from my father's side of the room and crossed to my mother's dresser. On an impulse, I pulled open her top drawer—socks and stockings—and reached into the very back, on the left side. The drawer was emptier than usual, but even so, it took me a second to find it. But when my fingers closed around something smooth and plastic, I knew that Charlie had been telling the truth. I pulled it out and saw that it was an ancient pantyhose egg, with L'EGGS printed on the side in gold script that was flaking off. I cracked the egg open and saw, as promised, that the egg was stuffed with cash.

Charlie had told me that he'd found it sometime last year—I hadn't wanted to ask how or why. But there was a piece of me that registered how desperate he must have been to have found the money my mother kept hidden in her sock drawer. That was about the time I started noticing just how far gone he actually was. Charlie had told me that he only dipped into it in case of emergencies and was always careful to put the money back, since he was sure Mom would notice. It always had six hundred dollars in it, mostly hundreds and fifties. Maybe Charlie had been too out of it by the end to care, or maybe he hadn't had time to replenish it before he found himself on a plane to North Carolina, but there was only four hundred dollars in it now.

I heard the front door slam downstairs and realized that Roger was probably wondering why it was taking me so long to get my suitcase. Not stopping to think about what I was doing, I pocketed the cash, snapped the egg shut, and put it back in its place. A piece of me was running through justifications—you couldn't trust these house hunters and shady Realtors, really I was just helping my mother out—but I knew none of them were the real reason I'd taken the money. So then why had I?

I pushed the thought away and hurried out of the room, closing the door behind me and dragging my suitcase down the stairs. When I reached the kitchen, I saw Roger standing in front of the fridge, staring at it. He looked at me as I thumped my suitcase onto the landing.

"All set?" he asked.

"Yep," I said, then immediately wondered why I'd just started talking like a cowboy. I pulled the suitcase toward the door and glanced back at Roger in the kitchen. He was back to looking at the refrigerator, which gave me a moment to study him unde-tected. He was tall, and the kitchen, which had been so quiet and still lately, seemed filled up with his presence. My mother had told me that he was nineteen and that he'd just finished his freshman year. But there was something about him that made him seem older than that—or at least made me feel young. Maybe it was the hand shaking.

"These are incredible," Roger said, pointing at the refrigerator.

"Oh, yeah," I said, crossing into the kitchen, knowing he was talking about the magnets. The fridge was covered with them, many more than were needed to hold up Classic Thai takeout menus and grocery lists. They were all from different places— cities, states, countries. My parents had started collecting them on their honeymoon, and they'd kept it up until a few months ago, when my mother spoke at a conference in Montana and came back with a magnet that was just a square of bright blue with BIG SKY COUNTRY printed on it.

"My parents—" I heard my voice catch a little on the word. Words I'd always taken for granted had turned into landmines, traps for me to stumble over and fall into. I saw that Roger had averted his eyes to the fridge, pretending he hadn't noticed anything. "They, um," I continued after a moment, "collected them. From all the places they'd been."

"Wow," he said, stepping back and taking in the whole fridge, as though it was a piece of art. "Well, it's impressive. I've never been anywhere."

"Really?" I asked, surprised.

"Really," he said, eyes still on the fridge. "Only California and Colorado. Pretty lame, huh?"

"I don't think so," I said. "I've barely been out of California." This was incredibly embarrassing, something I had told nobody except Julia. I'd been out of the country once—we'd all spent a very damp summer in the Cotswolds, in England, while my mother did research for a book. But California was the only state I'd ever been in. Whenever I had complained about this, my mother had told me that once we'd seen all there was to see in California, we could move on to the other states.

"You too?" Roger smiled at me, and as though it was an automatic reaction, I looked down at my feet. "Well, that makes me feel a little better. The way I justify it is that California's a pretty big state, right? It'd be worse if I'd never been out of New Jersey or something."

"I thought," I started, then regretted saying anything. It wasn't like I really wanted to know the answer, so why had I started to ask the question? But I couldn't just leave that out there, so I cleared my throat and continued. "I mean, I thought my mother said your father lived in Philadelphia. And that's why you're, um, doing this."

"He does," said Roger. "I've just never been out there before. He comes out here a couple times a year, for business."

"Oh," I said. I glanced up at him and saw that he was still looking at the fridge. As I watched, his face changed, and I knew he'd seen the program, the one held up by the ITHACA IS GORGES! magnet in the lower left corner. The program I tried to avoid looking at—without success—every time I opened the fridge, but hadn't actually done anything about, like removing it or anything.

It was printed on beige card stock and had a picture of my father on the front, one that someone had taken of him teaching. It was in black and white, but I could tell that he was wearing the tie I'd gotten him last Father's Day, the one with tiny hound dogs on it. He had chalk dust on his hands and was looking to the left of the camera, laughing. Underneath the picture was printed BENJAMIN CURRY: A LIFE WELL-LIVED.

Roger looked over at me, and I knew that he was about to say a variation on the same sentence I'd been hearing for the past three months. How sorry he was. What a tragedy it was. How he didn't know what to say. And I just didn't want to hear it. None of the words helped at all, and it's not like he could have possibly understood.

"We should get going," I said before he could say anything. I grabbed my suitcase by the top handle, but before I could lift it, Roger was standing next to me, hoisting it with ease.

"I got it," he said, carrying it out the front door. "Meet you at the car." The door slammed, and I looked around the kitchen, wondering what else I could do to delay the moment when it would just be the two of us, trapped in a car for four days. I picked up the plate from where I'd left it to dry in the empty dishwasher, put it in the cupboard, and closed the door. I was about to leave when I saw the travel book sitting on the counter.

I could have just left it there. But I didn't. I picked it up and, on impulse, pulled the program out from behind the Ithaca magnet and stuck it in the scrapbook section. Then I turned out the kitchen lights, walked out the front door, and locked it behind me.